FOOTPRINT UPON WATER

FOOTPRINT
UPON WATER

Barbara Fitzgerald

SOMERVILLE PRESS

Somerville Press,
Dromore, Bantry,
Co. Cork, Ireland

© Literary Executors, Dr Julian Somerville
and Mrs Christina Hoare 2012

First published 1983
This reprint 2012

Designed by Jane Stark
Typeset in Adobe Garamond
seamistgraphics@gmail.com

ISBN: 978-0-9573461-09

Printed and bound in Spain
by GraphyCems, Villa Tuerta, Navarra

PART ONE

CHAPTER ONE

Fellowescourt, as Susan remembered it from early childhood, was a genial brown house of Georgian design, standing almost on the village street from which it was separated by a low stone wall backed by a thick yew hedge. The hedge had been trained to form an archway, topped by a fabulous bird, over the narrow iron gate. The gardener, whom she used to watch in spellbound admiration while he applied an artless imagination to the science of topiary work, assured her that it was a peacock, but it was not fashioned in the likeness of any peacock that ever paraded this earth. After rain, by means of a stealthy nudge, it was possible to dislodge a shower of drops upon a person passing under the arch, and Susan soaked herself and one or other of her aunts many times before she was caught and punished.

A flagged path led up to the massive hall door which was painted a gleaming, almost luminous white. Above it was a fanlight more intricate than most of those of its period. Narrow hall windows flanked it, and beyond them three long windows on either side looked out across a gravel path on to formal flowerbeds; box edgings surrounded these, and outside them were small lawns of smoothly-shaven, intensely green grass. The beds were always planted with scarlet geraniums and lobellia in the summer and with wallflowers in the winter.

Behind lay the garden, surrounded by a wall and sloping towards the house. A line of Scotch firs formed a windbreak against the gales that swept down the bare and spongy slopes of the mountain at the back; it seemed that they alone, glistening in the rain-washed cold of the upland air, prevented the mountain from engulfing both Fellowescourt and the village of Glenmacool.

Thomas Fellowes had built the house in 1790, having amassed a fortune in the West Indies and married the daughter of an émigré French nobleman. The Fellowes were undistinguished Protestant merchants in the city of Cork, so Thomas, who wished to found his own dynasty, bought his fifty acres at the foot of the Ballyhoura Mountains, well out of range of his relations. From there, he sent his sons to be educated with those of the gentry and married his well-endowed daughters into good families; and there successive generations, after brief careers in the service of the Crown, settled down to do nothing at all for the rest of their lives.

Susan was unable to remember any home other than Fellowescourt; she was taken there at the age of three, in the year 1909 when her parents, so madly in love that the thought of their safety being of value to anybody but each other never entered their heads, were drowned together in a sailing accident off the coast of Galway. Her father, Lucius Fellowes, had been an only son and his death left her grandfather, old Captain Fellowes, with five spinster daughters on his hands, whom he kept in a state of unrelieved subjection; his wife had, by death, escaped his tyranny some years before.

Katharine was the eldest of his daughters, and Susan was aware of the imprint of her personality upon her from the moment of her arrival. She was kind in her own way, full of good works and humble about her own spiritual achievements; but she was obsessed with the consciousness of sin and the need for self-denial, and as ruthless with others as with herself when it came to the practice of virtue. Hell yawned before her and she continually described its horrors to her family, hoping to terrify them into observance of the strictest rules of Puritanism. So, with all her goodness, there was not much softness of temper or allowance for human frailty.

What grieved her most was the evident boredom with which her admonitions were received; her father did not pretend to listen and aired many irreligious principles so as to annoy her, while her sisters waited yawning till she had done. But Susan was young enough to be convinced that her aunt must be right and that, if she resisted her, she would be damned. All the same, even Susan was not good enough to please Katharine, who felt it her duty to pursue the souls of father, sisters and niece as relentlessly as the Hound of Heaven.

It was about this time that the Rector of the parish fell ill and a young curate from the town of Inish, five miles away, was sent regularly to Glenmacool to take the Sunday services. The Reverend Lawrence Weldon was a very good-looking young man, tall and straight, with an intellectual forehead, clear grey eyes and a most compelling sincerity. It was not long before he and Katharine had formed an attachment to each other. She became a devoted church worker and between them they contrived to enrage Captain Fellowes almost to the point of declaring himself a pagan. He took such a dislike to young Mr Weldon that he made no attempt even to be polite to him and once, when Mr Weldon had called just before tea-time and had been invited to stay, he was heard roaring to the maid-servant who was carrying the tea-tray into the drawing-room, 'Lizzie, when the Reverend Mister Weldon's here, bring me my tea in the study, d'ye hear? I'm telling you once for all, d'ye understand?'

No-one in the house could have failed to hear this outburst and after this the curate's visits became less frequent; but the certainty that the young couple were only awaiting an opportunity to ask his consent to marry, and the fear that in the meanwhile they might be conspiring for his salvation, so enraged the old gentleman that he missed no chance of ridiculing Katharine mercilessly about her admirer in the hope of driving a wedge between them. He had his own reasons for wishing to avert a match between his daughter and a penniless clergyman, however well-born, so he tried at all costs to avoid a declaration by the young man; but this was too much to hope for: Mr Weldon was very much in love and anxious to know his fate.

It was, however, some years before he was in a position to approach Captain Fellowes. A curate cannot support a wife without assistance, and Mr Weldon was not going to ask for Katharine before he was able to maintain her. They were obliged to wait until the death of the Rector and the subsequent appointment of Mr Weldon to fill the vacancy provided the long-awaited opportunity.

One afternoon, Susan had returned from a walk with Nanny and was dawdling in the hall, kicking the toes of the elephant's-foot umbrella-stand, when the bell rang and Lizzie admitted the new Rector. Awed by his black clothes, Susan gazed at him in silence, but so preoccupied was he that he did not appear to be aware of her at all. Thereupon she retired to the shelter of the shadows beneath a long narrow table in the back hall, hiding behind the immense bowl of pot pourri that stood on the floor there.

The Rector asked to see Captain Fellowes, and Lizzie, remembering her instructions about afternoon tea when he came to the house, was flummoxed by the problem of where to leave him. She dithered between the drawing-room and the way through to the back hall and study, finally driving him back to a point just inside the hall door with a whispered, 'Willya wait here, yer Reverence, while I tell the Captain,' and bolting towards the study door muttering under her breath, 'Oah! God help me! What'll he say to me at all!'

She knocked, and Susan, relying on her grandfather's doting affection which excused conduct in her that he would never have tolerated in his daughters, ran into the room as soon as the door was open to kiss him and be given a sweet as reward. As usual, he held out his arms for her to run into, but seeing Lizzie still hovering at the door, called out, 'Well, what is it?'

'Oh, Sir,' began Lizzie, shrinking at the thought of the displeasure she was about to provoke. 'Oh, Sir, the Reverend Misther Weldon's askin' for ye in the hall.'

He cast Susan away as if she had been a rattlesnake, pushed back his chair decisively and remained for a moment in thought, then said, in a voice that Susan had never heard used to her before, 'Run along now, up to the nursery. Quick.' And he gave her a little push and said to Lizzie, 'Show him in.'

Lizzie gazed helplessly at him, abject at her inability to understand where he was to be taken. Captain Fellowes roared at her, 'In here, girl. Show him in here.'

Susan fled to the back hall, hurt by the rebuff, then turned to watch Mr Weldon as he advanced, went in and closed the door. She marvelled at his calm; nobody, except herself, entered that room without dread. She felt that she was watching a victim entering the tiger's den, unconscious of his fate. His boldness was appalling.

Anyway, there it was. He was in, she was out and Lizzie had disappeared. She crept back behind the pot pourri bowl and removed the lid so as to investigate the contents. She had no desire to hear the conversation in the study; it was simply that she had to know whether Mr Weldon was going to emerge unscathed or suffer utter destruction.

Nanny called her gently from the nursery, but she preferred not to hear. Olivia, who was her lovely aunt, sped past noiselessly in a hurry; Charlotte and Daisy passed by together, silent and heavy-footed, as if their outing had really been too much for them. Harriet came by the other way, compact and busy as a mole. None of them knew she was there.

It had to be Katharine who discovered her; not only had she an observant eye, but she possessed an uncanny knack of surprising malefactors red-handed. Susan recognised her footfall before ever she saw her, the steps light but determined, purpose in every one. She never flitted, like Olivia, from room to room; she always set out for a reason.

Susan wriggled backwards and so attracted attention; her aunt bent down to look under the table.

'Susan,' she commanded, 'come out from there at once.'

She was not angry, which was a relief to Susan. She smiled at her in the way of people who are thinking what little things please little minds and said quietly, 'Run along up to Nanny, I don't like you to—' when there was a tremendous commotion inside the Study door.

Captain Fellowes was bellowing in a rage and demanding over and over again, 'Well, Sir, can you deny it? Tell me that, eh? Aha, answer me now, can you deny it?' He then laughed triumphantly, as if he had caught his visitor in a trap from which there was no escape.

Katharine put her hand nervously to her throat. 'Who's in there with Grandpa?' she asked fiercely, but she really knew the answer.

A strong voice replied from inside the door.

'I deny it absolutely, Sir.'

Katharine coloured up to her widow's peak as Susan answered her in a whisper, 'It's Mr Weldon.'

'I don't give that much for your denial,' thundered the voice of the old Captain, and they could hear the snap of his fingers. 'Parson and all as you are, you're after her money. Don't attempt to deny it, it's not a bit of good. It's her money you want, I know it. Well, when you can earn six hundred pounds a year you can have her, and not till then. And you won't get a penny with her, either.' He clapped his hands together and rubbed them noisily. 'Well, are ye satisfied? Will ye wait for her?'

Katharine stood there distraught, shaking her head for shame, humiliated at listening but unable to move on. They heard the quiet strong voice again.

'Captain Fellowes, I love Katharine whether she is rich or penniless, and I will wait for her until she can marry me. Will you allow us, then, to be engaged?'

There was a sort of explosion of anger at this, and they heard, 'Indeed, I'll do nothing of the kind! You can be engaged when you're in a position to marry, and not till then.' The door was flung open with a 'Now I must wish you good day!' Both men came quickly out and there stood Katharine and Susan revealed.

Susan backed against the table, ashamed to be caught and ashamed too for her grandfather who was bullying someone who deserved better of him. Katharine did not quail or excuse her presence there. She gathered herself together and took command, standing erect, a bright spot on either cheek, speaking in a voice that trembled a little with pride and love.

'Papa,' she said, 'Mr Weldon and I will not ask you for a penny. We shall be quite content to live on his stipend. We do not mind doing without all but the barest necessities of life if only we may be married. Oh, please Papa, will you give us your consent?'

'And a tribe of children in no time, to be clothed, fed and sent to school!' broke in the Captain, delighted at the discomfiture caused by this indelicate remark. 'No, Kate—the fellow's a pauper by our standards and he wants to turn you into a slave. That's not good enough for any daughter of mine! If he wants an unpaid housekeeper, let him look elsewhere!'

Mr Weldon moved towards the door and Katharine moved with him, as if she were being drawn along. They stopped to look at one another desperately, without speaking. Then Captain Fellowes handed the Rector his hat, in order to hasten his departure, said a peremptory 'Goodbye, Sir', and watched him down the path to the gate. Then he waved Katharine away from the door, shut it firmly and turned to march back to his study without another look or a word. The door banged after him and Katharine and Susan were alone again.

Katharine was for a moment stunned by the blow that had struck her, but suddenly she remembered that Susan was there, observing her. With icy repugnance she commanded, 'Go away, Susan, go upstairs to Nanny, you horrid little girl. Hiding and listening at doors like that!' She drove the child up the stairs and along to the nursery, while she herself ran further on to the cold privacy of her own bedroom.

Susan, hurt, resentful (for had her Aunt Katharine not also been listening at doors?) and frightened, buried her head sobbing in Nanny's lap.

'There, there,' comforted Nanny, in the voice that always made her feel better. 'What's the matter now? Tell Nanny. What ails y'at all?' As she spoke she smoothed Susan's hair in a slow rhythmic movement.

Nanny had been with Susan since she was a month old and had been nurse to her mother before her; she felt she had, as it were, inherited the child and brought with her to Fellowescourt a settled opinion that she, rather than the aunts, should have the direction of Susan's upbringing. Katharine, however, had her own very rigid views on the behaviour of children, so it was hardly surprising that she and Nanny should have regarded one another with indignant loathing from the moment of their first meeting. Nanny was never sorry to hear of Katharine's misdeeds, and Katharine blamed Nanny for all Susan's.

'It's Aunt Katharine,' said Susan haltingly. 'She . . . she says I'm horrid. She says I hide and . . . listen at doors. I don't, truly, Nan,' she added in a panic, lest Nanny should agree with her aunt.

'Of course you don't, lovey, of course you don't. Sure, Nanny knows that well enough. Arrah, don't mind what that ould Pope does be sayin' to ye, lovey; she's a quare crool one, so she is. Sure, she'd eat her young, th'ould Pope, so she would!' she finished with a note of triumph.

'What's a Pope?' asked Susan, intrigued.

'Arrah now!' cackled Nanny, 'Well I never!' She crumpled in consuming laughter as she tried to bring her ferociously Protestant old brain to work on a definition of a Pope. 'Well,' she began slowly, gathering speed as she advanced, 'a Pope's a quare one as is always right, so *they* think, mind ye, and likes to put everyone else right the way he is himself, and does always be rulin' the rest an' tellin' thim their sins. And he has a kind of notion he can speak for God, so he has. Arrah, you'll learn what a Pope is when ye're older. Now, tell me, dotey, why did yer aunt say that to ye at all?'

In a matter of minutes she had the whole story out of her. And, without a doubt, in a matter of hours it was known throughout the village and beyond.

The term 'Pope' became a sort of secret weapon of Susan's. When Katharine scolded her she would say wickedly to herself, 'You're just an old Pope!' and be so lost with her own daring that she would lose the gist of Katharine's admonition and be scolded again for that. But the name, although she did not comprehend its full meaning, and largely because of this, was too good to keep to herself for long and one day she brought it out in conversation with Olivia, her best friend amongst her aunts.

'Nanny says Aunt Katharine's an ould Pope,' announced Susan, watching Olivia narrowly in case she became so shocked that it was more prudent to alter one's meaning (aunts were odd like that). But Olivia's head tilted back and amusement crinkled her face against her will.

'A what, darling?' she queried in amazement.

'A Pope, an ould Pope,' repeated Susan, gazing at Olivia because it gave her pleasure to watch the expressions that passed across her face. She was the only fair-haired one of the family, with blue eyes, bright cheeks and a ripple in her hair.

'But that's naughty of Nanny,' she protested. 'She shouldn't say such things.' She covered her face with her hands and became quite helpless with laughter. Susan was delighted and laughed with her like a conspirator, alive to the fact that this must remain their secret. But in time Olivia told Harriet and she told the other two, so the name passed into circulation. Quite soon, Katharine was 'the Pope' to all the women in that household, and 'the Pope' she remained for ever.

Mr Weldon came to the house no more and he and Katharine had to content themselves with chance meetings in the street, and in houses where they were both invited, and with being aware of each other in church. Though there could be no engagement in her father's lifetime, there must have been an 'understanding'. She did not, however, bear a grudge against the old Captain for preventing the match: she accepted his decision in this matter as she did in everything. He was the Head of the Family, he was Papa, and what he said was Law.

All his daughters, except Olivia, were terrified of him. And such was his nature that he exploited their terror to the full. They had been reared to the belief that the male was a fierce and incalculable being whose wish was a command and whose reasons were indisputable, and that the female was created only to adorn, to obey and to spare him the nuisance of tiresome domestic proceedings. Captain Fellowes did nothing to disillusion them and delighted in summoning one or other of them for a scolding, accusing them of crimes which he well knew they had never committed, just for the pleasure of observing their wretchedness. Olivia he left alone; she had an independent spirit and might have stood up to him.

'Katharine!' he bellowed one morning from the hall, soon after the girls had dispersed from breakfast. 'Katharine!' So penetrating was his voice that nothing said by him ever remained secret. 'Katharine!' he bawled for the third time, and it seemed that if she did not come he must burst, either from frustration or from inability to increase the volume of sound.

But Katharine came flying before he had to call again, her brow wrinkled with nervous speculations, a victim ready for sacrifice.

'Katharine, why the devil have you hidden my umbrella? I left it here last night and now it's gone. How often do I have to tell you to leave my things alone?'

She, scarlet in the face, barely able to wait to justify herself, stammered, 'Oh, Papa, how tiresome for you! You shall have it in a moment, but it was so wet that I found it made quite a pool on the carpet, so I put it in the laundry.'

'Nonsense! A drop of water won't hurt the carpet. Bring it here at once. Goodness knows, I'm late enough as it is!'

She must have known that a delay of five minutes was never of the slightest consequence to him, but her sense of duty sent her streaking to the back of the house to return with the umbrella almost before the stir of her departure had subsided.

'Have we no servants?' he barked at her. 'Why couldn't you send one of the gerrls for it, eh?'

'I wanted you to have it quickly, Papa. It would have delayed you more to have sent Lizzie for it, so I thought—'

'You thought, you thought! Think a bit sooner next time and leave it where I put it, d'ye see?'

'Yes, Papa.'

The hall was long, dark and narrow, with a huge coat-stand on which hung not only garments in current use but also relics of Fellowes dead and gone which no-one had thought of removing. The walls were hung with an assortment of assegais, thongs, whips, poisoned arrows and shields, surmounted by an entire kayak and interspaced with heads of buffalo, rhinoceros and many types of gazelle. Here and there one or other end of a fox, the grinning mask or the brush, was visible. Clocks ticked and chimed endlessly throughout the house and a cuckoo clock called the quarters from the back hall. So it was no wonder that Katharine had failed to notice Susan standing in the doorway of the drawing-room, waiting quietly until her grandfather was free to attend to her. When he had done scolding, Susan came out and slipped her hand into his, but he put her away, telling her that he was about to go out.

As soon as he had gone Katharine found an excuse to speak sharply to her, to punish the child for witnessing her humiliation. When her father was not there, she became a different person, assured, quick-tempered, masterful, ruling the household with a rod of iron. Since the death of her mother, duty had obliged her to practise what to a nature like hers must have been the most exacting form of self-discipline, the subordination of her will to that of her father, regardless of whether his wishes had her sympathy, approval or consent. When his will was removed, her own came into play with increased force.

She was afraid of her father, though she had dutifully convinced herself that she loved him dearly. She did not perceive that a little stout-hearted opposition to the more absurd of his demands would have made him much more reasonable; even if she had realised this, she would have thought it wrong to oppose her will to his. So she continued to invite his oppression and her perpetual submissiveness only exacerbated his tyranny.

But such filial piety was beginning to show itself as an outworn manifestation of a passing age; her sisters next to her in age felt it far less than she did, and Olivia never felt it at all. Charlotte, Daisy and Harriet were their father's unwilling slaves, kept in servitude by fear alone.

Had their education been more advanced, the sisters might have held more daring views. But, as the three middle ones were barely literate and incapable of understanding anything more profound than love stories or the social column of the *Cork Examiner* they could not be receptive to the heresies of Mrs Pankhurst. It would have been hard to find girls with less knowledge of what was happening in the world, or greater satisfaction with the little that they had. This was chiefly due to their father, who disapproved of the education of women and had never sent any of his daughters to school. Instead, he had employed a succession of Miss Sullivans, Miss Nicholsons and Miss Pratts, who left only as the depths of their ignorance became impossible to conceal. During the twenty-odd years of these ladies' residence at Fellowescourt, the girls learnt to read, write and do elementary sums which did not involve the complications of pounds, shillings and pence; they also memorised a few French phrases in an accent unique to the County of Cork.

Katharine and Olivia alone profited from these slender advantages; both were readers and each had managed to supplement her education by sheer hard work, without direction or encouragement. The result was that Captain Fellowes, who expected all his daughters to win the approval of the County for their wit and conversation, was embarrassed by the vapidness of Charlotte and Daisy, the dullness of Harriet, and the dread that people might consider Katharine and Olivia to be blue-stockings.

When Susan was about five years old, Katharine began to wonder about her education. She approached Nanny one day in the nursery, to enquire whether she was capable of giving first lessons.

Nanny threw up her hands in horror at the very thought.

'Ah now, Miss, sure I couldn't do that at all! It's more than I'm able for to read what's on the newspaper, under the pictures. I could teach her a bit o' sewing, perhaps. She wouldn't be the first I'd taught her stitches to. But sums an' writing! That's too much for me altogether.'

Nanny, as Susan knew well, was only just able to read; when she read it was aloud, syllable by syllable in a flat voice. Katharine began to perceive how very elementary was her learning.

'We'll have to think it over, Nanny. You see, if we have to get a nursery governess, then there won't be anything for you to do, will there?' she said with inexorable logic.

At that moment a sword pierced the hearts of both Nanny and Susan. They had never been separated and had never imagined that they might be. Nanny refused ever to go for a holiday or to take an afternoon off, so they were perpetually together. The thought of Nanny not being there was torture to Susan, making the whole future dangerous and alarming. When Katharine had gone, she rushed at Nanny, pressing her face into her apron.

'Nanny, you won't ever leave me, will you? Ever, ever, ever?'

She had hoped for indignant reassurance. But Nanny sat down in an old, tired way and said nothing for a moment. Then, in a voice that did not deceive Susan at all, said over and over again as she stroked the child's fine, shining gold-brown hair, 'Arrah now, don't be talkin', lovey. We'll be able for her, we'll best her, so we will, th'ould Pope.'

Gloom filled the nursery for some days, but soon there came a slight change for the better. Nanny had begun to organise her defence.

Her trump card was old Captain Fellowes. She began to woo him in little ways, to flatter his judgement, inducing him to believe that only he and she could interpret the wishes of Susan's dead parents about her upbringing; she took care to impress him with her personal fidelity to Susan and, craftily, to cast shadowy doubts upon the motives and methods of 'the Pope'. It was easy for Nanny to be with Susan when her grandfather met her about the house, and to say a few respectful words to him while he patted the child's head or dug in his pockets for a lump of sugar.

One day when a streaming gale swept down the mountainside and Nanny, undeterred, had taken Susan for her daily walk, they met him in the back hall on their way in.

'Well!' he exclaimed, 'you must be soaked through!'

'Ah no, Sirr,' answered Nanny quickly. 'Sure, the rain'd never go through that mackintosh she has on, 'twould only jump off it. If I thought she'd be wet through, Sirr, she'd not be out at all. Sure, she's as harrdy as a thrush, so she is. She'll take no harm.'

'No, of course not,' he said hastily. 'Sure I know you take too good care of her for that, Nanny. Now,' he turned to Susan, 'if you get off those wet things and come to me in the study, I've got a surprise.'

Susan began to jump up and down with excitement but Nanny sniffed dissent.

'Well, I dunno, Sirr, could I let her down before tea at all, Sirr. There's Miss Kat'rine's ordhers that she's to stay in the nursery and learn her psalm, and I dursen't go against Miss Kat'rine.'

'Psalms, Nanny? What the divil is she doing learning psalms?'

Nanny's wizened little person emitted injured disapproval. So frail and small did she look that it seemed an act of gallantry for her even to hint disagreement with 'the Pope'.

'Oh,' she said slowly, as though unwilling to reveal the depths of foolishness to which Katharine had descended, 'Oh well now, I think it's some kind of a little punishment Miss Kat'rine's afther puttin' on her.' She stopped discreetly.

'Punishment!' Captain Fellowes was beginning to roar. Susan heard Harriet, her most timid aunt, murmur wretchedly 'Oh dear!' from the shelter of the morning-room, and it was as if every ear in the house was stretched to hear what might come next, the silence was so sudden and complete. The clatter of china ceased in the pantry, the cook stopped sharpening a knife and the half-fledged little kitchen-maid who had been running along the flagged kitchen passage stood still.

'But what's the child done, Nanny? You know as well as I do she's never naughty.'

'Arrah, not at all, Sirr! There's not a pick of vice in the child at all. ''Twas more of a little slip, like.'

The little slip had been a lie that Susan had been unwise enough to tell Katharine about how the china face of her doll had come to be broken. For once she felt that she had earned her punishment and was prepared to perform it without complaint, but listening to this discussion her heart began to harden. Of course she did not deserve to be punished! She pushed out her lower lip, ready to cry.

'Ah, look at the poor little thing!' exclaimed Nanny tenderly, pulling a handkerchief from Susan's pocket and dabbing at her eyes. 'Sometimes, Sirr, I do think maybe Miss Kat'rine's a little hard on her, and it's that that does be worryin' me when I think of the day I have to leave this house.'

'Leave this house?' he echoed in amazement. 'Whatever put that idea into your head, Nanny?'

'Well Sirr,' and Nanny disclosed the threat of the nursery governess and her own bewilderment at Katharine's assumption that there would be no further need of her own services. Such ingratitude for long service clearly grieved her deeply.

'Well, I'll be damned!' Such was the Captain's surprise that he began almost in a whisper, but as he continued his voice rose rapidly. 'I'll be damned if I'll have any nursery governesses in this house! Why, amn't I only just quit o' governesses without filling the house with them again? Now, listen to me,' he went on seriously, as though every occupant of the house was not listening with every nerve. 'While I'm alive, you stay in this house. D'ye understand? As long as I live you stay here with the child. Good Heavens! I should think Mrs Lucius'd be turning in her grave at the very thought! Tch tch tch!' He frowned so much that his immense eyebrows, like tangled silvery wire, nearly met. 'I'll tell Miss Katharine, don't you worry. Now take the child upstairs and get her ready to come down to me.'

'Yes, Sirr,' said Nanny meekly; 'an' not be doin' her psalm?'

'Pah!' was his only reply as he turned quickly and shut himself into the study.

Nanny and Susan went thoughtfully upstairs. The relief with which Susan had heard that Nanny would not be sent away in her grandfather's lifetime was tempered by her consciousness of his undoubtedly great age; like all children, she imagined that anybody with grey hair was very old indeed. Touching the centre of each pattern of stair carpet with her foot, whether it fell on the flat, or the rise of a stair, or under the rod, she prodded the future gingerly with her mind.

'Nanny,' she asked in a tight little voice, 'will Grandpapa die very soon?'

'Arrah now!' she cried in affectionate ridicule, touched more than she would admit. 'If God wills, he'll have many years in front of him yet. I doubt he's turned sixty-five, meself.'

Susan had thought him to be eighty at the least, and her troubles fled; Nanny would be with her for ever, almost. She was so elated that she ran ahead and flung herself on the nursery cat, curled up asleep on Nanny's armchair, and covered it with kisses. It remained coiled, but rigid, with one baleful eye open until she should leave it alone, as if trying to will her into believing that it was not really there.

She felt repulsed and cast about in her mind for a reason to explain this unfriendly behaviour. Her heart began to pound: the cat would have nothing to do with her because she had evaded punishment for telling a lie. It knew: God had told it.

Instantly, she assumed full responsibility for the lie, deciding to punish herself for it since her Aunt Katharine's retribution had been removed. That decision made, she forgot it at once. But she retained for a long time an association in her mind between an unfriendly black cat with a slitty, open eye, and her own guilty conscience.

After this, Nanny assumed an attitude of faintly servile superiority whenever 'the Pope' visited them in the nursery. For the present, her position was impregnable. But in the end nothing but a miracle could save her, and she knew it.

CHAPTER TWO

Whereas Katharine devoted herself to the formation of Susan's character, giving special attention to her faults, and Olivia treated her like a little sister, Harriet, whose chances of matrimony were becoming annually more remote, swamped her with a flood of unfulfilled maternal emotion.

It was all very well when she was quite tiny to be caught up, held tightly and smothered with kisses, but as she grew older this ruffled her dignity and offended her sense of propriety. If she struggled, Harriet would be hurt and put her down, and she would feel horrid and ungrateful.

'Don't you like to be loved, Susan?' Harriet would ask, her eyes full of pain.

And Susan would reply, 'Yes, thank you,' with a cold politeness that would have shrivelled anyone else.

'Then give me a kiss.'

Susan would edge towards her until she was close enough to poke her cheek forward to be kissed while avoiding the danger of being hugged.

'Poor little thing!' Harriet would exclaim. 'She's had so little love that she doesn't even miss it.'

Harriet had a squat, plump body, surmounted by a sallow face with dark brown velvet eyes and a tower of earth-coloured hair. Her eyes were the only beautiful thing about her and they were mild and liquid, like those of a Jersey cow. They conveyed all the hurt, joy and expectation that her dumpy little person and practical voice could not express.

To have children of her own was her dream of earthly bliss. To protect them, play with them, care for them and lavish affection upon them was her whole ambition. She would have married almost anyone for the sake of having a family, but, poor Harriet, hardly anybody took any notice of her. She envied Olivia her beauty because it might have brought her a husband, though Olivia did not seem to notice her admirers, which was such waste. But then, Olivia had everything; a lovely face and figure, intelligence, gaiety and courage, while she, Harriet, had nothing but a pair of soft brown eyes.

The dreadful thing was that children did not really take to her; they either shrank from her in self-defence or giggled at her in stupefied amazement.

Every Christmas there was a present from Harriet for every child and infant in the village. She prepared, all through the Autumn, queer little packages wrapped in crumpled paper and tied up with little bits of creased ribbon. She never gave dice, cards or knives, and she read through every one of the stories in each book to make sure that the moral tone was good. This bounty was distributed on Christmas Eve, and Harriet always took Susan on this mission with the double motive of making her feel sorry for children less fortunate than herself and of reflecting on her a little of the glory of the Lady Bountiful. But with the brutal intolerance of children for things not quite new, shining and perfect, Susan felt only shame as she watched her aunt hand out the messy little parcels. Not that the village children minded: they had too little to complain of minor imperfections.

The cottages, whitewashed outside, were dark and dirty within. The windows were tiny and never opened, and often geraniums, brought in to be safe from the frost, kept all the light out. There was a smell of babies, damp unwashed clothes, and steam from the potatoes that had been cooked there from the beginning of time. The only fresh air came in through the half-doors at front or back where sometimes, on fine days, an old granny would be sitting. Babies stayed indoors until they could walk, encased in layers of greyish, evil-smelling wraps, and astonishingly turned into beautiful children a year or two later. Small children tumbled about barefoot and plumped their bare bottoms on the stone steps without noticing the cold. Clothes boiled in the same kettle which, later on, would be used to heat the water to wet the tea. Roofs leaked, walls sweated and floors let the damp seep through into the overcrowded rooms where the young, the old, the diseased, the idiots and the healthy strove to keep alive. Hens walked unconcernedly over the door-sill, kittens darted to and fro, a linnet or goldfinch in a tiny cage made snatches of song, and lean, mean-faced dogs sniffed at strangers.

Harriet had to see every child in every home and discuss each with its mother. She loved them all, whatever they looked like. She picked up the babies, nursed them in her arms and meant every word of it when she told the mothers they were beautiful. Susan found the smell so nauseating that she would try to hold her breath; she was terrified of the two idiot children who would mouth noises and make unpredictable stampedes in bursts of unaccountable excitement, and she hated standing about while Harriet worshipped babies, being stared at by the other children.

Nanny, like all her kind, was an inexorable snob and resented her child being taken near dirt, disease or unpleasantness of any kind.

'If yer poor Mother was alive, Miss Harriet wouldn't be let take you into them nasty little dirrty cottages,' she would exclaim. 'The next thing ye'll be startin' scarlet fever or the whoopin' cough, and then who'll be to blame? Come here, now, till I wash yer head with carbolic and go through it wit' the tooth-comb. Sure, ye never know!' she would add enigmatically as she set to work.

Charlotte and Daisy used to tease poor Harriet about Captain Willoughby, the vet, who was a familiar figure in the village with his dogcart, Dalmation dog and lively black horse. He was an erect, military-looking man with very little to say, and he existed on the fringe of county society. Charlotte and Daisy thought him a great joke.

'If one didn't know about him, you'd almost think he was a gentleman,' Charlotte would say patronisingly, and Daisy would follow on with a shudder, 'Yes, but just think! Always smelling of the stable and the byre! Ugh!' And Harriet always rose to his defence, as they intended she should, replying excitedly that she had been told that he came of a very good family. Her face would be quite pink with anxiety.

'But,' the objection was always raised, 'if that's so, how does he come to be a vet?' And this was too much for Harriet; she could never explain how a gentleman could come to be a vet.

The first time he had come to the village Harriet had happened to be walking along the road between Fellowescourt and the convent; she noticed the smart dogcart, well-bred horse and spotted carriage-dog from some distance away and could not think whose they were. As they approached, she saw that the owner was a stranger and was greatly impressed by his consideration in slowing down as he passed her, so as to avoid splashing her clothes. She had looked up and smiled in gratitude and he had saluted her with his whip. She felt sure that he must be a Lord and could not stop talking about him, his distinguished bearing, pleasant manner and elegant conveyance. Some weeks later it was discovered that he was only the new vet. From that moment Harriet was unmercifully teased by her family about him, with the exception of Katharine and Olivia: Katharine thought it undignified to tease and Olivia thought it unkind.

Since then, there had been introductions but the acquaintance had never progressed very far. Harriet was shy and Captain Willoughby had never shown any but the most courteous and impartial interest in any woman.

Things were at this stage when Harriet and Susan set out on a mild and spring-like Christmas Eve to distribute the bounty. There was a dappled sky, with the sun pushing shafts of golden light through holes in the cloud that was soft-edged, ridged and hollowed like sand, and shining gold and grey. The spilt light fell on the green mountainside, on the furze clumps and granite boulders, the rough-coated cattle and tawny bog-grasses in a way that lit up the colour at that point alone and merged the surroundings with the distance in a blue and brooding foretaste of the dusk. Wind and rain would come with the night.

Each was carrying a basket, by now somewhat lightened, when, along the road from Inish and still a long way away, they saw Captain Willoughby's picturesque equipage approaching. At once Harriet was all of a flutter, looking self-consciously at her stout shoes and the mud splashes on her skirt, and trying to straighten her hat. She glanced at Susan to make sure that she was looking tidy, composed her face into unfamiliar lines of cheerful anticipation and went forward once more.

She had to dawdle a little so as to avoid being inside the next cottage when the Captain passed, but a convenient stitch in her side forced her to stop; she was looking very pink and confused when the dogcart rounded the bend at a brisk trot. The Captain, courteous as ever, raised his whip in salute, smiled and was gone. It was all over; he had been carried away without a word. But the encounter had done something for Harriet; her head was higher, her step lighter, and her eye brighter.

Susan turned to stare at the fast-disappearing Captain and was sharply nudged by Harriet who would have given anything not to feel it ill-bred to do the same. But Susan had seen something very disturbing and refused to look away: the spotted dog that had trotted between the wheels of the dogcart so gaily had suffered some weakness and was lying motionless on the road while his owner drove on in ignorance.

'Oh, look!' she cried.

Harriet, like Lot's wife, gave one swift and guilty look, but when she saw what had happened she stopped, turned and stood looking, calling and waving at the retreating Captain. But he did not look round and a moment later was gone beyond recall.

'Oh dear,' she said, looking at Susan, 'is it dead?'

'Dead?' echoed Susan, horrified. Death to her was unfamiliar, both terrifying and fascinating. The thought of having to discover whether the dog was dead or alive sent a cold shiver through her.

Harriet grabbed her hand. 'We must go and see,' she said.

They set off, Susan lagging behind, along the hundred or so yards to where the dog lay. Harriet went straight up to it and touched its ear, then its head and shoulder. There was no response and she began to fondle the smooth head, murmuring little phrases of encouragement and endearment. She spoke with such tenderness that it might have been the master she was addressing, not the dog.

She ran her hand down one leg and tried to move it, but it was too heavy. She stood up and looked around for help. Susan was close enough to watch without being within touching distance. The thought of its being dead or of its being alive was equally frightening. Harriet suddenly spoke.

'It's dead,' she said. 'We must get it off the road. Run to Christy Mahoney's house and tell him to come quick.'

Susan took to her heels, thankful to escape, and ran blindly until she reached the Mahoney's hovel. Her heart was pounding, her mind in a turmoil. She had never seen anything so newly dead. This lovely spotted dog, so elegant and lithe, so swift and shapely, smooth and spare, was now a muddy thing lying in the road, becoming every moment more cold and stiff, more rigidly unlifelike, further removed from warmth and vitality. She perceived how utterly gone are the dead from the living, how intangible is the essential being, how unfamiliar the body dispossessed. All this she felt with her being and knew without thought; she would not have been able to ensnare it with language.

Christy Mahoney's ancient face seemed to rush at her from the darkness of his stable as he looked out to see who was approaching with such haste. It was a face older than all time, flat as an ape's, with an ape's scarcely formed nose ending in two big rings of nostrils and an elongated, spreading upper lip. Two little shifting brown eyes, with lashes stiff as the spikes of a harrow, seemed never still; the ears were huge question marks above the fringe of tender beard that framed the jawbone like a line of mould. It was a face that had grown amongst the granite boulders and the thorn trees, the bog-holes and the furze bushes, the gales of wind and the rain, elemental as a leprechaun's. It came at her round his shoulder, as it were, as he held between his knee the donkey's hoof from which he was working a stone loose.

'Eh?' he enquired. 'Was it meself ye wanted, Miss?' His voice was thin, reedy and very old, his enunciation slipshod as is that of the toothless. Susan longed to escape. To her immense relief she suddenly heard the clip-clop of hooves and the Captain's dogcart reappeared. Ignoring Christy Mahoney, she rushed into the road and pointed to where Harriet, a little smudge half a mile away, was bending over the dead dog.

'Jump up!' he said, and hauled her up beside him. 'What happened?'

'It's dead,' said Susan.

'Ah, I was afraid of it. Poor old Tristan, poor old dog! Did you see what happened?'

She shook her head and neither spoke again until they reached Harriet. To her terror, he told Susan to hold the horse. She stood rigidly beside it, afraid that the slightest movement might make it bolt. It clanked and clinked, chewing its bit, and dragged her to the edge of the road where it threw down its head and began to eat grass, jerking the rein from her grasp and moving forward spasmodically every few moments to a new stretch. When she saw that it would not run away, she watched the Captain and her aunt, standing together, looking down at the dog. He felt it all over but could find no injury.

'Must've been his heart,' he said dejectedly.

'I hope he didn't suffer,' said Harriet with concern.

'I'd say not at all.' He shook his head again as though he could shed the melancholy of the situation. With difficulty he raised the body of the dog in his arms and staggered with it to the dogcart. Harriet went to help him and when she drew back found the front of her coat plastered with mud. Captain Willoughby was very upset; he insisted on using his handkerchief to wipe it off, thanking her all the time for her goodness by which he was genuinely moved.

'Why, Susan did more than I,' she said.

'Thank you, Susan,' he said gravely. 'I'm grateful to you both.' Susan felt that she was being addressed as an equal; at that moment she would gladly have died for him.

When he had gone, Harriet smiled at her with a sort of tranquil excitement in her expression, a gentle satisfaction, a tender determination; for once she made no attempt to kiss her. Indeed, had Susan not been there, she would have smiled in just the same way at the ancient bedstead that did service as a gate into the field beside them.

'The parcels?' said Susan soberly.

'Oh yes, the parcels,' she replied absently. They set off again on their round. The village babies suffered some neglect that afternoon, for they had been much delayed. As they neared Fellowescourt, Harriet slackened pace, grabbed Susan's elbow and gave it a little shake.

'Susan, darling,' she said quickly, pretending to brush the half-dried mud from her coat-front, 'I'd rather you didn't tell people about this . . . especially your aunts, and Grandpapa . . .'

Susan grunted and Harriet seemed reassured, but five minutes after they had reached home, Nanny had the whole story out of the child.

'You're not to tell a soul,' Susan warned her. 'She said so.'

'As if I would, lovey,' laughed Nanny. 'Oh, so that's the way of it, is it now? They do say as he is a very nice gentleman, all the same,' she added as though this were surprising.

Of course Captain Fellowes got to hear of the affair, and of course he teased poor Harriet about it far more than if she had told him of it herself.

It was Olivia who brought this persecution to an end. One evening when the family were all together round the drawing-room fire, after tea, the Captain became exasperated by Charlotte's benevolent inertia. She had eaten liberally, listened without contributing a word and was relaxing comfortably on the sofa when her father suddenly rapped at her: 'Penny for your thoughts, Charlotte?'

'What, mine, Papa?'

'Yes, you, child. How you can sit like a stuffed pig from morning till night! I'll wager you were thinking about some man or other, God help him.'

Charlotte stretched slightly and stifled the least perceptible of hiccoughs.

'Well,' she began in leisurely tones, 'no, I wasn't. I was thinking what a wonderful time girls must have in India, I mean married to someone in the Army or something. D'ye know, Flora MacCartney wrote and told Daisy that she has so many servants she doesn't even have to button her own shoes!' The smile of wonder and delight with which she ended this description of earthly bliss made her sisters laugh; even Katharine smiled. Not so her father.

'Well,' he blazed, 'if you want to live in idleness all your life you'd better find some rich man and marry him quick. I don't know what's the matter with all you girls: there's Olivia could marry young Loftus Maloney and won't, though he's as rich as Croesus and a damn nice young fella into the bargain, and yourself and Daisy stretched out on sofas all day, waiting to be waited on, and Katharine mooning after a penniless parson, and Harriet half-dead for love of a cow doctor! I'm sick to death of the lot of you; a more useless pack of women I never heard of, and goodness knows if I'll ever get any of you decently married now. You'll be spinsters on me hands for ever, I suppose, God help me!'

The unthinkable happened: Olivia lost her temper.

'Don't bully, Papa,' she cried, her blue eyes flaming. 'You ought to let Katharine marry Mr Weldon, and what does it matter if Captain Willoughby is a vet? It'd be hard to meet a nicer man. And as for that mean, shifty, rotten little Loftus Maloney, I wouldn't marry him if he was the last man on earth. How dare you go on at us all like this, Papa?'

Katharine was shocked to the depths of her being. 'Hush, Olivia!' she implored. 'Control yourself. Remember you're talking to Papa.'

'You blame Charlotte and Daisy for the way they go on,' continued

Olivia relentlessly, 'when it's your own fault.'

'Nonsense!' bellowed her father.

'Your own fault,' repeated Olivia. 'Look at the way you brought us all up, with idle, ignorant governesses who never made us do anything we didn't like. You can't blame them if they've turned out ignorant and idle themselves. It's too late now, Papa, to be angry with them.'

Harriet's face was buried in her hands, from dread of what might come. Charlotte and Daisy exchanged outraged glances. Katharine looked as if she awaited divine punishment to strike Olivia, so appalling was this revolt against authority; but as nothing happened she felt impelled to protest once more.

'Olivia,' she began, but her father suddenly whisked out of his chair and made for the door.

'Well, I'm off. If ye think I'm going to sit and listen to that kind of nonsense, you're mistaken.' His exit was astonishingly mild.

Katharine began again: 'Olivia, such wickedness! How could you, when you know that Papa always knows best!' The reproaches mounted up.

Olivia was quite calm now. 'But he doesn't know best, how can he? He's not even really interested in us. Aren't we ever to be allowed to grow up and decide things for ourselves? Why, it's ridiculous! We can't go on being steam-rollered for the rest of our lives.'

'But it's wrong,' laboured Katharine. 'He is Papa!'

Olivia remained unmoved and Katharine, distraught by her inability to counter such evil, turned away. Her eye lit upon Susan, whose presence everyone had forgotten, sitting on the hearth-rug beside a Chinese balancing toy with which she had been playing, and which was still rocking backwards and forwards from the touch that had set it in motion many minutes before. Susan had forgotten the toy; she was staring spell-bound at her Aunt Olivia.

'Susan!' snapped Katharine, scandalised that the child should have been a witness to such heresy. 'Are you still here? Go on up to Nanny this instant. Sitting there like a mouse, listening to things. . .'

CHAPTER THREE

Miss Flynn was an institution in the county. She was a visiting dressmaker of surprising skill who, after a fortnight in residence, would produce a collection of new and renovated clothes, and even hats, designed to see every female member of the family through every social engagement for several months.

She always came in an outside car from Inish station, five miles away, with a soft-topped case and her dead father's huge umbrella as her only luggage. She was whirled from one country house to another like a leaf in the wind, and wherever she was the sewing-machine whirred endlessly and pins covered the floor. Physically, she was insignificant and her spare little person was clothed in the cast-offs of the county ladies who were, on the whole, of a build more substantial than hers. Her eyes glinted through rimless glasses and every part of her face seemed to be in constant motion, giving her the look of a prism continually agitated by a draught.

At Fellowescourt she used to be given two attic rooms; one, a sewing-room, warmed by an oil stove, the other a bedroom. The sewing-room door had to be kept shut so that the noise of the machine did not reach the study; Captain Fellowes was inclined to curtail her visits if he thought they were too prolonged. Her status demanded meals on a tray and that she be addressed as 'Miss Flynn', though Lizzie much preferred to leave her standing in the back hall while she announced, 'The Dhressmaker.'

The morning-room used to be converted into a sort of fitting-room for her visits, littered with dresses, veiling, hats, beads, feathers and cards of buttons. On the sofa, warmed by a blazing fire, Charlotte and Daisy would settle after breakfast and await Miss Flynn in statuesque immobility; when she descended she would harry them into one garment after another without respite, then despatch them to fetch another sister.

One day, early in 1914, when Miss Flynn was installed at Fellowescourt, the family was assembled for prayers, which Captain Fellowes used to read before breakfast in the dining-room. In spite of his irreligious views he had never ceased to hold family prayers, perhaps because they were a tradition in the household, but he seemed to read them grudgingly, almost resentfully, and always fast. He expected the responses to be both loud and prompt.

There had been torrential rain in the night and the morning was cool, limpid and dripping, like washing hung out in the breeze, colours the more brilliant for being wet, drops glinting as they fell into the mirror pools below. A shaft of sunlight, diluted by the rain marks on the window panes, hit Susan across the eyes and made her toss her head as she listened to her grandfather's rasping old voice. Sitting on the broad, red leather chair and observing the pile on the carpet that grew all in the same direction, like fur, she saw Charlotte and Daisy smile secretly at each other, making faces that showed how much they wished Papa would hurry. She saw Olivia's shoulders fretting with impatience because her father had lost his place and did not recover himself well, and Katharine's look of concern.

'Our Father,' said the Captain and, 'Our Father,' echoed his daughters instantly. Had there been any delay he would have repeated it at the top of his voice, looking angrily round the table.

Prayers were over at last and everybody was glad. Captain Fellowes said Grace, and Nanny pushed Susan gently forward to be kissed. The watery line of sunshine strengthened and wavered against the red damask pattern on the wall, making the silver on the sideboard wink and gleam, and throwing globules of light on the furniture. Then, doused like a candle, it was gone. A moment later the rain drummed outside. Captain Fellowes cursed the rain under his breath, kissed Susan absentmindedly and kept an arm round her shoulder so that Nanny had to go without her.

'Katharine, I'm going to Cork today,' he announced. 'Sheehy must be round in plenty of time for the train, and I want a bag packed for three or four days.' He began to serve the porridge ferociously.

'Yes, Papa,' replied Katharine meekly. 'Perhaps I'd better see about it now,' she suggested, half-rising. 'If you'll excuse me, Papa.' She slipped out of the room.

Susan stood just behind her grandfather's chair, quite still lest someone notice her and send her away. She noticed how shiny and pink was the round bald patch at the back of his head, and how wiry the surrounding silvery hair. She could see the line of his cheeks swell as he blew on his spoon, and the little swirl of steam round his face. Unconsciously, she pulled at her fingers to make the bones crack, and the resulting sharp snap made the old man jump.

'What the divil!' he roared, turning half round. 'What the divil d'ye think ye're doing, child, making noises behind me. Go on off, now, back to Nanny.' He made a movement as if to rise and shook his table napkin at her. 'Go on,' he shouted, as she started to retreat.

Susan was deeply injured by this treatment; she was accustomed to hearing him speak so to his daughters but imagined that she was too precious to be bullied. She moved away so slowly that he sprang up, seized her under the arms, carried her out to the back hall and dumped her at the foot of the servants' staircase, roaring for Nanny to come and take her. Nanny came hurrying, shuffling downstairs in her old slippers.

'Nanny, for heaven's sake keep the child away from me this morning. I'm not fit for it, I tell you I can't stand it.' He passed a hand wretchedly over his forehead.

'Arrah, Sirr, I'm sorry now. . .' began Nanny, but the old gentleman had returned noisily to the dining-room. She turned to the weeping Susan. 'Ah now, lovey, sure he's not himself today. What ails him at all? What did ye do to vex him?'

'Nothing!' howled Susan, giving way to rage at the injustice. She threw herself on the floor and lashed out at Nanny with her heels. Nanny hovered round her, waiting for a chance to get her away upstairs.

'Leave her, Nanny,' commanded an icy voice. 'I will talk to her.' Susan stopped yelling for a split second from sheer surprise. 'You see,' continued Katharine. 'It's only temper.' She waved Nanny away up the stairs. 'Now, Susan, stop that noise this instant.'

Susan observed her through slitty eyes; she stood there as if she had all day to spare, resolute and composed, exuding authority. Susan had met her match; slowly, she stifled the sobs, making no attempt to move.

'Now get up.'

The impossibility of disobeying her, the hopelessness of refusal, the obliteration of her will under the impact of Katharine's made her weep tears of bitter defeat. She cried silent tears of mourning for her lost self-mastery.

'Go up to the nursery. I will come up later.' Katharine stood watching as the child turned blindly, scrambling up the stairs.

Some time later she went to the nursery and sent Nanny to the kitchen for her cup of tea; she sat in Nanny's chair by the fire and held out her hands.

'Come here, Susan,' she said with dutiful patience.

Susan remained flattened against the wall, as if she could in this way make herself two-dimensional and invulnerable.

'Very well. Stay where you are.' She shrugged her indifference. 'Grandpapa does not want you punished, but I want to see you tell him and Nanny you're sorry.'

'What for?'

She looked exasperated. 'For losing your temper; you know how naughty that is. And you kicked Nanny.'

'I didn't hurt her.'

'That has nothing to do with it: you wanted to hurt her. People who give way to temper sometimes end by committing murder. Every time you try to hurt someone you are crucifying Jesus and doing a very, very wicked thing.' She stopped to let the full horror of her sin appal the child. 'You see?' she added, after a proper pause.

Susan saw. The extent of her guilt overwhelmed her. Hell yawned, avid to receive her. She broke down in hopeless tears.

'Every time you wish harm to anyone it is a little killing,' said Katharine with quiet awe, 'and every sin is a little Crucifixion.' Her voice faltered; she was gazing at the fire with an expression of immense sadness and regret. 'But we are all sinners,' she added almost in a whisper.

This incredible pronouncement staggered Susan: she knew that her Aunt Katharine was always good, that she never told a lie, was greedy or worldly or lost her temper. Her goodness was insurmountable, an unscaleable wall between them; she was good all through, and Susan was bad, and that was that.

'Even you?' sobbed Susan, so sure of her facts that she did not even listen for a reply. Her crying irked Katharine.

'Hush now,' she said soothingly. 'When you've told them you're sorry we'll forget all about it.'

As if it were possible ever to forget! Susan marvelled at this piece of grown-up incomprehension. To say that she was sorry was pain and grief to her, worse than learning psalms, doing without pudding for a week or standing in the corner all day. When she was made to apologise she would think up ways of avoiding saying the words, 'I'm sorry.' She would pick little bunches of primroses and hand them silently to the person, or rush at them to hug them. They always forgave her. But this time she felt that there was no escape from full verbal admission of her guilt. She felt weighted down with despair.

'Nanny doesn't expect me to . . . she's been quite ordinary . . .' she countered, tailing off in tears again.

'I said both. Then we'll forget about it, not before.'

Katharine stood up, holding out an uncompelling hand which she could take or reject at her pleasure. Susan clasped hers behind her back.

Katharine smiled a little wryly, and they went downstairs.

Captain Fellowes was about to leave. When he saw Susan, he smiled, holding his arms wide as was his habit with her. She suddenly felt much happier and rushed towards him.

'There now,' he said, giving her a kiss on top of her head. 'We're friends again now. You mustn't mind when ancient old people get a bit cross, sometimes. They can't help it. Goodbye now, my love, remember your old Grandpapa when he's away, won't you?'

'Yes,' she promised, beaming.

'Susan,' reminded Katharine, 'you had something to say to Grandpapa.'

'Ah, don't be bothering me now,' said the old man irritably. 'I haven't time to be listening to things. Look after yer sisters and send me letters on to the Club.'

He was gone. Katharine looked at Susan in shocked disapproval. Susan was watching the trap disappear over the brow of the hill.

'I'm sorry,' she said in a flat, unrepentant voice as the last inch of Sheehy's whip was lost to sight. 'Now let's do Nanny.'

'That wasn't any good,' said Katharine tartly. 'It didn't cost you anything to say it like that.' She looked very put out as they went in search of Nanny.

They found her arguing with Lizzie in the back hall about who should have prior right to the use of the carpet sweeper.

As soon as she was aware of her audience she said loudly, 'If only Miss Kat'rine'd get another one for upstairs, then maybe we'd have a little peace. Ah, there you are, lovey! I'm after searchin' the garden an' stables an' all for ye. Quick now, get on yer coat and we'll go for our walk.'

'Susan!' said Katharine urgently, holding her by the shoulders. Susan began to wriggle, but could not escape. She said nothing.

'Susan!' repeated her aunt, bitter reproach in her voice.

'What is it, Miss?' said Nanny. 'What ails her?'

'Susan has something to say to you; she will tell you herself.'

Susan began to cry again. Nanny knelt beside her and took her in her arms. 'Arrah now,' she said, 'there, there now.'

'Oh, Nanny!' cried Katharine in exasperation. 'She was going to apologise for kicking you, but now you've spoilt it all.' She glared at Nanny in great annoyance. But Nanny began to laugh as though this were the best joke of the century.

'Kick?' she exclaimed, 'sure all she gave me was a little tip wit' her heel! She'd never hurt poor Nanny, sure ye wouldn't, lovey?'

'No,' wailed Susan, and that was the full extent of her apology.

Katharine hurried away with a little snort of impatience.

'Upsettin' ye!' grumbled Nanny as they went upstairs. 'Sins an' wickedness is all she sees, God help her.'

Susan recovered quickly, reassured by the way Nanny dismissed the incident as trivial. She felt safe in Nanny's presence. Nanny was able to laugh about it, so perhaps it was not so terrible after all.

The whirr of the sewing-machine reached them from the attic.

'Oh, let me go and see Miss Flynn!' begged Susan.

Nanny beamed at her. She would have let her do anything.

'Go on up,' she agreed, 'I'll just get the nursery done and then we'll go out.'

Miss Flynn was working with awesome concentration and rapidity. She smiled gently as Susan put her head round the door, her mouth was full of pins, her head shaking slightly and continually.

'Can I turn the handle of the machine, please?'

There was a certain hesitation; Miss Flynn could not permit even kindness to slow down her work and thus undermine her integrity.

'It would be such a help, dear, if you would pick up some pins for me,' she suggested. Susan crawled about, picking up pins and pressing them through holes of the filet-crochet cover of Miss Flynn's massive crimson pin-cushion. The oil stove had a reassuring smell and gave out a comforting warmth, and although Miss Flynn had scarcely said a word to her Susan knew that she liked children and was pleased to have her there.

She began to gather a collection of fragments of different materials, fingering them and allowing the light to play on them, grouping together those whose colours blended happily. There was a sudden light step outside and Olivia came in: she was the only one who ever ascended to Miss FIynn; the others made her come down to them.

Miss Flynn removed the pins from her mouth and smiled warmly at Olivia, whom she adored. She held up the half-finished frock on which she was working, and Olivia looked at it appreciatively.

'It looks simply lovely,' she said. 'I don't know how you do it. Is it ready to try on?'

Miss Flynn had pins in her mouth again; she was taking them out one by one to stick into the frock.

'Ffif. . . If you don't mind, ffif . . .'

Olivia began to take off her blouse and skirt. 'How's your mother, Miss Flynn?' she asked.

'Not too bad, thank you Miss Olivia, a great sufferer you know, always will be.' She bit off a thread deftly. 'Incurable, you know, thirty years in bed. Wonderful, isn't it? I don't know what I'd do if anything happened to her; she's all I've got.' Miss Flynn's fingers flew along as she finished off a seam by hand. She stood up and eased the dress over Olivia's head and shoulders, then stood back to inspect it.

'You're a wonderful daughter to her,' said Olivia humbly, her voice very gentle.

Miss Flynn's person vibrated all over as she shook her head.

'Oh, I ought to be with her more, you know,' she said, as if she had been accused of neglect, 'but what am I to do? I have to earn for us both.' She smiled suddenly with great sweetness. 'People are so good— so good to her. There's Mrs Mauleverer, our landlady, you know, looks after her as if she was her own mother, nothing's any trouble. Oh, I am lucky! Thank God, I always say, for our good friends.' With all the agitation, her hairpins were beginning to drop out from between the thin grey strands of her bun; she felt her head all over and pressed home the loose pins. 'Dear dear,' she murmured, as if in apology for such waste of precious seconds. She. was on her knees now, altering the hemline, the pins in her mouth like a cheval-de-frise, creeping round Olivia as if her life depended on doing it quickly.

'Look, this isn't quite right,' said Olivia, turning her head until she could touch her shoulder with her chin.

'Oh indeed! So I see! Tch tch tch. However did I make that mistake! Tch tch!' Horrified, Miss Flynn ripped the seam with one slash, grabbed a piece of tailor's chalk, marked the place and pinned it.

'Ah! that's better. I think that's done it.' She suddenly sat back on her heels and beamed shyly at Olivia. 'You won't mind my asking,' she said, and hesitated, then went on with a rush. 'Will you let me make your wedding-dress, Miss Olivia? When the time comes, that is, of course, ffif.' For a moment she sat looking up into Olivia's face and doing nothing at all, probably for the first time in her life.

'I wouldn't let anybody else touch my wedding-dress,' said Olivia, smiling down with great affection at the agitated little face.' You're the only person I'd ever let make it for me.'

'I hope it won't be long before you meet Mr Right!' sighed Miss Flynn happily. She turned to Susan. 'You've got such a lovely Auntie!' she said admiringly and, catching sight of an irregularity in the hemline of the blue ottoman laid across the end of the ironing table, set off, still on her knees, to put it right.

Susan was too shy to say a word; she pretended that she had not heard and pressed her nose against the window, gazing out at the sweep of the mountain down to the garden wall. A heavy shower was drenching the next line of hills, moving like a veil across them. In the garden there was the intense brilliance of a wet world between showers; there was a silvery bloom on the lawn grass and the trunks of the Scotch firs glowed ruddily in patches where the rain had soaked them. The ardent blue-green of the crowns of the trees was touched with gold in the vivid light, and lichen shimmered jewel-like on the deeply scarred bark. It was at this moment that Susan was first aware of the power of beauty to lift the heart and pierce it at the same time. Quite suddenly she knew that she had a secret thing, a source of vitality and of great joy that no one could take away from her, a thing to be guarded and nurtured and never mentioned to anyone and which even her Aunt Katharine could not touch. From that day, the line of Scotch firs against the mountain was, for her, the essence of Fellowescourt, the delight of her eye, and refreshment in her memory when she was away from home.

She swung round again, into the room. Olivia was nearly ready.

'Don't you get very tired, Miss Flynn?' she was saying. 'You always seem to be sewing half through the night, getting things finished.'

'Me?' asked Miss Flynn incredulously. 'Oh, I'm never tired.' There was a shade of impatience in her voice for those who allowed themselves the luxury of fatigue. 'Besides, I don't like to disappoint people; they want something for a special day and they've got everything planned to go with it—I can't let them down. And I love my work, always making pretty things!' Her fingers were darting along as she spoke, tacking a long seam; she made a quick back stitch and broke the thread with a little jerk. In a matter of seconds the material was rushing through the sewing machine, which rattled excitedly with the speed at which she drove it without a stop, so expertly did she guide the stuff and feed it to the needle. 'Dear me!' she laughed as she finished off the stitching. 'I wonder where I'd be if I allowed myself to feel tired! It's different, of course, if one is ill, but thank God I've got my health and a home to work for and my mother still living, so what more could I want?'

Indeed, her irregular old face, agitated perpetually by some interior motive force, radiated contentment.

'How wonderful to feel like that,' said Olivia, so quietly that Miss Flynn could not hear her, having set off on another lengthy run; but she seemed to sense Olivia's warmth and sympathy and raised her head in full flight, as it were, to smile back at her. In another second she was lost in her work again.

Olivia held out her hands to Susan. 'I'll dance you down the passage,' she said.

They set off in a rollicking polka, Olivia humming the tune of 'You should see me dance the polka' and breaking into song as soon as she remembered that her father was not at home. Up and down the passage they went, until they were so out of breath that they had to lean, panting, against the wall at the top of the stairs. After a moment, laughing, they set off again, both singing this time at the top of their voices. Then, hand in hand, they ran down the stairs and danced another polka on each landing, so that when they reached the ground floor they were panting, flushed and giggling, and making more noise than anybody, except the Captain, had dared to make in that house for years.

They almost fell into the morning-room, where Charlotte and Daisy awaited in static calm Miss Flynn's descent from the top floor. As ample and well-fitted as a couple of tea-cosies, they sat amongst all the dressmaking paraphernalia. They had the unusual gift of being able to remain in complete silence almost indefinitely without the slightest embarrassment; they seemed to have no nerves. Charlotte was, if anything, even less active than Daisy, and less liable to be surprised into movement. She was the first to complain that they were being put upon, that people expected too much of them, and Daisy always supported her. Charlotte was the larger, darker and less pleasant-looking, a little too fat, with an expression of bovine impassivity that was only dispelled by the prospect of what she described as a lark. Daisy's face was more open but no less vacant; her eyes were blue, like a doll's, her hair chestnut-coloured and coarse, and her mouth never quite closed over two white and slab-like upper teeth.

Daisy said, rather condescendingly, 'Whatever have you been doing, Olivia? You seem to be enjoying yourselves.'

'We quite thought,' announced Charlotte, as though it was inconsiderate of them to have deceived her, 'that you were Miss Flynn. We've been waiting for her all the morning.' She relapsed into an affronted silence.

Olivia picked up an enormous black straw hat that was lying on the sofa-head, and a feather boa, and put them quickly on Susan, turning her round to face the others.

'We were just having fun, Susan and I,' she said, 'dancing a polka. Look, who's she like?'

'Not like any of us,' said Daisy with distaste, 'she's too pale and wispy. She's not even like poor Lucius. I think she takes after *her* people.' Daisy always alluded to Susan's mother as 'her'; they had never liked one another and even now Daisy would not pronounce her name.

'No. Look!' laughed Olivia. 'Can't you see a look of Katharine? Something about the chin. Look now!' She whipped off the hat with its enormous pink rose trimming and cast about for something more sober. Her eye fell on Katharine's blouse with a boned net top and black velvet neckband and she seized it and put it on Susan. 'Now your hair,' she said, pulling off the ribbons and screwing the mouse-gold plaits into a prim bun. 'Now look at me as if I was being terribly naughty. No, you mustn't laugh, Susan! Now, oh do look! Isn't she the image?'

The likeness was unmistakeable in the brow, the nose, the set of the chin. Katharine's eyes were dark blue, her hair was nearly black and her skin clear and pale; Susan was fairer and her eyes were grey, but she had the look of a mezzotint miniature of Katharine. When she tried to look censorious her mouth took on the same line as Katharine's. Her aunts all rocked with laughter. Susan climbed on a chair to make faces at herself in the mirror, pretending that she was Katharine reproving her, and this made her laugh so much that she had to come down and collapse on the sofa. Charlotte had an extraordinary laugh, loud and coarse when she let herself go, and now she emitted peal after peal of merriment, making such an odd noise that her sisters were rendered almost paralytic with mirth. The noise they all made was like that of a flock of hens attacked by a fox. The door suddenly opened to admit Katharine.

There they all were, rolling about in an orgy of laughter, and Susan dressed in her very clothes with her hair arranged like hers. Susan tried to duck behind the sofa, but it was no good.

'Come out from there, Susan,' she ordered quietly and as the child emerged shame-facedly she added with some asperity, 'Why should you want to hide, I wonder?'

Olivia was unabashed: 'We dressed her up to look like you, and d'ye know, she really does. Come here, darling.'

But Susan's heart had failed her and she could not move.

'I don't expect,' commented Katharine tartly, 'that she feels like putting on the same expression when I'm here.' There was a moment's uncomfortable silence while she looked at them all. Then she said to Susan, 'Take off my blouse now and fold it tidily. Ask Aunt Olivia if she will plait your hair for you and tie your ribbons, and then you can run along.'

Susan began to obey her with almost exaggerated care, smoothing every crease out of the blouse before laying it on the table, and while she was so occupied, Katharine frowned at Olivia and complained in a loud whisper, 'How you can be so . . . irresponsible, Olivia, making a mock of me before the child! No wonder she rebels against my authority! And all this noise, too, the moment Papa is out of the house! Behaving like servant girls! I think it's disgusting.'

Daisy giggled behind her hand, Olivia grimaced and said, 'You're so stuffy, Katharine. We were only having fun.'

'Yes, about me. Before the child.' She sniffed. 'Please do Susan's hair for her now.'

Olivia sat Susan on the edge of her knees and began to separate her hair into strands. Katharine went to the door but turned back with a gesture of confusion.

'Oh!' she cried. 'All this has made me forget what I came in to say. Did you think Papa was well this morning? I was shocked at his appearance, he looked so ill. I wish he had not had to go away.'

'I thought he looked terrible,' said Olivia.

'Oh,' said Charlotte, 'is he ill then? I thought him very cross.'

'Papa is never cross,' snapped Katharine. 'He gets irritated.'

'I hope he's not going to be ill,' said Daisy thoughtfully. It would be such an upset.'

'If he got ill in Cork,' said Charlotte with awe, 'you'd have to go and look after him, Katharine.'

'Then,' giggled Daisy, 'you'd have to do the housekeeping, Charlotte.'

Charlotte stretched out her neck in annoyance, like an affronted swan.

'You know quite well I shouldn't ever think of such a thing,' she protested. 'We should have to have a housekeeper.'

'I wish,' said Katharine, 'he would have seen Doctor O'Brien. But then, he won't hear of going to a doctor.' She shrugged expressively. It was not disloyal to say that Papa did not pay enough attention to his health.

There was a tap on the door and Miss Flynn appeared, a load of dresses over one arm. She perceived the uneasiness in the room and hovered in the doorway.

'May I come in?' she enquired, nervously pressing home her hairpins.

'Oh, come in. Miss Flynn,' said Charlotte grandly. 'We've been waiting for you.'

Miss Flynn's head wobbled distressfully on her little stalk of a neck; she was horrified to think that she should have kept anybody waiting. 'Oh dear,' she said, 'I'm so very sorry. Ffif!'

'My fault,' said Olivia, smiling. 'I went and had a fitting upstairs.'

Charlotte was bored by apologies and excuses. 'It's quite all right,' she said graciously. 'We understand.' She felt disinclined to move at that moment. 'Daisy, let her start with you,' she said. 'Susan, bring me that red frock there. No, not that one, that's pink, that one.' She pointed. Olivia and Katharine left the room, too busy to stay. 'Now, Miss Flynn, do you think you could alter this neck without my trying it on?'

'Ffif! I'm afraid we must try things on if we're to get them right, Miss Charlotte,' protested Miss Flynn, seeing a threat to her integrity.

'It won't take us a minute when the time comes,' she added persuasively.

Nanny opened the door with a little fumbling knock and beckoned to Susan. 'Come on, now,' she whispered. 'We're past our time.' Susan began to move towards her. With a sudden exclamation of dismay Nanny cried, 'God save us, Miss Daisy, is it mournin' ye're all getting fitted for? I never saw so much old black . . .' Her eye wavered on the red frock on Charlotte's lap and she began to laugh. 'Sure, I don't know what took me at all. I must be goin' blind!' She led Susan off, cackling.

As it turned out, she was not far wrong. Captain Fellowes returned after two days, a sick man. Within a week he was dead of pneumonia.

CHAPTER FOUR

Susan was nearly eight years old when her grandfather fell ill, old enough to sense the terror with which Charlotte and Daisy regarded the prospect of a death in their very home, where they could neither ignore it nor escape from its impact, nor indeed concern themselves with anything else. They were so uncertain of themselves, being moved by awe rather than affection, yet wishing to conform to the proprieties, that they were afraid to laugh or talk above a whisper in case they should be thought wanting in respect. Their inner resources were inadequate, their spiritual beliefs unsure; they mistrusted their spontaneous reactions and felt it safer to spend their days cocooned unnaturally in hush and gloom.

Katharine, on the other hand, was admirable. She nursed her father devotedly, day and night, and when she could no longer do without sleep handed over to Harriet and Olivia, who sat up with him together. Charlotte and Daisy utterly refused to take their turn, so terrified were they that he might die while they were in charge. The very suggestion drove them to the verge of hysterics. But Katharine was unafraid, spoke of him always with compassion, moved about with calm and bore all the vexations and responsibilities with fortitude and self-control. Never for a moment did she give way to fatigue.

Susan was aware of her strength, just as she could feel the bankruptcy of Charlotte and Daisy and the sense of duty that drove Harriet and Olivia, shrinking, to do their share of the nursing. The household was really in two camps; the one led by Katharine included the servants who, being Roman Catholics, had learnt not to evade the thought of death and prayed without embarrassment for the soul of their master, and Harriet, Olivia and Susan; the other, without direction, afraid and despairing, swayed by superstition and ready to panic, consisted of Charlotte, Daisy and, oddly enough, Nanny.

Nanny knew that her days at Fellowescourt were numbered; she knew that Katharine, with every justification, regarded her as a cause of disunity, a scoffer at her piety and an instigator to rebellion in the nursery.

Nanny aged years in that single week. She dragged herself miserably around, babbling prayers for her master's recovery and terrifying Susan with descriptions of what would befall her when Katharine had her in her clutches. Her entire preoccupation was not with the Captain's death which became daily more inevitable, but with its consequences.

'Oh, what'll I do, what'll I do at all?' she muttered as she swept, ironed, or merely gazed into the fire. She wiped her eyes ceaselessly though she never appeared to be actually in tears.

Susan felt miserable, appalled and consumingly frightened. Nanny's misery, Charlotte and Daisy's alarm, Katharine's courage and serenity and the desperate determination of Harriet and Olivia to do their duty all reminded her constantly that something dreadful was happening. Nothing was natural or ordinary. Waking and sleeping, there drummed upon the taut skin of her consciousness the awful certainty that soon Nanny would be sent away, for although she prayed hard for her grandfather's recovery she had not the slightest faith that this would come about. She knew that he would die.

Mrs O'Brien, the doctor's wife, suggested to Katharine that Nanny and Susan should spend the days with her and her children until, as she put it, Captain Fellowes was better. Katharine was thankful to get them out of the house, so they walked the half-mile to Myrtle Lodge and back every day until the old gentleman was dead and buried.

Mrs O'Brien was a kind, Mongol-faced woman, with stringy dark hair. She had a whole tribe of little children from the age of ten downwards who spoke incomprehensible English and were all flat-faced, sloe-eyed and had quantities of straight black hair. Even the baby had been born with brown eyes.

Nanny was disgusted by the confusion that was both general and permanent at Myrtle Lodge. The nursery was in the charge of a girl called Bridie, aged sixteen, who toiled unsuccessfully from morning till night in the hope of keeping the four older children clean, fed, exercised and amused while she occupied herself largely with the baby. Discipline was non-existent, the noise was appalling, the floor was littered with toys, books, shoes, crusts and bits of coal plucked from the scuttle by the crawler, and dust lay thickly wherever it was undisturbed.

Mrs O'Brien, her ample person unrestricted by corsetry and seeming to lap like a tide against the yielding boundaries of her spacious and shapeless garments, trailed in and out with a perpetual air of being half-dressed. She would pick up the baby, settling momentarily on the edge of a chair to bounce him on her knee, and exclaim with cheerful unconcern, 'Bridie, the child is soaked!' She would then replace him, still soaked, in his cot until Bridie should have time to change him.

'Would you like my baby?' she electrified Susan by enquiring on the first day she was there. She made as though to thrust him into her arms. 'Will I give him to ye, will I?' Susan backed desperately away, embarrassed beyond expression, and Mrs O'Brien and Bridie went into fits of laughter. 'Ah, but it's sad now, isn't it? The poor little thing!' Mrs O'Brien exclaimed inexplicably, adding, 'Sure, the only one never has a chance!'

Susan thought the baby dreadful; he was always soaked and his face and hands were permanently smeared with butter from the slice of bread that was generally in one hand, or else had fallen amongst his coverings. He grizzled all the time. Susan really believed that Mrs O'Brien would foist him on her.

'Sure, Mammy'd never give y'away, now would she?' she crooned then, hugging the baby close. 'Ah, not at all, Mammy'd never spare ye to that little gerrl. Och, the pain of his teeth has him near out of his mind!' She wiped his running nose lovingly and kissed his greasy little face. 'Give me a little bit of a crust for him, Bridie, to cut his teeth on.' The baby stopped crying and smiled up at her. 'Ah, sure, Mammy'd never give y'away!' She cuddled him close, laid him back in his cot with a kiss and stooped to take Susan's face between her hands. 'Aren't you the poor wee lonely one?' she said tenderly and kissed the top of her head as if she pitied her more than words could say.

Nanny was too dejected to be of much help to Bridie. She suffered in a stiff-backed snobbish silence and protested to Susan all the way home, each evening, about the dreadful way in which the O'Brien children were being brought up, ending with, 'Mind now, never let me see ye wipe yer nose on yer sleeve, the way I seen that little Barry do it, though I must say when ye see how much lookin' afther them poor childhren gets, and that's none at all, it's a wondher they're as nice as they are.'

Barry was the one nearest to Susan in age, and no duenna could have been more concerned to prevent undesirable attachments than was Nanny to make sure that she had no illusions about Barry's suitability as a playmate then, or at any time in the future. She made out that she pitied the O'Brien children, but there was no compassion in her pity. When she and Bridie took all the children out for an afternoon walk, she always kept slightly aloof so that no one could imagine they quite belonged to the same party.

Susan admired Barry but he found her an unsatisfactory companion; she was too good, he said disgustedly, too frightened of getting dirty, too ignorant about birds' nests, tadpoles and stickle-backs, and much too easily made to cry. She persuaded him to take her looking for frogspawn and carried a jar of it home under her coat, only to get soaked with filthy water and to have jar, frogspawn and water hurled on to the rubbish heap by Nanny. He shinned up trees, expecting her to follow, and issued contemptuous instructions from aloft when he discovered that she had never climbed a tree in her life. But she was determined to impress him, if not by her skill then by her courage, and made such rapid progress that he was forced to admit that one day she might be all right.

Early in the morning of the fifth day, Katharine went to the nursery to say that her father was dead. Her face was grey with exhaustion and the early-morning light accentuated her pallor, but she did not weep, which was a great relief. Susan began to cry with a mounting compulsion to mourn not only her grandpapa but the end of her happiness. Nanny wept and wept without a word.

When they reached Myrtle Lodge, Susan felt half-dead and her face was swollen with crying. Nanny could only sit in misery by the fire.

Surprisingly, Mrs O'Brien made Susan feel much better. She sat in an armchair and pulled the child against her knee, stroking her hair and talking gently about death and immortality with a homely familiarity that took all the fear out of the subject; the next world seemed to be already a part of her experience and her quiet reassurance and natural way of speaking set Susan's feet on the ground again.

As soon as she saw that the child was calm and had stopped crying, she took off her shoes, laid her on her own bed, covered with an eiderdown, and left her to sleep off the grief, fear and shock of the last few days.

All the world turned up at the funeral; if not beloved, the Captain had at least been a notable figure. Even some of the Cork Fellowes made the journey. Nanny and Susan stood outside the gate of Myrtle Lodge and watched the slow procession wind in at the Church gate; there were carriages, gigs, dogcarts and even a couple of motor cars, as well as farm carts and traps.

As soon as the funeral was over, the spirits of Charlotte and Daisy recovered miraculously. They felt it was no longer discreditable to smile or laugh in a restrained way. It was even permissible to discuss the plans that had been forming in their minds and which it would have been improper to mention before.

The next day, in the morning-room, they awaited one of Miss Flynn's lightning descents with some hastily-made mourning clothes; they agreed that it was most convenient that she happened to he in the house at just this time. They were, as usual, sitting before the fire in great comfort and complete immobility, their full, smooth faces in repose, not a finger moving, not a muscle tensed.

'I suppose,' began Charlotte, ending one of their prolonged and comfortable silences, 'that Katharine'll marry Mr Weldon now.'

'Well, what's to stop her, now Papa's . . . no longer here?' said Daisy crossly, disliking the prospect of losing such an efficient housekeeper. She could no more have said 'now that Papa's dead' than she could have convinced herself that one day she too would die. Death was too unpleasant and alarming to be allowed into language. 'Of course,' she went on, having left a suitable short pause, 'it wouldn't suit us at all, really. You'd have to do the housekeeping, Char.' There was a touch of malice in her sideways look.

Charlotte bridled angrily, 'You said that before, once, Daisy, and you know I shouldn't dream of it. I do wish you wouldn't be so unkind.' She sat, looking very put out. 'Anyway, someone else could do it, Harriet or Olivia. It'd do them good.'

Miss Flynn's diffident knock prevented further discussion. Poor Miss Flynn was torn between the desire to get the Miss Fellowes suitably fitted out and dread that she might interrupt the course of grief. To her relief the sisters appeared quite composed and her admiration for the courage with which they bore their bereavement was unbounded.

'Would you like me now?' she asked timidly, 'I can come later if you like.'

'Come in, Miss Flynn,' said Charlotte graciously. 'We were expecting you.'

The spidery old hand flew to her head to press home the displaced hairpins as Miss Flynn advanced, her lips pursed with nervous concern.

'I don't expect you feel up to much,' she said sympathetically. 'Tch

tch tch, when we buried my poor father, forty-two years ago, I remember what I went through.'

The girls were nonplussed; they were ashamed to admit that affection for their father had never been a big thing in their lives, yet it was difficult and tiresome to assume a grief they did not feel. Eventually, Charlotte said, 'Yes,' in a tone of dismissal, but Miss Flynn was undeterred.

'Yes,' she reminisced, 'I was only twenty when he died, and never a penny was he able to leave us, poor man. Oh, we did have a struggle, I can tell you, but we won through. I've no complaints, no complaints at all. Though, mind you, I'm sure it was all that worry and hard work that brought poor Mother to the state she's in now—flat on her back for thirty years, she's been, and never a word out of her about the pain, isn't that wonderful, now?'

'Wonderful,' commented Charlotte affably.

'Of course you're safe from that worry, the money, I mean,' said Miss Flynn with genuine relief. 'It'd never do for ladies to have to earn their livings.' She drew in her breath with a sharp little 'ffif' as soon as she realised that the mention of money put her on dangerous ground.

'Earn our livings!' said Daisy in a shocked voice. 'I should hope not, indeed! Why, I know quite well I never could. I should simply starve to death.' She looked quite upset.

'No,' murmured Miss Flynn, 'that'd never do, never do at all. Now I'll just take that up a shade on the shoulder, Miss Charlotte. It's hard on Miss Katharine, now isn't it?' she went on. 'With so much to see to and no man in the family now. She's looking badly, I thought her looking very badly today, poor thing. I hope she'll take it easy now for a while.'

'Oh, but she's got a lot to do,' explained Charlotte pompously. 'Business and so on, you know.' She spoke as if such things were outside Miss Flynn's experience.

'The lawyer's here now,' added Daisy impressively, 'Mr Blair. He came down from Cork this morning. He'll be here for the night.'

'Ffif . . . yes, I'm sure there must be plenty for him to do. Still, you don't want strangers in the house at a time like this . . .' Miss Flynn's voice wavered a little as she remembered her own position in the household. She spoke no more, and her fittings completed, was gone in a moment.

The two sisters began to discuss their father's will, which had been read to them that morning. Fellowescourt had been left to them all, but any sister who married forfeited her share in her ownership. If they all married, Susan was to have it; it was to go to her in the end, anyway, as she was the eldest, and at the moment the only, grandchild. All money was to be divided equally between the sisters and Susan, in trust, the whole reverting to Susan as her aunts died.

'If Katharine marries Mr Weldon, then there'll be less for us to keep the place going on,' said Charlotte with a sniff.

'Susan's going to be quite a catch when we're all dead,' said Daisy in a grieved tone. 'I don't think it's fair. Why shouldn't *my* children have their share? Susan always was Papa's favourite just because he didn't know what our children were going to be like. I know I wouldn't spoil mine like he did Susan. It's a shame they'll have to be paupers, poor little things.' Her children seemed to stand around her, in penury.

'Rich husbands are what we need,' said Charlotte firmly. 'It's the only thing for us, Daisy.'

'Yes,' Daisy agreed, 'if only we could meet some. We're so stuck in the country here, we never meet anybody, and if we do they get smit on Olivia, not us.'

'When we're out of mourning, we'll go to Dublin, Daisy, just you and me. We'll stay with funny old Cousin Sib in Merrion Square, and she'll give a dance for us, at least. I'm sure she will. She knows everybody, and there are thousands of rich officers, with titles too, in Dublin, besides all the people who live there anyway. I'd like to marry an earl,' added Charlotte sedately. 'I think I'd make rather a good countess, don't you?'

Daisy ignored this question. 'Certainly I'd never consider a clergyman, unless he was a bishop, or anyone to do with trade. A lord of some kind, or a general, or even an admiral would do me very well. I don't want anybody too young; not old, you know, but over thirty-five and not too much of a gadabout. I should like him to stay at home with me. I shan't do anything at all; the servants will do everything.' She flicked a speck of dust fastidiously from her skirt. 'And I certainly don't intend to stay here all my life, taking orders from "the Pope".'

Such were their plans. But upstairs, Olivia and Harriet were also making arrangements for the future. They sat on the edge of Harriet's bed, the eiderdown spread over their knees for warmth.

Harriet was desperate: marry she must, and Captain Willoughby it must be. She admired him, he admired her, and Olivia must help to bring the match about. So much she had brought herself to declare, blushing all over. If Olivia had dared to smile, Harriet would have fled from the room.

'But what can I do?' she queried earnestly. 'Papa was so . . . discouraging to him that I think he was quite put off. I don't expect he'll ever come near us again. You see, Olivia, I'm almost thirty, and he's not getting any younger either.'

Olivia kissed her with real affection. 'I'm so glad you told me about it,' she said warmly, 'I always thought you and he ought to get married, but of course Papa wouldn't hear of it. And Katharine . . . well, we'll just have to get round her.'

'Yes, Katharine,' repeated Harriet glumly. Getting round Katharine would be no simpler than persuading Papa.

'Well, if she's difficult, you shall marry him in spite of her.'

'Oh, Olivia!' Harriet cried in delicious terror.

'Yes,' Olivia nodded as she spoke, to stress her determination. 'In spite of her! You're not to be timid, Harriet. You're not to let her stop you. After all, I expect she will marry Mr Weldon herself, so she won't have a leg to stand on . . .'

'You do think Captain Willoughby's a gentleman, don't you Olivia?

I mean, you don't feel like "the Pope" does about him being a vet?'
Harriet's face was pink with anxiety.

'Harriet, darling! If he was a chimney sweep and you loved him, I
wouldn't care, so long as he was a nice man and would make you happy.'

'Olivia!' exclaimed Harriet, giggling delightedly.

There was no doubt about it, the Captain's death had given his girls
a sense of liberation. And while Harriet and Olivia plotted the capture
of Captain Willoughby, Katharine was still engaged with Mr Blair in
the study.

Mr Blair was a dusty-looking little man with a moth-eaten
appearance about the hair; he was not dirty, yet he would have been
improved by a good spring-clean. He was unmarried and lived by
himself in rooms in Cork, so it was the concern of no one to keep his
clothes and his person in good order. He had a very bright grey eye,
as sharp as metal, and a great liking for gossip. He disliked dealing
with ladies, finding it difficult to educate them in an appreciation of
legal procedure, delays and phraseology. If they were left money, they
wanted it that very minute and made a fuss if they had to wait. They
had no patience, no discretion and no sense—or so he had imagined
until he had had to deal with Katharine Fellowes.

She had grasped every detail of the will with ease; her questions and
comments were remarkably intelligent and once or twice he had been
hard put to it to satisfy her by his replies. He could see that she knew
when he was hedging, and this made him a little frightened of her.

'Now, about the money?' she said coolly. Mr Blair gave her a quick
look of alarm, recognising signs of trouble to come.

'M'yes, Miss Fellowes?' he enquired, with simulated composure. In
his discomfort he crossed one snuff-coloured tweed leg over the other
and gazed at the lack-lustre toe of his shoe, moving it about as if it might
shine if only it could catch the light. 'How much is there?' she asked.

Mr Blair was a little shocked. Ignorance compelled him to evade
the issue.

'You've taken me by surprise, Miss Fellowes. It's hard to say at this stage, of course. Your father, you know, never chose to tell me the extent of his fortune. Did he never . . . I mean, you have no idea yourself?'

She gave him a quick, direct look. 'He never mentioned money to any of us, unless,' and she gave a tight little smile, 'he thought we were spending too much. But I am anxious to find out how we stand as soon as possible: there will be expenses to be met, wages and tradesmen's bills, and so on, and we have no more than a couple of pounds in the house. None of us has a bank account; you see, my father did not believe in women handling money. He paid our necessary bills, but we never had anything to spend. So I shall need to be able to draw upon some.'

'Tch tch tch!' worried Mr Blair, amazed by these revelations. 'Indeed you will, Miss Fellowes. No bank account, eh? Well, well! We must open one for you straight away. There will be no difficulty, I assure you. Close on eighty thousand pounds your grandfather left, if I remember rightly, when he died in '89. The family has always been . . . well-to-do, shall we say?'

'I suppose that is something to go on. Now, supposing I were to marry, Mr Blair?'

'You are to be married, Miss Fellowes?'

'I did not say so. All I said was, "supposing I were to marry".'

'Mm er . . . I beg your pardon, Miss Fellowes. Yes?'

'I would still receive my income from the Trust fund?'

'Certainly. Oh yes, indeed. Only you would no longer have a share in the house.' There was a short, uncomfortable silence. It was plain that Mr Blair was about to say something unpleasant.

'Yes?' enquired Katharine mercilessly.

'Er . . . you will forgive me, I know, if I speak as your legal advisor and your very true friend, Miss Fellowes.' He looked wretchedly at his feet again. Katharine's head shot back in quick defiance.

'I don't promise to take your advice, Mr Blair,' she said.

'No. No, naturally not. Nevertheless . . . if you were contemplating marriage you would take care to be very . . . sure of your partner, wouldn't you? I mean to say, a young lady of means, like yourself, with a personality as pleasing, and coming of a good family, and . . . er, as personable as yourself . . .'

'The Pope' cut him short. 'That's enough Mr Blair. I know I am no beauty, so you needn't perjure yourself on that account. I hate pretence in any form, or flattery.' Mr Blair uttered uncomfortable protests without actually speaking. She went on, 'You're afraid someone might want to marry me just for my money, is that it? It's kind of you to show so much concern, but perhaps I might be able to perceive such motives for myself.' She gave him a hint of a frigid little bow. 'As it happens . . . Mr Blair, what would you say to me if I told you I was going to marry a penniless clergyman?'

Poor Mr Blair winced; he could envisage nothing more calamitous. He shook his head before exclaiming with some warmth, 'I could not recommend it. I fear you would be heading for disaster.'

She looked at him stonily. 'Money isn't everything.'

'Ah, that's what people say while they have some, Miss Fellowes. When they have none, they talk differently. But do you mean to tell me that this . . . clergyman would be content to live on your income? That seems to me . . .' He was so agitated that he could not continue. He took out his handkerchief and blew his nose with a good deal of noise.

Katharine looked at him searchingly. 'As it happens,' she said, 'my mind is quite made up, so nothing you say will make the slightest difference. My father, like you, was very much against it and in deference to his wishes I did not marry in his lifetime. My duty to him, I think, is done and I propose to please myself. That is how things stand. I didn't mean to tell you all this, but things led up to it somehow. Please keep this to yourself: even my sisters know nothing of it yet.'

'But, my dear Miss Fellowes, are you sure that you can trust this man? I implore you, consider. Consider what you are doing.'

'Consider what you are doing, Mr Blair. You want to keep two people apart who, but for lack of means, would have been married this long while. You want to spoil their lifelong happiness by insisting on a conventional detail—that the man should have the money. You're a materialist, and suspicious without any grounds to be so. If you only knew the man whose motives you so mistrust, you would soon change your mind. Dinner will be at eight o'clock. Good afternoon.'

She had left the room before Mr Blair had even struggled to his feet. Her usually pale cheeks were very pink, her mouth was tightly set and her dark blue eyes blazed as she swept out, rather short of breath, not really thinking where she was going. Outside the morning-room she came upon Susan, hopping along on one leg with a message for Charlotte from Miss Flynn. She stopped and withered her with a look.

'So,' she said, anger clipping her words and making them difficult to understand, 'so this is Grandpapa's little pet! And the day after he's buried, she's dancing round the house.' There was no reply so she went on, 'Go back to the nursery and do your Sunday crochet. That may make you reflect!'

'I have to tell Aunt Charlotte—'

'Where's your crochet?'

'In the nursery, but—' Susan's mouth was dry.

'Go there and stay there, then. What a disobedient little thing you are! 'Pon my word, nobody's going to spoil you now. Go on, shoo!' She drove the child up the back stairs, pushed her inside the nursery door and closed if quickly, then took refuge in the chill calm of her own room. She took a cold sponge and pressed it against her burning eyes.

'Oh!' she exclaimed suddenly, aloud. Then 'Oh!' she cried again, 'God forgive me, I'm behaving like Papa!' Loyalty made her qualify this quickly. 'No,' she thought, 'I don't quite mean that, but I was a little bit unjust, perhaps.'

The discovery of her own capriciousness had dispelled her temper. The face that she saw in the mirror as she re-dressed her hair smoothly on either side of the centre parting was eager, resolute and shadowy with fatigue.

In the kitchen they were saying that there was no doubt about it, now Miss Kat'rine would marry the reverend gentleman. After a decent interval, of course, the way her poor father'd not be turning in his grave at the goings on.

Nanny, stirring a cup of dark oily tea, saw a ray of hope in this. Perhaps if Miss Kat'rine married she would not get the sack, since there'd be no one else to devote their time to poor little Susan. Gracious! thought Nanny, just imagine Miss Charlotte running the house! That'd be a queer set-up and no mistake, with herself and Miss Daisy stretched out on the sofas and chairs, losing the use of their legs, she wouldn't be surprised. Beef to the heels, the pair o' them, like Mullingar heifers! Now, if it was only Miss Olivia, she'd make a great job of the housekeeping, so she would. But with Miss Charlotte in charge what a time the cook would have, takin' home little bits o' this and that on her day out, and no one to say a word to her!

The cook, Mrs Flood, was holding forth loudly. The Mrs was a courtesy title, bestowed *ex officio* on cooks of settled age regardless of whether they were married or single. Mrs Flood was, in fact, at the age of fifty-seven still a 'gerrl' as all unmarried women are in Ireland until the day they die. She was short and immensely fat, with arms like hams, as pale as lard. Her hair was pale, of a discoloured grey, yellowish in streaks and wispy. Her eyes were pale, of a dull blue with eyelashes as white as a pigs. Her faded blue print frock had burst at every seam and her apron was far from clean.

'Oh, there'll be some changes now, so there will! Wit' the Masther gone. God rest his soul, an' Miss Kat'rine gettin' marri'd as I've not a doubt she will, who's to keep the rest o' thim in ordher? Sure, they're not fit to look afther thimselves, so they aren't, and I think Miss Kat'rine'd have a right to stay here mindin' thim and gettin' thim marri'd before herself. Sure, it wouldn't take her long: a couple o' years an' she'd have the lot off her hands; some gentlemen is terrible fools! Mary, have ye the peraters peeled for me?'

'I have, Mrs Flood,' came a terrified voice from the scullery where the candle light flickered in the draught from a broken pane. 'Sure, they're terrible bad.'

'I'll mash thim, so. What d'ye think now, Nanny? Will she marry him or will she not?'

'I'm in hopes she will,' was Nanny's heartfelt reply as she sipped the first cup of tea that she had been able to relish for many days.

Mr Blair felt ill-used and dejected. After Katharine had swept herself out of the room he stood with his hands in his pockets for some minutes, staring at the fire while he considered.

Miss Fellowes thought nothing of his character, that was plain. Yet he had only done his best to save her from disaster. It was always the way, people resented it when you tried to help them. But ladies were queer, you never knew with them, changeable, unpredictable and obstinate as the devil. He had hoped for better things from Miss Fellowes at first; she seemed to have a great grasp of essentials. But what a temper! And what . . . well, call it determination—'pig-headedness' is not a pretty word.

He straightened himself and set his head back; he felt imprisoned in this houseful of angry women, for having seen one in a temper he feared them all, and he decided to go out for a walk. He had a notion, nothing to go on, just intuition, that Miss Fellowes' penniless clergyman lived pretty near at hand, and who could tell what a visit to the church might reveal? He felt very curious about Miss Fellowes' admirer, and not a little suspicious. He could justify a good long look round by his interest in the family memorials and graves. If the church was locked, he could even go to the rectory and ask for the key. He hoped that the rectory and the church were not five miles apart; he would go into the village and ask where the Rector lived, and his name.

He went into the hall and took his coat from the stand and his cloth cap from amongst the headgear of his late client. What on earth would that girl do with all these coats and hats dating from before the Golden Jubilee? His eye fell on the collection of sticks and umbrellas in the elephant's foot and he stood coveting the noble and massive umbrella that had been the Captain's. Without a doubt, if he were alive to attend the funeral of any one of these young ladies, that umbrella would still be there, mouldering from prolonged idleness. It was a great waste.

At the gate, he looked about him; the village was down the hill, the church up the hill and beyond. He turned and went down the village street.

He was no country-lover but he did not mind an occasional short trip out from Cork, provided he did not have to walk through too much mud or meet too many unaccompanied animals. His natural distaste for squalor, dirt and poverty began, however, to assert itself before he had gone far from the gate of Fellowescourt. He was aware of curtains twitching in tiny windows as he passed, of barefoot children asking for a copper, of unwelcoming dogs and filthy gutters. He left the footpath and took to the middle of the road.

He stopped at the post office and peered inside. A vast man sat behind the counter with hair and beard of rippling, curling, flaming red, so profuse as to give the impression of a torrent of flame. On his knee sat a baby boy, perhaps two years old, the image of his father with a sort of burning bush of fiery curls surmounting a green-eyed face of most clear and delicate beauty. A whole tribe of red-haired children fled into the dwelling quarters, screeching until the door was banged shut.

The man rose with the boy in his arms and set him down as gently as if he had been a basket of eggs; the child held on to the man's knees and the man rested his huge hand on top of the little flaming head, so lightly as not even to depress the curls with its weight.

'Can I help ye, Sirr?' he asked, in the deep, soft voice of the countryman.

Mr Blair's attention was so held by the spectacle of this flamboyant pair that it took him a moment to remember why he had come in.

'Oh, er . . . yes indeed, thanks. Where is the rectory, please, and what is the name of the Rector?'

The postmaster lifted the boy on to a chair. 'Stay where y'are now,' he said, and made his way to the street doorway. He seemed to fill the little post office, not only with his huge size but with the exuberance of his entire being. Pointing up the hill he gave his directions.

'Thank you,' said Mr Blair, and hesitated. Then he said something that it had never occurred to him to say to anyone before. 'That's a beautiful child. What's his name?'

'He's a lovely child, God bless him. His name's Malachy, Sirr.'

'What age is he?'

'Two year old, Sirr.'

'Well, thanks.' Mr Blair found it difficult to break off. 'He's a fine boy,' he added awkwardly, and made his escape. He felt oddly moved by this encounter. The enormous strength of this ardent giant and his great gentleness with the child affected him against his will. He grunted at himself as he set off up the hill.

The last house on the left was a dejected-looking pub. Over the windows was a board, barely legible, on which 'Peter Cavanagh. Select Bar' had once been painted. The grimy window displayed advertisements of branded whiskeys, beers and porters, very fly-blown and dingy, on which the dust lay thickly. Behind these, a discreet partition sheltered the bar from public gaze whilst admitting a certain amount of light above eye-level. The smell of porter wafted across the street and made Mr Blair look up as he passed.

At the door stood a seedy-looking individual dressed in a stained and shiny blue serge suit, a collarless flannel shirt and a bowler hat. The head was melon-shaped, with dun-coloured hair. The face, in both colour and texture, was like an old newspaper blown along the road and brought up against some obstacle where it had started to disintegrate; the eyes, like holes in the paper, were of a dull cod-fish blue, faintly rimmed with red. Although the face was quite expressionless, it had a kind of awareness that seemed to hold it together. Mr Blair thought both the establishment and its owner undesirable and quickly looked the other way.

'Good evenin', Sirr.'

This could only have come from Mr Cavanagh who, however, gave no sign of having spoken. The face looked vacantly at him and the lower lip hung outwards.

'Good evening,' replied Mr Blair coolly, and walked a little faster.

The figure in the doorway half-turned, propping itself against the doorpost, the better to observe the stranger. The head nodded once or twice, confirming a thought.

'That'll be himself,' murmured Mr Cavanagh. 'That's me boy all right.' He went into the bar and poured half a pint of porter down his throat without appearing to swallow, wiped his mouth with the back of his hand, the back of his hand on his trousers, and returned to his observation post in the doorway.

Mr Blair was glad to top the rise and disappear from the gaze of Mr Cavanagh. When he had reached the end of the cement wall of the convent, he paused to find his bearings. To the North, behind the line of leaning Scotch firs, was the church, neither old nor new, built of brownish-grey stone. It was small, austere and weather-stained with a patina of orange in patches, with a narrow, square tower a little too tall for the rest of the building. The roof was of purplish slate. There was not an extravagant line or a hint of embellishment anywhere. In the graveyard there was not a cross to be seen; instead the graves were marked by slabs and humps of stone amongst the tussocks of grass. The winter sunlight fell coldly on the diamond-paned windows of clear glass. A mass of flowers and wreaths marked the newly-occupied grave of old Captain Fellowes. The church door looked firmly shut.

Just beyond was the rectory, a square Georgian house of weathered brick with stone steps leading up to the pillared portico and open front door. Store cattle grazed in the field beyond the gravel sweep. A grass verge surrounded the house, extending down the slope of the area to the semi-basement windows. The place had a look of gentility maintained with the minimum of expense. There was no grandiose bedding-out, no extent of flower garden or clipped hedges. Wherever possible, the grass was kept rough, showy cultivation restricted and the fences made of undemanding wire.

He decided to see if he could enter the church. There was no one in view as he stepped over the stile into the graveyard. He paused to read the cards on the wreaths that covered the roughly-filled grave of his late client, then walked slowly across to the church door.

It was locked securely and he started to go round the building in the hope of finding a lesser door that would open. He had nearly completed his unsuccessful round when he saw two people walking up the short drive from the road. They were talking most earnestly and he felt sure that they had not seen him. When he perceived who they were, he ducked hastily behind a monument to avoid detection.

The two were Miss Fellowes and an unusually handsome young clergyman. Mr Blair felt like rubbing his hands together in self-congratulation on his astuteness. But he also felt most anxious to escape. Miss Fellowes was angry enough with him at present, but if she discovered him hiding behind monuments and spying on her, he trembled to think what might happen. Not only would she wither him with her scorn, but she would certainly change her lawyer.

People who do not know they are being watched seem to hang about in the most tormenting way. Katharine and Mr Weldon kept poor Mr Blair on the damp grass, concealed from them behind the black stone of a pretentious monument, for a full half-hour. They looked at the grave endlessly, re-arranging the wreaths and flowers and tidying the edges of the sods. They returned to the church in search of something, and this made Miss Blair very uneasy indeed as they could not find what they wanted in the toolshed, so they separated and began to look amongst the graves. At one moment he felt that he was lost as they converged upon him from different sides, but he was preserved from disaster by a cry of 'Got it!' from Katharine, as she picked up a rake and set off with it back to the grave.

When they decided to leave, they said goodbye interminably at the gate. Then to Mr Blair's relief, Katharine set off towards the village. He was about to emerge from his retreat when, to his horror, he saw the young man walking again towards the church. Fuming with impatience and anxiety, he remained concealed while the Rector fumbled for the key under a scraper, opened the door and entered the church.

For the moment, Mr Blair was safe from view. Brushing moss and grass off his coat and wiping his wet shoes carefully with a tuft of grass, he came out of his hiding place and, summoning all his dignity, walked slowly down towards the road.

He had gone only a few yards when he heard the door being closed, the clink of metal on stone as the key hit the ground and the scraper was pushed over it again, and the appalling sound of footsteps pursuing him. It was only by using the utmost self-control that he did not take to his heels and flee. He felt certain that Miss Fellowes must have told the Rector about him and his advice on marrying penniless clergymen, so his pursuer could hardly be well-disposed towards him. As the footsteps came nearer and nearer to him he shrank from the clutch of a hand on his shoulder. He very nearly panicked. Suppose this young man wanted to fight him? Reason reasserted itself. A clergyman brawling, and on the church avenue?

He forced himself to stop and look round. Mr Weldon walked up to him with outstretched hand and said, 'Have you been anxious to get into the church? I can open it up for you in a moment. We have had to keep it closed recently as we have had thieves twice within a few months.'

Mr Blair's relief left him temporarily speechless, but he grasped the hand held out to him and murmured his thanks.

'I was just interested in a few of the monuments . . . I er have a kind of a business connection with the Fellowes family and . . .'

'It's odd that I didn't come across you then, for I've been here for the last hour,' said the Rector in genuine surprise.

'I know,' said Mr Blair with feeling, 'but as you were busy talking to Miss Fellowes I kept out of your way. Don't trouble to open up the church now,' he added quickly, 'for I must be getting back.'

'Are you, then, Mr Blair?' said the Rector.

'Er, yes,' admitted Mr Blair, relieved to have survived exposure. 'Then you must be the Rector?'

'Yes, my name is Weldon. How do you do?' There was a glint in the Rector's eye that Mr Blair found very disconcerting. Could it be possible that this young man was amused by him? Before he had finished murmuring politenesses, Mr Weldon said boldly, 'Miss Fellowes tells me that you know she and I hope to be married.'

'Er, yes. Miss Fellowes told me herself, in a roundabout way, you understand. No names were mentioned.'

'And you gave her some very prudent advice, Mr Blair. Of course you were perfectly right; it was most necessary that someone should warn her against adventurers.'

Mr Blair cleared his throat with some difficulty while casting about for some reply to this disarming speech. But Mr Weldon, smiling now outright, had not yet finished.

'If Miss Fellowes were a person of only average character and capability I think you would have been right to persuade her against marrying a man in my position; on the whole I think it does not do. I am leaving out of account the whole question of my wishing to marry her for her money, Mr Blair, as I feel you no longer consider it a serious one. Am I right?'

Mr Blair hastened to reassure him, uncertain why he felt able to do so, yet confident of this man's integrity.

'If I had met you, Mr Weldon, I would never have said that. I trust you will not hold it against me . . . that it did occur to me?'

Mr Weldon gripped his elbow. 'On the contrary, I congratulate you,' he said. 'It is such a pleasure to see that someone really has got Miss Fellowes' interests at heart. But to go back to where we were: I feel that she is so capable, so used to managing on a small allowance, that we shall manage very well, and she will still have her own money. Do you know that that old . . . that her father never gave her a penny piece to spend on herself? It pleases me greatly to think that at last she will be able to have something to spend, of her own. So will you give us your blessing, Mr Blair? I should like to have you on our side.'

Mr Blair smiled and held out his hand. 'It's odd,' he said, 'for the blessing to be this way round, but what blessing I can give is yours, Sir. I am sure you will be happy.'

That evening, in the drawing-room at Fellowescourt, Mr Blair felt himself very ill at ease. There were so many ladies, and they looked so critical that he soon excused himself on the grounds that he had to catch an early train, and went upstairs to bed.

When he had gone, Katharine sat idle for a moment, her work lying on her lap. She looked from one sister to another, seeing Daisy's yawns, Olivia's concentration on her book, Harriet's head bent over her crochet and Charlotte gazing idly into the fire. She gathered them together in one comprehensive glance of affection, pitying them that they could be unaware that this was a moment to remember. She herself was desperately tired, but for that reason conscious of much that was invisible and intangible, perceptible only to a mind receptive to the unseen. She felt the life within her burning like a flame, the thread of family attachment that drew her and her sisters together in spite of their differences, her consuming delight at the prospect of marriage with a man whom she could both love and admire and of whom she felt deliciously unworthy, and regret at the passing of a period which, now that it was over, she could see had not been really unhappy. 'Oh,' she thought, watching her sisters' unseeing heads, 'I am so happy!'

'I want to tell you all something,' she said, savouring the delight of the moment. 'Mr Weldon and I are to be married. It is to be a secret for the present, so I know you won't tell a soul.'

She smiled at them, leaning back a little in her armchair, looking even a little beautiful in her happiness.

They all looked at her in amazement, astonished that it should have come so soon. Now that she had told them, fatigue invaded her whole being. So tired was she, that their congratulations and good wishes hardly penetrated her consciousness. She was only aware that she was happy.

PART TWO

CHAPTER FIVE

Patrick Quinn, the Glenmacool postmaster whose exuberant red hair and beard had so fascinated Mr Blair, knew pretty well all there was to know about the affairs of the village whose people he served. Not that he resorted to any of the practices of unscrupulous Post Office servants such as steaming letters open or gossiping with servants, but it was almost impossible for a man in his position to remain ignorant of the import of what passed through his hands.

When Mick the Post, the man who cycled in daily with the mail from the market town of Inish, five miles away, flung his bag down on the counter, Patrick Quinn would take it up and quietly sort the letters while Mick sprawled on the wooden chair in an attitude of exhaustion.

He found it helpful to read the names on the covers aloud during this operation, but in a sort of recitative, not wishing to communicate anything but merely to expedite the performance of his duty. Sometimes he would add a comment, generally of a compassionate nature, but sometimes explanatory, always in the monotone in which the whole was said.

'Mrs Mahony, the Reverend F.X. Walsh, P.P., Mrs Power she's in desperate throuble poor thing so she is God help her, Mr Peter Cavanagh the dhirrty rascal, P. O'Brien, Esquire, M.D., the poor man he was out till all hours last night wit' Mrs Maguire and she havin' the baby I wondher now is she alive yet God save her,' then, his deep voice modulating to an enquiring tone, 'Did ye hear, Mick, did Mrs Maguire live through the night?'

'I did not, now, but I'll surely hear when I'm goin' round wit' the letters.'

The incantation would then be resumed until all the letters had been sorted and bound in bundles ready to be put into Mick the Post's bag.

Patrick Quinn knew that Mrs Mahony was trying to establish a claim to the estate of her brother who had died last year in the army in India, that Mrs Power was nearly out of her mind because her boy in America never wrote home now and she was sure he was dead, that Peter Cavanagh was in correspondence with a Cork firm of lawyers, the same firm as the one that wrote so frequently to Miss Fellowes, that Mrs Maguire, mother of seven, had been warned that she would probably die if she had another baby and that the Reverend Mr Weldon was in the habit of posting bulky manuscripts to publishers and receiving them back again after a lapse of time. He knew the handwriting of most of the regular letter-writers and very often he himself wrote letters for the illiterate at their dictation, posted them off and read the replies to them at their request.

He was a kind man, and the troubles of his neighbours weighed heavily upon him. Sometimes, when a telegram arrived with bad news he would take pains to deliver it himself, with some kind of a spoken warning to soften the blow. When young Sheehy, son of the Fellowescourt coachman, was lost overboard in the Mediterranean, Patrick Quinn sought out the boy's mother first, knowing she could stand the shock better than the father who was given to bouts of being 'not himself at all'. But with all this, he was the soul of discretion; though he heard endless gossip he never made use of his official knowledge to add to it and only in extreme cases to deny it. But it worried him when he knew that his neighbours were in difficulties, and still more so when he was aware that in their folly they were becoming more and more involved. 'Oh, boys-a-boys!' he would murmur sadly as he postmarked a letter to a firm of Cork money-lenders. He was a sort of public conscience, counsellor, father of the people and one-way information bureau.

He had watched Mr Blair walk up the village street and over the hill on the day before he left Fellowescourt; he had had an eye on Peter Cavanagh at the door of his 'Select Bar' as he greeted Mr Blair and had judged that the publican was up to no good. Having lived opposite Peter Cavanagh for twelve years, he had come to know something of his activities. The man looked a fool, an idiot almost, with his dull codfish eye and flabby lips, but that was his best asset—to look a fool and not be one. He was, in fact, exceptionally astute, especially where there was a chance of making a bit of money out of the weakness of his neighbours. Patrick Quinn knew him to be a blackmailer, gombeen-man, and oppressor of the undefended and he longed for the day when Cavanagh would make a mistake and find himself in the hands of the law. But there was little he could do without proof, except utter a gentle warning to those in trouble to 'give that fella across the road the go-by if ye want to keep outa more throuble'.

The postmaster knew who Mr Blair was just as well as did Peter Cavanagh: had not the telegrams from Fellowescourt to him and back all passed through his hands? So it was with a feeling of uneasiness that, only a few days after Mr Blair had departed, Patrick Quinn wrote out a telegram for delivery to Miss Fellowes.

'Regret must see you urgently as situation not as anticipated arriving midday train unless you telegraph—Blair.'

'Tch tch tch,' grieved the postmaster, 'there's somethin' up. It's a shame now, sure those poor young ladies has no one to protect thim.' Sealing the yellow envelope, he called his telegraph boy, a barefoot streak of a lad called Danny, who became a servant of the Post Office when he put on the official cap and armband and mounted the red bicycle provided by His Majesty's Government. In his spare time, which was abundant, Danny did a milk round, measuring out pints and half-pints from a large milk-can set in a soap-box on wheels. If a telegram arrived while Danny was beyond range of the postmaster's bellow, then it simply had to await his return.

Danny happened to be half-way down the hill with his milk when the summons arrived; he screeched back to show that he had heard, carefully ran the soap-box against the curb of the footpath so that it should not run away down hill, and abandoned it to the care of his woolly dog.

'Fellowescourt,' said Patrick Quinn gently, handing Danny the telegram, 'and don't come away till ye see is there anny reply.'

'Ay,' replied Danny, pulling the cap on to his head and sprinting up the street to the long brown house at the top.

Danny stood in the doorway while Lizzie took the telegram to her mistress, looking without curiosity into the hall that was so different from any house that he had ever entered. The fantastic crowding of objects made no impression on him; the ticking clocks and thick carpeting, the hunters' trophies and varied weapons excited him not at all. They were the sort of things you saw in the houses of the quality, they did not belong to his world and never would. The things the quality did were unpredictable, they collected a terrible lot of useless stuff and surrounded themselves with it. It was a queer way to live.

Lizzie came pounding back to the hall door, her cap bobbing up and down on her springy mass of black hair to which it was attached by a single inadequate hatpin at the front.

'There's no answer,' she panted. 'Go on round the back an' Mrs Flood'll give ye a bit o' dhrippin' for yer mother. She said to tell ye.'

'Tanks, I will then,' said Danny, and looking as if legs and arms might fly off at any moment, he gallivanted down the stone path, out under the yew arch and back to the stable gateway, which he entered with every appearance of guilt.

Inside the house, 'the Pope' was meditating about the message received from Mr Blair. She felt seriously alarmed and depressed. While she made preparations for his reception she wondered if she should show the telegram to her sisters. She decided to do so: they would see Mr Blair arriving and know that something was wrong.

Charlotte and Daisy received the news with stoicism; their comfort was not threatened as far as they could see, and if Mr Blair had to come and bother Katharine with tiresome business it was nothing to do with them; she was good at that sort of thing and they were quite hopeless. Olivia sensed that 'the Pope' was frightened and tried to reassure her, but this was not really possible without knowledge of what had gone wrong. Harriet repeated what 'the Pope' said to her in a puzzled enquiring voice, but her mind was not really attending to the matter. She had been wondering ceaselessly how 'the Pope's' engagement and marriage would affect her own chances of inducing Captain Willoughby to propose to her.

Sheehy was sent to fetch Mr Blair from the station. When the trap stopped outside the gate, Mr Blair made his way up the flagged path as if he were going to his execution. Sheehy followed him with a bag.

'So,' thought Katharine, nervously touching her throat, 'he has to stay the night. It's going to take a long time, then.' She sent Lizzie flying off to see that a spare room was made ready and came down from the upstairs window whence she had been watching events.

She reached the hall as he was hanging up his coat and welcomed him almost with affection; they were beginning to understand and respect one another.

'When you are ready, will you join me in the study, Mr Blair?' she asked, as she herself went into the room. While she waited for him she looked at the daffodils bending and bowing in the March wind, the brilliant green of the young grass on the lawn and the watery velvet bloom on the mossy slope of the mountain in the sharp spring sunshine. She had lived here all her life and had never left Fellowescourt for more than a few days at a time, and she felt now that she was seeing it for the first time as it really was. She watched the lights on the mountain changing with the cloud shadows; the pale almond green became brown, became pink, became a brooding opaque blue as she stood there. She sighed, because it was very beautiful and because it offered nothing else but its beauty to humanity. The land on the mountainside was a saturated sponge, and 'the Pope' resented waste.

Susan and Nanny were crossing the garden on their way in to luncheon. Susan had a ball and was making Nanny throw it for her to catch. Nanny was quite useless at throwing and did not even try to do it properly, but just jerked it half-heartedly in one direction or another. She saw Susan miss the ball, which rolled across a flower-bed. With a quick glance at the morning-room window, Susan walked over the bed to fetch it. 'The Pope' saw Nanny shake her head, though she said nothing.

Katharine was suddenly angry. She banged on the window-pane and shook her fist at Susan, who stood looking up guiltily. Then she flung up the bottom sash, leant out and called stridently, 'Susan! You thought I wasn't looking, so you could do wrong! Come here. Come here,' she repeated more loudly as Susan hesitated. 'Now you know that wrong is wrong whether anyone is looking or not. Don't you?'

Susan nodded despairingly, tears brimming. 'I'm sorry,' she gulped.

'I'd rather you'd kept your sorrow till you say your prayers,' snapped 'the Pope'. 'Go on with Nanny, now. I don't want to see little girls who are deceitful.'

As she pulled the window down Mr Blair entered the room. He closed the door, then opened it again and, leaning out into the passage, looked up and down to make sure that they would not be overheard. This time he shut the door firmly, went up to Katharine and pressed her hand with impulsive sympathy.

'Miss Fellowes,' he said regretfully, 'er, Miss Fellowes . . . I would give anything I possess not to have to make known to you the intelligence I bring you. Believe me, Miss Fellowes, it is most painful . . .'

'The Pope' stood with her back to the window, her hands clasped before her. 'What has happened, Mr Blair?' she asked. 'Can you tell me in a few words now? We can go into details after luncheon.'

'I can, I fear, in a very few words. It is that your father's affairs have been found to be in a state of chaos; a great deal of his capital had been sold out, and now I have received this,' Mr Blair took a thick envelope from his pocket, and handed the contents to Katharine, 'from a publican called Peter Cavanagh.'

In her hands, 'the Pope' saw a wad of greasy papers, creased, grimy and dog-eared; she tried to open them out so as to see what they were, but they had been so long rolled that they sprang back into position. Handling them as though they were a nest of vipers, she flattened them on the window ledge. There was a number of sheets inscribed identically, 'IOU', followed by varying sums from £100 to £300, and the flamboyant signature, 'Thomas Fellowes, Fellowescourt, Glenmacool,' and the date.

That they were genuine was indisputable. 'The Pope' could not delude herself even for an instant. She turned back to Mr Blair and in a voice of horrified amazement asked, 'How did these come into your hands?'

'The . . . er . . . the creditor brought them to me in person, yesterday. I had a good mind to put them in the fire, I can tell you. But that would have given him grounds for blackmail against you and all sorts of unpleasant practices, and I thought it better to hold on to them. Mind you, he's a slimy sort of a customer as I'm sure you know, and I should think he's crooked enough to hide behind a corkscrew, but he wouldn't have a leg to stand on if this came to the courts. An IOU has no legality.'

'Yes, but I suppose Papa must have had the money and used it?'

'Oh, I haven't a doubt of it,' said Mr Blair.

'Well then, we must consider it a debt,' said 'the Pope' with great firmness, adding, suddenly afraid, 'What do they amount to?'

Mr Blair chewed his lips for a moment, holding his chin in his hand. 'I'm afraid the amount is considerable, Miss Fellowes—about four thousand pounds in all—and if it is to be paid it will make a considerable hole in your father's depleted capital. It is my duty to tell you that I cannot see how you and your sisters can continue in this establishment. In fact I wish I could see how you are going to live on your means at all . . .' He shot a quick glance at her face to see what effect this news was having.

Katharine was almost dumbfounded. 'Are you serious, Mr Blair? Can it really be as bad as that?' Her mouth felt dry and her throat contracted, making her swallow repeatedly. 'I must sit down,' she admitted. 'Won't you, too, Mr Blair?' Only with a great effort could she make her voice audible, her words coherent. The thought that was drumming in her mind was, 'Now Lawrence and I cannot marry,' and it made so much actual noise in her ears that she found it almost incredible that Mr Blair did not hear it.

'Oh!' she thought remorsefully, 'can I only think of myself! What is to become of us all? And Susan, how is she to be educated? And where can we live?' Like circles spreading from a stone dropped into a pond, the terrors of her situation followed one another, widening and growing until the whole scope of her consciousness was filled with them, and behind them all, the dinning noise in her head.

Mr Blair stared into the fire for several minutes to give her time to recover from the shock of his disclosures. Then he said quietly, 'I'm afraid it is only too true, Miss Fellowes, only too true. And that reminds me that your sisters are equally beneficiaries under your father's will, and your niece too, though she is too young to have any say in what is to be done, so I think we should have them all—that is, except your niece—in here after lunch to explain to them what has happened and to see whether they will consent to honouring these . . . er documents.'

'Honouring them? Of course they'll have to honour them!'

'Er . . . it isn't everybody who would agree with you, if I may say so, Miss Fellowes. Not everybody by any means.'

'But Papa had the money, and used it, and that horrible creature Cavanagh lent it to him, so of course it is a debt. How can anyone think of it as anything else?'

'Hm,' said Mr Blair shortly, and was silent for a moment. Then, with an almost sly glance at Katharine, he asked with great courage, 'I suppose, Miss . . . er . . . Fellowes, you have no idea how all this money was . . . er used? Were you aware that your father was living so very much beyond his means?'

'No.' It was clear that Katharine resented so intimate a query. 'His movements were entirely his own business and, as I have already told you, he never spoke to any of us about money. He used to go and stay in Cork periodically for a few days, but he never told us what he did there.'

'Ah!' thought Mr Blair, 'gambling and drinking, I haven't a doubt of it!'

Aloud he asked diffidently, 'Was he a drinking man at all, Miss Fellowes? I mean, did you ever see him the worse for—?'

'No, indeed I did not!' exclaimed Katharine with some heat. 'Really, Mr Blair, my father may have been eccentric, but he was not a drunkard.'

'Ah, come now, Miss Fellowes, you mustn't take me up wrong! There are many gentlemen in this county who are given to taking a drop now and then, and no one thinks the worse o' them. I'm afraid men are rarely as good as their womenfolk like to think them! Did he play cards at all, then?'

'The Pope' sat looking at him with stubborn distaste: she felt now that her original aversion to Mr Blair was justified. The man was low, given to suspecting even the dead of tastes as low as, no doubt, were his own. He had no decent impulses, all his thoughts were tainted.

'An odd game of whist,' she said so coldly that Mr Blair could not bring himself to ask the next question, which was delicately framed in his mind as, 'Well, do you think it could have been a case of *"cherchez la femme"*?'

'Hm, er, hm,' he said, but he could not risk it.

Katharine felt quite numb now, answering questions about things that were as fantastic as the truth that Mr Blair had disclosed to her.

The truth was not true; it was all a nightmare, it could not be true.

She closed her eyes for an instant, greatly wearied and unable to believe any of it. Suddenly, little thoughts and speculations about her father began to creep into her mind: what if Mr Blair was right about him after all and he had been nothing more than a disreputable, besotted old gambler? Little incidents came to light, times when he had come in late at night, though no one even knew he had been out, and banged the front door with violence, shaking the house and his daughters in their beds; on one such occasion Katharine had heard him knocking against the furniture in the hall and nearly came down to see if he was ill. Had she done so, she thought with a twinge of bitterness, she would only have been sworn at. And she remembered that he used often to go to races; perhaps he lost a lot of money backing no-good horses. Then there came into her mind something she had once heard of Peter Cavanagh, the very words and the voice of the speaker, though at the moment she could not recall who had spoken them. 'Ah yes, Cavanagh keeps a book all right—he'll take a bet on any race, big money too.'

She opened her eyes and, seeing again the familiar things around her that had been part of her daily scene since birth, she dispelled the evil thoughts as suggestions of the devil. She saw her father as she always had seen him; as Papa—odd maybe, erratic, quick-tempered, arbitrary, but Papa, the head of the house and therefore beyond criticism and never wrong.

She stood up, feeling really very ill, and invited Mr Blair to make his way to the dining-room when she heard the sound of the gong.

'My sisters and I will meet you here after luncheon,' she said, and left him to repent his offensive insinuations.

They had had to bring more chairs into the study, which was an intimate room furnished to accommodate only three or four people in comfort. Charlotte and Daisy settled on either side of the fire, holding up newspapers to prevent their faces from being scorched. Harriet and Olivia sat on dining-room chairs, upholstered but not designed for indefinite sitting-in. Katharine was in her father's large, red, leather-covered chair with the awkwardly high arms, turned outwards to face the room from the desk. Mr Blair stood before the fire.

He described rapidly the situation he had discovered. Katharine could see Olivia and Harriet becoming every moment more appalled, Charlotte and Daisy only half-listening and taking nothing in. When he said 'er' or 'mm' they were inclined to giggle.

He completed his statement and there was a horrid pause; Katharine could feel her heart pounding wildly.

'How much money is there left, Mr Blair?' she asked quietly.

'With all claims met, er . . . legal and moral,' said Mr Blair as shame-facedly as if he himself had spent their fortune, 'the capital remaining would amount to just under ten thousand pounds. You will agree that the income from that, amounting to nearly four hundred pounds a year at, say, four per cent, will not go far in maintaining an establishment like this. The share of any one of the six beneficiaries will not exceed sixty-six pounds annually, and I am forced to warn you that the marriage of one sister would impoverish the rest by that amount every year. If more than one were to marry, I fear the situation would be untenable. You would have to sell the house. I beg you to consider this lamentable state of affairs before you make up your minds to marry.' He spoke very sternly, taking care to avoid Katharine's eye. But, for the moment, her mind was not on marriage.

'Sell the house?' she said incredulously. 'You can't mean sell Fellowescourt?'

'Dear lady, I'm afraid I do,' he replied apologetically. He felt very nervous; Miss Fellowes was beginning to look as if she might get angry again.

'But no one has ever lived in it but our family! It was built for us, and by us. How could we sell it? It isn't possible!'

'Ladies, ladies!' lamented Mr Blair to himself. They would not be realists. Sentiment, contrariness or plain obstinacy made them insist that the only, the obvious, course was barred. Patiently he protested, 'Families do find themselves in these predicaments, Miss Fellowes, from time to time. To sell property is one way out.'

'I daresay,' cried Katharine, pink with indignation, 'but not Fellowescourt! Not while I'm alive, even if we have to live in the stables.' She looked from one sister to another. 'Don't you all agree?'

Harriet and Olivia nodded violently; so did Daisy after a glance at Charlotte. Charlotte was the only one to speak.

'If you sold Fellowescourt, then we shouldn't have anywhere to live and that would be silly,' she said rudely to Mr Blair.

'I said, "if more than one sister married", Miss Charlotte,' protested Mr Blair. He sighed. He felt greatly tired. He was doing his best to help them and they only disliked him for it. 'Retrenchment is the only other course, and one that you will have to adopt in any event; but before we discuss that, I—'

'Mr Blair?' said Daisy.

'Yes, Miss Daisy?' It bothered him to be interrupted and his voice was a little sharp.

'Do you say I can have sixty-six pounds a year?' Daisy's face glowed with pleasure; she had never handled so much money in her life. She envisaged a glorious spending spree in Dublin.

'On that sixty-six pounds you will have to be fed, clothed, housed and everything else; doctors' bills, stamps, charity and your share of the rates on this house will have to come out of it before you can spend any of it. It must cover all the costs of keeping you alive.' Mr Blair spoke politely but quite ruthlessly.

'You mean Katharine's going to try and take it from me for housekeeping? But she can't! It's mine.' Tears stood large in Daisy's eyes.

Exasperated, perceiving that Daisy was ineducable, Mr Blair shrugged his shoulders and threw out his hands.

'Try living on sixty-six pounds a year anywhere else, dear lady, and see how you get on.'

Nettled, Daisy took refuge in recrimination. In a hurt voice she cried, 'I do think you are unkind, and Katharine too, taking all my money from me. I don't believe you've any right to.'

'It is the circumstances that are unkind, I'm afraid,' said Mr Blair regretfully. 'Now, Miss Fellowes, we must settle what is to be done about the IOUs.' He put the dirty bundle on the table.

Charlotte and Daisy looked at it with repugnance as Mr Blair told his story. When he had finished. Charlotte said, 'But those filthy bits of old paper can't be worth anything! You've only got to look at them to see they're not the real thing.' What the real thing was like, she did not say. She smoothed her skirt grandly as though her command of the subject was complete and she handled 'the real thing' every day.

Mr Blair opened out the roll of filthy papers, to show her father's signature and other essential details.

'How he could sign those!' said Daisy fastidiously.

'I expect,' said Mr Blair patiently, 'that they were cleaner when he signed them.' He shook his head gently. He was finding the going very heavy.

'Well, I vote we don't pay them,' said Daisy. 'Mr Blair says we don't have to if we don't want to.' She looked round with a bold little smile and awaited the unanimous approval of her sisters.

Charlotte backed her up. 'I agree with Daisy,' she said. 'Why should we? Papa left the money to us, so why should we give it to that wretch Cavanagh? It gives me the shivers just to look at him.'

'The Pope' was suddenly at her most hierarchic.

'Of course it must be paid,' she flashed. 'It's a question of common honesty. If we don't, that miserable Cavanagh will have the right to say that the Fellowes don't pay their debts, and you may be sure he will, too. He lent the money to Papa and now he has to be paid back. There's nothing else we can do but pay it.'

'But why,' complained Daisy, 'did Mr Blair say we needn't? I don't see why you want to make paupers of us all, Katharine. It's most unkind.'

'Mr Blair said the papers were not legally binding, that was all. But if we dishonour them we shan't ever be able to hold up our heads again in our own village.'

Mr Blair nodded approval of this. 'Your sister is quite right, I'm afraid. Miss Daisy. There is a moral obligation.'

'Well, I think it's too bad,' pouted Daisy, looking at Charlotte for support.

'So do I,' glared Charlotte, thinking of her vanishing chances of going to Dublin in pursuit of a rich husband.

'But you agree that it must be done,' said 'the Pope', with no tone of query in her voice; she was making a statement.

There was no denial; Charlotte and Daisy glowered at the carpet but said nothing. Harriet said nervously, 'Oh yes, I feel it must be done.' Olivia, who had made up her mind at the beginning and had since allowed her thoughts to wander, pulled herself back with a little smile and said, 'Yes, of course.'

'Hm,' said Mr Blair, 'I think you have made the wisest decision, unpleasant though it is. Now, I feel that we must discuss the immediate future. Hm. How many servants have you. Miss Fellowes?'

'Servants, Mr Blair? Well, counting Nanny and Sheehy and the gardener, eight, I think.' 'The Pope' counted them off again on her fingers to make sure she had left nobody out. 'Why? Oh, I see,' she added sombrely, 'you think we should manage with fewer.'

'I think you should manage with none,' said Mr Blair brutally, 'but as I suppose that's out of the question, how many can you do without?'

They all looked at him with horror. That he could even envisage their doing without servants showed how completely unalive he was to the needs of the gentry, how low-born a creature he must be, how barbaric and unfeeling. Even Katharine was shocked; it had never occurred to her that it was possible to live without servants. Considering it, she knew it was not possible: she and her sisters scrubbing floors and peeling potatoes, washing-up and handling raw meat and fish! Surely they were not going to be as poor as all that!

'I must have a cook,' she put in quickly, 'and I suppose some cooks would be prepared to do without a kitchen-maid.'

'And Lizzie,' suggested Harriet, 'she wouldn't mind doing upstairs as well as down—she's very willing.'

'The Pope' sniffed: she considered Lizzie more willing than effective.

'Did you say there was a Nanny?' enquired Mr Blair; 'I should have thought a child of eight . . .?'

'Nanny must go,' announced 'the Pope' in a voice that forbade argument.

Charlotte had a sudden vision of Susan hanging about all day in the morning-room and making a nuisance of herself to her aunts. 'Who's going to look after Susan?' she asked sharply.

'I am,' 'I will,' came at the same moment from Katharine and Harriet.

'We all will,' said Olivia.

'Not me,' said Daisy. 'Charlotte and me haven't time.'

'You'll have to find time for a lot of things you aren't accustomed to doing, from now on,' said Katharine menacingly. Daisy shrugged her shoulders and looked away.

'You realise that the horses will have to go,' said Mr Blair. 'That will mean that you can do without a coachman.'

Daisy regarded him witheringly. 'But how can we get to tennis parties?' she demanded, as if she were supplying an irrefutable argument for the retention of coachman and horses. She smiled pityingly at Charlotte.

Mr Blair had had enough of Daisy's contempt. 'I think if you each had a bicycle you would manage very well,' he suggested, with a sharp look at Daisy and Charlotte as they drew themselves up to look like affronted pigeons.

'Bicycles!' they gasped together. 'Really!'

'I'd love to have a bicycle,' said Olivia. 'We could go—'

'Pooh!' said Daisy. 'Think what we'd look like when we got there—all hot and untidy. I'd rather stay at home than ride a bicycle, thank you!'

'The Pope' took no notice of her sisters. 'It's going to be very difficult about Sheehy,' she said. 'He's the coachman, you know. He's been here since he was a boy, and he goes out of his mind from time to time, and besides that, he's so old now I don't think anyone would want to take him on. All the children are out in the world, now, of course, but he's got an old wife. How can I turn them out at their age?'

'He'd be eligible for the old age pension,' stated Mr Blair. 'I'm sorry, Miss Fellowes, but you cannot afford to indulge in sentiment.'

'Five shillings a week!' 'the Pope' blazed. 'A long way they'll get on that, with rent to pay. I know,' she exclaimed, 'why shouldn't they go on living over the stables? We don't want to put anybody else in there.'

'Hm,' said Mr Blair, 'we could consider it; he should, of course, give certain services in exchange for free accommodation. Hm, it might be quite a solution. He will probably be able to get odd jobs to augment his income, don't you think?'

'I hope so' said 'the Pope', filled with dread at the thought of having to give notice to this old servant who should be given a family pension instead of his dismissal. The thought so cast her down that she thrust it away from her until circumstances should force her to consider it again. Instead, she found the vision of poor Nanny come to torment her; where could Nanny go? She too was old, really too old to go to a new post. Dislike Nanny as she did, justice compelled her to think of her with compassion. She shuffled her feet in an effort to shake off the torture of what faced her. 'Oh,' she thought, 'where will all the awfulness end?'

Mr Blair was now considering the garden; there could be no full-time gardener, so perhaps the ladies, with a little help from Sheehy, could manage that too? The reaction was not favourable on the whole. Daisy and Charlotte were becoming really put out. Charlotte permitted herself to grow very heated and, flushed as a turkey cock, let herself go.

'I don't know who you think you are, Mr Blair,' she said offensively, 'but you can't treat us like this. It's too bad. You want us to do all the work in this house, and ride bicycles everywhere, and get freckles in the sun, and now you want us to ruin our hands and our complexions and get lumbago digging. If Katharine and the others are ready to be put upon like this, I know Daisy and me aren't. We simply aren't going to do all these wretched things for you and have you treating us like servants.' Encouraged by a nod from Daisy, she stood up and with a great show of indignation they both prepared to leave the room. But Mr Blair called them back with almost syrupy politeness.

'Ah, come now, come now, Miss Charlotte, you mustn't blame me for trying to help you. I assure you that the circumstances demand the greatest possible retrenchment: there simply won't be the money to pay for all the servants you're accustomed to having about the place. When the devil plays we have to dance to his tune, worse luck. Come on back now and sit down, there's good girls. I tell you I'm only making all these suggestions so that you can afford to go on living in this house, though I don't even know if that's going to be possible. So the only hope is for you all to work together and do your best.' He slid between them and the door and propelled them back to their seats, as if they were a couple of outraged broody hens. 'Now, that's better,' he beamed, rubbing his hands gently. 'That's more like it.'

The two girls would not look at him; they were furious with him for having overcome their obstinate determination to impede, delay and in every possible way prevent the fulfilment of his horrid threats. But he had not yet finished with them.

'Give me your word, now, Miss Charlotte and Miss Daisy, that you'll back your sister up. She has a grievous burden enough, without you making it more difficult for her.' He appealed to them with a direct look from his brilliant grey eye, impossible to ignore. The girls looked at their feet and made circles on the carpet with the toes of their shoes. They said nothing. Charlotte looked up, after a moment, to see if he was still looking at them; when her eye met his, she blushed and pouted, and stole a glance at Daisy's sullen face.

'Oh, come on Char,' said Olivia, smiling. 'We could have quite a lot of fun doing things together.'

'The Pope' did not say a word; she was not going to let Mr Blair see her in a rage for the second time. But when he had gone, she would strip the hide off those idle hussies; she would make them do just what she required of them, and if they rebelled she would larrup them. She was her father's daughter after all.

The silence was heavy and Mr Blair took care that it should continue until one of the two girls spoke. He could see that it weighed on them and made them fidgety. They could not keep it up much longer.

Daisy suddenly turned tear-filled eyes towards her sisters, avoiding Mr Blair's piercing glance.

'It's not fair,' she gulped, dissolving into tears.

'Yes,' agreed Charlotte, beginning to cry in sympathy and self-pity, 'it's too bad!'

No one could induce them to say another word.

CHAPTER SIX

Nanny had looked very small, old and defeated, but Katharine had been able to harden her heart until the old woman asked, 'Sure, couldn't I just stay on, Miss, wit'out anny wages? I do have a little bit put away and maybe I could manage if I just had me keep. There'd be little jobs I could do about the house, now the child is growin' up.'

She was watching her with such humility and anxiety that Katharine wavered, deeply touched. Reluctantly, she found herself forgiving all Nanny's past rebelliousness and secret opposition.

'I don't think that would be right, Nanny,' she said slowly, 'but I'll think it over. It's very good of you.'

'It'd be a charity, Miss, if you'd let me.' Her sincerity was so apparent that Katharine felt the tears pricking in her eyes.

'We'll see, Nanny. Thank you,' she had said, and taken refuge in her bedroom.

Now she was crossing the grass on her way to the stables, in search of Sheehy the coachman. She lingered in the walled vegetable garden, relishing the windless sunshine on the south wall and peering under boxes to see if the early rhubarb was nearly ready. But she could not delay indefinitely; it was only postponing the evil moment. She forced herself to go through the little green gate that led into the stable yard.

Here there was quite a different little world. There were cobbles underfoot, a smell of horses and straw and sounds of chewing, stamping and the hwish hwish of a horse being groomed. In the harness-room, brass winked and leather shone, there was the musty-dusty smell of oats and she could hear the dripping of a tap that had needed a new washer for years. She always hurried past the bins, because once, as a child, she had lifted the lid of one and a rat had jumped out at her face.

She went on through, until she came to the loose-boxes where Sheehy was wisping her father's chestnut cob, Dolly, with a rhythmic, polishing motion. Dolly was mouthing the back of his collar affectionately, while Sheehy uttered, from time to time, commands and advice that were understood and obeyed with the help of a nudge or a gentle push.

'Hwish hwish, that's it now . . . move over Wesht a bit Dolly boy, move over, errr . . . that's it. Hwish hwish . . .'

He was half-bent, his back to Katharine, dressed in an old brown tweed jacket passed on from his late master, ancient cord breeches, gaiters and a bowler hat that had once been black but was now dark green. Katharine watched him for a full minute, busy, devoted and perfectly happy. Then the course of his operations brought him round, slipping under the pony's neck, to face her. He was surprised to see her standing there, and a little embarrassed to have been caught murmuring to the pony almost like a lover.

'Good morning, Miss,' he said gravely, with a stately touch of his hat. He dropped his wisp of hay and came out of the loose-box towards her. Dolly stood nuzzling the hay in his manger, where lay the stable cat, feigning sleep. The pony blew at it in a friendly way until it opened one eye and closed it again, completely indifferent to the disturbance.

Sheehy nodded his head benignly when he perceived that Katharine had been watching the animals.

'Arrah, them's the quare old pair, Miss! Dolly and th'ould cat is great butties, so they are. She'd never settle wit' anny o' the other horses at all, only wit' Dolly.' He chuckled delightedly. His wavy grey hair and spare courtly figure, always a little curved as though he were about to bow, and the surprisingly nimble way in which he darted about on his old bow-legs gave him something of the air of a dancing-master, especially as he generally carried a little whippy stick under his arm, which made him look as though he had only forgotten his fiddle.

Seeing him so happy and at peace amongst the straw and cobwebs with his horses, Katharine's heart almost failed her.

'Sheehy,' she said, 'I'm afraid I've got something to say to you.'

His long old face became suddenly serious. 'Is it bad news, Miss?'

'Well . . .yes it is, Sheehy. Since the Master's death we find we're not able to afford all the things we used to have. I'm afraid we can't afford a coachman any more. . .' Katharine spoke very gently.

'Oh, my God, Miss! An' what'll become o' me horses?' The old man threw out his hands despairingly.

'I'm afraid they'll have to be sold. We shan't be able to keep any horses.'

'Sell the horses, Miss? Are y'asthray in the head? Sure, the Master'd be twistin' and turnin' in his grave if he hearrd ye.' He began to look very agitated and to breathe quickly and noisily.

'You must not get excited, Sheehy,' ordered Katharine with such authority that he made an effort to calm himself. She knew that she could make him obey her, even when he was suffering one of his periodic bouts of derangement. 'Now listen to me,' she went on. He stood before her, turning and turning his old bowler hat in his hands. 'Keep quiet, Sheehy.' The turning ceased. 'Now, I want you and Mrs Sheehy to go on living above the stables; we'll never turn you out, so you'll know that you'll always be safe. We shan't be able to keep Denny on in the garden, so I'd be grateful for a bit of help with the digging from you sometimes. Do you understand all this?'

He looked bowed and bent. His dancing-master's bravado had vanished and his voice was irregular and hurried. 'I do, Miss, I do. I'll be dhrawin' the pinshin now so 'tis good o' ye to leave us in the rooms, so it is. But,' and his voice rose in a crescendo of revolt against the injustice of adversity, 'what in the name of God'll I do wit'out me horses! Sure, me hearrt is broke.' He clutched the brim of his hat with both hands, gripping it as if it were trying to escape him, and looked over Katharine and beyond her. Dry sobs convulsed him.

'Sheehy, put on your hat,' commanded Katharine. When his hat was on his head he was subject to discipline. It was his badge of office.

He looked very mad as he clapped his venerable bowler rather forwards and sideways on his head. Katharine knew that he would do her no harm but she was afraid to leave him alone.

'Put it straight, it's all crooked,' she said, and his hands flew up to put it right. 'That's better. Now come with me.' She led the way to his living quarters, talking gently to him all the time.

'Mrs Sheehy!' she called.

A little old squirrel-faced woman put her head round the door at the top of the steps and in one quick desperate glance perceived what was happening.

'Oah! Glory be to God!' she shrieked. 'He'll have me life, he'll take the hatchet to me the way he did before!'

The door slammed and she was gone. Katharine could hear her barricading herself in. She turned to go down the steps.

'Come with me, Sheehy,' she said with a sigh, and doglike, he followed her quietly. She went into the harness-room.

'Now I want you to clean all the harness,' she said gently. 'It all needs doing, so you can spend the day at it. Just stay at it all day.'

She waited until he had brought out saddle soap, metal polish and a mountain of old rags, and had set them on the table in an orderly way. He began to lift down the tackle and pile it up at one end of the table.

'That's right,' she said, very quietly. 'You won't stir, now, Sheehy, promise me that.'

'I won't stirr at all, Miss,' he said meekly. He seemed hardly to hear her. Sitting at the bench with his legs crossed, he set to work, slowly warming to his task.

As she slipped out across the yard and into the garden, Katharine was trembling; she walked quickly across the walled garden and through the gateway. When she reached the seat on the lawn she sat down; her legs would not support her and she felt cold to her heart's core. Gathered to herself, arms pressed against her chest, legs and feet driven together in the effort to arrest the shivering that had taken possession of her body, she fed her weakness with self-pity.

'It's too much,' she told herself, 'for me to bear. Why must it be I who have to sacrifice everything? Why must I see my marriage elude me when it was in my grasp? Why must I break the hearts of faithful old servants? I have to think and plan and be strong when I am frightened to death of the future. I have to put things right for them all, they all count on me and it is too much. Oh, if only I could escape and marry Lawrence and forget about all the rest!'

Her mind fled along this beam of thought in an enchantment of liberation. Her heart leapt out in pursuit of the image of happiness that had been her fixed light, seeking to seize and hold it, to grasp the nebulous might-have-been and nail it to her consciousness. But it eluded her, just as the reality itself was evading her. Sick at heart, she recognised herself as the instrument marked out for the rescue of the blind and helpless dependants in her little world.

It was her destiny and there was no escape. Because she was she, moulded to her pattern, unique and designed for this very purpose, she could not run away. The question of happiness was irrelevant, she admitted in a moment of insight, since when it is pursued deliberately it is instantly in flight, and is only stumbled upon in the darkness or perceived in retrospect.

She was pressing down the wormcasts that abounded on the grass with a toe that had been instructed by her eye, without the conscious direction of the will. She suddenly became aware of this activity. She had stopped shivering. She sprang up in shame at such a waste of time.

She made up her mind that Doctor O'Brien should be told about Sheehy; she must get a message to him.

And Lawrence? She had not seen him since Mr Blair had left. He knew nothing of what had been going on. Unreasonably, she resented his happy ignorance while she suffered. But when she thought of all there was to tell him, her resentment ebbed away on a tide of sorrow and near despair. She knew that she had avoided him so that the vision of their future together could be held intact for a few more days because no word had been forged to shatter it. She knew this to be an evasion of the inevitable, but the stolen satisfaction it yielded was almost enough to justify it. Almost, but not quite.

Her selfishness smote her. That she could gratify herself by holding on to a myth while he was still persuaded of its truth made her feel ashamed. Then, from the shadow of her evasion emerged the real reason: she was afraid to tell him. She simply had not the courage. It was more than she could bear.

She sighed hopelessly as she looked at the truth. 'How can I ever do it?' she thought. 'I have used all my courage and I have none left. I don't think I even want to go on living.'

She hurried past the morning-room window in the hope that Charlotte and Daisy, arrayed in Miss Flynn's mourning creations and taking their ease by the fire, would not see her.

They did not see her; they were too busy examining the top layer of a box of chocolates. Heaven knew how they had come by it! Fascinated, she watched them each choosing a sweet, slowly and with as much care as if it had been a piece of jewellery, raising it meditatively to take an experimental bite, then savouring it with the same calm reflection, commenting on the taste to the other. The sight of them maddened her; she longed to batter them into a proper state of mind. She hurried upstairs unmolested.

In her bedroom she had created a little atmosphere of herself. It was chilly, austere and cell-like. Nothing was new but everything was serviceable. The chairs were functional rather than inviting. Her bed was narrow, high and had only a single pillow; the bedstead was of brass. Above it hung the framed text, *'Be still then and know that I am God.'* On the small table beside it stood a candlestick, a Bible and a varied collection of well-worn devotional books. There was nothing in disorder anywhere; her shoes, shabby but brilliantly polished, were ranged with precision under the dressing-table, and inside the drawers and cupboard her clothes were meticulously tidy. On the mantelpiece, faded photographs of her mother and father, taken at the time of their marriage, gazed placidly at each other across a box of matches and a small French clock in a discoloured leather case. The looking-glass on the dressing-table was dark and unflattering. Sepia reproductions of Pre-Raphaelite religious art were disposed round the walls and in the corner least exposed to the light stood a prie-dieu. There was always one window open, sometimes more, and when the door was opened the pictures shook and rattled on the walls.

There was no fresh, bright colour and no cosiness, no warmth and no sympathy there. The curtains and carpet were old and faded; Katharine liked them to be that way. She despised material beauty.

She closed the door and stood with her back against it for a moment, relishing her privacy. She took off her coat and hung it up, laid her half-galoshes together off the carpet, put her hat on the wardrobe shelf and stood at the mirror to smooth her hair. Then she made her way to the prie-dieu and flogged herself in prayer.

Katharine sent Nanny and Susan to Myrtle Lodge after lunch with a note for Doctor O'Brien. The doctor was out, miles away in his trap, but the soft-voiced little maid who answered the door promised to hand it to him the minute he came in. Nanny refused to trust her: little gerrls like that never remembered anything from one minute to the next, sure their minds was never on their work! But in the end she had to give in and leave the note in her charge.

Just as they turned their backs on the doctor's front door, they heard screeches of recognition from Bridie and all the children who were emerging for their walk. Barry came rushing out to Susan and grabbed her gloved hand in his own bare, warm and sticky one.

'Com'ere till I show ye,' he whispered, pulling her after him till they had rounded a corner of the house. 'I've a blackbird's nest wit' four eggs in it.'

Susan's eyes grew round with excitement. 'Oh, show me!' she begged.

'Come on, so!' He scampered across the lawn and she after him, through a shrubbery, across a bramble patch and over the wall into the orchard. There, in the fork of an apple tree high above her head, Susan saw the nest.

'Sh!' Barry whispered fiercely. 'She's on it.' He held Susan, in case she might rush at the tree and frighten the bird. Susan shook his hands off in annoyance.

'You don't have to hold me,' she said crossly.

'Isn't it a pity now ye can't look inside it!' he said wistfully, unconscious of her vexation.

'I'm going to,' she announced, and began to scramble up the tree.

'Ye can't,' he screamed, frantic at her disobedience. 'She'll desert.'

'What d'you mean?' Susan continued to advance. She had never heard the expression before. She felt that it was time to assert herself with Barry. She looked down at his little round, sallow face with its black sloe-eyes beseeching her to come down, and she went on upwards.

The bird, which had been sitting to her eggs as close as a boat to the water, swooped off and out under the boughs. There, she and her mate set up a desperate whooping and throbbing to scold off the invader. But Susan was almost at the nest; one more heave and she was able to look right into it.

'Don't touch it,' shrieked Barry. 'Don't put yer hand to it, Susan.' He danced up and down beneath her.

Susan was quite ignorant about birds' nests. She imagined that Barry did not want her to touch it because it was his discovery. She looked at the nest in wonder for a moment, at the four smudgy eggs lying on their smooth mud floor, so secret, so contained. It was infinitely exciting. She put out a finger and touched an egg; it was warm and had a thick, almost greasy feel. She picked it up between finger and thumb and held it out for Barry to see.

'Look!' she commanded. And to prove that she was doing it no harm, she held it out farther.

'Put it back, oh put it back now, do,' begged Barry in despair.

The birds swooped near her hand, shrieking, and Susan was frightened. She lost her balance, dropped the egg and fell out of the tree.

Physically, she was quite unhurt but Barry's disgust at her behaviour wounded her most deeply. He went up to her and rolled her over with his foot as he would if he had found a dead pigeon in the field. When he saw that she could sit up, he withdrew and looked stonily at the broken egg on the grass.

'I'll never show y'anythin' again,' he said stolidly.

Susan cried bitterly, filled with remorse and shaken by the fall.

'I'm sorry,' she gulped. With Barry, she could bring herself to say it.

'Ye shouldn't have put yer hand to it,' he said sullenly. 'Didn't I tell ye not to?' He looked upwards at the nest. 'They'll never go back to it now,' he stated. 'You've spoilt it for them.'

The contempt in every word turned her spirit to dust.

'But what'll happen to the eggs?' she asked, horrified. 'Won't they hatch?'

'The magpies'll get them. They'll suck them.'

'But why won't they go back to it?'

'Because you put your hand to it,' he repeated ruthlessly.

'Would it be the same if you'd touched it?'

'Of course.' He looked at her disgustedly. 'You'd best g'wan back to Nanny now,' he advised coldly.

She picked herself up and started off quite humbly, feeling ashamed of herself. Then the desire to reinstate herself in his opinion made her turn back. 'I didn't know all that,' she said; 'I won't do it again. I know now.'

He muttered something and began swiping at the grass with a stick.

'You will show me things sometimes, still?' she pleaded.

He made an extra savage lunge at a tuft. 'If ye swear ye'll do as I tell ye.' He would not look towards her.

'Oh yes I will; I promise.'

He threw the stick down. 'All right, so,' he said, and escorted her back to the front door.

Susan longed to make amends for this disgraceful episode; inspiration came suddenly.

'Would you like to see a dead cat?' she asked eagerly.

'How long is it dead?' he asked, slowing down. The subject was so absorbing that they stopped walking altogether.

'Oh, ages,' said Susan impressively.

'Is it far?'

'Near our stables, in the hedge at the back. If Bridie'll let you come for a walk with us I can show you. Oh, come on!'

Barry agreed doubtfully. He suspected Susan's discernment in differentiating between the irresistible and the prosaic.

'What colour is it?' he asked as they began to move on.

'Black and white,' replied Susan with pride.

That settled it. He thought it would be worth seeing. They broke into a run as despairing screams from Nanny and Bridie reached them. Nanny was furious; that little Barry was making Susan as wild as himself. Defeated, the children turned back.

'Well, you're a nice pair!' Nanny scolded, ostentatiously brushing bits of grass and moss off Susan's coat. 'An' where's yer hair ribbon?' While Susan patted her head in a vain search, Nanny turned to Barry. 'You've no call to be leading her off like that, Barry. I've a good mind to tell yer mother on ye.'

'Barry, ye're terrible bould,' said Bridie in support.

'I'm sorry, Nurrse,' said Barry, his little face quite empty of expression. The threat to tell his mother did not carry much weight; she would have been unable to see the harm in it all.

Susan hugged Nanny's waist. 'Don't be cross!' she pleaded, 'Barry was showing me a nest. Nanny's heart melted. 'I want to whisper,' went on Susan, reaching up to pull Nanny's face down to her level. Nanny bent her head. 'Can Barry come for a walk with us? Please, oh please!'

'All right, my lamb, if Bridie says he can. Will ye be good, the pair o' ye?' she added in a threatening voice.

The children beamed at her. 'Oh, yes,' said Susan. 'We will so,' said Barry.

Bridie agreed with enthusiasm. Barry was becoming something of a handful and she could not manage him when she had a baby and three other children to mind.

'Sure, he can run home by himself,' she said. 'He does often go to the shop by himself, an' he'll come to no harrm. Will ye come straight home, Barry?' she demanded, bending to his level and speaking right into his face.

'I will, of courrse,' said Barry. So it was arranged.

The children ran along together ahead of Nanny, chattering. When they reached Fellowescourt, Susan asked, 'Can Barry play with me in the garden for a little?'

Nanny's old bones ached from the walk. 'Ye can, indeed,' she agreed. 'I'll just go in an' get me coat off an' put the kittle on. Sure, I can keep an eye on ye out o' the winder.'

She sent them up the way to the stables instead of through the house, thinking of their muddy feet. She herself turned off and went in by the back door.

Susan and Barry skipped along to the yard, which they had to cross to reach the green garden door. Susan took Barry's hand importantly but he shook her off.

'Leave me go,' he said gruffly.

'Would you like to see the horses?' asked Susan, diverted by the sound of a whinny.

'I'd love it,' he replied with feeling.

They went through the harness-room. There was a huge pile of gear on the table, saddles, bridles, traces, bits, all thrown together in disorder with Sheehy's ancient hat, badly dented, beside it. There was no sign of Sheehy himself.

Susan led the way into the stable. The two old hunters were munching quietly in their loose-boxes. Dolly's head was over his door and he was half-whinnying at them in a friendly way.

'Those were my grandpapa's hunters,' announced Susan grandly.

Barry was more interested in Dolly; he stroked the velvet nose with gentle confidence, laughing when Dolly wrinkled his lip and pretended to nip his shoulder.

'What's his name?' he asked.

'Dolly.'

'Sure, every pony's called Dolly,' commented Barry with disgust.

'The hunters are called Brandy and Shandy,' said Susan, hoping that he would be impressed.

'Our harse'd ate ye,' stated Barry with pride, 'but I can handle him all right. He'd never touch me, so he wouldn't, not even if I put me hand in his mout'.'

'Why wouldn't he?'

'I suppose I do have a way wit' me wit' harses,' he explained happily. He continued to stroke Dolly's nose. He reached up to touch the cob's forelock but Dolly backed away with a clatter of hoofs, turning completely round, and returned to the door with his ears back and eyes staring. At the same moment, Susan became aware that the stable was darker. Something was blocking the light in the doorway.

'What ails y'at all?' said Barry, mystified by Dolly's behaviour. He felt suddenly afraid, not of the cob, but of a something that was making Susan gaze at the doorway and stand frozen-still. He turned quickly to see for himself.

Old Sheehy was standing there, hatless; his whole body swayed as if rocked by waves that drove him first one way and then back again. In

one hand he brandished a carving knife and with it he smote the air as
though his wild blue stare saw enemies on every side. When he saw the
children, he began to murmur, laughing slyly and chuckling, advancing
a little nearer every moment, still cleaving the air with his weapon.

The children made a sudden dash, out through the harness-room,
across the yard and into the kitchen garden. And, moving like a horse
on a tight rein that longs to show his speed, Sheehy followed them. He
took long steps and rose high with each one as if he were walking in
water. He waved the knife with a circular motion as he ran, exulting,
shouting with laughter. The children tore through the gate on to the
lawn and he followed them.

The children reached the back door, screaming, and in her panic Susan
could not open it. Sheehy was coming nearer and her screams rose higher.
Mrs Flood, in great alarm, ran to open the door. She did not know what
was the matter but the children's terror was so evident that there was no
doubt that something frightening had happened. As the two children fell
in at the doorway she saw Sheehy approaching and with a shout of 'Oah,
my God!' banged the door and shot home the bolts.

This done, she prepared to have hysterics, but the sight of Sheehy
dancing outside the window, shouting, 'I'll get ye! I'll get ye!' and
flourishing the carving knife drove her to further action.

Mary, the kitchen-maid, who was under notice and disinclined to do
more work than was necessary, was slumped in a chair in the servant's
hall, half-asleep. She stumbled to her feet in a great fright when Mrs
Flood screeched to her from the kitchen, 'Mary, Mary, com'ere now
quick or my God we'll all be murdhered.'

'What ails ye, Mrs Flood?' Mary came shuffling in with the laces of
her black shoes undone and her fat feet bursting out.

Pointing at the menacing figure outside, Mrs Flood waved an
imperious arm: 'Go on up and fetch Miss Kat'rine, Mary. Tell her the
coachman's afther us all wit' the carvin' knife an' I dunno how long
can I keep him out. Go quick now, or we'll all be dead.' She gave the

panic-stricken Mary a great shove that propelled her along the flagged passage. 'Quick now!' she repeated as Mary streaked through the green baize door into the hall.

Mrs Flood returned to the kitchen, patting her bosom and breathing loudly. The children had backed against the wall and were quite silent, huddled together. Outside, old Sheehy danced at the window, gurgling and pointing at them all inside. Suddenly, inspired by a new and cunning thought, he wagged his forefinger solemnly against his brow and disappeared towards the conservatory.

'Oah!' shrieked Mrs Flood. 'He'll be in on us!' She sped along the passage herself now, and through the hall to the morning-room, where Charlotte and Daisy were sitting in contented silence. Without a word to them, she flung herself at the outer door, locked and bolted it, then fled to the front door and locked that too. The frustrated Sheehy, finding himself barred from entering the morning-room by the conservatory, slid cunningly out of sight.

As Mrs Flood returned from the hall door, Harriet, Nanny and all the servants poured down both back and front staircases, Nanny was moaning at the thought of Susan's experience.

'Is the little boy wit' her?' she asked Mary anxiously.

'He is. Sure, I've told ye twice,' replied Mary unsympathetically.

Charlotte and Daisy, who had seen Sheehy threatening their lives with terrible sideways cuts through the air, moved out of the morning-room with unusual rapidity to join the party on the stairs. They all herded together on the bottom steps, feeling safer there than where they could be seen from outside. Nanny pushed her way through them and went to the kitchen.

'Oh, thank God ye're safe my lamb!' she cried as she saw Susan. 'Come on, Barry, child.'

She drove them gently before her to the hall as Katharine hastened down the stairs.

'At last!' they all thought, 'at last she's come!' They trusted her blindly, certain that she would deliver them. They had no notion of what they expected her to do, but they knew she would do something.

She stood at the morning-room door, peering through the conservatory.

'Where is he?' she asked. 'I can't see him.'

'Hidin'!' cried Mrs Flood. 'Waitin' to lep out on us!' She felt able at last to give way to her emotions. She burst into unrestrained and noisy tears.

'Stop that at once, Mrs Flood!' commanded Katharine, and as the noise continued she picked up that morning's newspaper, rolled it into a baton and beat the cook with it about the head until she stopped.

'You ought to be ashamed of yourself,' she rebuked her. 'It's for you to set an example to all the other girls.' Then, turning her back on them all, she marched to the outer door of the morning-room, unlocked it, walked quietly through the conservatory and stood waiting for Sheehy on the lawn.

They crowded into the morning-room after her, unable to keep away. An instinct of self-preservation made them press back against the inner wall, away from the unlocked door which nobody could lock again for very shame. There was a horrified gasp as they watched her standing, very small and upright, looking about her for the maniac who was seeking a victim.

Katharine did not feel afraid as she waited. Indeed, she experienced a kind of elation. 'I want him to kill me,' she admitted to herself. 'I don't want to live any more. God forgive me! I have had more than I can bear.'

She saw Sheehy then, swinging round the corner of the house with the knife raised in his hand. She went towards him, and some remnant of sense in his old brain brought his hand, still clutching the knife, up to his forehead in salute, even as he advanced.

Laughing and swaying, he was almost up to her and she had not moved. The knife swung dangerously near her and she saw how sharp it was, with its concave edge worn from years of use. She ceased to think. She acted only from instinct and outraged authority. Above all things, now, she wanted her life.

'Sheehy!' she cried, suddenly consumed with indignation. 'How dare you! Give me that knife at once.' Anger was bubbling out of her, making her feel swollen and twice as big as herself.

The old man dropped all his wild, threatening manner and stood quite meekly before her.

'Yes, Miss,' he said and held out the knife for her to take. He looked aged, shrunken and bewildered.

'Thank you, Sheehy,' she said severely. 'Now you must stay here until I come back. You are not to move.'

'No, Miss,' promised Sheehy. He passed his hand anxiously across his brow.

With a most compelling look to make him obey her, Katharine went into the house to dispose of the knife. At the conservatory door she looked back and shook a raised finger at him. He touched his forehead respectfully.

In the morning-room there was a scene of wild disorder. The servants, with the exception of Nanny, had fallen on their knees and maintained continuous prayer during the whole of the crisis. Now, giving thanks noisily, they struggled to their feet.

Nanny, a protective arm round the shoulders of each child, had kept up a monotonous stream of reassuring speech, half-croon, half-gabble, which rose and fell with her agitation and relief. Now, with a loud cry of, 'Oah! thank God ye're safe, Miss Kat'rine!', she lay back in her chair, abandoning herself to her emotions.

Harriet was weeping silently and looking deathly pale. Charlotte and Daisy presented the only static feature. They had suffered extreme fright but the happy outcome had convinced them that their agitation had been unnecessary and they were now quite recovered. Like a group of statuary representing order in the midst of chaos, they sat, heavy, impassive and inert.

There were shrieks of gratitude for her deliverance when Katharine brought the knife in. Harriet threw her arms round her kissing her repeatedly. And now Susan, swelling with admiration and sudden affection, rushed out from the shelter of Nanny's arm and, throwing her arms round Katharine's waist, raised her face to be kissed.

Katharine was touched most deeply by this evidence of affection, but she could not show it. Disengaging the encircling arms, she kissed Harriet and Susan in a preoccupied way, and laid the knife on the table.

'Katharine, you were brave,' said Charlotte admiringly, 'but we knew you would be, didn't we Daisy?'

'Yes,' admitted Daisy, 'but we never really thought he'd dare to hurt you. We felt sure you'd be all right.'

Katharine made no comment; she did not feel that she had been brave at all. It was an access of cowardice that had driven her out to meet the homicidal Sheehy. She knew that she must attribute the sudden upsurge of the will to live only to the grace of God. She felt immensely humble, thankful and ashamed.

So it was not from modesty but from shame that she refused to let them make her a heroine. Their adulation embarrassed her and she asked them, with some irritation, to desist.

'Someone must go and fetch some men to stay with Sheehy,' she went on. 'Then, if he gets violent they will be able to deal with him. Mrs Flood, would you go down to the village and . . . what is that?'

The hall door bell was being rung repeatedly. The din within the house had been so incessant that no one had heard it.

Lizzie heard it now, open-mouthed. It was her duty to open the door but she did not move. She could see Sheehy standing quite mildly on the lawn, so she knew that it was not he who was ringing the bell. Nevertheless, she could not suppress her dread of the unseen; it could only be another assassin.

'Oah, I can't, Miss,' she said miserably.

The other servants caught her panic; as the bell continued to ring, their screams rose.

Katharine pointed to Sheehy standing on the grass. 'You're perfectly safe, Lizzie,' she said quietly. 'Look!'

'I know, Miss,' wailed Lizzie, and covering her face with her apron, she wept despairingly.

Katharine swept them with a withering look and went to open the door herself.

The Reverend Lawrence Weldon, who was on the other side of it, had become seriously alarmed when his repeated ringings had brought forth no response in spite of the fact that he could hear female voices in evident distress within. He had tried looking through the letter box but had been able to see only the hall floor. He had peered through the small windows flanking the door but had been able to see no one. So he had kept on ringing with loud persistance in the hope of being heard eventually. When he heard bolts being withdrawn and the huge key turned in the lock, his apprehension increased.

The door opened and he was faced by Katharine, flushed, a little disordered about the hair, but apparently perfectly sound. His relief was immense.

He threw back his head, smiling, and began, 'Tell me, what has been . . .' but he was unable to continue.

Katharine grasped his elbows tightly, looked into his face with ineffable devotion and exclaimed, 'Oh, Lawrence, I have been in such need of you!' So dependent did she seem upon his support, so empty of her usual self-confidence, that his whole being swelled with the desire to protect and assist her.

'My love,' he cried, 'tell me what is the matter?'

But she only bent her head over his hands and wept.

CHAPTER SEVEN

Harriet was no mechanic; to her, a bicycle was a self-willed monster as enigmatic as the Sphinx and less predictable than any horse. She had learnt to ride with difficulty, in constant fear of her malevolent machine, and having reached the stage of being able to mount, dismount and pursue a wavering course along the roads, was now considered fit to ride short distances by herself.

Hills, either up or down, terrified her, so for them she dismounted; she did the same for any moving object on the road from an ass-cart to a steam-roller, quite certain that if she tried to pass anything she would collide with it, or cause the horse to bolt, or be crushed under the wheels. Her progress was therefore slow but she always arrived in the end, heated, windswept and as nervous as a cat.

She had an uncomfortable notion, as she pushed her machine up the hill about three miles out of Glenmacool, that something had gone wrong. The front tyre was a curious shape and the wheel rattled over the bumps and holes in the road in an unfamiliar way. When she reached the top she bent down to examine the tyre before proceeding and found that it was quite flat; it was, in fact, punctured and Harriet was no more capable of repairing it than she was of flying.

It was a great nuisance; she was on an errand of mercy to the Maguire farm, taking a bundle of little garments for the new, motherless baby, the youngest of six. She had made them all herself and she had stitched enough love into them to encompass the little creature for the rest of its childhood. She had also brought a bag of sweets for the other children because she could not bear to think of their disappointment if they were left out. Nobody at Fellowescourt knew where she was; she had just slipped out after luncheon, as secretive as if she were planning a crime.

She leant the bicycle against the bank, so as to examine it better, but it slipped and shuffled away until finally it fell into the road, lying on the pedal. The wheels spun wildly and the handlebars were in such an unnatural position that when she tried to pick it up they seemed to want to face the rear of the machine. She became very confused, the more so as her skirts kept impeding her movements. Standing back to study its anatomy, she felt certain that it was now broken beyond repair and that she would have to abandon it in the ditch. It had a contorted, agonised look which made her pity it against her will. She tried again to stand it up, and this time succeeded by leaning it against a gate. Then, optimistically, she decided to try and pump up the tyre.

She had seen people pumping up tyres before, but she had never observed the essential preliminaries. First, she had to detach the pump from the bicycle, which was not easy unless done correctly. It took her many minutes. Then the pump had to be prepared for use, and this defeated her. She tried to attach it as it was, quite flushed with triumph at having first located the valve and recognised it as the strategic point of the operation. Neither persuasion nor force worked, and she sat on the grass bank in her hot black clothes turning the pump over and over in her hands and marvelling at its cunning in resisting her. Even prolonged study revealed nothing of its secrets and she laid it on the white dusty road while she considered what to do.

She was quite determined to reach the Maguire farm, having come all this way. It was only about half a mile on, and she thought that if she could push her bicycle that far someone there might be able to help her. With difficulty she replaced her pump; then, feeling hot, dirty and frustrated, her hat pushed backwards on her head, her clothes dusty and untidy, she began to toil onwards.

It was May. The fields were of a green so brilliant that it made the heart rejoice; the grass seemed to drink in the sunlight, to hold it and still release it with living radiance. Dog daisies stood flat and steady as little plates at table, open to the sun. Buttercups, glossy as wet paint, glowed and shone in the grass, white hawthorn plastered the hedges, its sweet-dusty smell warm on the air, and the ash-trees that accident had sowed amongst the thorn, dishevelled as a girl's wet hair, were soft-edged with pale tufts of infant leaves. Life was thrusting upwards, an irresistible force erupting, possessing, overwhelming; evident in the way the lambs butted their ewes for milk, all but upsetting them in the onslaught, and drank as if they might never drink again, tails wagging, heads up, intent; and in the way the young birds in the nests stretched upwards gaping, hungry beaks.

Harriet was not aware of much beyond her discomfort, which was aggravated by the warmth of the day. She was puffing wearily when she reached the crown of the rise and stopped to lean against her machine for a moment while she looked around and recovered her breath. The beauty of the afternoon struck her then and she watched and listened and sniffed the air, receptive to it all. The lambs delighted her; propping her bicycle against the bank again, she stood and watched them. It was not until Captain Willoughby's dog-cart was almost upon her that she awoke to the fact that there was anybody else on the road.

She was annihilated by innumerable conflicting feelings; she started to call out to him for help, as she would have done to any passer-by, then stifled the cry for fear that he would think her forward; she was tremendously excited by meeting him, yet aware that she was flushed and perspiring in her unbecoming black and, after greeting him as warmly as decorum permitted, she cast around for a means of escape.

He had saluted her with his whip and was preparing to pass, when his eye happened to fall upon her punctured tyre and he was down in a moment.

'My dear Miss Fellowes,' he reproved her, 'do you mean to say that you were going to let me go past you without calling upon me to get you out of this trouble?' He shook his head at her as though he really admired her for her unselfishness. 'Is it a puncture? We won't try to mend it here. Where are you going? Wherever it is, I will take you there.'

Without a moment's hesitation he had hoisted the bicycle on to the back of the dog-cart and before she could say a word he was securing it with a rope for which he had delved into the box.

She looked up at him with a gentle trusting expression in her liquid brown eyes, so amazed, so stimulated by what was happening that she could not put her words together.

'You are . . . too kind. Really I . . . not going beyond Maguire's.' Within, a volcano of excitement threatened to engulf her at any moment. Outwardly, she seemed a little dazed.

He helped her up: 'I am going there myself,' he said. 'Will you be long?'

'Oh no,' she protested. 'I only brought . . . for the children . . . a few little things. Their mother died so tragically.'

He looked appraisingly at her: 'I think you are a blessing to these people round here,' he said thoughtfully. 'I wish there were more like you.'

'I love the children,' she said, 'and they get so little.'

'Hm,' he said, preoccupied. They turned into the narrow lane that led up to the Maguire farm; it was rutted and muddy, becoming worse as they reached the farmyard. Hens fluttered before them, incapable of deviating from the straight, and so were pursued until the gate brought the horse to a stop. Within, pigs weltered, cows waited to be milked, geese dragooned the strangers off their land and children darted round the drier regions, barefoot and caked with mud. The buildings were whitewashed but the thatch was dark and thin with age and scummy with green, and there was an all-pervading smell of horses and cows mingled with the stink of pigs.

'Surely, Miss Fellowes, you were not going to come all the way up here in those thin shoes?' exclaimed Captain Willoughby. 'It really is too much for a lady to go through such filth. Now, you must stay here; I will not hear of you dismounting. I will send someone out to you.' He was gone before she could protest, through the gate and leaning in at the open half-door of the house, calling Maguire.

The man appeared from a byre and a woman, a pot of potatoes steaming in her hand, came anxiously to the door. The Captain, after a word with the woman, disappeared into the byre with Maguire, and the woman put down her pot on the step and picked her way across to Harriet.

She was not a young woman, but younger than she looked. She was tall, sallow and scrawny, seeming concave from ceaseless overwork and the bearing of burdens too heavy for her. She had the drawn-up, sickly look of plants reared in the dark and her garments were dark, ragged and half-protected by a filthy apron. But her manners were beautiful.

"'Tis very good of you to call, Miss Fellowes, and 'twould be a pleasure if you'd come in but I couldn't ask you, sure wit' such oceans of mud between you and the door.'

'Now,' said Harriet, perplexed, 'tell me, who are you?'

'I am Michael's sister, Miss Fellowes, and when poor Mary died, God rest her soul, he wrote to me out in New York to know would I come home and mind the childer for him. So of course I came.' There was no trace of heroics in the last phrase. Amongst the Irish peasantry, family needs are met without reserve and outweigh personal considerations.

'You were in New York?' said Harriet wonderingly. 'And how long have you been here?'

'Four months, Miss.' She had a fleeting smile of great beauty.

So that, thought Harriet, was what four months in a hovel surrounded by mud with six children and a man to look after could bring you to. The woman looked so ill that Harriet was disturbed.

'And your name is?'

'Brigid Maguire, Miss.'

'What did you do in New York?' she asked gently.

'I was a lady's maid, Miss.'

'Did you get good wages?'

'I did indeed, Miss, very good. Very good indeed, they were.'

'Do you ever go out, here?'

'Well,' the woman hesitated, 'to hang up the clothes, like, on the line, and to carry in the turf and collect the eggs—little things like that. And on a fine day I do roll the baby out along the road a little way. But, sure, what would I be goin' out for?'

'You know, I'd love to see the baby,' begged Harriet wistfully. 'That's what I came for. I have one or two little things for him here.'

'I'll bring him out to ye of course,' said Brigid Maguire. ''Tis terrible kind o' ye, Miss, to be bringin' things for him.' She tacked across the farmyard from stepping stone to stepping stone and was back in a minute with a grey bundle in her arms. When she reached Harriet again, she propped the baby upright, so that he could be better seen, and bent her own head over him, smiling and talking as she drew away the grimy shawl from his face.

'Arrah now,' she crooned, 'smile now, smile for the lady!'

Harriet held out her arms. 'May I hold him?' As the woman held the baby up, she took him and nursed him, smiling down into the minute pale face almost with adoration. His skin was of a delicacy alarming in its transparency; under the eyes and round the upper lip there was a blueness which, with the deep blue of the eye, was the only colour to be seen. He was not a very clean baby and his wraps smelt horrible.

Harriet turned a beaming face to Brigid Maguire. 'Isn't he lovely!' she exclaimed, quite unaware of his filthy coverings.

'I don't know is he clean now,' said the woman anxiously. 'I wouldn't like ye to be destroyed with him,' and she held out her arms to take the baby back again. 'He is a lovely baby all right, Miss, God bless him. Five gerrls before him and he the only boy.' She waved her free hand round the yard to include all the watching children who stood, fingers in their mouths, in complete silence and immobility.

Harriet gave her the bundle of clothes and beckoned confidentially to the other children. They came one step nearer and stopped, then another step. They were too shy to come right up to her. Harriet held out the bag of sweets to the eldest.

'There is something in here for all of you. Won't you come and get it?' The girl's face was scared but with encouragement she approached, gasped her thanks and retired with the bag. All the children clustered round her, heads bent, peering into the mouth of the bag.

'Only one, now, one at a time I tellya,' admonished the eldest. They obeyed her and stood about in the yard with lumps in their cheeks, sucking. Harriet smiled at them and they smiled shyly back. She was satisfied; it was all the reward she wanted.

'Do you miss New York?' she asked Brigid Maguire.

'Well, I do and I don't,' was the reply. ''Tis great altogether to be back home; 'twas terrible lonesome over there in the States and though there was great luxury there was no comfort in it. Ach, I'm glad to be home, so I am,' she concluded, nodding to give weight to her statement and smiling her rare, swift smile.

She looked so ill that it pained Harriet to see her. 'You must get out in the sun with that baby as much as you can, now the weather's nice,' she advised. 'Sun is good for babies,' she added with some diffidence, knowing that fresh air and sunlight were thought to be dangerous to infants.

'Yes, Miss,' said Brigid Maguire, but from her tone Harriet knew that she was unconvinced and would never take her advice.

The men emerged from the byre. Gazing at Captain Willoughby, Harriet thought how distinguished he looked, with his straight bearing and the military cut of his clothes. His face had a kindly expression and, talking to Maguire, she noticed how he gave him his whole attention. She swelled with pride at the thought that he admired her. 'I don't care what Katharine thinks of him,' she declared stoutly to herself. 'I think he's wonderful.'

When Captain Willoughby made up his mind to do something, it was half done before he had finished thinking. He said goodbye and they were gone, down the bohereen and out on to the road. He looked at Harriet with some concern.

'You are not too cold, Miss Fellowes? There is not much protection up here, I'm afraid.'

Harriet, who would gladly have endured a blizzard for the sake of sitting beside him, quickly reassured him.

'It is so very pleasant up here,' she said. 'It is quite the nicest way of seeing the countryside, so much better than a trap. I am sick of flying along between the hedges and seeing nothing at all. And I am very warm,' she added. 'I never feel cold.'

'Ha!' he exclaimed with great interest. 'Just my own feelings! A dog-cart is the way to see the country; I have always said so.' He looked at her with some warmth in his regard: 'I think that you and I have many things in common, Miss Fellowes.'

She glanced up at him quickly, almost afraid that he might be teasing her; their eyes met and his were perfectly serious, even admiring. She smiled a little shyly at him, surprised at his perception. She had remarked to herself a long time ago that they had much in common, but had not expected him, a man, to be aware of it. He was a person so practical, so very much inclined to action rather than to thought, that his having considered their relationship at all, touched her deeply and gave her great solace. She felt that she must be very much in his mind, and this emboldened her to speak with more frankness than decorum.

'I know that we have,' she said. 'I would like so very much to know in what ways you think . . .'

He did not hesitate for a second: 'But it is quite clear to me that we have the same view of the people of the countryside, the farmers and labourers and their families; you are devoted to them and their children; I try to help them by looking after their stock and telling them of new and more efficient farming methods. I want these farmers to improve the quality of their animals, to breed healthy stock and sell clean milk and decent meat. I want to see every farmer his own master, out of the hands of the bank and the gombeen-man, with enough to keep his family decent and his farm up-to-date.' He shook his head angrily. 'But look what happens! You get people like poor Michael Maguire put to the pin of their collars to keep going at all, with a string of children' growing up like savages and a wretched over-worked woman to look after the lot of them, and she riddled with consumption from the look of her. They're doomed, the ones like that; they're so poor that they can't afford to live, let alone improve their land, so everything deteriorates until it even stops being productive.'

He stopped talking suddenly as if he had caught himself saying far more than he had intended. After an amused look at Harriet, which seemed to ask her how much of this kind of talk she could stomach without protesting, he said in a gentler tone, speaking more slowly, 'Ah, Miss Fellowes, you must think me an odd fellow, to lecture you like this on farming. You must stop me, you must indeed, for I should know better than that. There is no other lady of my acquaintance who would put up with it for a moment—not, indeed, that I am acquainted with many ladies, but no lady will listen to farming talk. The trouble is,' he continued confidentially, 'that I am a plain man who cannot talk to amuse. If I am to talk at all it must be about something that interests me. I cannot contrive to talk. I am no ladies' man, Miss Fellowes.'

Having unburdened himself of this statement, he watched her until she should reply. Harriet felt that it had cost him something in self-esteem to make the admission, that he was a little afraid that she would think less well of him for it and that on her reply might depend his attitude towards himself.

She smiled at him to give him confidence. 'But surely small talk is only a sort of bridge to carry people over the emptiness of having nothing they really want to say to each other, Captain Willoughby. I am not good at putting things clearly, Katharine says I am too stupid, but perhaps you will be able to understand me.' She could see with such clarity in her own mind the thought that words could so easily distort, so that he might even invest them with a meaning that she had never intended. 'I do not think that you and I are in need of small talk,' she added, 'when we say things, they mean more than that.' Her gentle brown eyes, now so full of sympathy and anxiety to be understood aright, melted his last uncertainties.

It was clear that he was making a great effort to control his emotion. He reined in his horse, seeming to be unable to keep himself in check unless he restrained it also. But when he had brought the horse to a standstill he was in danger of looking very foolish unless he explained himself at once.

Harriet was so agitated by the suddenness with which all that she had imagined and desired was overtaking her, had actually caught up with her and threatened to carry her far beyond anything she had been able to envisage, that she could not look at him or assist him in any way.

He looked at her and away again, as if he feared that she might be laughing at him after all. 'Miss Fellowes,' he began, and found it difficult to express his feelings; 'I can only tell you what is in my heart, I cannot make speeches. Would it . . . does it matter to you that people despise me because I am what they call a cow doctor? I am asking you to marry me, Miss . . . Harriet; I cannot find words to tell you how deeply I love you. If you will have me I will do my utmost to make you happy. Please . . . try to give me an answer quickly; waiting is such torture.'

He had said it and he felt the better for it; he had spoken and she had not rebuffed him yet. He turned to her anxiously just as she turned towards him, and the sight of the love and happiness in her face filled him with gratitude.

'Indeed I will marry you,' declared Harriet joyfully, with her hat on the back of her head and her hair blown into wisps and streels by the drive, her hands oily and her clothes dusty. She put out her arms and lifted her face to be kissed in delightful surrender.

At Fellowescourt, tea was over and no one knew where Harriet was. 'The Pope' felt a little anxious when she discovered that Harriet's bicycle was also missing. Motor cars were becoming much more plentiful on the roads now and they were driven much too fast; she had heard of several accidents attributed to the recklessness of chauffeurs. She grew frightened as the afternoon wore into evening and Harriet did not return. She found that she could not settle to anything, she was forever jumping up to look out of the window or stopping to listen to an unfamiliar noise, so she took her sewing to her bedroom and sat at the open window, with the first blue shadows of the evening creeping over the grass below and the hint of the sundown chill beginning to encroach.

She laid her work down in her lap as her eye fell upon the neglected flowerbeds and grass edgings of the front garden; the summer geraniums had been put in, but weeds were showing amongst them and a fringe of green overlaid the edges of the flagged path; there were even tufts of grass between the paving-stones.

So many things were deteriorating around her that when more evidence of neglect struck her, she suffered something near to despair. Whenever she reflected on the present way of life at Fellowescourt there rose to the surface of her mind the rebellious thought, 'Oh, it is too much for me!' She would have to find the dividing line between unnecessary upkeep and essential maintenance, but the sight of dust in the house and unchecked luxuriance in the garden frightened her because she knew that even the minimum was beyond her. Now that Sheehy was in the lunatic asylum at Inish, she had no man to keep the garden and only an untamed village lad to do the rough work for her; he needed constant supervision if he was to be prevented from doing more harm than good, and this she had not the time to give him.

She put her sewing away, changed her shoes, ran downstairs, and, taking an ancient coat from the hall, made her way to the toolshed. Picking up a pair of long-handled shears, a weeding-fork and a rake, she set to work to tidy the front garden herself. As she worked she experienced a grim sort of contentment at the thought that she was catching up with circumstances, that she was still undefeated; she leant on the handle of the rake for a moment to admire the order that she had restored, then continued to work with a ferocity born of the desire to do more in the time at her disposal than could really be achieved.

As always when her mind was not actively occupied, her thoughts dug into the question of her engagement, toiling and striving to find a means of marrying soon. Since the day when she had discovered that, in spite of the malignant operations of fate, in spite of fear, despair and exhaustion, life was still sweet, she and Lawrence Weldon had spent many hours in wistful discussion of their future and of how soon, if ever, their marriage would be possible. He had refused to contemplate breaking their engagement, had been resolute in his determination not even to discuss such a calamity, but force of circumstances had obliged him to submit to a postponement of their marriage. 'We will put it off,' he had reluctantly agreed, 'but nothing will induce me to give it up, so long as you love me.'

That was how the matter now stood, and she probed and thrust at the obstacles to her happiness, in the constant hope that they might be found to be less solid and less durable than they appeared. But always round her neck, dragging her to perdition, was the dead-weight of her human obligations: Charlotte, Daisy, Harriet and Susan. Olivia she did not regard as a burden; she was a great help to her and besides she would probably marry one day; but what hope was there of the other three sisters ever becoming independent of her? The more she observed them, the more oppressive seemed her responsibility. Harriet meant well but she was unable to perceive what needed doing and what she tried to do had generally to be done again. Charlotte and Daisy were obstructive, selfish and too ignorant to earn their own livings. They did not want to learn anything more than they already knew. It took far more energy to make them do things than to do them herself; yet, for their own good, she tried to drill them into shape, resisting and resentful though they were.

She straightened her back and again tried to remember if Harriet had said anything about going out for the afternoon. It was now so late that she began to feel serious alarm. She was about to go into the house to see if Olivia would search in one direction while she herself went in the other, when she heard a horse-drawn vehicle approaching at a brisk trot. She ran quickly to the gate under the yew archway and leant out to see what was coming. The spectacle that she saw took her breath away.

Captain Willoughby's smart dog-cart was coming into the village from the direction of Inish; the horse, that lively black high-stepper, was the sole reminder of its usual trimness, the only remnant of past glory. Side by side, elevated to a position so conspicuous that they were visible from all sides, sitting very close together, holding hands and gazing with rapture into each other's eyes, were Harriet and the Captain. Behind them, roped to the back of the dog-cart, in an attitude of sprawling abandon that parodied the freedom with which they themselves were behaving, was Harriet's bicycle. Harriet's hair was down her back, her hat on the back of her head; she looked like a tinker after a day at the races.

'The Pope' was so horrified that she stood where she was, her head sticking out beyond the hedge, staring at them in a way that only the extreme shock she had suffered could excuse. She gaped at them as does a servant who perceives the caterpillar in the cauliflower that she is handing round. Suddenly aware of the impropriety of her own behaviour, she withdrew her head, and with mounting anger began to gather up her tools.

She had worried herself nearly sick about Harriet, dreading the news of some accident, and here she was, perfectly all right. She had no right to be all right, worry should be justified by events, though 'the Pope' had spent the entire time hoping that this would not be so. The inconsistency of her own attitude disturbed her not at all; she was not in a mood for thought, her whole course of action was being determined by her feelings. She hurried to the shed with the tools, then back to the gate, new causes for anger bubbling to the surface with every step she took.

How dare Harriet come home looking like this, she raged. Behaving in public in a way that no little servant girl would dream of going on! Her hair falling down, looking at that dreadful man in that besotted way—it made one wonder what had been taking place. She could see the horse, standing outside the archway, but never a sign of Harriet or of Captain Willoughby. What on earth could they be doing that so delayed them? Here she was, waiting for them, waiting and waiting, and they not in the least concerned, dawdling the evening away. With a snort of disgust, she leant out into the road again.

Harriet had her back to the gate; she was watching adoringly while Captain Willoughby released her bicycle. He put it on the ground and bent to examine it, and together they discussed its repair in the most leisurely way. He wheeled it slowly to the footpath and propped it against the hedge. Then he saw Katharine.

He raised his hat and stepped forward briskly to greet her. 'Ah, Miss Fellowes,' he said, shaking her hand warmly, 'you must not blame me for keeping Miss Harriet out so late; her bicycle was punctured, so I took her along with me in the dog-cart, and now we have decided that we like it so much that we never want to be separated again.' He was looking more at Harriet than at Katharine, or perhaps he would not have spoken with such confidence.

'Indeed,' said 'the Pope' scorchingly.

Harriet, like a mouse in the power of a cat, observed her with guilty fascination. The expression on Katharine's face brought home to her the disorder of her appearance, the want of decorum in her arrival and the general thoughtlessness of her behaviour.

When Captain Willoughby, carried away by enthusiasm, took her arm and demanded, 'That is so, is it not, Harriet?', she was speechless and could only nod her head at Katharine.

'Are you trying to tell me that you want to marry my sister, Captain Willoughby?' blazed 'the Pope'. This last impertinence, that they should be able to marry while she was condemned to spinsterhood for heaven only knew how many years, caused her such rage that she could hardly speak. Her head was bursting and she felt as if hot coals were behind her eyes. She wanted to hurt them, to make it as difficult for them to marry as it was for her, to make them suffer so that they should know the extent of her own suffering. She scarcely heard the Captain when he replied.

'I am, Miss Fellowes, and I hope we have your good wishes. But this is hardly the place to discuss it and I trust you will allow me to drive over in the morning, as it is now so late, and ask you more formally for your approval.'

Harriet gave him an imploring look. 'D'you have to go now?' she whispered, terrified of being left alone with 'the Pope'.

'I should not have thought my approval was of any consequence,' snapped Katharine. 'You bring my sister home holding hands on top of a dog-cart, and at dusk, moreover, looking as if you'd been love-making in the hedges, and then try to make me believe that you are proposing honourable marriage to her. How often has this kind of thing happened, Captain Willoughby? How long has it been going on?'

For the first time he seemed aware that she was angry with him. His surprise was evident.

'Why, Miss Fellowes,' he protested, without the smallest sign of annoyance, 'indeed you mustn't be imagining such things! Why, your sister is not that sort of a girl, as you well know, any more than I am that kind of man. We met today by accident—you must believe that because it is the truth and your sister gave me reason to admire her even more than I already did, for I have always thought her a fine girl, and I proposed to her. That is the story. I am very sorry that we have come home so late in the evening, Miss Fellowes, but on an occasion like this, time is inclined to be forgotten.'

He spoke with such sincerity that 'the Pope's' heart smote her; she knew that he was speaking the truth, that he really loved Harriet and that she loved him; yet she felt that it was all too easy for them. It was unfair that things should go so right for them and so wrong for her. But in this moment of hesitation she suddenly perceived the wrong that she was doing them; she caught a glimpse of herself with the eye of truth and all her rage collapsed in self-condemnation. She felt bitterly ashamed and so anxious to do violence to her pride that she blushed crimson to her hairline. She closed her eyes, held her breath and, all in one moment of time, prayed in complete abasement, 'Oh God, forgive me!'

She held out her hand to Captain Willoughby. 'You must think me an ogre,' she said shakily, 'to be angry with you when all you have done is good. Thank you for taking care of Harriet—I'm sure she will always bless that puncture! Will you lunch with us tomorrow? I hope by then to have recovered from the shock you have given us.' She smiled.

He took her hand delightedly, shook it several times as he thanked her, accepted her invitation, and released her.

'Perhaps,' he said, as he raised his hat in farewell, 'one of these days you will fall in love yourself, Miss Fellowes. I hope so, indeed.'

Katharine started back as if she had been struck in the face; she was quite unable to speak. She drew in her breath quickly and held it for a moment, then looked at Harriet as if imploring succour for her wound. But all she found in Harriet's glowing face was a desire that she would be gone and leave her and her lover to say their goodbyes in privacy. Her back stiffened, her head went up and with a brusque wave of the hand she marched up the flagged path and into the house.

When Harriet wandered in several minutes later, she was so dazed with the day's events that she was unprepared for 'the Pope's' swift slaughter.

'You slut!' raged Katharine. 'Just look at yourself. I'm disgusted with you. Have you no reserve, no sense of decency? How can you let yourself be seen like that by all the countryside? Look at your hair, right down your back, dust all over your clothes, oil on your hands and that besotted expression on your face! You make me sick. How any man can want to marry you looking like that is beyond me.'

Harriet surveyed herself with some dismay in the hall mirror, holding back the coats that nearly covered it the better to see herself. She sighed, for her appearance was really most disreputable, but with the wisdom of fresh experience replied mildly, 'You know, if someone's in love with you it doesn't seem to matter what you look like. They love you just the same. I don't think they see.'

'The Pope' snorted. 'I can tell you this, then,' she snapped indignantly. 'If you get married thinking that it doesn't matter looking like a slut, you'll discover that it does when it's too late.'

'I just couldn't help it today,' explained Harriet with complete calm. 'It was all so . . . unexpected. I got dirty trying to do my bicycle and if I'd known he was coming I would not have let him see me. But I just couldn't help it,' she repeated. 'You can't always look your best.'

'The Pope' said no more; she was annoyed because Harriet was no longer frightened of her. She seemed to have gone beyond the range of her authority. Rage at her as she might, the effect was negligible. With a shrug of her thin shoulders she accepted the inevitable. 'Oh well,' she thought, 'that's one of them nearly off my hands, anyway!'

CHAPTER EIGHT

While she despaired of Charlotte and Daisy, Katharine felt that in Susan lay her hope of moulding a character who would be a glory to God and a credit to herself. So upon Susan she lavished many prayers, much discipline, advice and reproof, and an affection so well-concealed that Susan herself was unaware of it.

She was determined to bring home to Susan the fact that she was no longer the indulged and petted darling of a capricious old man, but the least important member of a large family. At last her efforts seemed to be bearing fruit. Susan was more obedient and submissive, less subject to violent fits of temper and much less noisy than she used to be.

Nanny was still at Fellowescourt, but on sufferance. Katharine had allowed her to stay on, unpaid, on the condition that she ceased to incite Susan to rebellion.

'Oh yes!' Katharine had insisted sharply as Nanny's old head shook disingenuously in denial of this charge. 'I know how you used to try to put her against me when the master was alive. D'you give me your word there'll be no more of that, Nanny?'

'I do, Miss,' Nanny had mouthed toothlessly, defeated by the insecurity of her position. She had come to know on which side her bread was buttered.

Katharine and Olivia were teaching Susan between them; Katharine taught her reading, writing, scripture and the Arts, with a smattering of English history; Olivia tried to teach her how to do sums and English grammar. Now, within a few days of her eighth birthday, Susan could very nearly read, and was able to recite the dates of the kings of England, a number of hymns, psalms and passages of the Old Testament, most of them about sin, and draw a book lying on the table with some regard to perspective. In her copybooks, pothooks and moral sentences were reproduced in triplicate beneath the original examples. In fact, so good had been her progress that Katharine decided to give her a Bible of her very own for her birthday.

The year was 1914, and the month August. Susan was tall for her age, rather angular, with a pointed pale face, fine mouse-gold hair and large grey eyes that regarded the world with candid solemnity and some uncertainty.

Harriet had arranged her wedding for the 6th, Susan's birthday. Susan and Olivia were to be her bridesmaids, and Miss Flynn had altered an old frock of Charlotte's to fit Susan; new dresses were out of the question, Katharine had said, and she was a very lucky little girl to be a bridesmaid and have such a pretty frock to wear. Susan, looking at the floor, had agreed.

Now there was a great scare that war might break out before the wedding could take place. Captain Willoughby was on the Reserve of Officers and ready, with loyalty so ardent that Harriet was piqued to find herself taking second place, to go to the ends of the earth in the service of King and Country. It was no wonder that poor Harriet was in a frenzy lest she be cheated of her husband, perhaps even of her wedding, by an accident of malignant fate.

To pay for the wedding, Katharine had sold some pieces of jewellery that her mother had left her and which she never wore. With the proceeds of the transaction, which had been conducted by Mr Blair for her, she had been able to instal Miss Flynn for a week with the makings of a modest trousseau, invite the immediate relatives and close friends of both parties, and arrange for their refreshment with moderation proper to their reduced circumstances. Now that she was in command, it was characteristic of her that she told her sisters nothing of the ways and means she had used to find the money; it never entered her head to do so, even when Charlotte and Daisy protested that if she could afford such outlay now she could easily have let them go to Dublin in the spring.

Katharine had been gratified to discover that Captain Willoughby's relations were quite as distinguished as her own. His mother was Lady Willoughby, widow of the General Sir Hercules Willoughby whose direction of the campaign to stamp out insurrection in one of the African colonies had aroused such public admiration. The list of guests to be invited that she sent Katharine contained many impressive names. Nevertheless, it annoyed Katharine to think that she would have a vet for a brother-in-law.

The news of the outbreak of war did not reach Fellowescourt until the eve of the wedding. It was received quite cheerfully by everybody but Harriet, who imagined that her Eustace would be killed by the first shot. The general opinion was that the Kaiser was about to be taught a most salutary lesson and that the war could not possibly last longer than six months. Old soldiers rummaged for their uniforms and prepared for mobilisation. There was an air of gallant expectancy, splendid preparation and certain glory.

Harriet quite lost heart that night; she wept in Olivia's bedroom, refusing consolation. She would find Eustace snatched from her on her wedding day, she would be left waiting at the church, or she would be a widow as soon as she was a wife, and how could she endure to live alone in Brandon Cottage for the rest of her days, tormented by loneliness and misery?

Olivia found it difficult to be encouraging. The future was so obscure.

'You could have Susan to stay, if you're alone, or one of us,' she suggested. 'Or perhaps there'll be jobs for women to do in the war—you never know.'

'But I don't know how to do anything,' objected Harriet. Olivia could only agree. None of them knew how to do anything.

'You could come back here to live while Eustace is away,' said Olivia. Harriet showed some spirit for the first time.

'What!' she exclaimed, 'and put up with "the Pope"? Not me, I've had enough of that. Of course,' she admitted, 'she's really been awfully nice about everything, but still. . .'

'Perhaps you'll have a baby,' suggested Olivia comfortingly. That, she knew, would be consolation for Harriet, utter and complete.

'Oh,' sighed Harriet dreamily, 'wouldn't that be lovely!'

Comforted by this thought, she allowed Olivia to put her to bed.

'Don't tell "the Pope"!' were her last words, uttered with imploring urgency and repeated until Olivia swore that she would not.

Susan woke very early the next morning, tremendously excited. She could not stay in bed; the fact that day had dawned meant that every minute spent in bed was wasted. Nanny was still asleep, so Susan slipped past her to the open window.

There was great mystery in the garden. The grass was plushy with dew, pale and silvered, alluring as untrodden sand. A thrush, brilliantly spotted, its outline blurred by immaturity, pulled resolutely at a worm until, its elasticity exhausted, it was drawn from the earth to be swallowed greedily. Blue shadows lay mistily under the trees, impenetrable and secret. Flowers, refreshed by the cool night, glowed with the brilliance of pebbles seen through water. Susan felt the dewy chill of summer morning and sniffed the evanescent scents of the first hours of day. It was irresistible. She brought her head back into the room, dressed quickly and ran downstairs without making a sound.

With the aid of a chair she was able to loosen the bolts of the conservatory door; outside, she darted about, making tracks on the virgin surface of the grass, smelling the chilled, freshened flowers, and looking back at the closed smugness of the sleeping house. Her shoes dripped with water and she bent to scoop up the dew into her hand and fling it away into the air. She began to pick some flowers for

I larrlet as a surprise; a child's mixed bunch, sweet-peas and dandelions, a dahlia and a full-blown rose, daisies and feathery grasses, all the stalks too short.

But then she saw the mountain, with the sidelong gleams of the sunrise throwing a golden light on the velvety slopes. The heather glowed crimson-purple under the crossways beam, illumined with quicksilver flashes and softened with the bloom of the dew and the moss. Little green patches where the grass was boggy, and sundew and bog-cotton flourished, shone out smooth and lustrous. She watched it briefly, enchanted, then ran to the end of the garden, climbed the low wall beneath the row of Scotch firs, and ran towards the mountain.

Once over the wall, she felt that she was beyond recall from the house, that she had entered a forbidden paradise where no one could reach her.

Colour was pouring into the day now; blue in the sky, streaks of mist in opalescent bands encircling the higher parts of the mountain, saffron lichen glowing on the granite boulders, and flecks of quartz glittering like little mirrors. There was a magical quality in the light, glistening and sparkling on the bloom of the morning.

Susan pushed her way through the high bracken that covered the foot of the little valley, ducking under the umbrella-like foliage and emerging on to a rushy piece of ground where brambles thrust over the rocks, and stunted ash-trees grew at random.

It was going to be a perfect day. On the ash-bark the flies sunned themselves exuberantly, shining blue-black and green, and dashing off noisily to whirl an exultant circuit before settling again and shaking their wings in the sun in constant enjoyment. Spiders' webs were dew-encrusted on the brambles, the leaves of which were turning crimson and gold as the fruit was taking colour.

Susan went on, climbing further afield. She came to a mass of rose-pink honeysuckle strewn over a pile of boulders, in full flower.

'Oh!' she cried, marvelling. She laid down the wilting bunch that she had picked for Harriet and began to gather the elegant, tenuous clusters with their crimson stems, breathing in the smell of them as she picked. When her hands were full she went on until she reached a shoulder of the hill, and branched off through the heather to surmount it. She could hear running water and wanted to find the stream.

She saw it as soon as she was over the hump, a silver thread of a mountain torrent gushing and shooting down the mountainside, spraying the ferns on the banks and making a little mist of its own where there was a sheer fall of a few feet. It was deep-set and its peaty water foamed and roared as it rushed the barriers of granite boulders in its path.

There was a gravelly verge at one spot, a little backwater where the stream was forced aside by an enormous flat-topped rock and seemed to ease itself back round its base, lapping the little stones amongst the gravel, flecked with foam. The water was golden at the edge, over the sand; beyond the great rock it was dark as molasses.

Susan was drawn to this rock as by a magnet; it was of granite, most beautifully pitted and marked. She reached its flat top by a bound from a lesser rock, spread-eagled herself on its surface and, edging up to the part that overhung the fast water, lay gazing into the torrent.

The ceaseless discipline of the water-pattern fascinated her. A tiny whirlpool, a jet of water, a boiling deeper patch of treacly surface were endlessly renewed and continued, the insubordinate licked into the shape designed for it in nature. She watched and watched, throwing in honeysuckle leaves to be swept along, becalmed, floated off and brought up against a barrier in the end.

She was perfectly happy. She lay face downwards, her legs kicking lazily in relaxed pleasure, arms under her chin, her body warming in the sun as she listened to the repetitive chain of sound and watched the changeless pattern of motion.

A flash of metallic blue caught her eye and looking up she saw dragon-flies darting about like rockets, whizzing through the air in straight, undeviating flight. They landed with such impact that they were like little clockwork flying machines shuddering with the shock of collision and winding up again to start on a new journey. Their radiance was astonishing.

Susan rolled over and looked into the blue of the sky and the now resplendent sun, one eye shut and the other the merest slit, but the piercing brilliance stabbed at her and she turned back until she was looking into the calm, silver-floored water on the shore side of her rock. The sun drove deep into the water, making it glow golden, barred with beams of light and sparkling wherever the surface was broken. Nothing was still: the water lapped in continuous disturbance, perpetual motion of small degree, the sunlight flashed and winked on the ripples and the ferns dipped their leaves eternally in the shadowed water, agitated in a regular, ceaseless rhythm.

Susan had not a thought in her mind. She felt a delight in the beauty that surrounded her so intense that it filtered through the porous surface of consciousness into the fabric of her being, leaving there a reflection of itself that could be lit up and reproduced on demand. Intuitively, she knew that what she was taking into herself could not be taken away by anyone.

Suddenly, she felt hungry. She began to wonder if they would have missed her at the house. She had no notion of the time. Hurriedly picking up her flowers, she bounded to the ground and set off towards Fellowescourt.

Climbing over the wall into the garden, she dodged behind the bushes until she could appear near the house, looking as if she had never been out of the garden. But she happened to reach the conservatory at the same moment as Katharine, who had come to fill a can of water for the flowers in the drawing-room. It was actually only breakfast time and if she had been more fortunate no one but Nanny need ever have known of her expedition.

She started so guiltily that Katharine was instantly suspicious. But as it was Susan's birthday, Katharine decided to show clemency.

'Happy birthday, Susan,' she said, holding out her hands. 'Come and give me a kiss.'

Susan approached and held out her cheek. 'Thank you, Aunt Katharine,' she said.

'Why, how untidy you are! And your feet are soaked! And how did your legs get torn like that? They're all bleeding, child.'

Susan's heart was thumping and she felt cold. She held out the honeysuckle, now beginning to droop.

'I went to get these for Aunt Harriet.'

'But where did you find them.'

'Oh, they grow all over some rocks on the way up the mountain.'

'On the way up the mountain?' echoes Katharine incredulously. 'Then you've been there before?'

'No, Aunt Katharine.'

'Then,' said Katharine in a voice of triumph, 'you couldn't know the honeysuckle was there, could you?'

'No.' Tears swelled under Susan's eyelids, distorting her vision, threatening to fall and shame her. It was the old, wretched, miserable story. She had been found out. She was a liar and she would go to Hell. She tried to think why she had felt the need to lie and could not find sufficient reason. She could not account for it at all. It had never been necessary. She must be at that stage in the destruction of the soul of which Aunt Katharine had so often warned her, the stage when a person is so dead to the truth that the corrupted mind cannot distinguish between truth and lies.

'The Pope' dealt with her sorrowfully, the fact that it was Susan's birthday increasing the burden of her grief. Susan knew how God hated lies, didn't she? Then how could she go on telling lies? In very truth, Susan did not know.

'I was going to give you a Bible for your birthday,' said Katharine, regretfully shaking her head, 'but you are not fit to have it. You will have to wait for it until you have shown that you want to be good, that you can say no to the Devil . . . And I had thought that you were so much better,' she added with infinite reproach.

In a frenzy of remorse Susan begged to be forgiven. 'I'll never tell a lie again. Aunt Katharine,' she almost screamed. 'I promise I won't, ever.' She meant every word of it. She was horrified at herself; if she started so badly on her birthday, was not the whole year doomed?

Nanny came shuffling along the passage, half-demented with worry, searching for Susan in every room. But when she saw Katharine talking to her she slipped away to the nursery, shaking her head and muttering about the queer notions some women had of persecuting innocent little children.

While 'the Pope' considered her offence and its proper punishment, Susan stood meekly before her, hands behind her back, eyes downcast and brimming with tears. So often had this kind of scene been repeated that she could only think of herself as something so vile that not even God would think her worth saving. Nobody else in the world was quite so awful as she, because she had the inestimable advantage of having been instructed about right and wrong, yet still continued to do and want nothing that was right. And so often things that seemed quite harmless to her were later demonstrated by 'the Pope' to be of surpassing wickedness.

How often had Aunt Katharine cautioned her: 'You know how God hates lies?' She knew. She also knew how God hated greediness, vanity, laziness, disobedience in children and the challenging of grown-up authority. Particularly did God hate people to do anything pleasant on Sundays. God liked to see people rejoicing in pious literature and charitable works, like making hideous crochet shawls in dark grey hairy wool for poor Mrs Sheehy. And if you were the child of God you loved, you really enjoyed, singing hymns round the piano on Sunday evenings after Evensong, when you had spent the morning at Matins and half the afternoon learning the Catechism and repeating it until you were word-perfect. God expected his children to listen to Mr

Weldon's sermons, which lasted for three quarters of an hour, without peeping through the carved holes in the pew-front at the woodlice perambulating on the black and red tiled floor, or playing trains with the hymn-books, or looking round to see who was in church. And it grieved him if your attention wandered during the Litany.

Susan knew, therefore, beyond all doubt, that she was no child of God. She practised all the vices which He abhorred and none of the virtues which came naturally to the good, unless it was with loathing, impatience and resentment and under duress from 'the Pope'.

'Susan,' enquired Katharine sorrowfully, exercising great forbearance, 'why did you tell me a lie? Look at me.'

Susan raised her head but could see nothing for the blur of tears. She experienced the same heart-pounding, paralysing fear that had possessed her before. She wanted to protest, to say anything that would excuse her, to avoid trouble at all costs and escape from the all-knowing eye of 'the Pope'. But she had only just sworn to Katharine that she would never tell another lie. She held back the excuses and for a moment perceived the truth: that it was fear of 'the Pope' and weariness of her censure that drove her to prevaricate. Had there been any fragment of her moral fibre of which Katharine could say a kind or hopeful word, she might have been able to bear it, but Katharine always made her feel that she was bad all through, a hopeless case. So escape, not truth, had always been her incentive.

She gulped, seeking courage to say what was in her heart.

'I think I was afraid,' she said in a small voice.

'Afraid?' queried Katharine incredulously. 'Afraid of what? You know that you have nothing to fear so long as you tell the truth. I have always told you that, Susan. That cannot be the reason.'

If Aunt Katharine would not believe the truth, what use was it to go on? It did not seem to matter what you said, nothing was any good. Susan could only stand unhappily and wait for what Aunt Katharine should choose to say.

Katharine, on the other hand, was feeling her first qualms about her dealings with Susan. Like many forceful people she was quite unaware of her own formidableness. It was perfect nonsense for Susan to say that she was frightened. What had she, Katharine, ever done to frighten her? Nothing, nothing at all, except . . . except to expect the worst of her and to pounce on her wrong-doings with severity.

She was a little flushed as she said coldly, 'You were afraid . . . of what?'

'Of your being cross and going on and on.' Susan was petrified by this terrible admission. She dared not imagine its effect. She held her breath, awaiting sentence.

Katharine's face was red. 'Cross? I don't get cross, Susan. I do get very grieved, sometimes, but that is not the same thing. And what do I go on and on about, as you call it?'

'God,' said Susan, as though she never wanted to hear the name again.

Katharine's whole face and neck flared up with a blush of absolute horror. Never, in all her life, had she been so deeply shocked.

'Go up to the nursery!' she thundered, driving Susan to the door. 'I don't want you near me, blasphemous little thing! Don't let me see you again until you're truly sorry. Go on, go!' She gave her a push.

Susan bolted up the back stairs and flung herself hysterically at Nanny.

'She says I'm . . . she won't believe me when I tell the truth . . . she says I'm not to come down until I'm sorry, I won't ever be sorry . . . she won't ever let me down . . . I shan't be able to be a bridesmaid. . .'

Nanny was sitting at the window in her low chair. She pulled Susan towards her.

'There now, lovey,' she murmured again and again. 'Don't you mind that ould "Pope". Sure, she's got vinegar where she ought to have blood, that one. Sure, she'd ate her young, so she would, if she had any!'

'She says I'm no good and God hates everything I do. And she won't believe the truth. I've never seen her so angry. I'm so tired of her talking to me about God, and she says I'm blasphemous. What's that?'

'Blasphemous, was it? Begob, that's a new one!' Nanny began to laugh, throwing back her head and cackling until the tears ran down her face. 'Oh dear!' she cried, unable to say more, 'oh dear, dear, dear!' When she had laughed her fill, she gave a quick suspicious glance at the closed door. 'Look now, lovey,' she said, crossing the room to shut the door tightly, 'just you listen to Nanny for a moment. That ould "Pope" has got sin on the brain. She's not right in the head about it. When she goes on at you the way she does, just you say to yourself—to keep your spirits up, like, "she doesn't know all about God". Precious little she knows about God, if you ask me! If ye believed all she told ye you'd think that God had no mercy at all, so ye would, nor love. Now it seems to me that there's no two people sees God in quite the same way, and maybe there's a little bit o' truth in each one's way of seein' Him, but none of us sees the whole o' Him, d'ye see? So ye'll find yer own way o' seein' Him as ye get older, an' don't be mindin' her at all. She's got a mind to make ye the same as herself, but ye mustn't let her. D'ye hear me, ye're not to let her!'

Such heresy made Susan's skin tingle with apprehension, but it reassured her as nothing else had done before. She felt the wisdom in Nanny's sentiment, and the warmth of her voice drove away all the terrors of hell. She felt like a child again, instead of a monster. She smiled up at the wrinkled old face that was watching hers.

'Oh, Nanny, I'm so hungry,' she said.

'There, there my lamb!' beamed Nanny, 'wait now till I . . .' She sped downstairs to fetch Susan's breakfast on a tray from the kitchen. When she returned, she made the child tell her the whole story of the expedition to the mountain and of how she had been met by Katharine on her way into the house. She shook her head when she thought of Susan's punishment.

'That's no way to be spendin' yer birthday,' she exclaimed contemptuously, 'broodin' over yer sins in the nursery! And yer auntie's weddin' day, too! Tch tch tch!'

Susan's heart failed her as she remembered her dilemma: if she did not tell Katharine she was sorry, the alternative was perpetual punishment in the nursery. Her birthday would be over, and the wedding, and she would be condemned to spend all the rest of time here in this room . . .

'She won't let me out for the wedding,' she said wistfully.

'She might an' she mightn't,' was all that Nanny would say.

She felt suddenly tired. She stood at the window for a little, watching the play of light on the mountain, and when Nanny left the room to do her odd jobs round the house, she settled into her low chair and went fast asleep. She must have slept for a couple of hours, because the morning was well advanced when the door burst open and the room was filled with her chattering, gesticulating aunts. They were all there, with the exception of Katharine, and they rushed up to her, kissed her, wished her a happy birthday and told her to come downstairs with them. They pressed parcels into her hands and told her to wake up or she would miss all the excitement. Even Charlotte and Daisy were quite animated and, spurred on by the desire to be quits with 'the Pope' at last, very nearly showed some affection to their niece.

Olivia took hold of her hands to pull her up, saying, 'Come on, we want you to help us get Aunt Harriet ready, and you are to help me with her bouquet.'

Susan gave them all a scared look. 'I'm not allowed to leave the room, Aunt Katharine said.' She was nearly in tears. She longed so much to go with them and to be in all the excitement.

'She knows we're here,' explained Charlotte. 'We told her we were going to get you.'

'Didn't she mind?' asked Susan, wide-eyed.

'Yes, very much,' said Daisy with some relish, 'but your Aunt Harriet said she wasn't going to be married without you, and we all said we weren't going to have you punished on your birthday, not when it's her wedding day as well.'

'But she'll be so angry with me if I . . .'

'No, she won't,' promised Olivia.

'We just told her we weren't going to have it,' stated Daisy.

'And in the end she gave in,' added Charlotte.

'She did? Really and truly?' Hope and incredulity alternated in Susan's expression.

'Yes,' Olivia assured her solemnly, 'she did.'

Like a flower opening to the sunlight, Susan responded with happiness to their affection. 'Oh!' she cried, holding the toe of one shoe and dancing round on the other. 'Oh, how lovely! Aunt Harriet, look what I've got for your bouquet.'

From the bedroom jug, where it had been stuffed by Nanny, she pulled out the honeysuckle. Harriet nearly wept, so touched was she, but Olivia swept them all from the room, declaring that if they wasted another second they would be late at the church.

Watching Lawrence Weldon as he performed the marriage ceremony, Katharine wondered if he felt the same bitterness and despair as she did. Who could blame him if a little human envy stole into his heart? She saw only him, as she stood there, thinking how she loved every inch of him, from the high forehead with the dark hair that grew so thickly above it with irrepressible vitality, to the long, rather bony hands that were so quick in movement and so capable in action. She loved him so much that she felt actual pain in the certainty that he was thinking, not of himself and her, but of Harriet and Eustace, with such affection and pleasure in their happiness that it showed in his face. And what had Harriet done to deserve her good fortune? Nothing at all, she told herself; she simply had not earned it.

Harriet's happiness became her. Katharine looked away quickly to Olivia and Susan. The child's frock was too short, but Miss Flynn had insisted that she was only a child and should look like one instead of like an old woman. Katharine did not want to think about Susan either. The child was an enigma. Behind all the bravado, she knew that Susan was afraid of her; but the only reason for fear could be that the child had a guilty conscience. Otherwise, she could have no cause for fear, surrounded by love as she was, in a happy home. Of course, she told herself, it had been necessary to teach Susan a sharp lesson; Papa had spoilt her so, making so much more of her than he had ever done of his own daughters, that correction had inevitably been painful. It did not enter her head that the correction might have been less severe had jealousy not caused her to resent Papa's preferential treatment of Susan, any more than it occurred to her that she was herself inherently alarming. Certainly, she thought grimly, Susan was a bitter disappointment.

Self-pity and envy devoured her, souring all the good will that she would have liked to feel. Why must she watch Harriet, stupid, kind, timid, hopeless Harriet being married to the man she loved when she herself could not marry because she was capable and responsible and saddled with the burdens of all the family? And why should everyone be against her?

Searching the faces round her in the hope of finding one that might perceive the extent of her suffering, she was repelled by their blankness. Neither from her sisters nor from the Willoughby relations could she glean a grain of warmth. Their faces were all unseeing: they were looking inwards at themselves. They were no more able to discern her troubles than to cure them.

She felt humiliated by the morning's defeat: she ought not to have given in; Susan should have had her full punishment. But things had been taken out of her hands and, through weariness she had capitulated. She had been taken by surprise. And, in the end, she had sheltered her surrender behind ill-humour.

'Susan may come down, since you are all so set upon it,' she had snapped, 'but don't bring her near me, I'm too busy.'

Eustace was slipping the ring on to Harriet's finger. A glimmer of hope lightened Katharine's heart. Perhaps, she thought, Lawrence and I will be the next! With all the strength of her will she projected her love and resolve towards him, so that she might compel him to share them.

This permission to hope which she had granted herself dispelled her bitterness. As the service drew to a close, she was able to wish from her heart all that was good to Harriet and Eustace. In penitence for her evil thoughts she abased herself. And one of the first war weddings was over.

Afterwards, at Fellowescourt, the festivity was a little forced. Laughter was louder than it need have been, congratulations more hasty, conversation unnaturally cheerful. The recent discovery by Olivia of three cases of champagne in the cellar gave the party its only authentic sparkle; even so, Katharine kept a sharp look-out in case any of the guests should become unduly merry. Drunkenness she would not tolerate. She fixed old Admiral Moloney, father of the Loftus Moloney whose wooing had been so repugnant to Olivia, with an icy stare, convinced that he was tipsy. He was swaying gently, glass in hand, as he told a doubtful anecdote to the puzzled Harriet. But Olivia assured her that he always stood and talked like that, owing to his need to stand up to rough weather at sea and his delight in making young ladies blush.

Eustace took her aside. 'We shall have ten days honeymoon, Katharine, only ten days. Harriet does not know it, but after that I go to my regiment. I thought it too unkind to say anything to her today.'

'Ten days?' she repeated blankly. 'What will Harriet do?' For the first time the war became real to her.

'I don't know. We must think of something: it will be harder for her than for me. I know you'll be good to her. Forgive me.' He slipped away before Harriet could notice that he had consulted Katharine.

Lady Willoughby came up to discuss Harriet. She was an ample woman with a full, warm voice and a Roman nose. It was clear from her manner that she was used to having her wishes treated as commands.

'I see that Eustace has told you,' she said in a contralto whisper. 'May I call you Katharine,' she added, 'since we are to be connected? Ah, I knew you would not mind. Now Harriet, dear girl that she is, must come and pay me a long visit when Eustace has to . . . go: you know what I mean. I will not take no for an answer—she must come! I feel they have so much in common. I never thought Eustace would marry, myself; he was such an odd boy! Of course he has made a queer choice of a profession, but he is none the worse for that.'

'Harriet will be delighted to go to you, I'm sure. She will feel the separation dreadfully; it is very hard for her.' All this, Katharine uttered while thinking to herself: she is ashamed to think that her son is a vet. It saddened her to think that his mother should despise his profession and have to make excuses for him. From that moment she ceased to look down upon him for being a vet, feeling an almost protective anger against Lady Willoughby.

'She is a good girl, I can see that,' said Lady Willoughby, throwing the words away as if this was hardly a compliment. 'She will not make a fuss, I can see that. She is not that sort . . . Like Eustace. He never showed his feelings, even as a child.' She looked narrowly at Katharine. 'As a matter of fact,' she said confidentially, 'he and his father could never agree. My dear husband was perhaps a little *difficile,* but Eustace and he . . .' She shook her head as if the memories were too painful to discuss. 'I hope his marriage will make up for much that was distressing in his childhood.'

Katharine longed to be rid of her. She was aware of Lawrence, waiting for a chance to speak to her. But Lady Willoughby drew out her lorgnette and scanned the company.

'Your sisters?' she said. 'I cannot see them. There is a pretty one, I understand. It is odd that Harriet should be the first to marry. And who is that little girl?'

'My niece, Susan,' said Katharine. 'Her parents are dead and she lives with us.'

'Hmph. She is like you, though she has the look of an orphan.' After examination of Susan through her glasses, she announced, 'She will never be a beauty, I'm afraid. But she will improve, I've no doubt.'

Katharine was nonplussed by these remarks. With a growing feeling that Lady Willoughby was not impressed by the family into which her son had married, she offered to present some of the Cork Fellowes to her. One glance through the lorgnette sufficed.

'Katharine, dear girl, I know you will understand, but I do not feel up to it. I know we should not have a word to say to one another; they are so woefully provincial. And the son has drunk too much champagne. Take me to see the wedding presents.'

There was nothing for it but to obey. Lawrence pursued them at a distance. Lady Willoughby made many comments, few of them complimentary, but her tone was never disparaging and mitigated their acidity. Olivia and Susan appeared in the doorway and Katharine presented them but they were dismissed in a moment.

'A pretty face,' commented Lady Willoughby of Olivia, 'such a pretty face!' She sighed. 'Of course it must be difficult to dress well, buried in the country as you are. And that reminds me, my dear; Harriet is a naughty girl to fix her wedding for Horse Show week. It was too thoughtless of her. I nearly did not come! No wonder so few of our friends are here. They are all in Dublin, at the Horse Show.' She smiled and patted Katharine's hand. 'But since it is war time I will not say a word.' She raised the lorgnette again, seeking a way of escape. 'Ah!' she cried suddenly, 'there is dear Lady Mountowan—I did not think I should find her here.' She was gone.

Lawrence came up and held Katharine's hand so tightly that it hurt.

'Lawrence, let go! Everyone will see.' She was embarrassed and delighted.

'I do not care who sees. I want them all to know how much I love you. Katharine, were you thinking how it might have been us?'

'I had to drive the thought from me: it was more than I could bear.'

'I had to do violence to my thoughts of you: I could not do my duty properly for thinking of you.'

Katharine's heart melted with love for him at this admission.

'Ah, and I watched you, thinking how far from me you were,' she said regretfully. 'Lawrence,' she continued, her voice vibrant with excitement, 'ours must be the next wedding in your church. We must not let it get put off and off. Promise me we shall find a way to make it possible!' She looked so intently into his face, with eyes so full of confidence in his power and a smile so tremulous with disappointment and longing, that he felt he could refuse her nothing. He shook his head and smiled at her.

'You know I want it as much as you do.' he said. 'We must not let circumstances defeat us, you are quite right. But until the time comes, we must not lose heart. That is the great thing, not to despair.' He had been going to say more, but Charlotte was beckoning them from the doorway.

'They are drinking Harriet's health,' she called. 'Come quick, or you will be too late.' She herself was gone at once.

'We must go,' said Katharine, still smiling up at him.

'We must.' He smiled down at her.

They held the moment, imprisoning it, refusing it escape. They stretched it to its ultimate limit, then simultaneously released it. Together they went to stand at the doorway of the crowded dining-room where speeches were being made and healths being drunk.

'Harriet has only ten days with him before he is called up,' she whispered, 'but you must not say anything; she does not know it yet.'

He looked grimly across at Harriet, her soft brown eyes lit up with happiness.

'It is like the guillotine,' he said. 'But she is happy now, poor child. She will always have today.'

'The war may soon be over,' said Katharine hopefully.

'Do not imagine that the war will be over until the nations are bled white,' said Lawrence. 'It will go on for years. Susan may well be in her teens before it ends. It will go on until one side has no more blood to spill.' He looked suddenly angry. 'The boasting and bravado sicken me. I can only wonder how many of these men who are so ready to go, so cock-a-hoop about the glory of war, will ever come home.'

He pushed his way through the press of people to take two glasses from Lizzie, who was taking round a tray.

'Here,' he said shortly, 'they need all the luck we can wish them.'

Katharine looked at him in near-terror. 'Can it be possible?' she thought. 'Surely he cannot be right!' She raised her glass to Harriet and Eustace, gulped a mouthful of champagne as if it were medicine, and felt her heart grow cold with fear.

CHAPTER NINE

People talked war, lived war, dreamt war, but on the whole it did not press very closely upon Susan; she had no father to fear for in France, no brother to pretend that he was of an age to join up. But there were certain aspects of it that she would remember for ever.

There was Olivia's departure to work for the Voluntary Aid Detachment in France; this happened very soon after Harriet's wedding. Susan felt that with her had gone her last defence against 'the Pope'. When she had gone there was no life in the house. Susan mourned her as if she were dead, missing her gaiety and affection. When she came home on leave it was to say that she was engaged to be married to a Major Frank Heathcote, whom she had nursed, and that, when the war ended, her home would be in Dorset. Susan found her tired, preoccupied and tense, absent in mind and old in heart compared to the Olivia who had danced her round the house in a polka.

'Will you bring Uncle Frank here?' begged Susan. 'Will you bring him to Fellowescourt to see us all?'

'Of course I will,' Olivia assured her.

'You're quite sure? You promise you will? You won't let anything stop you, anything at all?'

Olivia hesitated, suddenly afraid, then laughed quickly.

'Just let anything try to stop me,' she said, trying to hide her alarm from Susan. But even Olivia who was so brave and clever and gay could not stop the shell that fell into Frank Heathcote's trench and killed him with fifteen of his men a month after his marriage. Olivia went on with her nursing, but she came less and less to Fellowescourt and when she did only a part of her was there.

Susan kept to herself the guilty thought that her insistence had forced from Olivia the defiant cry that had been only tempting Providence. For many nights she cried herself to sleep, tortured by remorse. It was not until she heard a chance remark of Lawrence Weldon's, blaming people whose faith fell back with the advance of superstition, that she ceased to believe that she might have brought the tragedy upon Olivia.

There were 'the Pope's' chickens. The lawn was covered with them, the house smelt of incubators, the eggs piled up in the storeroom, awaiting despatch. Harriet was amazed at her success. 'How did you learn about chickens?' she asked naively, and Katharine looked at her down her nose and said grandly, 'I was born knowing about chickens.'

There was poor Harriet's anxiety during the evacuation of Gallipoli. Eustace was there and she had had no word from him for weeks. How could she know if he were dead or alive? She left Brandon Cottage for Fellowescourt until she should have news. She was expecting a baby and for the sake of the child tried to suppress her fears, but only drove them inwards to devour her in secret. By the time she heard that Eustace was safe, she had lost the baby and nearly lost her own life into the bargain. Susan would always remember her despairing cry, not meant for her to hear, 'Oh, if only I had not worried so! I think worry destroys everything it touches. I wonder how many women have died of it since the war began.'

Katharine was very gentle with Harriet and her patience was extraordinary. By the time Harriet was recovering from her grief and disappointment, nursed all the time by Katharine, Eustace was due home on leave and Harriet rushed over to London to spend it with him, which took her mind off the loss of the baby. She was really grateful to Katharine and kissed her with genuine affection when she left, trying to encourage her by saying, 'I do hope you can be married soon, Katharine. But even if you can't, you have Lawrence here and you do know that he is safe.'

'Safe indeed!' snorted Katharine. 'He's made up his mind to be a naval chaplain and the Bishop has released him from next month. Safe, indeed!'

Harriet was flustered as she always was when she had ruffled Katharine's temper.

'Oh dear,' she said again and again, 'oh dear! I wish I had said nothing. I had no idea of it.' But, knowing how irritable anxiety made her herself, she forgave Katharine for snapping at her.

There was the sinking of the *Lusitania* with the loss of 1300 lives, and the feeling that decency in war was a thing of the past.

There was the landing of Sir Roger Casement near Ardfert and the Easter Rebellion of 1916, with people in the village showing themselves to be rabid patriots although they had never before revealed their political bias. No one knew whom they could trust. Terrible stories of siege and bloodshed, murder and shootings filtered through from Dublin. People were thrown into a state of uncertainty and dismay by the sight of a strange face, by unusual activities or unfamiliar noises, afraid that the trouble was spreading throughout the country.

There was the aeroplane, the first that Susan had ever seen, which passed over the Glenmacool valley towards Cork. Everyone in the house, even Charlotte and Daisy, pressed round the open door to watch it, shading their eyes with their hands until it was out of sight.

'Oh God, Miss!' exclaimed Lizzie, ready to dart for cover at the first sign of danger. 'I hope it's not a Hun!'

It was not, of course, a Hun; but the party watching it from the Fellowescourt steps felt that war had reached even Glenmacool.

There were the expeditions to the mountain, not merely permitted but organised by Katharine, to gather sphagnum moss to be despatched to the Red Cross for dressings for the wounded. Sackloads of this left Fellowescourt, with parcels of socks and mufflers, bandages and dressings, all collected by 'the Pope' with press-gang ruthlessness from family and neighbours. She persuaded Daisy to start knitting a muffler. Daisy knitted four rows of it. Charlotte knitted one and Katharine completed it contemptuously.

Katharine would have liked to turn Fellowescourt into a convalescent home for the wounded, but the house was too remote, the plumbing too primitive, and Katharine withdrew her offer after taking offence at the tone of an official letter which pointed out these deficiencies. Charlotte and Daisy were bitterly disappointed; they had envisaged themselves coaxing wounded officers (always of course young, rich, handsome and unattached) back to health and receiving proposals of marriage from them. So when the idea fell through, they decided to try their luck elsewhere and wrote to ask Lady Willoughby if she could help them. It so happened that she had just converted her own spacious house on the outskirts of Dublin into the most modern convalescent home imaginable and was looking for nice girls of good family to assist her. She made it clear that the girls would not have to nurse any really unpleasant cases, such as those suffering from shell-shock or serious mutilation, since she had stipulated that she was not able to receive these into her home as the inconvenience and even the danger of having such people about would be too great.

Charlotte and Daisy could not start work quickly enough. It all sounded so agreeable, and they were even to be paid. So off they went to Dublin, where they were enslaved by a dragon of a Matron, made to work so hard that they became quite thin, and kept away from the more eligible patients by their superiors who considered that first pick was their own due. Lady Willoughby humiliated them by constant quips about their country ways, provincial accent and idle habits. Before the end of the week they had had enough. They wrote to Katharine, begging her to insist on their return, to come and rescue them, to tell Lady Willoughby that they were not strong enough for the work, anything, so long as they could come home. But she wrote firmly back to say that they must just stick it until the end of the war because she had promised their rooms to a family of Belgian refugees.

They fumed and stormed, sending letter after letter describing their miserable plight, but 'the Pope's' heart was as hard as iron. In the end, they settled down. Disciplined into routine, they learnt how to appear industrious without being so. They acquired a veneer of fastness by discreet swearing, powdering their faces and smoking cigarettes so that the less desirable patients came to regard them as 'good sorts' and to enjoy their company at races, dubious dance halls and raucous parties.

In the meanwhile the Belgian refugees, Professor and Madame Albert, Madame Albert *mère* and Jeanne, aged eight, arrived. Katharine had an ulterior motive in inviting them; Jeanne would teach Susan French and perhaps the good Professor would offer to instruct her in other subjects. Katharine was finding difficulty in keeping ahead of her lessons with Susan as she was forced to learn the matter for the next day's work every night, when she was already tired.

The Alberts were to be fed and lodged in return for the cost of their keep. The ladies were expert needlewomen and were to earn a modest income by dressmaking and embroidery. The Professor promised to help in the garden.

They were whirled from Inish station to Glenmacool by outside-car, a horse-drawn vehicle peculiar to Ireland with a terrifying tendency to pitch the passengers on to the road unless they could hold on with strength and skill. Old Madame Albert nearly died of the experience, and her daughter-in-law from watching her. They were only prevented from going straight back to Cork by the terror of the drive.

Katharine felt sorry for them, homeless in a strange land, almost destitute, and with their home in German hands. So she and Susan came out to greet them, ready with carefully rehearsed French phrases of welcome.

They were quite unheard, for the Albert family swamped them in a torrent of abuse about the vehicle, the driver, the wildness of the horse and the distance from the station. Old Madame Albert was slowly detached and lifted down by her son, then supported up the flagged path by both him and her daughter-in-law. Jeanne, stout and pasty with brown ringlets round her shoulders, followed wordlessly.

Before they had been in the house an hour, Katharine had apologised for the cold damp climate, the unhealthy air and rural situation of Fellowescourt, the curious hours of meals, and the neuralgia that had already attacked Madame Albert. How was it that they had been so deceived? No one had explained to them that they were to be entombed in the remotest regions of uncivilised Ireland; they had expected to be in a city where they could live a cultured university life as they had done in Liège.

Susan had never seen anything like this family in her life. Their language was utterly incomprehensible to her, yet they spoke with such fire that they could be partially understood. She led Jeanne to the nursery where Nanny, having discovered that the child spoke no English, announced querulously to Susan that she looked as if she were in need of a dose.

Their beds, how could they sleep in them? Their meals—uneatable! Naturally, they were not complaining of the food, only of its unfamiliarity. They had eaten some queer food since leaving Liège, but nothing like this: no beer with meals, no coffee at breakfast, no garlic, no flavour in anything—vegetables cooked in water and, moreover, served in it. *Tiens*! And, again and again, the moan about this sepulchre of a house in the wastes of the mountains. It might be on the moon! There were no concerts, no lectures, no theatre: it was oblivion!

The old lady sat all day by the fire, nursing her sorrows and shuddering at every sound made by the children. Her son and his wife, both of them martyred by neuralgia, wrote impassioned letters in French applying for situations with more cultured families and stipulating that they must be in a town. They earned nothing and paid nothing. They did nothing in either house or garden. Katharine began to wonder how she could induce another family to take them.

Her wish to get rid of them became a fixed purpose when, three days after their arrival, she happened to walk up the village street from the Post Office to Fellowescourt, and see emerging from the doorway of Peter Cavanagh's unsavoury premises, the Professor and his lady. Her embarrassment was equalled only by her consternation, for in Ireland the public house was merely a drinking shop and frequented by men only of the labouring and racing communities, never by the gentry. They greeted her without shame, complained of the lack of gaiety in the bar, and walked the few remaining steps with her. As soon as they entered the hall she sensed, nauseatingly and unmistakeably, the smell of beer. She tried to explain to them in French why they should not go to Cavanagh's Bar.

'Ees no good,' agreed the Professor amicably. 'You are right, ees too . . . *triste. Demain* we buy beer, drink eet *à la maison.*'

'No,' protested Katharine. '*Non!*'

'*Mais oui, mademoiselle!* Ees alright, you will see.' Before she could say another word they were halfway up the stairs.

Susan did learn phrases from Jeanne, who possessed a pack of cards. They used to spread the cards out on the nursery hearth-rug and play one game after another for hours on end. Jeanne always won.

The Albert family spent only one Sunday at Fellowescourt; the manner in which they spent it was the decisive factor in Katharine's determination to expel them.

They had to walk to Mass through inches of putty-coloured mud and this had distressed them greatly. When next seen, however, they had a holiday air about them. They were wearing their best clothes, talked without ceasing and were inclined to break into song. At lunch, the Professor, generously including his hostess and Susan, produced beer for all. Katharine, who refused it with determination, was too shocked even to protest when he poured some into Jeanne's glass. How terrible if Susan were to see the child drunk! She could envision no greater depravity than that of children drinking beer. The fact that

Jeanne showed no sign of intoxication made it worse; the child must be so used to alcohol that it no longer affected her!

When Monsieur Albert actually poured beer into Susan's glass, Katharine sprang up, seized the tumbler and flung the contents out of the window, without a word. She rinsed the glass with water and sent that flying after the beer. Then, with an admonitory glance at the Professor, she resumed her meal. The Alberts, unaware till now that they had done anything reprehensible, twittered apologies, but 'the Pope' remained in silence until the meal was over.

When Susan asked if she and Jeanne might get down, Katharine watched them go with relief.

'You have twenty minutes before your Catechism,' she warned Susan. 'I shall be in the study.'

'Yes, Aunt Katharine,' said Susan demurely.

Upstairs, Jeanne brought out her cards and they began to play on the rug as usual. Time passed and Susan forgot all about her aunt waiting for her in the study until the door opened and 'the Pope' stood looking at them.

'Susan!' she cried, with dreadful sternness. 'Cards on Sunday! What are you thinking of, child?'

'Is it wrong?' asked Susan in surprise. 'I didn't know.' She had never handled a pack of cards before Jeanne's arrival.

Katharine was infuriated by Susan's failure to know by instinct that it was wrong to play cards on Sunday. The child had no right feeling; she ought not to need telling about such things.

'You didn't know?' she said sharply. 'What was your conscience doing? Of course it's wrong to play cards on Sunday.'

'I can't see why,' murmured Susan, more to herself and Jeanne than to Katharine. But Katharine heard.

'It's made you forget your Catechism-time, for one thing,' she snapped, 'and it's . . . unseemly on a Sunday when your mind should be on better things. It's bad enough on a weekday, but on Sunday!' She was still irked that Susan could not see that it was wrong. 'How is it that you can't realise these things without being told?' she complained suddenly. 'That's the part that makes me sad.'

'We can feenish ze game?' asked Jeanne coaxingly.

'No!' roared 'the Pope', suddenly very angry. 'We'll have no continental Sundays at Fellowescourt. Put your cards away Jeanne, and go to your mother. Susan cannot play again today.'

'Please?' said Jeanne, her head a little on one side, meaning that she did not understand.

'No, I said!' repeated Katharine furiously, still more annoyed at having to explain while she was angry. 'You,' she pointed accusingly at Jeanne, 'have made Susan naughty. Susan may not', now she shook her head and pointed at the cards, 'play cards on *Sundays — le dimanche.*'

'*Suzanne est méchante?* It is I,' Jeanne dug two fingers into her chest, 'who . . . *vous dites que c'est ma faute, mademoiselle?*' Her expression was one of utter amazement. Katharine nodded emphatically.

'You say... no *cartes* today, Sunday? Why is zat, *mademoiselle?*'

'It is wrong. It is not good, Jeanne. God does not like it.'

'But on Monday, yes?'

'If you want to.'

Jeanne shrugged her shoulders and grimaced, turning out her hands in a gesture of hopeless incomprehension. She began to make comments to Susan in an undertone, so that Katharine would hear.

'Ees bad today, ees not bad *demain—ça c'est imbecile, voyons!*' With a pouting look at Katharine she picked up her cards, carried them to the window-seat and spread them out for a private game of her own, taking care to turn her back on the others and making a great show of counting aloud.

Katharine looked as if she might explode. With a kind of enraged snort she strode over to Jeanne, picked her up round the waist and hauled her to her grandmother's room. Jeanne was a lumpy child and the effort made Katharine breathless. Then she returned, picked up the cards and dropped them inside the door of the room where Jeanne was throwing a tantrum, shutting the door firmly on her yells.

'They must go,' she said to Susan, 'they must go. We can't keep them here.'

'Oh,' said Susan disappointed. It had been fun having another child to play with.

'Surely you can't like that little . . . pagan?' said Katharine in amazement and indignation.

'I do, rather,' admitted Susan, thereby putting herself in the wrong again.

That sealed the fate of the Alberts. Jeanne was a corrupting influence on Susan and go they must.

Go they did, five days later; this time in a trap, not an outside-car.

The only satisfaction and profit that Katharine could hope to glean from their stay was the allowance which she claimed from Peter Cavanagh for the empty beer bottles which the Alberts left all over their bedroom floor. Naturally she did not make the claim in person: she and Peter Cavanagh never communicated with one another except through an agent. She sent the garden boy. He brought back a bill for the beer.

The war dragged on and on. Katharine put aside the profit from her chickens into a little secret fund that was to provide for her trousseau and all the expenses of her wedding. She kept it in a locked drawer of her father's desk in the study, adding to it little by little and counting it over like an old miser, gloating over what it would achieve for her. With all her sisters gone, she no longer had Lizzie or a cook; one girl called Julia did all the work with Nanny. The garden boy came twice a week for a pittance. Olivia, always returned her allowance to Katharine, and sent her something out of her earnings besides. She said she had more money to live on than she could use. Harriet too was generous. Charlotte and Daisy sent only enough to cover their share of the rates, and that under protest.

By the beginning of 1918, Katharine felt that, in the matter of teaching Susan, she had reached the end of her tether. Susan was a clever child and read avidly, so she needed more advanced teaching. Katharine could not pretend to know the answers to her questions and Susan's mathematical knowledge far exceeded her own.

Harriet, now also nursing while Eustace was in France, came home to Fellowescourt on one of her short leaves, and Katharine discussed Susan's schooling with her.

'She ought to be at school, there's no doubt about it,' she said, 'but there's no money, I just can't manage it. I've sent for several prospectuses.' She handed these to Harriet.

After reading through them, Harriet was very quiet, thinking deeply. Suddenly she leant forward excitedly and put her hand on Katharine's arm.

'I think I could do it, Katharine. I'm sure I could. I've got a little money saved up, all my very own, not Eustace's. I'd love to do something for dear little Susan with it. And I could keep it up as long as I go on nursing.'

'It'll mean going on for at least five years,' said Katharine doubtfully. 'Of course it can't be an expensive school, but it must be somewhere where she'll be properly taught.'

'Perhaps she could get a bursary,' suggested Harriet doubtfully.

'We could try for one,' agreed Katharine.

They worked out, that even with Harriet's help, there would still be about fifty pounds a year to make up if they sent her to a school in Cork which they had in view. Katharine decided to write to the headmistress in the hope that special terms might be arranged.

The reply was not discouraging. A bursary could be available for a suitable applicant if the resources of her guardians were proved to be inadequate to meet the full charges. Would Miss Fellowes bring her niece to sit for a test paper at the school?

Katharine wrote to accept, and a date was arranged.

Susan had never left Glenmacool even for a day since she had been brought there to live with her aunts and her grandfather. The journey to

Cork, the interview with Miss Knox and the subsequent examination in an empty classroom, under the supervision of a junior mistress, all contributed to make the outing a major experience. When they reached Fellowescourt again, late in the afternoon, she was dazed with exhaustion but so stimulated by the variety of things she had observed that she could not sleep until the early hours of the morning.

While Susan was doing her examination, Miss Knox showed Katharine over the school. She was a pleasant-faced woman in her fifties, with straight brows and a straight nose, particularly candid brown eyes and a generous mouth; her grey hair, rapidly whitening, was combed back into a bun, but stray wisps wreathed about her ears with an agreeable freedom. In repose her face very nearly smiled. She wore a dark blue skirt with a striped blouse and a trim waist-belt which gave her a very neat appearance. Katharine was impressed by her; she thought her both kind and capable and she had an air of integrity that pleased 'the Pope' greatly. The girls rose and stood with such respectful politeness whenever Miss Knox and Katharine entered a classroom that she felt no doubts about the discipline.

Katharine asked many searching questions. How many times did the girls attend chapel on Sundays? Naturally they would attend morning and evening prayers daily. Were cards allowed? How did the girls occupy their spare time on Sundays and on holidays? Was French taught by a native of France? What school rules were there, and what punishments? And was it essential for a girl to bring every article prescribed on the clothes list?

Miss Knox was used to parents and had some experience of aunts, but it astonished her to find a Victorian so comparatively young yet so set in her period. She herself was a Victorian, probably a good twenty years older than Katharine, but she could see things with an awakening eye. Katharine's eyes, she felt, had closed with the old Queen's.

She answered each question fully. Katharine was dismayed to learn that, once the girls had writen a letter home, the rest of their Sunday free time was at their own disposal.

'You don't give them some useful handwork, making things for the poor, or for missions, or give them special Sunday reading, then?' she queried in alarm.

'No,' said Miss Knox firmly, with a glint of humour in the eye that glanced quickly at 'the Pope'. 'They can do either of those things if they wish, but we find that compulsion sickens them of good works for the rest of their lives. In fact, we find they do more voluntarily than if we made them work for good causes.'

'If you haven't tried both methods I don't know how you can tell,' said Katharine stuffily.

'Last year,' announced Miss Knox, 'the girls had a sale of their work and made seventeen pounds for the waifs and strays.'

Katharine thought of Charlotte and Daisy, wondering how much voluntary work Miss Knox would have got out of them.

'From my experience,' she said coolly, 'girls waste their time unless they are made to work.' She sighed and raised her shoulders in a little shrug. 'Perhaps you are more successful than I,' she suggested in a disbelieving tone, 'and I hope that if Susan comes here she will keep herself occupied.'

'We trust our girls,' said Miss Knox, 'in many ways, and we have never known them abuse our confidence. We make them responsible for their own behaviour, then when they leave school they are more ready to order their own lives. They become guardians of their own characters, which means in effect that they are in far better hands than if they were under the eye of a duenna; girls can always give a duenna the slip, Miss Fellowes.' Her candid eyes looked straight at Katharine with a hint of a smile. 'I assure you that it works,' she added.

'I believe in a rule of life myself,' flashed Katharine, 'laid upon them from infancy and rigorously enforced throughout childhood. Otherwise, there is no discipline, they do just what they like.'

'We find they like to do right, if they are trusted,' said Miss Knox quietly. 'It is compulsion that drives them to evade their duty.' She sighed. She knew that nothing would convert Miss Fellowes to her point of view. She went on in a more practical tone. 'Miss Fellowes, it has just occurred to me that in about a year's time a bursary left by a Mr Alfred Fellowes of Cork in 1862 will become available. If Susan should come here, I think the Board would consider her application for the Fellowes Bursary, in view of your circumstances. I think they would, in all probability, award it to her. That is, of course, if you think you would like her to come here, and if she does sufficiently well at her test. How has she been taught up to now? Has she had a governess?'

'She has been taught at home,' replied Katharine stiffly, afraid to confess that she herself had been the teacher for fear that the result of the test might disgrace her for ever. Miss Knox asked no more questions and Katharine felt the dangerous moment was over. 'How much is the Fellowes Bursary worth?' she asked.

'Fifty pounds a year,' replied Miss Knox. 'Of course, you understand I cannot commit the Board in this matter, I can make no promises. I can only tell you what I hope and believe they would do.'

Katharine smiled. 'It is really very kind of you,' she said, 'to think of it.' With a feeling that she was taking a desperate risk she decided to forgive poor Miss Knox her dangerous principles and give her a trial. It would not take her long, she thought grimly, once she was in charge of Susan, to discover that with certain characters compulsion was the only way. 'If she passes her test,' she said, 'and you will have her, I should like her to come here.' She spoke fast, afraid of changing her mind.

They parted on the best of terms. Katharine did not hear from Miss Knox for some days. Then a letter arrived to say that Susan had passed her test. This was such a relief to Katharine's self-esteem that she laid the letter down for a moment before reading further. The achievement, she felt, was hers, not Susan's. But in justice she had to admit to herself that she had had an apt pupil.

She picked up the letter again and read on. 'It is clear that Susan has considerable ability and her work is neat, but we feel that she has been taught by methods that are old-fashioned in the extreme, especially in mathematics. Her knowledge of the Old Testament is extraordinary.'

'Well!' exclaimed Katharine under her breath, blushing with shame at the stinging comment, yet full of pride at the last remark. Sitting with the letter open before her, she recalled her own sketchy education and the succession of incapable women who had struggled to appear fit to instruct her and her sisters. She marvelled at the amount she had learnt by having to teach Susan, and she had to smile when she remembered the evening she had embarked on Algebra for the first time, and her difficulties with Euclid. Considering all this, she felt a certain pride in her own achievement; after all, ignoramus that she was, she had succeeded in schooling a child sufficiently for her to win a bursary at a good school. Some of the credit must go to Susan, but a great deal of it was hers.

There was another paragraph of the letter which she had not yet read. It informed her that the Matron refused to consider any modification of the clothes list for any pupil, as this was inclined to reflect on the credit of the pupil concerned, and also because no girl could manage with fewer garments than the number prescribed. So, with infinite regret, Miss Knox must insist . . .

Katharine read through the clothes list with horror. It demanded three of everything, special blouses, tunics, coats, hat, scarf, shoes . . . It seemed to go on for ever. How could she ever buy all these things for Susan? Where could she find the money?

It was no good trying to hide from the answer; there was no money sufficient to cover this large outlay apart from her private fund, the fund set aside for her wedding.

She longed for Lawrence to be there so that she could force him to say that of course the money must be used only for the purpose for which she had designed it. If she wrote to him there was no knowing when the letter would reach him, and if she wrote with honesty she knew that she would lose the battle. He would reply straight away that of course Susan must go to school. He would not have considered the alternative.

Susan was her life's work, her hope of glory. On what she made of Susan she must herself be judged. She could not deny the child the chance to prove herself, to stand on her own feet, to put into practice the teaching that should by now permeate every atom of her being.

The sacrifice was to her so appalling that she desired to make it while she was still blindfolded by the good that it would bring forth. She could not consider the loss by itself.

Pulling the blotter towards her, with the bold, rather flowery hand of her father still on the top sheet, she wrote quickly to Miss Knox. Susan, she said, should have her full wardrobe according to the clothes list. September was the time chosen for her to go to school and to this Katharine agreed. Until the Fellowes Bursary fell vacant Susan was to have a reduction in fees of twenty pounds a year. She stamped the letter and put it on one side until she had answered all her correspondence. She let it lie in her hand for a second, trying to assess the weight of its content upon her heart. She did not hold it long; her heart was as heavy as lead.

There was another letter for her, in a business envelope postmarked Cork. It took her a moment to realise that it was from the lawyer who had taken Mr Blair's place until the end of the war should bring back the dusty-looking little solicitor who had always conducted the Fellowes business.

With some hesitation he was compelled to inform her that the firm had been approached by an individual called Peter Cavanagh, a publican in Glenmacool, who had required him to transmit the following message to her. This he was doing with great distaste. Seeing, the message ran, the dilapidation which now reigned at Fellowescourt, Mr Cavanagh had concluded that Miss Fellowes was having difficulty in maintaining the property in its old condition and he wished her to know that if she was ready to part with the property he would be equally ready to offer her a fair price at any time. The lawyer concluded with a number of prayers that Miss Fellowes would not take this message amiss, though the firm had felt in duty bound to transmit it to her.

They were confident, naturally, that she would take no action.

'Well!' said 'the Pope', aloud this time, her cheeks suddenly pink and a flash in her eye. Her dark, rather heavy eyebrows rose in a curve of indignation. She glared at the letter.

'Naboth's vineyard,' she exclaimed. Standing at the door of his Select Bar all day he could observe the big house unceasingly, watch the growth of every blade of grass in the gutters, the flakes of paint that fell away, and each slate as it became dislodged. He could await its decay. Gradually he had laid his hand on property all over the village. He owned a farm here, a cottage there, a little business or a thriftless shop wherever prosperity dwindled. He was by far the biggest property-owner in the village and he was a rotten landlord.

Katharine was furious—as if she would ever sell Fellowescourt to such a man, even if she had the power to do so! She would rather watch it crumble to dust. She wondered why he had considered this moment ripe for putting forward his proposal.

And how dared that unspeakable little lawyer have the effrontery to put such insolence on paper. Had he had his wits about him he would have acquainted himself with the terms of the will and learnt that Fellowescourt was not hers to sell; even Mr Blair would have known that, she thought contemptuously.

She immediately wrote off a blistering reproof that was to make the solicitor think of Miss Fellowes with respect and alarm for the rest of his life, and picked up both letters. She would take them to the post and have a good look at the exterior of Fellowescourt, observing its condition with the eye of a surveyor, on her way home.

Even as she left by the hall door, she was shocked by the deterioration, now that she was looking for it. The once gleaming, almost luminous white paint was dull, and ribbed and veined all over, like a skeleton leaf. The flowerbeds that had been so trimly kept in her father's time were planted with purple irises that flowered in June and were untidy for the remaining eleven months of the year. The earth in the beds had a used-up exhausted look. Even the weeds did not thrive. The yew-hedge ramped leggily upwards, and the little gate that was corroded with rust had shifted so that it no longer shut properly. Dandelions flowered under the hedge and between the coping-stones of the little wall, and tufts of grass humped between the flag-stones of the path. The house needed re-pointing and there was a broken pane in the fanlight.

Katharine sighed heavily. Dilapidation was the right word for it. Not one penny had she spent on maintenance since her father's death and not one penny could she find to spend on it now.

The little iron gate groaned as she let herself out. Across the road, lower down, she could see Peter Cavanagh standing at the door of the Select Bar, not looking in her direction. She swept down the street, head erect, looking straight ahead yet conscious of Cavanagh even as he blinked. He saluted her as she passed without appearing to notice her and she took care to pretend that she had not seen him do it.

He was still there when she returned. His almost imbecile stare was directed upwards towards the roof of Fellowescourt as he saluted her again. She could scarcely restrain herself from crossing the street to see what had so gripped his attention. From the little gate she did look up at the roof; there was indeed much to be done there: slates were loose, gutters choked and one great chimney was badly cracked. Green stains of damp ran down the cinnamon-coloured walls, grass grew on the ridges and at the base of the chimneys. The whole house looked as shabby as an old clothes shop.

Frightened, Katharine silently let herself in and went up to her bedroom. While she was taking stock of the ravages of time she would examine her own face. She drew a hard-backed chair to the dressing-table, sat on the edge of it and leant forward to peer into the dark looking-glass that needed resilvering.

She tried to see herself as Lawrence would see her when he came home at the end of the war, which please God would be soon. She saw a face sharper and thinner than it used to be, with lines across the wide, rather shallow brow; the mouth was set, as though she had made it her habit to resist and repress, and never to savour or enjoy. It was a weary face, resolute, tough and courageous, not pretty, not even very pleasant. It was alert and practical but there was in it a hint of self-approval that dispelled every trace of its early innocence and charm.

It was a depressing examination. Katharine sighed deeply as she had done earlier at the dilapidations of the house. She leant forward, suddenly aware of grey hairs, not just one or two, but quite a sprinkling of them on either side of her parting. She eliminated them, one by one. Ruefully, she remembered a favourite expression of Nanny's. 'Well, I suppose I wouldn't tear in the plucking,' she remarked to herself. 'After all I am thirty-five. Thirty-five! If we don't get married soon I shall be too old to have any children.'

Fear looked out of the mirror at her; fear of growing old before she had ever been young and of being swept past all that she desired by a face too old for her heart.

She sat there, plunging haphazardly into the past, picking out memories of the times when happiness had taken her by surprise. The time when Sheehy had fetched her from a children's party after dark, in the trap, and she had sat with her face upturned, marvelling at the heaven full of stars. The time when Lucius, Susan's father, and she had gone mushrooming at dawn. The night when her mother had brought her downstairs late, because she could not sleep, and read to her in the drawing-room until she began to yawn. The day when she was first aware that she was in love. . .

She pushed back her chair impatiently, with a frown of disapproval at her thoughtlessness. She had not told Susan about the letter from the school. It was not fair on the child.

She went to the nursery.

'Susan,' she said smiling, 'you've passed your test. You did very well. You'll be going to school next term.'

'Oh, good!' said Susan with fervour. Then she smiled back at Katharine. It was the first time she had ever heard herself praised by 'the Pope'.

CHAPTER TEN

The war was over, Lawrence was due home in a matter of hours, and he and Katharine were to be married in January. Olivia's generosity in promising her share of the Fellowes income to the unmarried sisters at home had made this possible. With such happiness almost within her grasp, Katharine was afraid to let herself savour it for fear that it might even now elude her. Nevertheless, her heart lifted at the thought of it so that she found she could not take a deep breath for excitement.

There was only one week till Christmas and the whole family was to be reunited at Fellowescourt. Charlotte and Daisy were coming home for good by the same train that was to bring Lawrence home from his wanderings. Olivia was crossing from England that night and was to bring Susan down with her the next day. And Harriet, poor Harriet, was coming over from Brandon Cottage until the New Year.

Katharine suddenly envisaged Harriet as she always was now, seated at the drawing-room window of her home, only five miles from Fellowescourt, looking up and down the road in the hope that Eustace might come along it. He had been reported missing after the Sambre advance, while Harriet had still been nursing in France. Since then there had been no word of him and no one knew whether he was alive or dead. Katharine believed him to be dead. Harriet, her face belying her words, proclaimed that she knew, she was positive, he was alive. But Harriet had said one day to Katharine that until she was told for sure that he was dead she would continue to say that she knew him to be alive, lest her lack of faith sever whatever tenuous thread might still be holding him to life.

But just before Harriet's return a dreadful thing had happened. The railway had delivered all Eustace's kit and dumped it on the doorstep of the cottage, unheralded, unexplained and unaccompanied. There it was left in the rain, muddy, battered, damp and as personal as an old pair of shoes, infinitely afflicting to behold. Katharine, summoned by a neighbour, had made a special journey there to stow the things decently away before Harriet came home, but the sight of them, so shabby and dejected, had filled her eyes with tears. Harriet busied herself with a desperate and terrible courage over preparations for Eustace's homecoming. She was knitting socks for him, making Christmas puddings, going over all his clothes and mending them. She had made new curtains for the dining-room and was fashioning a pair of carpet slippers for him with a care more loving than skilled. The more she did for his possessions, the more she could assert that he was alive. In making things for him and going about his business as if he were only away for a while, she felt that she might cheat death of him and wheedle him back from fate.

She had no child to make her loneliness bearable; she had lost her only baby prematurely. She was quite odd about other people's children now, turning away when they were discussed. It looked as if she would never have one now.

Katharine felt ashamed of her own joy and relief when she thought of Harriet, but its intensity drove everything else out of her mind. She looked years younger than when she had inspected her face in the glass with such brutal candour a few months ago. Her eyes were vital and sparkling and the ageing expression of restraint had given way to one of expectant delight. She had even begun to think excitedly about clothes and Miss Flynn was booked to come into residence early in the New Year.

Sitting at the big desk in the study to snatch a moment from time that could not be spared, she fingered the bunch of patterns that had arrived by post that morning. They were of serviceable material, suitable for a coat-frock that the Rector's wife could wear for many years. She had abandoned the idea of being married in white after a dreadful incident which she blushed to recall. She had been making up Daisy's bed, ready for her return, when the idea had suddenly come to her to throw the sheets round her and over her head so that she might envisage herself in her wedding dress. She had advanced to the long mirror with a tremulous sense of excitement only to be confronted by the sight of a middle-aged, sallow face, lined across the brow and round the eyes and reflecting a greenish light from the harsh whiteness of the sheets. So shocked had she been that she had flung the sheets on to the bed in a frenzy of haste, her face suffused with shame.

The patterns in her hand were of colours more becoming to her. She stroked one of dark blue that matched her eyes, ran her fingers over the surface to gauge its quality and, with a sigh, decided upon it for her wedding dress.

She would have liked to be married in something more dressy. In silk, perhaps, or at any rate something with pretty touches about it. But such had been the demands upon her secret fund that one new dress was all that she could afford. And bright colours and frills would not do the Rector's wife for all occasions.

She was going to be so good to Lawrence! She, the tyrant, the dominating personality who was the terror of them all, would be his willing slave. She would take a delight in making herself of no account so that he would be the more exalted in comparison. His slightest wish would be her command, to be fulfilled with a sense of privilege. So excellent was his character that she could trust his motives unhesitatingly and be assured of the wisdom of his decisions. That he was a clergyman gave him added authority in her eyes and she felt prepared to accept anything that he said or did as unquestionably right. She could even feel a pricking sense of anger against whoever might dare to dispute his judgement. Her face grew quite flushed at the thought and she could see herself rushing to his defence as fiercely as any tigress to her young.

All the thirty-six years of her life seemed to have been passed in waiting, in a kind of chrysalis state from which she was now to emerge into a resplendent perfection of living. It was difficult to imagine the present as no longer something to be endured, with the future the only time when she could hope for happiness.

She was so excited that she could not stay still. She put the bunch of patterns back on to the blotter and ran upstairs to tidy her hair. She felt sure that Lawrence would not get out at the rectory, but would come on to Fellowescourt with Charlotte and Daisy after dropping his luggage. He would not be able to resist coming. And she was going to be looking her best, although of course she did not expect him to come. She did not expect him, yet she would be bitterly disappointed if he did not come. She smiled secretly at her own illogicality. Had anyone else dared to smile, she would have turned and rent them.

She could hear Nanny padding along the corridor in search of her, muttering because she had had to look in so many places and her feet hurt her. Nanny was as excited about Susan's return as Katharine was about Lawrence's, and every remark she made referred to it in some way. 'Arrah, it'll be fun for the child to see a bit o' life in the house again,' she would say, nodding her head and thinking back to the old days. 'Sure, it's been desperate dull for her all this long time wit' only yerself and me' (she did not count Julia) 'in the house along wit' her till she went off to school.' Katharine did not like this. It was unseemly of Nanny to consider her such dull company.

She heard the old woman outside her door, listening for any sound that might reveal her presence, and she felt irritated that Nanny did not knock as the other servants did.

She called out, 'Come in, Nanny,' a little tartly.

'Och, there y'are; now! I've been lookin' and lookin' indoors an' out, Miss, an' never a sign o' ye.'

Katharine ignored this. The slightest sympathy would engender a recital of ancient and grievous wrongs.

'Did you want me?' she asked mildly, and so happy was she that she had to smile into the mirror at Nanny standing behind her in the shadows.

'Yes, Miss.' Nanny's old and wrinkled face softened. 'Don't ye think now the child could have an ideydown on her bed, an' she nearly a young lady? There's a nice little one in the press and never used since I was in this house, an' maybe it might stop the moths gettin' into it if it did a little turn on her bed. . .' Her voice tailed away as she realised that this suggestion was not meeting with approval.

'Hm,' said Katharine shortly. Nanny had no right to go prying in the linen press, going over things without permission. 'All right, Nanny,' she conceded, to her own surprise. Then, carried away by a sudden impulse, she added, 'Come round here, Nanny, I want to speak to you.'

With an astute glance at her, Nanny edged round and stood, hands clasped in front of her huge stiff apron.

'In a month's time,' began Katharine, and hesitated. 'In a month's time Mr Weldon and I are going to be married.' She only glanced momentarily at Nanny as she spoke, watching her own image in the glass. As she put her happiness into words she could see it shining from her face.

'Arrah now, I was thinkin'!' shouted Nanny in triumph, rushing forward to grasp both Katharine's hands in her own and shaking them up and down. 'I was just thinkin', Miss, did I ever see Miss Kat'rine so happy lookin', an' I thought to meself wit' the war over sure Misther Weldon'd be home anny day now, an' I wondhered, I just wondhered, Miss.' Overcome by the exuberance of her reaction, Nanny suddenly released her grasp and stood back decorously. 'I hope ye'll be reel happy, Miss. Sure, isn't it time it came to ye,' she added beaming.

'Thank you, Nanny,' said Katharine a little shakily, for the warm sincerity of Nanny's outburst had touched her greatly. She swallowed quickly and continued, 'We must decide about you now, Nanny. I don't quite know what'll be happening about Miss Susan in the holidays after I'm married, but wherever she is I expect you'll want to be.'

'That's right, Miss,' said Nanny soberly. 'Is it Miss Charlotte who'll be the boss here, then?' she added in some alarm.

'I think so,' said Katharine, her voice so crisply practical that Nanny would not dare to venture any comment.

'I see, Miss,' was all that Nanny said. She looked ancient and insecure again, as she had at the time of Captain Fellowes' death.

'Don't worry,' said Katharine with unaccustomed gentleness. 'You and I are old friends now, Nanny. I'll see that you're all right.'

'Thank ye, Miss, ye're reel kind.' The old woman stood there waiting to be sent away, looking so humble and dependent that Katharine felt like a slave driver.

'All right,' she said, almost with tenderness. 'Mr Weldon and I will talk it over.'

Nanny shuffled out of the room and Katharine considered what would be the best thing to do for Susan. Fellowescourt would be hopeless as a home for her, once she, Katharine, had left. She would grow up a slut if Charlotte were her example. Charlotte and Daisy would establish themselves, like lumps of statuary, in the morning-room as they always had done, and the dirt would settle round them while they complained that nobody did anything about it. They would stir neither hand nor foot themselves to keep things going. And she, Katharine, would have to watch the downfall from the rectory, knowing that all that she had slaved for in the house and garden was being let go to rack and ruin through sheer idleness.

On the other hand, she did not want Susan to come and live in the rectory with herself and Lawrence; she wanted to be alone with him to enjoy their happiness without observers or critics. With Susan there, she would be afraid to show her devotion to Lawrence, she could not be natural with him in front of a witness. Nevertheless, she saw that Susan must come to live with them.

After all, it would be only during the school holidays.

She kept getting up and darting about, unable to keep still. She took a scarf out of a drawer and arranged it to conceal the tiny holes worn by her brooch in the front of her dress. She brushed her hair and rubbed her pale cheeks to make them pink. There were still three hours to live through before Lawrence could possibly arrive, and she felt it beyond her power to endure them.

She sat through one course of her lunch, then told Nanny to clear away. Nanny looked at her as if she were still in the nursery and over-excited about Christmas, but dared make no comment.

Afterwards, Katharine took an armful of torn sheets to mend in the drawing-room and lit the fire for the first time since her sisters had left. The cold in the huge room was paralysing. The chimney was damp and the flame dwindled and went out. Grey smoke billowed back into the room in a turgid, evil-smelling cloud. Katharine knelt to look up the chimney for jackdaws' nests but could see nothing. She relaid the fire and tried again but it did not thrive until she drew it up by holding a newspaper in front of it. Suddenly it took hold with a roar.

The drawing-room at Fellowescourt was a long room with three high windows facing towards the street. Muslin curtains restricted the view of passers-by. Flowers sprawled in undisciplined profusion on the wallpaper but were scarcely visible since every inch seemed to be covered by mezzotints, silhouettes, semi-sacred oil paintings in ornate gold frames, miniatures and the sodden and spidery flower-studies of Victorian water-colourists. Cabinets and glass-topped tables were filled with curios of every kind from pumice-stone gathered at Pompeii, to the medals and decorations awarded to long-dead Fellowes in exchange for their lives, sacrificed on distant battle-fields, or their health, forfeited on political service in the far corners of the Empire. There were Indian brass pots, tear-bottles from Palestine, Chinese plates and Venetian glass fishes; a Swiss cowbell stood beside a Red Indian scalp, and a set of Japanese ivory balls, carved one inside the other with an industry and futility passing human comprehension, stood upon a cloisonné box containing seeds discovered in the tomb of one of the Pharaohs. Mirrors reflected one another, glass winked from unexpected corners and prisms tinkled against each other at the slightest disturbance of the air. Hangings collected the dust in carefully arranged folds and each black bobble on the edge of the red cloth over the table shook at every tread. On one side of the fireplace was a gilt Irish harp and on the other a what-not, crowded with knick-knacks and crowned by an Eastern balancing figure that swayed and bowed at a touch but never fell off its stand.

The mantel-piece was a triumph of indiscriminate arrangement. In the centre was a French clock of great beauty, flanked by tall marble candlesticks of a dull blackish-green made to look like Corinthian columns and hideous beyond description. Beyond this central piece there was infinite variety: a soapstone horse, a small case of stuffed kingfishers, a Chinese tea-bowl containing a collection of the Miss Fellowes' baby-teeth, a china light-Sussex hen sitting on a nest of eggs, a number of snuff-boxes, amethyst chippings, tropical shells and inferior specimens of mother-of-pearl and onyx.

The fire made no difference whatever to the temperature of the room. It would take more than a single fire, burning with a chilly yellow flicker in a cold grate, to disperse the accumulated damp of the last three heatless years. Mildew had formed in patches on the walls, the picture-glass was cloudy and the red table-cloth had a musty smell. There seemed to be no brilliance left in colour or texture, no shine on anything. Even the little Irish harp was losing its gilt and its strings were loose; Katharine could remember her mother plucking at them as she sang the words of Thomas Moore's melodies.

Katharine sat at a little table near the window so that she could see and hear what went past the gate. The thickness of the yew hedge prevented a clear view but the sight of the legs of a horse or pony through the railings of the little gate was enough evidence for her to make out whose they were. Most of the carts passed down to the village and back again at the same time day after day. They were an essential part of the Fellowescourt background, as familiar as daylight and dusk. The jingling tripple of donkey-carts made a quick, light sound-pattern in contrast with the loud and heavy clop-clop of farm horses, as regular as the ticking of the kitchen clock. The half-clipped pony that brought in the trap from the convent had a wild trot, irregular and unreliable, and there was the quick, smart, even sound of Doctor O'Brien's ill-tempered chestnut hunter as he passed on unpredictable journeys. Katharine and Nanny knew them all, the regulars and the less-regulars, the market-day bustlers, the bulging traps that meant a family outing, the parish priest's steady-trotting strong grey cob and the carrier's slippery-sounding and quick-stopping little mare. 'Oah!' Nanny would sometimes exclaim with shocked surprise, 'is that Michael O'Leary I hear gone down the hill already? Sure, I'll never get me ironin' done be dinner-time, so.' Or, 'That's three times Mrs Mahoney's afther goin' in an' out in the one mornin'! Wouldn't it surprise ye, Miss, the way some people does pass their time?'

Katharine was seaming a worn sheet, sides to middle, but the icy chill stiffened her fingers till they were bloodless and rigid as stone. She knelt at the fire, rubbing her hands until the blood began to circulate again. Then she returned to her sewing.

The placid occupation began to soothe her. She was able to think without emotion, settling her mind on one thing at a time. She set a term to her work. 'Four o'clock,' she said to herself, 'if they are not here by four o'clock, I shall stop then.'

She heard the bump-bump on the uneven road surface of Mick-the-Post's bicycle on his way back to Inish with the letters. He was wheeling it up the hill and just at the upper end of the yew hedge he would leap on to it to free-wheel down the other side of the rise. In a month's time, a quarter of a mile down the road, she could watch the same people passing by, but the tempo of their going would be different; they would be rattling along on a straight, flat run, having gathered speed on the downgrade from Fellowescourt.

At half-past three agitation drove her to action. She could sit no longer. She dashed to the kitchen to soak her cold hands in warm water, lay the tea-things on the silver tray, and carry it back to the drawing-room. She laid on it an extra cup and plate. Just in case Lawrence should come, she told herself.

She began, with panic, to remember the countless things to be done. She must fetch a pot of jam from the store-room. The spoons had been put away so long they needed polishing. The bread was too fresh to cut thinly, the butter too hard to spread. What was Nanny thinking of that she had not attended to all these things?

In a frenzy she worked to get all done before they should arrive from the train and find her unready. She bit her lips and tensed herself for the struggle with time. She called Nanny irritably and sent her flying to do half-a-dozen jobs, muttering protests as she sped about.

At last all was ready. The kettle, over the methylated spirit flame, was on the boil, the tray on the table before the fire, the silver gleaming and winking with the flicker of the flames. Within six feet of the fireplace the temperature of the room was bearable. Beyond that it was like a tomb.

She stopped rearranging little things to listen: there was Crowly's outside-car briskly trotting into the village, slowing down to top the rise then taking it easy down the short slope to the gate. They were here!

She could not breathe. She held her right hand pressed against her heart as she ran to the hall door. She fought with the latch but it was obstinately resistant and would not open. She wrought with it as with an enemy, hurting her fingers in the struggle to force it into obedience before they had all passed through the gate and up the flagged path to the door.

She ceased to wrestle with it and, panting with exertion, stood back for a second. Then with no difficulty at all she opened the latch. No one had yet come inside the gate and she hurried to open it, peering out to see who was there as she pulled it, groaning, towards her. Crowly was lifting the luggage down. Charlotte and Daisy were watching him. No one else was there.

She could not believe it. It could not be true. So sharp was her disappointment that she was thankful to be faced by the broad backs

of Charlotte and Daisy, unconscious of her presence. She stole back to
the house and made a quick dash to the tea-tray in the drawing-room,
snatched up the extra plate, cup and saucer and sought wildly a hiding
place for them until after tea. As her sisters sauntered up the path she
stuffed the china behind a cushion on a chair that was never used.

There was no warmth in her smile as she kissed them at the door.
There was no feeling in her at all. Lawrence did not love her, or else he
was dead. Nothing else could explain his not being here.

Charlotte and Daisy were very quiet. They evaded her eye. Daisy
kept giving Charlotte sly little looks and as they dawdled through the
door into the drawing-room she nudged her and was irritably told to
leave her alone.

'You must say something,' she whispered.

'Yes, in a minute,' glared Charlotte.

Katharine heard them and saw every movement. Her heart shrivelled
with apprehension. Something so awful had happened that they were
afraid to tell her what it was.

'Tea's ready in the drawing-room,' she said in a thin little voice.
What could it be? Lawrence had told them he no longer loved her, he
was drunk, he was dead, he was married to some dreadful creature who
had ensnared him at some foreign port, he . . . Katharine stopped dead
and, holding on to the door-post spoke in a voice so tightly controlled
that it was scarcely audible.

'Charlotte, is anything wrong? You must tell me.'

'Lawrence sent you a message,' said Charlotte. 'Oh, I'm so tired, I
simply must sit down.' She moved with dignity to an arm-chair at the
fire and remained silent.

'Tell me,' demanded Katharine fiercely. 'Daisy, if Charlotte won't
tell me, you must.' She agitated her clenched fists with impatience.

'You tell her, Char,' said Daisy flatly. 'You're the elder.'

'Oh, all right,' snapped Charlotte, cornered. 'He's not ill,' she added
for Katharine's benefit. 'He came to see us at the train, in Cork.'

'Didn't he come to Glenmacool?'

'No. His father died last night and they caught him by telegram, in Cork. He's had to go home to see about the funeral. He won't be here for several days; he says he'll have to pack up for his mother and see about somewhere for her and his sister to live. He sent you his love.'

'His best love,' corrected Daisy.

'He said there was a letter for you in the post,' went on Charlotte, offering little crumbs of comfort as if they were sweets, with an air of meriting great thanks by her generosity. But she would not look directly at Katharine; she and Daisy exchanged glances.

So, thought Katharine, the old Dean was dead! And his widow must clear out of the deanery and find somewhere for herself and her almost invalid daughter to live on a pension of fifty pounds a year. Where could they afford to live? Where else but in Glenmacool rectory with Lawrence? Plenty of room there! It was a solution so obvious that once it had presented itself no other was worth considering.

She found herself hating them with such bitterness that she was shocked at herself. She had not imagined that she was capable of such evil. With loathing and repugnance she envisaged the Weldon ladies as thin, black wraiths of women, always ailing but infinitely tenacious of life, and with all her heart she wished them dead.

Her mind penetrated the future with terrifying foresight. These women would hate her, and for many reasons. They would hate her because she hated them, because she wanted them out of the way and because she wanted to steal Lawrence from them. They would watch and criticise every single thing she did, just as she would lie in ambush for their failures. But chiefly they would hate her for her power over Lawrence and for the knowledge that if she really exerted her influence she could drive them out to fend for themselves in the cruel world, that only by her charity might they stay.

She could think of nothing to say that would not condemn her. She could not conjure up one kind or compassionate word. She could only look at her sisters, and through them, and beyond. She saw the figures of the two bereaved women descending, with the desperation of those who have no resources, like vultures to snatch her happiness away.

The inadmissible thought, the impossible certainty that once more her marriage must be postponed hammered at her consciousness. I can't think about that now, she thought, I must wait until I can be quite alone. It may not need to be true. I must think of Charlotte and Daisy; I haven't said a word to them yet.

She could feel the siege of her despair being lifted for a period of truce. The room became real to her again. The yellow light from the high oil lamp flowed over and around Charlotte and Daisy and they were in it as in a pool. Outside, the dusk was blue against the high, paned windows and soon the darkness would come pressing against them and would have to be turned away by drawing the curtains. Once the curtains were drawn the room was safe. The darkness could not get in.

Never an imaginative person, these odd thoughts that crowded upon her frightened her. That inanimate things should possess a personality shocked her. She thought it wicked to feel their influence. Quite suddenly she perceived that the image of the encroaching, menacing darkness seeking entry to the unguarded room was only an illustration of her own condition. 'How like me,' she thought. 'I won't let the dark in; it's got to be kept out. But there's light in the room, and a fire, and that's a core of warmth and comfort. There's nothing like that inside me: I think the dark has got in in spite of me.'

She jumped up so quickly that Charlotte, on whom her gaze had been fixed, started with a little cry of 'Oh!' Katharine darted to the windows, one after another, and tugged the heavy curtains across, making sure that they met, lifting them off the ground to ensure that they fell straight.

She realised that she had said nothing at all. Charlotte and Daisy must think that very odd. They were looking at the tea-things in an enquiring way, wondering if they dared pour out without asking her permission.

She picked up the tea-pot and began to fill the cups, casting about for something to say. The tea was well stewed and had an oily darkness. She wondered how long she had sat there in abstraction.

She was not going to utter a word of sympathy for Mrs Weldon and her daughter, for she could feel none. In choosing this moment to die, the old Dean had exercised a malevolence startling in its ingenuity. It was as though he had perceived the need to die quickly, before Lawrence married, so that his wife and daughter might still have first claim upon him, upon all that he was and all that he had. And they would exercise that claim, batten upon him, eat up all his livelihood, swallow him up in their avidity and leave nothing of him for her.

'Poor Lawrence!' she said, choking with the effort of breaking the crust that had formed on the silence.

'It's very sad,' sympathised Daisy, who thought that death and sadness must be synonymous. She looked piously at the floor while she chewed bread and butter. After a few seconds she felt that her gesture had lasted long enough and that she could begin to be natural.

'Yes,' agreed Charlotte, denying herself the pleasure of spreading jam on her slice of bread while she harboured distressing thoughts. 'He was very upset. You couldn't help feeling sorry for him.' She felt that it was now permissible for her to spread her jam, provided that she did so without haste, so she set to work ponderously after she had self-consciously pushed back an undulation of her Marcel-waved hair from her forehead. She was surprised that 'the Pope' had not remarked upon her coiffure.

'I suppose you'll have to put off your wedding, now,' suggested Daisy, the thought having just crossed her mind. 'It wouldn't do, really, so soon after, would it? Tch! It is a nuisance, him dying just now. I must say, it's going to upset everything.' She looked accommodatingly put out, now that she had realised the inconvenience of the Dean's death.

'Did Lawrence say anything . . .?' began Katharine nervously.

'I told you—he sent you his love,' repeated Charlotte with a trace of annoyance.

'His best love,' corrected Daisy again.

'Yes, I know,' said Katharine quickly, 'but I meant . . . about plans. Did he say anything about the wedding, or about where he thought Mrs Weldon and his sister might go?' she added hopefully.

'He didn't say anything about the wedding,' said Charlotte doubtfully, 'but I do think you'll have to put it off.' She sat back and pushed her feet out before her to consider the propriety of weddings during mourning. 'I mean it isn't war-time any longer, so you haven't got that excuse, even.'

'Yes, yes,' chid Katharine impatiently, 'but what about his plans? Did he say anything about them?'

'It looks as if he'll have to bring them back to the rectory to start with, anyway,' began Charlotte cautiously. 'He said his mother had no relations left, except him.'

'I expect they'll have to live at the rectory with you and Lawrence,' said Daisy, as though all their destinies were in her hand and the matter was now settled. 'It won't be very nice for you, Katharine, to have them in the house with you all the time. Of course, I've never met them, but still—'

'If they were angels from Heaven, I still wouldn't want them in the house,' snapped Katharine, flushed with the effort of keeping back all the things she felt about the Weldon women but could not, for very self-esteem, be heard to express.

'Yes, it is a pity,' commented Daisy graciously, her head on one side, 'but there it is, it can't be helped.' Her slow, unlit smile conveyed that she thought enough had now been said and that it was time to turn to something else. She leant forward to cut herself a piece of cake, narrowing the segment a little when she thought Katharine was watching her, then widening it just before she cut as she realised that she was not being observed. The slice safely on her plate, she lay back heavily against the cushions and munched contentedly.

Katharine was consumed with the desire to speak her mind. She needed to express her rebellion against this final malignancy of fate. She could neither eat nor drink. She could only sit behind the tea-pot, gripping her fingers together in her lap and stuffing back down her throat the words that demanded utterance, her mouth clamped tightly shut.

Charlotte had finished her tea. The moment had now arrived that gave her much enjoyment. It was time for her after-tea cigarette. With a surreptitious look at Katharine, she lifted her handbag off the floor and set it on her knee while she searched for her needs. Then, quite quickly and almost silently, she struck a match and lit what she described as 'a gasper'.

The smoke drifted lazily towards the fireplace and it was not for some moments that a wisp of it reached Katharine.

'Goodness me!' she exclaimed, sniffing. 'Charlotte, you're smoking!'

Charlotte blew out a plume of smoke as she leant back and rested her head against a cushion.

'Yes' she said, 'we both smoke a bit.'

For the first time since their return, Katharine really looked at her sisters. She saw now the over-rouged cheeks, the lipstick that was not only on their mouths but had come off on their cups and had spread to make a crimson streak on one of Daisy's rather prominent front teeth; the greasy look of their faces after the journey, which exaggerated the mauvish shade of whatever powder still remained, and the rippling artificial waves that abounded so exuberantly on both their heads.

'What on earth do you think you look like?' she demanded.

They looked affronted and did not reply. She could feel their resentment rising, swelling within them. But it was her duty to put them right however much they might dislike it. All her frustrated rage against the Weldon women gushed up to be liberated in this digression.

'You look like barmaids!' she spat the words out, almost suffocating with the torrent of speech that needed release. 'No, worse than barmaids, much worse than that, like women on the streets, horrible evil women. What sort of girls have you become? What sort of people have you got amongst in Dublin? Do you drink now, too? And swear? And play cards? I suppose you think yourselves modern!' After allowing them a moment in which to refute these accusations, she continued, 'People may put up with that sort of thing in Dublin, but it won't do here. You're back amongst decent people again and the sooner you realise it the better.'

Daisy had become red in the face. She sat upright and said loudly, 'We don't know any people who aren't decent.'

'Honestly, Katharine,' protested Charlotte, 'I'm thirty-four and Daisy's thirty-three and we're old enough to choose our own friends and make up our own faces without being told we're like bad women. You're so old-fashioned, you just don't know—'

'It's too unkind, just the minute we get home,' continued Daisy, her voice strident with grievance, 'And I tell you if you go on like this we won't—'

'We won't put up with it,' said Charlotte stoutly.

'No,' repeated Daisy, 'we won't. We simply won't stand it. It's damned unfair.'

After this pronouncement, they both sat bolt upright, glaring at her in silent indignation.

Katharine could scarcely believe her ears; the worms had turned and her authority was in dispute. She had not believed that they possessed the initiative to rebel against her, but it seemed that their stay in Dublin had altered them in many ways. As her father had done when he found himself opposed, she crumbled. She looked at them, speechless.

'You're buried here in the country and you simply don't know how people go on,' Daisy continued to object. 'Nowadays everybody uses rouge and lipstick and if you don't use powder you look just silly. And all the girls smoke. You're years behind down here.'

'Yes,' Charlotte supported her. 'The war has changed everything. Nobody thinks anything of girls smoking and having a little drink nowadays. You're not really to blame for being so out-of-date, I suppose. You just can't help it, stuck down here at Fellowescourt and never going anywhere.

They rammed home point after point. If she did not defend herself with some counter-weapon they would annihilate her altogether and trample on her dethroned authority. Her self-esteem came creeping back. Was she not now the head of the family ? Her head shot up, her chin stuck out.

'It's wrong to paint your faces and smoke and say damned, Daisy. Even if all the world does these things that does not make them right. Wars always sweep away moral standards, and if it's old-fashioned to believe in right and wrong, then I'm proud to be old-fashioned.'

'But why is it wrong to make up your face?' demanded Daisy with maddening insistence. 'Tell me that? I think it's wrong to look uglier than you have to.'

'God gave you your faces: do you imagine you can improve them? And if you think you look nicer with all that muck on your faces, just have a look in the mirror. Your lipstick's all over your teeth, Daisy, and the china as well, and your rouge is all raddled and greasy—I never saw such sights!'

Before she was half-way through this speech, they had grabbed their pocket mirrors out of their handbags. Katharine, they perceived, had caught them at a disadvantage. Out came powder puffs, lipsticks and combs.

'Now, that you cannot do in here!' raged Katharine. 'Out you go! You can do it in the men's cloakroom if you must, but the drawing-room is not a dressing-room.'

She drove them out by the force of her indignation. They grumbled, but they went. Daisy lit a candle in the hall, then returned for a second, complaining that one did not give them light enough to see what they were doing.

Charlotte put her head in at the door. 'Lady Willoughby has electric light,' she announced. 'We ought to have it put in here. It's lovely, you just turn on a switch. I shall never get used to candles again, and smelly oil lamps.'

Katharine still sat at the table, staring into the fire. When she did not reply, Charlotte went away. The sound of her lamentations could be heard trailing away. She was going to find it so dull without any cinema, or races, or bridge, or dancing. The flickering of her candle and the sound of her voice faded simultaneously; the last words Katharine heard were, 'My, but we're going to miss a lot of things now we're home!'

With any luck they would go straight up to their rooms. Nanny and Julia had toiled up the stairs with their luggage. So accustomed were they to having everything done for them that they would not lift a finger for themselves until someone chose to leave some work for them to do. Tomorrow, thought Katharine, tomorrow they can start making their own beds, washing their own clothes and doing their own mending. Tomorrow they can think how we're going to get the house done up and the roof mended.

After so much fret and strife, the silence seeped round her protectively, filling in the gaps where there had been noisy and ill-natured talk, driving away the echoes of anger that still swung inside her head. She pressed her fingers against her closed lids, bringing thick slow-moving patterns of purple and orange to climb before her eyes. She spread her fingers apart, relaxing the pressure, and gazed between them at the firelight.

'Oh,' she thought, 'I am so weary I could die!'

Now that her sisters had left the room she could think. Of course it was true that her future was menaced. Lawrence could not hope to support three women on his stipend and Mrs Weldon's pension of fifty pounds a year, added to the pittance she would bring. His mother had a natural claim upon him which could not be denied, but his sister, his useless, delicate sister was another matter. Not strong enough to work yet always ill enough to run up doctors' and chemists' bills, she would be a mill-stone around his neck for ever. The two of them would come to Glenmacool and between them they would dissipate his resources, order his life, prevent his marriage, and keep her, Katharine, whom he loved and who loved him, at bay for the rest of their lives.

That sister of his would be in his house until she died. And she could be relied upon to suffer from every disease that was not fatal; she was the kind who lived to a ripe old age of ill-health. And she, Katharine, would be expected to want to keep her alive, to cherish her as her nearest and dearest and to grieve for her misfortunes. If she appeared harsh or thoughtless there would be complaints to Lawrence.

Marriage to Lawrence with them in the house would be unbearable. There would be no sincerity, no happiness, no peace. There would be only jealousy, hypocrisy, resentment and utter misery.

Katharine pushed the tea-things from her, laid her head on her arms and wept.

'If they come,' she said to herself, 'I shall break it off. It's too much to ask of me. It is more than I can bear.'

Whatever she chose to do, it was going to be unbearable. To break off the engagement and still see Lawrence daily as he went about his work in the parish would be too painful to contemplate. If he asked for another parish and moved away from Glenmacool, right out of her life, that would be worse. She felt bowed down with hopelessness.

She raised her head and saw the firelight swim through her tears. 'If they come, I must break it off,' she said to herself. 'And I shall spend the rest of my days here in Fellowescourt, an old maid, persecuting the life out of Charlotte and Daisy, punishing them for my not getting married. And instead of children of my own, Susan must be my life's work. I shall make her my justification for living, my work for the glory of God. That is . . . if I have to break it off,' she concluded grimly, nursing the declining hope that perhaps all might yet come right.

CHAPTER ELEVEN

Olivia was shocked by the shabbiness of the house. She went all over it and inspected it outside from every angle. One of the chimneys had a list like the Tower of Pisa, and the whole of the roof needed attention. The outside painting had last been done in 1907, so it was not surprising that most of it had flaked and weathered off. The inside of the house had not been decorated since Susan's arrival, in 1909.

The rooms along the top floor were damp and festooned with cobwebs. Dead blue-bottles lay on the cracked window-ledges. There was a musty smell and patches of damp disfigured the walls. The ceiling of one room had come down altogether and lay in pieces on the bare boards below. No window had been opened up there since Miss Flynn's last visit, and lumps of soot that had been dislodged by storms and jackdaws had tumbled out of the empty grates over the floors. There was a wet patch on the passage ceiling where the lead valley had cracked above it.

The more she saw, the more alarmed she became. She tried to show her sisters how desperate was the need to do something even to keep out the weather, but Harriet was altogether preoccupied with her anxiety about Eustace, Katharine seemed remote and despairing, and Charlotte and Daisy were interested only in the inconvenience of having only one fire to sit at, and that in the drawing-room. The fact that the walls still stood and that the rain did not enter their bedrooms was proof enough that nothing serious was the matter. Olivia, they said to each other, was just being fussy.

Olivia went down the street a little way to peer at the leaning chimney from a distance and was surprised to find herself being watched with deferential contempt by Peter Cavanagh. He was standing, rather less steadily than usual, at the newly-painted doorway of his Select Bar.

'Goo' mornin', Miss,' he ventured with half-coherent affability, bringing his forefinger to the brim of his bowler.

'Oh, good morning,' said Olivia, edging off.

''Tis a long time since you was home, Miss . . . Ma'am.' He wiped his nose with the dark blue sleeve of his coat, well-stained from previous use. 'That ould war was terrible long,' he ruminated, 'an' crool. Many a one has suffered from it like yerself, Ma'am.' He took off his hat, to show respect for her widowhood, then replaced it with a slight flourish. Olivia murmured something inaudible and turned to leave him.

'Are . . . are ye home for good now, Miss?'

As if the effort of boldness required to ask this question had unsteadied him, he felt with one hand for the support of the door-post, behind his back, and ranged his person against it so as to spare his legs the joint burden of upholding him and keeping him balanced. This achieved, he sighed with relief. He kept one hand firmly on the door-post as a kind of stabiliser. His lower jaw sagged and his watery blue eyes were shot with pink. He had reached the sodden stage of intoxication when the supreme need is to talk.

'No,' replied Olivia, revolted by the smell of stale porter.

''Tis a great pity, now, about that ould house,' he said irrelevantly.

'Old house?' queried Olivia, mystified for the moment.

'About Fellowescourt, Ma'am. Tell me, now, d'ye get the rain comin' in yet?'

'No!' replied Olivia hotly, forgetting that this was scarcely true.

'Ah, no matter, ye will soon then.' His head shook as he contemplated this dismal event. 'Sure, whatever is Miss Fellowes thinkin' of, lettin' it go to rack an' ruin the way it is?' Olivia noticed that he was observing her with increased attention, his bleary eyes fixed on her face. She was becoming annoyed.

'We mean to see about it almost at once,' she said stiffly.

'It's not the money, then?' he leered.

'The money? What are you getting at, Mr Cavanagh?'

'Oh, I had a notion the money was a bit tight up there, but I could be wrong,' he conceded magnanimously. 'It mightn't be that at all. No, I only wanted to do yez all a good turn, but there's Miss Fellowes won't even turrn her head to me, and thim lawyers o' hers druv me outa their office on to the streets of Cork last week, so what can I do only speak to yerself?'

Olivia refused to comment upon these discourtesies. He waved a vacillating forefinger towards the roof of Fellowescourt.

''Twon't be so long now before ye'll be gettin' the gales,' he announced nonchalantly. 'They could sthrip that roof for ye, so they could. One gale could do that—'tis desperate the damage they do. Sure, that ould chimney'd kill yez all in yer beds if it blew down, Miss.'

'Do you think so?' said Olivia coldly.

'Oh, not a doubt of it! But I suppose Miss Fellowes knows what she's doin'. Maybe it's stronger than it looks, Ma'am?' He fixed her with a look of triumphant enquiry. There was a pause.

'What was it you wanted to say?' said Olivia directly.

'Maybe it'd be waste of time to tell ye,' he said, hoping for encouragement. 'Ah well, I'll tell ye now, Miss.' He waved his finger towards the crown of the rise where there was a long, narrow field flanking the Fellowescourt garden. 'D'ye see that little field, Miss? Now, what good is that to Miss Fellowes at all? Sure, 'tis alive with thistles an' tansy and the seeds does be blowin' on the wind an' contaminatin' the land. It's my belief the polis could be prosecutin' her for that, Ma'am. Sure, all the farmers is ragin' wit' the thistles that does come from there.'

'That field is let for grazing,' said Olivia.

'Ah, don't be talkin'. Ye'd be hard put to it to find two decent blades o' grass in it, so ye would. I doubt Christy Mahoney'll be wantin' to renew when the time comes, Ma'am.' He pushed his finger under the crown of his hat to give his brow a contemplative scratch.

'You mean you want it?' said Olivia bluntly.

'I wouldn't say that, Ma'am,' countered Peter Cavanagh, shocked by Olivia's directness. 'All the same, I suppose I might be able to find a use for it if Miss Fellowes'd like to be shut of it.'

Olivia frowned. 'What d'you want it for?' she asked, searching for the reason for all this talk. 'Is it for building?'

He looked deeply hurt. 'Arrah, no. Sure, I know Miss Fellowes'd never let it go for that. Sure, I wouldn't do that to her at all. What? Build that close to the big house? Ah, no, not at all. I was thinkin' maybe I could get a crop o' fodder off of it for me horses.'

'You want to rent it, then?'

'I'd buy it off of her,' he said quietly. 'It might come in handy for me fodder.'

'I'd buy it off of her for old times' sake,' he continued. 'Sure, it'd be doin' her a kindness. But I'd do more than that for yer father's sake. God rest his soul! Arrah, that was a reel gentleman, Ma'am. I do miss him still, so I do.' He raised his eyes to heaven. 'Ye'd not see his like now.'

Thinking of the roll of filthy IOUs made out by her father for Peter Cavanagh, Olivia was not surprised that he should miss him.

'I'm sure my sisters and I will not want to sell the field,' she said, ignoring his pious looks. 'Did you want to make an offer for it, or what?'

Peter Cavanagh gripped the door-post with both hands as if the moment had come when he needed additional support. He looked, not at Olivia but at the telegraph pole across the street.

'I thought maybe we could arrange that,' he said. 'I wondher now, what she'd say if I was to do up the house in exchange for the li'l field. I'd make a good job of it, so I would.'

'Do up the house?' said Olivia in amazement.

'Yes, Miss,' said Peter Cavanagh with an air of humility.

''Twouldn't be meself'd do it. I'm afther taking over a contractor's business and it'd give the poor fella a job o' work to do. Sure, he'd've starved to deat', only for me. Oh, if it wasn't for me kind heart I'd ha' been a rich man this long while.' He sighed wearily.

Olivia happened to look towards Fellowescourt. At the little iron gate stood 'the Pope', beckoning furiously.

'Come quickly,' she called. 'Come at once.'

Peter Cavanagh let go of the door-post with one hand and saluted her gravely. She ran up the street towards the house.

'What's happened?' she asked anxiously.

'The Pope' looked her up and down. 'You've been talking to that man,' she said disgustedly. 'We don't speak to him.' She drove Olivia before her into the house.

Olivia told her of Cavanagh's proposition. Katharine snorted.

'We couldn't ever do business with that man,' she said with an air of finality.

'It's a way to stop the house falling to bits.'

'You couldn't trust Cavanagh: he'd give you the slip somehow.'

'Mr Blair could tie him up.'

'I hate the whole idea,' said Katharine.

'Beggars can't be choosers,' countered Olivia.

Katharine went to sit at her father's big desk in the study where she could consider in peace. The idea of having dealings with Cavanagh was utterly repugnant to her. And yet . . . and yet how else could they manage to have the house put in order? They would never find the money to pay for having it done.

There was a knock at the door. It was Susan, her hair dishevelled, eyes shining, face flushed. She had run all the way home from Myrtle Lodge where she had been to visit Barry.

'Please, Aunt Katharine, Mrs O'Brien wants me to go to their Christmas party on the fifth, can I?'

'Come right inside, don't stand in the doorway. And shut the door. Do you want to go?'

'Oh yes, please.'

'Why do you want to go?'

'It's sure to be great fun. I've never been to a party since before the war, and Barry says all his cousins are coming from Limerick. It's always fun with them there.'

'Hm. I'm sure the O'Briens are very kind to ask you. What sort of a party is it to be?' Katharine was looking doubtful.

'Oh, games, I expect, and sometimes Doctor O'Brien plays the fiddle and they do Irish dancing.'

Katharine frowned. 'You will remember they're not like us,' she said, 'if I let you go?'

'What do you mean ?' said Susan, mystified.

'They're not gentry, for one thing. And they're Roman Catholics. It wouldn't do for you to get too much in with them.'

'Oh?' Susan sounded disappointed and perplexed.

'It is most terribly important that you should understand this, Susan. I only let you play with Barry because there are no other children of your own age near us. He is not a suitable companion for you at all.'

'Oh,' replied Susan because she had to make some response.

Then, after a suitable pause, 'Can I go then, please?'

'Very well, but remember what I've said.'

Susan's face lit up again. 'Oh, thank you,' she said, and was about to leave the room when there was a fumbling knock and the door was flung open by fifteen-year-old Julia. She was not used to announcing visitors and clung on to the door handle, being dragged by it into the room and almost off her feet.

'The Reverend Misther Weldon, Miss,' she gasped and before she could recover her poise, Lawrence had passed her and was in the room.

'Lawrence!' Katharine started forward, flushed with delight and surprise, holding out her hands to him.

'Katharine!' He took both her hands and pressed them between his own, smiling at her, laughing a little because she was blushing and looked embarrassed that he would not let her go. She shook her head a little, laughing and yet frowning because Susan was watching them and it was not proper that she should witness such affectionate behaviour.

'Susan, you can run along,' she said, leaning sideways so that she could see past Lawrence.

He released her hands and turned to look at Susan.

'Is that really Susan?' he asked, unconvinced. 'Why, she's nearly grown-up! Katharine, she's the image of you.'

Susan smiled shyly and held out a hand to be shaken. He took it gravely, as if she were a stranger, smiling and inclining his head a little. He opened the door, holding it wide for her to go out. With a turn of the head and a quick smile she was gone. Lawrence shut the door.

'What do you think of her?' asked Katharine quickly.

'She is charming,' he said. 'I wish I had known you when you were that age.'

Katharine's resolution to resist him, to break off her engagement and dismiss him from her life, melted and ebbed away. She felt quite weak with love for him as she smiled and basked in the delight of his presence. 'How could I ever have thought I could do without him!' she wondered. 'Oh, what a fool I am!'

'I have come back to take the Christmas services,' he explained. 'Poor old Canon Law had promised to help out in one of the city parishes and couldn't stay. Oh, Katharine, how I have longed for this moment.'

He was looking at her so intently that she felt nervous. She knew she was not looking her best; she felt that he must be aware of her frayed cuffs and patched elbow, her shabby old shoes and her rough hands. If she had only known that he was coming how different she would have been looking! But he noticed none of her deficiencies; he was conscious only of loving her, and of her happiness that they were together again.

'Have you come back for . . . good, now?' she asked, hesitating because she dreaded losing him again, even for a few days.

'Ah,' he said sadly, looking suddenly quite wretched, 'Katharine, if you did not love me, I do not think you could bear what I have to tell you. . .'

'I know what it is,' she said. 'I have known all along. They are
coming to live with you.'

He shook his head slowly as if he could not bring himself to state
the full story of all that he must ask her to bear. She tried to help him.

'From the moment Charlotte told me of your father's death, I could
see there was no other solution. They cannot afford to live anywhere
else, isn't that so?'

He gave her a look of such gratitude for her understanding that she
felt ready to endure anything for the privilege of being loved by him.

'Yes, that is so,' he said, and paused. 'But that's not all. Mother is
so gentle and self-effacing that you could not find her difficult to live
with. She is devoted to you already and anxious for us to be married as
soon as possible. It is Esmé who is the trouble.'

She did not want to discuss Esmé; it would make her too agitated.
To make a delay, she said, 'But your mother does not know me. She's
never even seen me.'

She knew how he would reply, but she wanted to hear it spoken.

'I have told her so much about you that she loves you already.' He
smiled, as if the contemplation of so much that was wonderful in a
single person kept him continually amazed.

Katharine smiled, from the enjoyment of being admired. 'When she
sees me, she will be disappointed,' she said, knowing that this would
certainly be the case. But he would not have it so.

'Not for a moment,' he declared. 'What could there be to disappoint
her about you? No, she will love you from the start.' He looked grave
again. 'It is Esmé who . . . she is not an easy person.'

'She is jealous because you are engaged to me?'

'She does not want me to marry. I'm afraid ill-health has made her
rather self-centred. She feels that my marriage will be a threat to her
security, that we shall resent having her in the house, and that I shall
grudge spending as much on her health as my father used to do. She
thinks that she will be neglected and that her position in the house will

be an inferior one . . . It is most painful. Nothing that Mother or I can say seems to change her attitude. She becomes quite hysterical.'

'She'd better go and live somewhere else, then,' said Katharine, the colour mounting in her face as she considered the infuriating, impudence of Esmé. 'We don't want her if that is how she feels.' She could not keep the sharpness of her dislike out of her voice.

'Ah, but my love, she is ill, she is a sick woman,' protested Lawrence, confident that this explanation would soften Katharine towards Esmé. 'We must remember that her . . . contrariness is a part of her illness and think of her with compassion. She has not the strength to earn her living, and there is nowhere else for her to go, but to me.'

'If she had to, if you weren't there for her to sponge on, she'd soon find the strength to earn her living,' blazed Katharine. 'I know the kind of woman she is—a parasite, fastening on to anyone who will provide for her and driving off anybody who might threaten her comfort.' On and on she went, ignoring the warnings of her brain which told her to hold back, to go slowly, to control her indignation. With blistering scorn she concluded, 'I suppose she suffers from nerves!'

Lawrence was looking at her in distress and dismay. He had not expected this reaction from Katharine. But being himself schooled to excuse, to account for and to forgive unreasonable behaviour, he checked his impulse to answer her hotly and after a moment's pause spoke very gently.

'That is her trouble, I'm afraid, but you must not think that it is within her power to cure herself. The doctors agree that her condition is . . . pitiable.' He leant forward to plead with her. 'Try to think of her with sympathy, Katharine. What a terrible affliction it is that engenders suspicion of those who want to help her and brings her into conflict with those who love her best! Why, it must be Hell for her. Think of the misery she must endure in her incapacity to love. If you can only realise that she cannot help her disorder, that she cannot be otherwise than she is, I know that your resentment will give way to compassion.'

Katharine seethed with contempt and rage. Venom rose within her as she waited for him to finish. She despised him for being taken in by his sister, for encouraging her self-deception. She was as angry with him as she was with Esmé. So enraged was she with the hopelessness of trying to convince him that he could help Esmé far more by treating her with bracing nonchalance than by pouring out his compassion for her, that she could not pause, as he had done, to soften her answer.

'Everybody can help it; giving way to nerves is as bad as giving way to . . . greed or covetousness. Of course she can help it, Lawrence, but don't imagine that she's going to try to help it while she can keep you and your mother lavishing sympathy and wasting all your time and pity on her. Of course she laps it all up! I never thought that anyone with as much sense as you have could be such a . . . fool. I could have nerves too, if I liked, but I don't expect anyone'd be sorry for me.'

Lawrence was deeply hurt. It grieved him that Katharine could say such words to him at all, but it pained and alarmed him still more that her anger should drive her so fiercely that she was past caring what she said. But the core of his hurt, the weapon that drilled into him and whose pain he could not isolate was the fact that she thought he was only doing harm by his pity and his self-control, his love and compassion; that all his forbearance was not only wasted but injurious, and that he was nothing but a poor fool to treat his sister so gently. Her contempt lashed him into a desire, almost a necessity, to show her that he was not so foolish, that she could be wrong, that she had no right to judge when she knew so little of the case. He could feel the surge of temper flooding his face as his sense of injury strengthened. But he said nothing for a moment, and made a final effort to turn the edge of her anger.

'Don't judge yet, my love, I do implore you; wait till you see her and I'm sure you will think differently.' There was a grating quality in his voice that he feared might betray his emotion.

He looked so earnestly at her that she was almost touched, but when she perceived that he was on the verge of anger and that she had nearly unseated him from his long-suffering calm, she was possessed by a desire to overthrow him completely, to make him behave as reprehensibly as she had done, so that she would not be alone in wrong-doing.

'Well,' she said, her tone sharp with warning, 'you'd better choose. The rectory won't hold us both, I can see that. If she comes to live with you, I shan't. So you'd better make up your mind.'

He moved his head quickly, as if to avoid an actual blow and covered his face with his hands for a moment. The unfairness of her attack left him helpless. He could find no weapon with which to counter her intention to be unjust.

'You're not being fair,' he stated, with rising bitterness. 'I had not thought you capable of such injustice, Katharine.'

'Injustice! I like that!' she blazed. 'Do you think it's fair to foist a hypochondriac woman on your wife? Do you?'

'Katharine!' he leant forward to touch her hand, but she shook him off. 'Katharine, this is terrible. Just think—'

'Don't touch me,' she screamed at him, on the verge of tears. 'You think I'm unfair: well, is it fair to ask me to put up with Esmé for the rest of my life? I won't do it. I won't watch you being made into her lap-dog.'

'Believe me, I won't ever be anybody's lap-dog,' he protested quietly. 'Oh, Katharine, I cannot help what I am doing: I have no choice. Esmé is my responsibility. I cannot escape from my family commitments. If there were a way, do you not think I would take it?'

'Very well, this is the end of our engagement,' pronounced Katharine tonelessly, her voice shaking. 'There is nothing more to be said.'

'Katharine! Oh, my love, think what you are saying.'

'I can't help it. If you weren't . . . on her side it would have been different. You're determined to waste all your sympathy on her. I don't come in anywhere. It isn't fair. . .'

'All these years, Katharine, we have loved each other and waited for this moment. Must we throw our happiness away when it is within our grasp?'

'Our love has all been wasted too,' she said bitterly.

'Love is never wasted; you really believe that too, Katharine.'

'We should never be happy.'

He sighed heavily. 'Perhaps I thought you could rise above the limits of flesh and blood. I thought you were an angel, but you are human after all. And who can blame you?' He felt in his waistcoat pocket and held something out to her on the palm of his hand. 'That was for you: your engagement ring.' His fingers closed over it as he saw that she resisted the impulse even to look at it. 'Think, Katharine, think hard before you make up your mind. I love you and will always love you, even if you cease to love me. I shall keep this ring in the hope that one day you will relent, perhaps in a week's time, perhaps in ten years. I shall always keep it until you are willing to take it.'

She could not speak. She could only shake her head.

'I am going to leave you now,' he said wearily. 'Remember that I shall always love you. If you should change your mind. . .'

She made no sign to show that she had heard him. He stood up and left the room quickly, without looking at her again.

She was alone. Sobs tortured her, gripped and shook her. Fierce sobs without tears, like a dry thunder-storm. She had ruined her own life. She had only herself to blame.

Like the sting of a smack, the minor thought nagged at her, smarting: she would never know what her engagement ring had been like.

Wedged between Harriet and Nanny in the front pew, singing the Christmas hymns and listening to Lawrence Weldon's impassioned plea for goodwill towards all men, Susan was aware of currents of feeling and thought amongst her aunts which were quite new to her. They had been away long enough for her to observe them now as they were, instead of as the ageless, changeless grown-ups she had imagined them to be.

Harriet, the only one not in the choir, chanted tunelessly to her right while Nanny's ancient drone made a sort of bagpipe accompaniment on the left. Both were undaunted by their inability to follow the tune, pumped by Katharine from a wheezy harmonium. Behind the sexton's two small boys and in front of the sexton himself, were ranged Olivia, Charlotte, Daisy and one of the twin Misses Pratt who lived a good way out of the village on the Inish road. The Misses Pratt were so identically alike that no one ever knew whether they were addressing Miss Primrose or Miss Violet. There never seemed to be more than one of them in church, but whether it was the same one all the time, or whether they took it in turns to come was an unsolved mystery. They were angular, elderly and erratic, both rabid gardeners, always dressed in brown, and afflicted with long sight so that they had to hold their books at arm's length in order to read a note of music. They liked everybody but never went out or asked anyone to visit them. They were tremendous walkers and never went to church any other way than on foot.

Charlotte and Daisy sat with expressions of bland indifference on their smooth, full faces, chanting mildly while thoughts of new hats, Christmas dinner and the admirers who considered them 'good sorts', and had sent them chocolates, flitted through their heads. They sang without effort, joy or any kind of emotion, contained in a sort of windless atmosphere where they remained for ever undisturbed. Yet there was a change in them; they had had a blossoming, a stirring that had now subsided but that left good-time memories to bloom again in the altered colour on their faces, in the worldly look of their new hairstyles, and a coarseness when they smiled.

Olivia's delicate beauty had a melancholy tinge, yet she retained her old liveliness and sense of fun. But her response was less immediate, her gaiety slower to effervesce. She was at that stage when active unhappiness is giving way to the compensating action of time and natural vitality. Like one of the tiny fish that inhabit rock pools, she was withdrawn but watchful, ready to dart out at a propitious moment, but with her secret refuge always available.

Susan knew that her Aunt Katharine and Mr Weldon were no longer engaged and she felt awed by this momentous cleavage. It was clear that they were both desperately unhappy, yet they seemed incapable of mending their differences. Susan could not understand how two people so deeply attached to each other as they were should be able to quarrel irreconcilably in so short a space of time. Had she not seen them herself, each so warmed by the love of the other that nothing outside could touch them, yet within half an hour he had left the house a stranger.

Susan's sympathies were with Mr Weldon. Knowing her aunt as she did, she found it incomprehensible that anyone could fall in love with her; yet it was odd how being in love made people behave in quite a special way. Her Aunt Katharine had become a new creature the moment Mr Weldon had entered the study that day, soft and flushed and appealing, all her papal qualities submerged so that Susan wondered if poor Mr Weldon had ever even guessed at their existence. Now, she felt, he was discovering them but was determined not to be put off by them; he did not seem to want to believe in them.

His Christmas sermon, though applicable to all, had surely been designed to storm the bastions of her resistance, and break down the obstacles to her good will. But she, who in the old days used to gaze at him with rapt attention, had sat today with her head bent over the Psalter on her knee, her attitude proclaiming her preoccupation. She sat now, squeezing tunes out of the harmonium and looking, to Susan's critical eye, unlovely, formidable and bent on proving her own rectitude by paying exaggerated attention to the service. It did not occur to Susan to pity her, the sight of her did not move the heart, she had not the appearance of being in need of compassion. Yet, so apart did she feel in her wretchedness, that a single word of affection, or even a look, could have brought down the whole edifice of her self-sufficiency.

Harriet was miles away, gazing with unseeing eyes at the hideous east window of German glass, depicting Christ ascending against a background that resembled a plaice on the fishmonger's slab far more than the rays of divine light it was meant to suggest. Harriet looked sad, earnest and weary, but her face had the transparent remoteness of those whose experience of reality is spiritual rather than material. The completeness of her devotion suddenly moved Susan into the climate of worship as the admonitions and instruction of 'the Pope' had never done. The idea of God that had been imposed upon her from without was dispelled in a moment of perception. For the first time in her life she experienced the compulsion of religion and a spontaneous need and desire to worship.

So astonishing was this discovery that Susan was overwhelmed by its magnitude. Dimly she began to appreciate the flame-like quality of absolute truth which consumes the obscurities with which man surrounds it for his own convenience. She saw the indispensability of integrity as equipment for the person searching for truth. Without integrity the vision is distorted and perception cannot function. It was the shortcoming of the virtuous that they allowed their vision to be selective, excluding the unpalatable, so that they adjusted truth to themselves instead of themselves to see truth. That was where 'the Pope' went astray. Some aspects of truth were too uncongenial for her to accept; she chose what she wished to perceive. To choose was to exclude, and to exclude was to be subject to prejudice. A wider view would have frightened and confused her; it would have made her life too difficult.

Although Katharine's descriptions of the nature of God had contained repeated assurances of His love, the words had not been warmed by even a reflection of its fire and had fallen coldly on Susan's heart without leaving even a spark to smoulder there. So, as a small child, she had come to resent the God Whom she could not understand and Whose mind 'the Pope' alone seemed able to interpret. She had been driven to believe that 'the Pope' knew all about God and spoke with complete authority. Since Katharine's conception of the nature of God was terrifying and inspired nothing but dread in Susan, and since she also insisted that children must love this God with their whole hearts, Susan had felt wicked all her life, because love Him as 'the Pope' envisaged Him, she could not.

She felt suddenly liberated from all the terrors of Katharine's ideas, now that she could realise that her own relationship to God had nothing to do with that imposed upon her. The desire to worship came from within and no outside authority could canalise, confine or change its essential spontaneity. The relief of discovering that she could love God was infinite. She felt like a plant thrusting out from under a stone superimposed upon it, reaching the light at last.

She stretched her neck, moving her head about in an unconscious effort to assess the extent of her freedom. She gazed first at Harriet and then at Nanny, amazed that they could be so close to her on either side, yet quite unaware of what was happening to her. Neither of them even looked at her.

She looked at Katharine, playing the Amen to the hymn. Her shoulders were a little rounded, the set of her head dispirited. She looked diminished, as if a part of herself was no longer there. Susan felt a sudden smarting of pity for her because her papal sufficiency was now inadequate. Exposing her limitations had dispelled the myth of her infallibility.

The discovery of weakness in a human being who has always appeared to have none is a little tragedy, filling the observer with guilty shame and a desire to compensate for the knowledge by a display of affection or appreciation that is probably unprecedented in that particular relationship. Susan felt frightened and ashamed that she should see 'the Pope' brought so low. 'I'll be nice to her,' she thought. 'I'll make something for her and I'll give her a kiss when I hand it to her.' She longed to show her new-found compassion.

When they reached home, she begged some scraps of material from Nanny. Laboriously, she fashioned her offering.

'What are ye makin' at all?' asked Nanny gruffly.

'A pin-cushion,' said Susan shortly, dreading the next question.

'An' who wou'd it be for?'

Susan blushed. 'Aunt Katharine.' Her look dared Nanny to make any comment whatsoever. Nanny made none, but her amusement was unconcealed.

When she had finished sewing she asked Nanny, 'What do I put inside it?'

'Bran, or maybe silver sand.'

There was a little box of sand in the potting shed, used for rooting cuttings. Susan used nearly all of it. She rushed back to the nursery to sew the few remaining stitches.

Before tea she went to the study door and knocked. Katharine's voice said wearily, 'Come in.'

She was seated at the big desk, writing to Mr Blair's partner about Cavanagh's proposition. She pushed the blotter away from her with relief.

'Well?' she said.

From behind her back, Susan produced the present. 'I made this for you,' she announced, laying it on the desk and smiling. The kiss was too much to achieve. She simply could not do it. The physical barrier of the huge chair was magnified by the rigidity that froze her. She stood, acutely embarrassed, twisting her hands tightly together in utter inability to make the gesture she had planned.

Katharine was touched. She smiled.

'Thank you, Susan,' she said gently, picking up the pin-cushion and, from sheer force of habit, turning it over to examine the neatness of the sewing. She stopped herself in sudden awareness. 'What a nice Christmas present!'

Susan smiled back. There was a difficult silence. Then a coldness came over Katharine's face.

'Did you say that Mrs O'Brien had asked you to a party on the fifth?' she said.

'Yes.' Susan knew instantly that she was not going to be allowed to go to it.

'But that is a Sunday.'

'I know.'

'But of course you can't go to a party on a Sunday, child. Did you know that when you asked me if you could go?'

'Ye-es.'

'You never mentioned it to me. I should never have considered it for a moment if I'd known it was a Sunday. I don't think that was very straightforward of you, Susan.' There was infinite reproach and condemnation in Katharine's look. In her voice there was despair.

'I didn't think of it. Can't I go then?'

'Of course not. Not on a Sunday.'

'What am I to say? I told them I could go,' Susan said desperately.

'They will understand if you tell them you aren't allowed to go to Sunday parties. Mrs O'Brien should have known better than to ask you.' Katharine gave a little sniff.

'I can't say that. They'll think. . .'

'What will they think?' Katharine's voice was severe.

'They'll think we're silly.'

'I really don't mind if they do.' Katharine paused. 'If you had been more open about it to me, you would not have got yourself into this difficulty. That is the trouble with deceit—it always leads you into difficulties.' She paused again to let this truth sink in.

Susan's eyes filled with tears of disappointment and injustice. Her compassion was utterly forgotten and anger rose up in her.

'I hate you,' she cried, stamping her foot. 'I can't do anything without you spoiling it. I hate you.'

She picked up the pin-cushion and flung it into the empty fireplace. Then she ran out of the room and into the garden until she was beyond the sound of Katharine's angry calling.

CHAPTER TWELVE

This was the day on which old Mrs Weldon and Esmé were to take up residence at the rectory and Katharine gloomily counted it as the blackest of her life, for once they were actually installed there could be no change of plan; hope would then be dead. Up till this moment she had wildly cherished the hope that something might occur to prevent their arrival, that God might have pity and lift this burden from her, but nothing had happened and a quick glance at the old French clock in the drawing-room told her that they were probably at that instant being driven up the avenue to their new home.

Katharine knew perfectly well that no window in Fellowescourt but the passage one in the attic would give her a view of their arrival, yet she hovered restlessly between the hall door and the long drawing-room windows, peering out to see what traffic was going past. This was a fruitless occupation, since the rectory was outside the village and there was not the slightest chance of their coming past the house. Nevertheless, the uncertainty of their arrival tortured her so that she could not keep still; until they had been seen in the village and she knew that they really had come, her mind could not be at rest in its despair.

She felt irritated by her own stupidity and still more so by the complaints of Charlotte and Daisy who were being disturbed by her constant flitting to and fro. They sat before the fire, feeling the draught from the open door and resenting the constraint that her presence laid upon their chatter, yet unable to remember during her brief absences what they had wished to say.

She had just made up her mind to accept the arrival of the Weldon ladies as a *fait accompli* when her still listening ear recognised the diminishing trot of the station outside-car drawing up at the gate. She dashed to the window again and saw that she had made no mistake. Her heart leaped up with the wild hope that Lawrence would come in at the gate to announce that at the last minute his mother and sister had decided to go elsewhere.

The little gate groaned as the driver pushed it open and held it wide for someone to pass. There was momentary flutter beyond it while a figure darted back to fetch something and then reappeared to advance uncertainly up the flagged path. It was Miss Flynn. She looked up at the windows as if for a sign that she was indeed expected, found no reassurance there and reached the hall door in a state of great trepidation.

When Katharine recognised the little darting figure of Miss Flynn she gave a shriek of annoyance so heartfelt that Charlotte was stimulated to ask, 'What's happened, Katharine? Who is it?'

'It's Miss Flynn,' said Katharine wretchedly. 'She's come to make my trousseau. I forgot to put her off. Whatever shall we do? There's no bed made up or anything, and we haven't got any work for her to do now that I'm . . . now that there's no wedding.'

'She can do some things for Charlotte and I,' suggested Daisy helpfully. 'And I expect Olivia could use her too. We can easily use her up between us.'

Before anyone could say another word, Julia had pushed the door open and announced breathlessly, 'The Dhressmaker.' With a demented look at Katharine, in the forlorn hope that her actions would earn some token of approval, she pushed her cap right to the back of her head, goggled at Charlotte and Daisy and with a despairing giggle fled to the kitchen.

Miss Flynn, dressed in deepest black with a purple scarf round her neck, stood in the doorway, clutching her dead father's enormous umbrella in one hand and a little soft-topped case in the other. Every portion of her vibrated with agitation and her rimless spectacles gleamed now and again as they caught the light.

Katharine went towards her, holding out her hand.

'Miss Flynn,' she began, 'you must forgive me. . .'

'Ah, I thought as much!' Miss Flynn replied with triumph. 'I said to myself when there was no one at the station, they're not expecting me, I said. Ffif . . . But I came out, just in case. There might have been a breakdown, I thought. Or the carman might have forgotten, they're not all very reliable. And I was lucky: there were a clergyman and two such nice ladies on the train who were coming all the way to Glenmacool, such a lucky chance, and when they saw me stranded they insisted on squeezing me on to their outside-car. So kind. They all got out at the rectory and I came on here, but I feel sure I'm not expected, Miss Fellowes, I . . . is it true that. . .' Her wrinkled old face was screwed up with anxiety and perplexity in case she should say the wrong thing or express herself in a way that would cause pain to Katharine.

Katharine strove to put Miss Flynn at her ease even while her inner consciousness was proclaiming that Mrs Weldon and Esmé had indeed arrived. She felt quite hollow now that the blow had fallen; the tension that had kept her darting to and fro as if on wires subsided absolutely, leaving her without support.

'It's quite true,' she said bluntly. 'There will be no wedding.'

Her voice was hard and cold, forbidding any show of sympathy.

Miss Flynn looked crestfallen and at a loss. Say something she must, yet Miss Fellowes was very alarming. Her hand darted to push in the loosening hairpins under her black hat.

'Ffif . . . Believe me, dear Miss Fellowes, I am so very sorry,' she said quickly; then after a short pause she continued in a more practical voice, 'Of course you will not want me now, I quite understand. If I could just . . . ffif . . . if I could spend the night somewhere—I don't believe there's a train before the morning.'

'I must confess that I quite forgot to put you off, Miss Flynn.

It is altogether my fault,' said Katharine, speaking fast so that the unpleasantness of apologising should be quickly done with, 'but my sisters would like you to stay to do some work for them. I'm afraid that the top floor is very much out of repair just now—we will fix you up in the morning-room. We will put a camp bed in there for you.'

'So kind. So kind! ffif . . . Ah, Miss Charlotte and Miss Daisy,' said Miss Flynn beaming at them from the doorway as Katharine swept her back into the hall.

'And how is my favourite, dear Miss Olivia?' asked Miss Flynn as they reached the morning-room. 'She always was my favourite of all my ladies everywhere. Such a really beautiful person she was, I'm sure she is still and always will be, indeed.'

'She is Mrs Heathcote now; she married and was widowed in a month,' explained Charlotte. 'She lives in England but she is here just now.'

'Ah! Poor dear Miss Olivia, tch tch tch!' Miss Flynn grieved for her with little noises of distress. 'I know so well how she feels, Miss Fellowes, for my own dear mother died only last Thursday.' She wiped her eyes unashamedly. 'That dreadful Spanish 'flu' it was; it carried her off in two days though I did everything I could to save her. She was very old and quite helpless, bedridden for thirty-eight years and never a word of complaint out of her, wasn't it wonderful! Oh, but what am I going to do without her to look after? She was all I had and now I have no one to love.'

Her lined old face crumpled up and she subsided on to a chair in a flood of grief, mopping the tears valiantly as they fell.

Katharine was nonplussed. She disapproved of such open manifestation of sorrow. She considered it scarcely decent. She went to the bottom of the stairs and called Olivia, her voice a little shaky.

After a short explanation she begged Olivia to go in to Miss Flynn.

'You'll be able to comfort her,' she said edging away. 'She's so devoted to you; she'd do anything for you. I'd be no good.'

Olivia went into the morning-room and closed the door quietly. Katharine stood for a moment gripping the voluted rail at the foot of the stairs. She felt that her own need to give way to tears was as great as Miss Flynn's but she refused to permit herself the luxury. Weak women might weep and show themselves to be inferior and undisciplined, but she, Katharine, could hold herself in check. By her strength she would show her contempt for Miss Flynn's feebleness.

She called Julia and sent her scurrying for blankets and bed linen. She called Nanny and told her to help Julia to bring down the stretcher bed and air the mattress at the kitchen range.

The door bell rang and Katharine was aware that through the other sounds she had heard that of a motor-car drawing up outside the gate; such an unusual noise at any other time would have stirred her to wonder who could be arriving, but today she had ceased to hope or expect anything from outside.

The bell rang again and she went to open the door. She stood on the mat inside without moving and stared at the person who faced her on the step. She could not believe her eyes. It could not be Eustace! She must be seeing what was not there. She was quite unable to speak.

Eustace was smiling, looking at her with some of his old gallantry as he raised his hat and kept it in his hand in preparation for entering the house. He was painfully thin and his face was the colour of buff paper. He looked as if he was only just well enough to stand.

'Where's Harriet?' he asked, taking her hand and patting it reassuringly. 'There there, Katharine, can't I come in?' He moved forward so that Katharine had to retreat. 'Didn't you get my telegram?' he asked suddenly.

'No.' Katharine suddenly smiled and now tears did come to her eyes as she turned her back and rushed to the staircase again.

'Harriet!' she called brokenly. 'Harriet!' she hammered on the rail.

Harriet came out of her bedroom and leant over the banisters, alarmed by Katharine's odd appearance and uncertain voice.

'What is it?' she asked anxiously.

Katharine could only beckon her down; her face was contorted with emotion and she could not say anything. Her gesticulations became quite wild and I Harriet hastened to her help. Halfway down the stairs, where the bottom flight began, more of the hall was visible and Harriet was suddenly confronted with her husband who was advancing from the shadows behind Katharine. She stopped dead in utter amazement but he continued towards her and with some effort mounted the stairs to where she stood. He took hold of her elbows and together they collapsed to sit on the stairs and recover from the agitation of the moment. Harriet kept fingering his coat to reassure herself that he was really there and repeating again and again,

'Oh, Eustace! Is it really you?'

The commotion was sufficient to rouse the interest of Charlotte and Daisy who opened the drawing-room door, leant out and called querulously to Katharine, 'What's happening? What's going on?'

Katharine struggled for command of herself. She drew herself up, took a deep breath and proclaimed, 'Eustace has come back.' Then she opened the morning-room door and called, 'Olivia, Eustace is here!'

The enormous effort she had made to control her emotion left her weak. She sat on the bottom stair and watched them all as they came to see for themselves whether she had gone out of her mind or was speaking the truth. She was trembling with cold.

Nanny, helping Julia down the back stairs with the stretcher bed and making full use of the opportunity to instruct, admonish and threaten the girl as is the pleasure of the old, came tottering along the corridor to the morning-room just as Miss Flynn and Olivia emerged. One glance at the group on the staircase was enough for her. She threw up her hands and cried, 'Oah! Thanks be to God, if it isn't the Captain home!' Abandoning Julia and the bed she skipped up the stairs and wrung Eustace warmly by the hand, beaming at both Harriet and him in turn. Then, overcome by her own daring, she darted cackling back to Julia and scolded her for having made no progress by herself.

Olivia ran up to them and kissed them both. Charlotte and Daisy felt a little stranded by the tide of emotion that had swept everyone away. They stood at the bottom of the stairs, near Katharine, feeling foolish and awkward, and smiling because they felt some evidence of pleasure was expected of them.

'I say!' said Daisy, 'What luck!'

'Yes,' said Charlotte in agreement, 'just fancy!'

'Ffif,' murmured Miss Flynn, 'Ffif.' Her tear-stained face began to beam again. She retired into the morning-room to take off her coat and hat, carefully keeping out of sight. She felt that she would be intruding if she remained with the family.

The bell rang again. Julia, determined to prove to Nanny that she was quite able to do her job without advice or prompting, flew to open the door. Patrick Quinn, the postmaster, stood there, his red beard luxuriant as a tropical creeper, his hair flaming with a light of its own, a broad smile of satisfaction on his face. He handed a telegram to Julia.

'I t'ink de news is before me,' he said. 'God be praised!'

'It is so,' confided Julia. 'Isn't it great?'

'It is great indeed! Sure, I saw the cyar stoppin' outside the gate and the Captain steppin' out and the next minyit didn't the telegram came t'rough. 'Tis good news all right.'

He turned and went smiling down the flagged path while Julia, leaving the door open, went giggling to Harriet and handed her the telegram announcing her husband's return.

The relief at finding something to laugh at was enormous. They all rocked with mirth, shaking wordlessly. Eustace was the first to recover.

'Pack your things,' he ordered Harriet. 'The car's outside to take us back to the cottage.'

'Car?' said Harriet.

'I hired a car to bring me down from Cork. It was such a near thing my getting back at all I thought I'd do it in style. And when I got to the cottage, me wife was out and away, so I came here.'

'What did happen to you?' said Harriet tremulously.

'I got typhoid on the Sambre. Some French people looked after me.'

There was silence. Olivia pulled Harriet to her feet.

'Come on; I'll help you pack.'

They all dispersed. Charlotte and Daisy went up to fetch their clothes for Miss Flynn to alter. Charlotte hummed a contented little tune; it was so convenient, Miss Flynn turning up like this, because she had been wondering what to do about last year's coat and skirt; the seams were now a little tight.

Katharine went to the study. She too was thinking about Miss Flynn. They must have been talking, she thought; the Weldons must have told Miss Flynn that her engagement was off. Unless . . . what a terrible thought! Unless Miss Flynn had chattered to them in her artless way and told them she was coming to make Miss Fellowes' wedding-dress. Then with what pleasure they would have set about putting her right. And Miss Flynn had described them as 'two such nice ladies'. If that was what had happened she could never hold up her head again.

Susan was not at home on that day; kind Mrs O'Brien had asked Katharine to let her spend the day at Myrtle Lodge in an effort to compensate for the bitter disappointment of missing the Sunday party. 'The Pope', a little alarmed by the violence of Susan's anger, a little afraid of the censure of Olivia and Harriet should they be drawn into the fray and even a little ashamed of herself, had been gracious.

During the days between Christmas and the O'Briens' party, Susan had simmered with resentment against 'the Pope'. She had sat on the window-seat in the nursery sourly watching the light changing on the line of Scotch firs at the foot of the mountain and nurturing a growing sense of injury. The more she dwelt on the wrongs done to her by 'the Pope' the more she found to resent. It had taken her two days before she could bring herself to confess to Mrs O'Brien that her aunt disapproved of Sunday parties. To her disappointment, Mrs O'Brien had been tolerance itself and declared that of course she understood, that it didn't matter at all only it was a pity she'd miss the party, but she must come another day to make up for it. She had been so full of generous understanding that Susan's wrath, maintained by the thought of what Mrs O'Brien would think of them all, had deflated instantly for want of sustenance. But so angry had been her face and so rebellious her attitude that Mrs O'Brien had felt impelled to reprove her.

'Come here to me now, Susan,' she had said, patting the chair next to her own. 'What sort of a face is that I see at all? Now, you've no call to be feeling that way about what your auntie says you can do and cannot do: sure, it's nothing to do with you at all and 'tis all for your good she does it.'

'She won't let me do anything,' grumbled Susan, 'not even things that nobody else would mind, ever.'

'There now, it's because she loves you so much, she wants to turn you out a credit to the family, that's what it is, and you mustn't be letting those bad feelings get the better of you. It isn't right, Susan, to let bad feelings eat into you that way, and the one it does the most harrm is yourself. Promise me now that when you get home you'll give your auntie a kiss and forget all about it.'

Susan looked into Mrs O'Brien's plate-like face with its kind, dark eyes and untidy black hair that roped over the brows in hanks and loops, and said in a shocked voice, 'But I couldn't ever kiss Aunt Katharine, Mrs O'Brien. I tried to on Christmas Day and I simply couldn't.'

'What stopped you?' asked Mrs O'Brien in amazement. Her expression darkened with the realisation that all families were not as full of affection as her own; such a thing in her own home would have been unthinkable. 'Don't you love her enough for that?'

'I don't love her at all,' said Susan with cold solemnity, 'and she doesn't love me, she hates me.'

'Ah, not a bit of it!' exclaimed Mrs O'Brien, horrified. 'Don't be talking to me like that at all. It's not right, Susan, I tell you it's not right to be thinking like that of your auntie. You do love her really, you only think you don't. And as for her hating you, why I never heard such nonsense: how could she hate a little bit of a motherless child like yourself?'

Susan shrugged her shoulders. 'I don't know,' was all she would say.

And Mrs O'Brien had let it go at that, afraid that worse revelations of family dissension might follow.

'We'll fix up for you to spend a whole day here before you go back to school,' she said consolingly. 'Don't you say a word to your auntie, leave that to me and I'll get round her.' She had fixed her slanting eyes reflectively upon Susan and suddenly enquired, 'Are you happy at that boarding school?'

'Oh yes,' said Susan with enthusiasm,

'Are you not lonesome, then?'

'Lonesome?' asked Susan. 'What for?'

'For your home, child,' said Mrs O'Brien impatiently. It exasperated her that there could be a child in creation who would not be lonesome away from home.

'No,' replied Susan, 'but I miss the country.'

'Tch tch tch,' had grieved Mrs O'Brien, making a stout effort to refrain from condemning Miss Fellowes as a hard-hearted tyrant. 'What kind of a household can it be at all.'

She had kept her word and now Susan was back at Myrtle Lodge for the day, surrounded by O'Briens of every age, tugging at her skirt, begging her to do up their shoe-laces, blow their noses, kiss their bumps and tell them stories. Barry was shooing them away so that he could tell her of his plan to climb the mountain with her, Bridie was chiding the ex-baby for persecuting her and Mrs O'Brien was driving them all out of the room so that she could have a private word with Susan herself.

'Go on, now, go on now,' she was saying, 'sure you'll have her soon enough, I only want to talk to her for a little minute.' She waved them out and closed the door, standing against it for a moment and raising her voice to cry, 'Go on now, didn't I tell you to let us alone for a moment. Go on, will you.'

She sat down slowly at one end of the shabby sofa, patting the space beside her until Susan sat also. She looked at Susan with great and affectionate concern.

'Well,' she asked gently, 'and did you make it up with your auntie?'

'Well,' said Susan, squirming because she could not claim to have made any real effort to put things right between herself and 'the Pope', 'not exactly. It all sort of passed over.'

With a wise nod Mrs O'Brien said, 'Until the next time, I've no doubt, then it'll all be dragged up again. And in the meantime you're uncomfortable and she's uncomfortable and you keep out of each other's way.'

It so precisely described the present way of life at Fellowescourt that Susan could only agree.

Outside, in the hall, the tide of life ebbed and flowed as the children screamed and jostled, bumped against the door, called shrilly for their Mammy and devised new games with Susan's coat and gloves. Mrs O'Brien seemed quite unaware of all the movement without, as if she had discovered a peaceful oasis in which she was determined to settle, but Susan's mind was half inside, half outside the room; she was listening to Mrs O'Brien with one ear and to the throbbing activity of the children with the other.

'Now, that won't do, Susan,' said Mrs O'Brien reprovingly. 'That will never do. Sure, you'd get no peace of mind that way at all. Wait till I tell you now what you must do: you must make it up with her. Will you promise me now you'll do that?'

Susan looked at her feet with embarrassment then back again at her finger following the outline of a pattern on the sofa cover.

'I'll try,' she conceded. And with that resolve she smiled up into the broad flat face so earnestly looking into her own.

'That's a good girl!' said Mrs O'Brien, beaming delightedly. Then, in order to dismiss the unpleasant subject she said quickly, 'And what'll you be when you grow up? Have you made up your mind?' She stood up and began to flick dust off the ornaments with her handkerchief, moving slowly about the room.

'That's another thing,' said Susan gloomily, 'Aunt Katharine wants me to be a missionary.'

'And you don't want to be one, is that it?'

'Yes, but she goes on and on.'

'Tch tch tch! Now, listen to me child. Don't let any one turn you into something you're not meant to be, d'ye hear me? It'd only be a sin against yerself. No one has a right to do that to you. Will you remember that?'

She spoke with such unusual vehemence that Susan was impressed.

'You don't think I ought to then?' she said hopefully.

'Of course I do not, unless you want to do it yourself.'

'Oh no, I couldn't do it. I keep saying no but she seems to think I'm wicked not to want to. At the beginning I felt I was right but she talks so much I don't know what I want by the time she's finished.'

Mrs O'Brien tapped her on the chest to emphasise the importance of her words, 'Just you go on saying no, Susan. Unless you change your mind. You owe it to yourself.'

'I will,' promised Susan. 'Thank you. I'm glad you said that; I was beginning to wonder how much longer I could go on saying no.'

She experienced once again the elation of Christmas Day, the conviction that she had resources within her. She smiled at Mrs O'Brien, filled with the resolution to resist.

Mrs O'Brien kissed her affectionately. 'That's a good girl,' she said once more. 'Just you stick up for yourself.'

'What's Barry going to be?' asked Susan, preparing to go.

Mrs O'Brien regarded her with smiling pride. 'He's going to be a priest, thank God!' she announced. 'It was his own idea entirely.'

'A priest!' echoed Susan in astonishment; the idea was so strange to her that she could not conceal her surprise.

'What better could he be?' demanded Barry's mother, a trace of challenge in her tone. 'Will you tell me that?'

'Oh, nothing,' said Susan quickly. 'I just didn't expect it, that's all.' She thought of the tadpoles and dead cats, the birds' nests and animals that had been Barry's chief interest when he was smaller. She was suddenly aware that she and Barry were scarcely children any longer. She did not like to think that he was to be a priest: it meant that she could not be the most important thing in life to him and it made her feel deprived and unloved, although until this moment she had never realised that she wanted him to need her. She felt awkward and foolish, angry with herself and disappointed in Barry.

Mrs O'Brien looked at her shrewdly. 'You wanted him for yourself a little bit, I'm thinking,' she said, not unkindly. 'Ah, we all get notions and the half of them never come to anything. Sure, you're only children yet, there's no harrm done.' She opened the door, leant out and called, 'Bridie, will you get the baby dressed and into the pram. I'll roll her out meself this morning.' Leaving the door open, she turned back to Susan. 'Go on now, child, Barry has sandwiches packed for your lunches on the mountain. He'll be mad with me for keeping you all this long while.'

Gratefully, Susan emerged into the seething turmoil of the O'Brien hall. She was glad to be ignored for a moment, to be amongst beings who had no reason to observe her closely but who were glad to have her with them. She was baffled by her own emotions. The sense of loss that she felt showed up her lack of independence; it annoyed her to think that she had counted upon Barry's attachment to her without cause, that he had never thought of her in any special way. Her nose was out of joint and she did not like it.

She tried to look at Barry from a different viewpoint, shifting her ground from one spot to another, like a photographer who wishes to take the best picture possible. She began to perceive him as a creature who had his own personality distinct from hers, private and contained, so distinct in fact that she realised suddenly that the Barry she thought she knew so well and over whom she had exercised a sort of benevolent despotism did not exist at all. She had been harbouring a myth.

He was coming out of the kitchen with a rucksack swinging from his arm; his long, thin body looked as if it had been flung together by accident and by some miracle of cohesion had not fallen apart again;

his wrists and knuckles were flat and bony, his elbows and fingers double-jointed. The characteristic plate-like face was smooth and pale, barely broken by the unobtrusive nose and slight outward thrust of the lips. His eyelids enclosed the bright black-brown eyes so smoothly that they had the air of being able to close without a sign of a crack beyond the fringe of the lashes lying like copperplated wire over the flat cheeks. There was an oriental repose about the planes of his face, an inscrutability belied by the ready smile and the merry light in the eye. The surprising features were the very large and even teeth, so white that the sight of them in the pallid face was a shock, and the dark hank of hair falling over the eye, copperplated like the lashes.

Kevin, the ex-baby, ran at him laughing, trying to climb up his legs; Barry held out his free hand to pull him up, then put down the rucksack and tossed the child high in the air, laughing with him all the time. After a minute or two of this he pretended to dodge the child, picking up the rucksack and holding it before him as a shield.

'Are ye ready?' he called to Susan across the hall. 'We'll go, so. We'll have to make a run for it or we'll never be quit o' this fella.'

He caught Susan's hand and pulled her after him out at the door and over the gravel to the gate, Kevin staggering behind them and emitting little gurgles of laughter. Barry shut the gate firmly and poked at him playfully through the rails.

'Gwan back to Mammy,' he commanded. 'Gwan now.'

He waited to see his order obeyed, then set off with Susan.

Susan had watched him coolly, taking no part in the game herself. She would not soften until she had his whole attention.

'Race you to the trees.'

'Oh no!' cried Susan, but he was already yards ahead of her and she must follow or be left hopelessly behind.

He paused at the gate into the little field that Peter Cavanagh wished to buy and they took a short cut to the line of trees beyond the Fellowescourt garden.

It was one of those mild January days when there is kindness in the air and the sunshine falls gently with the same benign quality as a shower.

Susan was always moved by the beauty of the mountain; the vexations and bothers, the complications and perplexities of life at Fellowescourt were sponged away like the scribblings on a blackboard, by the beneficent action of unhindered air and open sunshine on the receptive, waiting earth. There was a life on the mountain slopes so distinct from that of the inhabited countryside that there might have been miles of space and thousands of years between them. In fine weather there was a slow serenity that impregnated the being; when the wind was rough and the rain drenching there was an elemental excitement in surviving the unbroken onslaught.

Susan was suddenly happy, excited and smiling; she had a sensation of immense well-being, and there was not a thought in her head. She bore no grudge now against Barry, she no longer felt the need to be his chief preoccupation, yet his companionship was pleasant. She wished everybody well, even 'the Pope'. She was quite free of the prickly jealousy she had felt earlier.

The two of them swung along, jumping from tussock to tussock across the marshy places, from boulder to boulder over the streams. They chattered amicably, without a trace of self-consciousness, perfectly happy, each in their own way.

When Susan reached home that evening she was tired but relaxed, a little dazed with fresh air, and full of her promise to Mrs O'Brien that she would make her peace with Katharine.

She went in by the back door, where there was no need to ring the bell, and found Nanny and Julia gossiping over the day's events. Nanny was still filled with excitement over Captain Willoughby's return and kept Susan listening to her account of it followed by a description of Miss Flynn's arrival.

'Ah! Ye'd be sorry for her, so ye would!' exclaimed Julia compassionately. 'Sure 'twas only yesterday she buried her mother and she was desperate fond of her, the creature. She wouldn't have come here only she didn't want to disappoint Miss Fellowes, she said, and when she gets here she finds she isn't wanted afther all only no one told her not to come. So, it's no wonder if she has a little bit of a cry now and then, ye couldn't blame her, now could ye?'

Susan listened, mystified at the discovery that grown-ups could cry, and determined to avoid witnessing such a calamity as Miss Flynn weeping, fond of her though she was. To be seen crying was to her such humiliation that she was unable to envisage anybody who could weep without suffering agonies of shame. For both Miss Flynn's sake and her own she would keep out of her way.

'Were y'out on the mountain?' asked Nanny querulously. 'I t'ought I saw the pair o' ye slippin' t'rough the little field across there, and there's only one place ye could be makin' for, so.' She looked down at Susan's feet and threw up her hands. 'Go on up stairs and change yer shoes, child, go on up this minit: sure they're saturated with the wet.' Like a broody hen she fussed and fretted until Susan fled up the stairs before her.

Pulling on clean, dry stockings, Susan asked,

'Where's Aunt Katharine?'

'Below, in the study, I'm sure,' said Nanny drily. 'Why, d'ye want her?'

'Yes.'

Nanny gave her an amused, curious look and nodded her head knowingly.

'There's no accountin' for tastes!' she remarked with a sniff. She resented the existence of any private matter between Susan and 'the Pope'. She hated to think that her child was old enough to act without her guidance, that she was becoming independent. It made her feel that she was getting past her work.

Susan knocked quietly at the study door; Olivia and 'the Pope' were sitting before the fire and their conversation stopped abruptly when she came in. Katharine looked as if she were trying to fix a thought in her mind so that when Susan left the room she could continue without a break.

Olivia smiled, 'Did you hear about Uncle Eustace?'

'I know, it's marvellous.' Susan smiled back at her. 'Nanny told me.'

'Did you want something?' said Katharine.

Susan began to blush, 'Well, not really. . .' She turned to leave the room but Olivia was at the door before her.

'I'll be back in a minute,' she called to Katharine round the edge of the door. 'I just want to see how Miss Flynn is getting on.'

'Sit down,' said Katharine, seeing that Susan did not mean to go.

Susan sat on the edge of Olivia's empty chair, carefully staring into the fire and holding out her hands to its warmth so as to avoid looking at Katharine.

'I'm glad Uncle Eustace is safe,' said Susan after a painful pause.

Katharine was well aware that Susan had not come to say just that. She glanced quickly at her, saw the tense expression and knew that she was trying to say something difficult that it would take time and encouragement to draw out of her.

'Yes,' she said, and Susan knew that more was to come and that it would be of a pious nature. There was a heaviness about the way she said the 'yes' that meant it was only the prelude to comment. 'God has been good to your Aunt Harriet,' continued Katharine.

'Yes,' said Susan, unable to say more. The tone of Katharine's statement was not altogether pious; there was a tinge of envy about the way it was spoken, a hint of feeling that God had not been good to her.

'Have you had a nice day?' asked Katharine after a further silence.

'Oh, yes thank you, lovely.' Susan's face came alive. She turned away from the fire to face 'the Pope'. 'We went up the mountain, right to the top.'

'You can see three counties from there, or so I've been told,' said 'the Pope'.

'You can see for miles. All the fields look so tiny, up and down all the smaller hills and valleys, with the farmhouses all looking so white and neat. They don't look like that near.' Susan stopped, suddenly aware that she was making no progress with her endeavour.

'Yes?' said Katharine encouragingly.

'I'm sorry I was so horrid on Christmas Day, and since.'

She had said it; her heart swelled with relief and she sat back in her chair, relaxed and at peace.

Katharine moved uneasily in her chair. She wanted to lean forward to Susan and put out her face to be kissed, but her relentless pride prevented her. She had in fact put her head a little forward on impulse and was hard put to cover up the gesture. She smiled at Susan with a little shake of the head as if only she knew the dreadful import of such malpractices as rebelliousness and want of respect for the head of the family.

'If you're really sorry, we'll say no more about it,' she conceded.

Susan swallowed. 'Yes,' she said, 'thank you. Aunt Katharine.' She suddenly felt quite exhausted. Now that she had fulfilled her promise and humbled herself, her mind was released and she was quite unconscious of her surroundings. She gazed unthinkingly at the fire, said nothing and let her thoughts wander pleasantly.

'How is your tray cloth getting on?' asked 'the Pope'.

'Tray cloth? Oh, tray cloth. It isn't getting on at all,' admitted Susan.

'But the Missionary Sale is next week.'

'Yes, I know.'

'It must be finished by Sunday: it has been promised.'

'I never seem to have any time.'

'You have plenty of time for things you want to do.'

'I suppose that's it,' said Susan, reproaching herself.

'Yes, and you never think that by your lack of application you may be denying the money to pay for the conversion of the heathen. The more things you make, the more money they make at the sale and the more missionaries they can send out to Africa.'

'Yes,' agreed Susan hopelessly. She felt that her lack of interest was almost criminal.

'You'll finish it then?'

'All right, Aunt Katharine.'

There was a terrible amount of work to be done on the tray cloth, she would have to spend hours every day embroidering if it was to be finished in time. The prospect appalled her, but her remorse for her rebellious behaviour to 'the Pope' drove her to agree.

The door opened quietly and Olivia, her face very serious, came in. She stood by the fireplace and said to Katharine, 'I'm afraid Miss Flynn is very ill.'

'The Pope' looked incredulously at her.

'Very ill?' she echoed. 'But what can be the matter?' As she spoke, the terrible truth became apparent to her. 'Very ill! But of course, she told me, her mother died of Spanish 'flu'.' Immediately she became practical. 'Olivia, go and gargle. Send Julia for Doctor O'Brien. Tell Charlotte and Daisy to gargle too, salt and water. Susan, go up to the nursery and keep away from all of us.' There was a pause. Katharine spoke as if there was no one to hear her.

'Spanish 'flu',' she said, 'and who is to nurse her?' She waited for a moment, considering, then announced, 'I will nurse her myself. It was for my sake that she came here. Olivia, make me a mask.'

'We'll nurse her between us,' said Olivia. 'You can't do it alone.'

Doctor O'Brien did not delay; he returned with Julia, driving her back to Fellowescourt in his trap.

'My God!' he said to Katharine. 'I'd hoped that old influenza was goin' to pass us by in Glenmacool, but it seems I was too soon. Let's hope it won't go the round o' the village now.'

He made no desperate predictions and showed no sign of panic; nevertheless he demanded observance of the most rigid precautions. Katharine knew that he was far more alarmed than he was prepared to admit.

'Is she very bad?' she asked him, after he had examined Miss Flynn.

'She is,' was all he said, but his voice was undefeated.

When he was gone, Katharine sat for a moment at the fire, planning the reorganisation of her household. The only member of it who had not even seen Miss Flynn was Susan, so she must keep to the nursery and avoid all her aunts. Harriet was really in no danger: she would not even tell her at present. Olivia and herself, Charlotte and Daisy were the most likely to catch the infection. Perhaps, she thought, considering the possibilities without a trace of emotion, I shall catch it and die. I have nothing to live for; yet when Sheehy tried to kill me I did not want to die, so probably I should find the same thing again. If I catch it and do not die I shall be forced to believe that God has chosen me for a special inescapable destiny. Surely he would not keep me in this torment of unfulfilment for no purpose? And surely, she protested to herself, surely he would not have chosen me out for affliction as he has, if it were not to refine me by suffering for some special end.

She felt very tired, purged of all emotion, able only to see without the slightest agitation or concern the likely course of events.

'I must find out Miss Flynn's next of kin,' she said to herself, 'before she gets too bad.'

She wrote 'next of kin' on a slip of paper and left it on the blotter. Then she went in search of Charlotte and Daisy.

They were sitting comfortably in the drawing-room, Charlotte in an armchair at the fire. Daisy stretched out on the sofa, discussing a letter which Charlotte held open and from which she was reading extracts.

As soon as Katharine appeared all speech between them ceased and Charlotte laid the letter down on her lap, covering it with her hands. They both looked flushed and excited. Katharine could never quite prevent a feeling of resentment at their secrecy in her presence. It was as if she were a prying duenna instead of their sister.

A little sharply, owing to the smart of injury she felt at their reserve, she said, 'You'll be able to go on talking in a minute—I shan't keep you for very long.' She paused to let them feel embarrassment, but they showed no sign of it and with a little sigh of impatience she continued,

'Did anybody tell you that Miss Flynn has been taken ill?' She came up to the sofa and waited for Daisy to make room for her. Daisy drew her feet up, and Katharine sat down.

'Oh, I say!' exclaimed Charlotte. 'That's not like Miss Flynn, she's never ill. What's the matter with her?'

'It's Spanish 'flu'.'

Daisy sat upright. 'Spanish 'flu'! But we've been with her, very close to her. She'd no right to come here.' She brushed her skirt down with her hands as if she could thereby brush away the infection. She glared at Katharine. 'I hope she's done my skirt,' she said resentfully, 'I need it badly.'

Katharine took no notice of her remarks.

'Doctor O'Brien says she's very bad,' she said quietly, and proceeded to instruct them in the precautions to be taken. 'Olivia and I will nurse her between us,' she finished.

'We'd better keep out of the way, then,' said Charlotte.

'You won't want any help from us, will you?' said Daisy, but the query was merely formal; she was really making a statement.

Katharine sighed. 'We shall manage,' she said.

Miss Flynn died, and on the same day Olivia fell ill. Susan was sent to end the holidays at Brandon Cottage, with Harriet and Eustace. Nanny helped Katharine to nurse Olivia until Katharine herself caught the infection, then Daisy. Mrs Sheehy, still living above the stables, came in daily after that and looked after them all with great devotion.

None of the sisters was seriously ill at first. Olivia recovered quickly. Daisy complained bitterly that Charlotte did not come to see her and sent messages that brought no response. Charlotte was taking no risks: she wrote a little note to Daisy telling her that it was dreadfully dull without her and that she must get well quickly and join her again, but not before it was safe to mix with people.

As soon as Daisy began to get better, she determined to take matters into her own hands. She was bored to death in the solitary confinement of her room, she could not wait for details of the answer Charlotte must by now have sent to the letter they had been reading together when Katharine had surprised them; and the opportunity to follow her inclination, now that Katharine was unable to supervise the household, was irresistible. She had been up in front of the fire on the previous day and was to get up again later, so she did not ask Doctor O'Brien if she might visit Charlotte in the drawing-room: he was as fussy as Katharine and would be sure to refuse permission.

After luncheon, when Daisy had been left to sleep while Nanny and Mrs Sheehy took a little rest themselves, she put on her dressing-gown and made her way downstairs. The chill of the house struck her, but she had soon reached the drawing-room where she hoped to find Charlotte.

The room was empty. The fire was low and Daisy attended to it, but it would be hours before it began to give out any warmth. She felt the cold of the room acutely, her knees were weak and her disappointment at not finding Charlotte made her feel very sorry for herself. She gave up the attempt and crept back miserably to bed.

When Doctor O'Brien called that evening, he was shocked to find that Daisy had suffered a most serious relapse. No one could tell him the cause of this and Daisy herself remained resolutely dumb. She was by this time a very frightened woman and knew that her wanderings round the icy house had done her great harm; she did not wish to add the Doctor's condemnation to her troubles.

Doctor O'Brien was in a quandary; if he told Katharine that Daisy was now seriously ill with double pneumonia, she would undoubtedly insist on getting up herself and thus lay herself open to the threat of a relapse; but if he said nothing to her, he dreaded the lash of her tongue when she finally discovered that he had withheld the truth from her. He decided to wait for a day and watch developments; in the meantime he warned Charlotte that Daisy's condition was causing him anxiety.

Charlotte's panic was alarming.

'You must tell my sister,' she commanded shrilly. 'I can't take the responsibility of her not knowing. It isn't fair to me, Doctor O'Brien. You've no right to put me in this position.'

'It's yer sister, Miss Daisy, who's in the bad position, not yerself,' he admonished her. 'D'ye want to have Miss Fellowes in the same case? Sure, it might set her right back.'

'Have you told Olivia? I'm not going to be the only one to know.'

'You're the eldest, after Miss Fellowes, isn't that so?'

'Yes, but you must tell her, not I. She might think I was making too much of it. Is she going to die? You must tell me what to expect.'

He looked at her with an air of not knowing how to steady her. He was as much afraid of saying too little as of saying too much. He shook his head as if the jerk would bring him wisdom.

'While there's life there's hope,' he said. 'Now, you're the only one who's fit to stand shocks and do anything at all. Ye must pull yerself together, Miss Charlotte. Sure, Miss Fellowes'd never go on the way you're doing.'

'Oh, but she's different,' insisted Charlotte. 'She's used to being at the head of things. It's much worse for me.'

'Y're makin' it worse for yerself, that's the truth of it,' he said bluntly. 'I'll be back before bedtime, maybe in two or three hours' time.'

Charlotte set up a noisy weeping as soon as he had gone, but it availed her nothing: there was no one at liberty to hear it, no one in a position to take the burden from her. At last the moment had come when her responsibilities could not be shifted on to anyone else. She buried her head in one of the sofa cushions and abandoned herself to terror and despair.

It was plain that Doctor O'Brien thought Daisy unlikely to recover. Charlotte's mind went ahead and she envisaged life at Fellowescourt; alone with Katharine she would go mad. The comfortable silence that she and Daisy had been used to share over so many years could never be recovered without her companionship: its emptiness would shriek at her.

And the funeral! There was not a soul to arrange it but herself. The thought of it appalled her; she had not the slightest idea how to set about it. She had made none of the arrangements for Miss Flynn's funeral, for that had been organised and paid for by Mrs Mauleverer, devoted landlady to her and her mother for over thirty years. And a very grand funeral it had been: Miss Flynn would have been in a great flutter had she been there to see it. Ladies from all over the county had sent the most wonderful flowers and some had even gone to the church; the names on the cards had read like a page from Debrett. Charlotte and Daisy had agreed in secret that it had all been very wasteful, especially when Katharine had asked them for money to buy a wreath, but they had not dared to say so, since Miss Flynn had died in the house, and to make a fuss would have been bad form.

Now, it seemed that Daisy was going to die; her funeral, Charlotte knew, would have neither the number of mourners nor the mountains of exquisite flowers that had marked Miss Flynn's; it would create much less stir and when she was gone hardly anyone would miss her. This was not right, for Miss Flynn had been an insignificant little person and Daisy was a gentleman's daughter; it was not right, but it was nevertheless true.

Something of the barrenness of her own life and Daisy's loomed out of the prevailing darkness. They were unloved by anybody but each other and even that love was a convenient, hand-in-glove sort of affair with no spark of sacrifice or self-denial in it; it was merely a companionship of like with like, completely passive; like a couple of termite mounds in the desert they had stayed close to one another because that was how things had fallen out.

Now she was to be left alone. Daisy was deserting her. It wasn't fair! In a crescendo of self-pity she gulped and sobbed into the cushion. It wasn't fair; she was to be left more alone than anybody else in the world. Nobody but Daisy understood her; the rest all blamed her for things that were not her fault, such as her dislike of exertion. And now they were all going to expect too much of her, making no allowances for her natural disinclination to do things and the resulting ignorance about how anything was done. They would expect her to do everything and then blame her for not doing it all properly. It was too much and she could not face it.

She raised her head speculatively, half-prepared to see Katharine's baleful eye fixed upon her in condemnation. But Katharine was still incarcerated in her bedroom and there was no one to observe Charlotte or to care what she did. She wiped her eyes, blew her nose and then, warily, leant across to pick up her handbag from the floor.

What a mercy that she had not answered the letter! She and Daisy had laughed about it so much. The impertinence! They had exclaimed, the presumption! Who did he think he was, anyway? Charlotte had been awaiting Daisy's recovery to concoct with her a suitably crushing reply.

She found it difficult, so suffused were her eyes from weeping, to put her hand on the letter amongst the papers in her bag. But after a momentary panic during which she felt sure that it was not there but had fallen into the hands of Katharine, she lit upon it.

The letter was ill-written upon inexpensive lined paper of an exaggerated blue; the hand was inexperienced though not illiterate.

7th January   10, Rockbrook Terrace,
                                              Kilburn,
                                              London, N.W.6

Dear Old Girl,

Have been thinking of you off and on a good deal & felt better late than never so don't be surprised hearing. Remember the fun we had at Lady W's, especially the races at the Park. Laugh! I thought I'd never stop, that day I was wearing your apron and the old lady caught us. My, was she angry!

Bilko and I get together sometimes at the local but its no fun now. Ireland was just my cup of tea but now even that seems to be going bad on us. You'd almost think we wasn't nice to know the way foreigners seem to dislike us. Haven't seen Ricky since that day on Kingstown Pier. Haven't run across any of the old crowd over here either.

Soon as I get my demob which won't be long now because of my foot I'm going to Australia, apple-farming with old Wilf. He's got himself engaged to a real hot-stuff little piece from Worthing. Which set me thinking. Like to take the plunge and get spliced up with yours truly? You were a good sort always. Me and Wilf and you and Doris could knock a good time out of the trip out and make a go of it out there all of us together. Plenty of gee-gees to make our fortunes for us there, I'm told.

Don't keep me too long for an answer. Tell Dais she can pay us a visit one day. Mum says if you like to come and take a look at her and Dad before you say yes or no that will be all right. I say yes it will put you right off. Ha. Ha. We could get married over here if you'd rather. Well, here's hoping!

Yours ever

Pongo

P.S. How is your sister 'the Saint' ?

Charlotte sat thinking for a little. Marriage to Pongo Bates would be trying beyond belief; he was that anathema of all ambitious mothers, the ranker-officer; his vocabulary was composed largely of slang and clichés, he never called anything by its name if it was possible to describe it otherwise and he had an abiding affection for pubs, races, 'good sorts' and music halls. He had good looks of an inferior kind; his eyes were dark but a little too prominent and with a bloodshot tinge; his complexion a little too florid, his mouth just too curved, with a tendency towards rabbit teeth. He was always wiser than anyone else on how things should be done, food ordered or people addressed. He was the kind of man who prides himself on teaching people a lesson, putting waiters in their place and never taking an insult lying down. In spite of his swagger he did not look at home in uniform and cultivated slickness in details of dress and personal cleanliness.

Pongo had been wounded in the foot in France and had arrived at Lady Willoughby's convalescent home in Dublin towards the end of the war. His attachment to Charlotte dated from his discovery that her sister was Lady Willoughby's daughter-in-law, for he was rapturously devoted to the aristocracy and landed gentry by whom he desired, more than anything in the world, to be accepted. It had occurred to him that marriage with Charlotte might effect his entrée to the world of country house-parties and Hunt Balls, but his prospects were at that time too uncertain for marriage; now that he was about to emigrate he thought it worth trying.

Charlotte rather liked the thought of going to Australia. So elementary had been her education that she imagined it to be a land something like India, where it was always hot and swarms of native servants existed only to do the bidding of their masters and mistresses; she envisaged the lovely idle life that she would lead, going to race meetings, playing cards, dancing and dining out. The only drawback to it would be Pongo Bates, but with any luck his apple-growing would keep him very occupied.

She fetched writing paper and began her reply: she would say nothing definite in this letter.

Dear Pongo,
Fancy hearing from you after all these months. Daisy and me were talking about you only a few days ago, remembering old times at Lady Willoughby's. It was nice of you to suggest our getting married but you mustn't mind if I dont make up my mind one way or the other just now as we are in trouble as Daisy is very bad, the doctor says it is pneumonia and he thinks she wont pull through. I'll write again in a few days. I can't seem to think just now.
All the best,
Charlie
P.S. Our sister's nickname is 'the Pope', not 'the Saint'. She's ill too.

She addressed the envelope, sealed it, stuck the stamp on crookedly and thumped the letter with her fist to make sure that everything was tightly gummed. Then, with an uncertain look round the hall she walked out, leaving the door ajar, and posted the letter at the post office. She was able to slip into the house again without her little expedition having been noticed by anyone other than Peter

Cavanagh who saluted her with unsteady dignity.

When Doctor O'Brien called that evening, Charlotte forced herself to go with him into Daisy's room. She was terrified of the infection and kept well away from the bed, but she could see at once that her sister was very ill indeed. Doctor O'Brien waited till they were in the passage to shake his head at her. Charlotte had tried not to breathe while in the sick room and was now filling her lungs. He looked at her with curiosity.

'Well, I'll be damned,' he muttered. Aloud, he added mercilessly, 'How is it ye're not nursing Miss Daisy yerself, Miss Charlotte?'

'Well. . .' faltered Charlotte, 'somebody's got to keep well.'

'Sure, poor old Nanny is dead on her feet; you ought to take a turn wit' the nursing, so y'ought, and give her a night's sleep.'

Charlotte appeared not to have heard him. 'Is she worse?' she asked. 'She is.'

'Then you must tell my sisters.'

'An' what if Miss Fellowes goes gettin' up and has a relapse herself?'

She resented his unrelenting stare that bored into her, seeking to uncover her motives and expose her selfishness.

'She won't have a relapse. She wouldn't let herself have one. She won't, I promise you,' said Charlotte quickly. 'If anything . . . happened and she hadn't been told, I can't think what she'd say. She'd be mad, really. . .'

'Hm. She would indeed.' He experienced a certain sympathy with Charlotte. 'Very well, I'll tell her, so. And Miss Olivia. And let you sit down and write a note to Mrs Willoughby. I'll be passing the cottage in the morning and I'll drop it in for ye. Maybe the Captain would be some help to ye.'

He moved towards the door of Katharine's room, his shadow grotesquely elongated by the light from the oil lamp on the table.

'Thank you,' said Charlotte graciously. 'I'll be in the drawing-room.' She walked quickly away so that there should be no question of her being drawn into Katharine's room.

'I suppose that's as far out of range as ye can get!' murmured the doctor indistinctly from the doorway as he knocked.

Charlotte took no notice of this comment, pretending to herself that she did not understand it. She looked resentfully at the neglected fire in the drawing-room, shuddered and sat down on the sofa with her writing things. She wrote Harriet a piteous story of their sufferings and insisted that she and Eustace come over every day to help her until matters should improve. It was all too much for her, she said, and everything was being left for her to do so that she was quite ill herself with worry and overwork. Of course they could not sleep at Fellowescourt, that would be too difficult to arrange, but they could spend the day there during this crisis; it was the least they could do. Harriet, she thought, could help to nurse Daisy; the doctor said that Nanny was dead on her feet and it would not do for her to get ill herself at this time. She had no time for nursing, but would expect to see Harriet and Eustace the minute they could come. She sealed the letter and stared blankly into the cinders.

The recitation of her woes stirred her to feel deeply sorry for herself. Her situation was really dreadful, and instead of trying to help her that horrid man, Doctor O'Brien, kept making sarcastic remarks that were most unkind. Tears welled up in Charlotte's eyes, brimmed and rolled down her cheeks in a steady stream.

It was thus that Doctor O'Brien found her on his way out. He looked at her without surprise and made no effort to sympathise with her.

'Miss Fellowes has promised me she'll stay in her bed till tomorrow, anyway,' he announced. 'Miss Olivia . . . that is, Mrs Heathcote . . . can leave her room tomorrow if ye can get this room warm for her. Ye'll be sittin' up with Miss Daisy yerself tonight: I've sent Nanny to bed.'

Charlotte sat upright and swelled with indignation. She mopped her eyes and cheeks hastily.

'I must get some sleep,' she gulped. 'Look at the state I'm in. I can't possibly sit up all night.'

'Was it a nurse ye called yerself in the war?' he asked scathingly.

'What kind of a nurse were y'at all, eh ? So on in, now, to yer sister. My God, what kind of a family is this at all? I have almost to tie Miss Fellowes down in her bed to stop her going to Miss Daisy, and I have to drive you to her at the point of the bayonet! Go on, now, Miss Charlotte, there's a good girl.' He put a hand under her elbow and helped her up, pushing her gently in front of him to the door.

Charlotte was protesting desperately, 'I can't, oh I can't. What'll I do if she . . . gets very bad. I shan't know what to do. Oh, I can't. . .' and she backed against the hand that was driving her forwards, her shoulders heaving as she sobbed.

Doctor O'Brien gripped her shoulders and shook her till her teeth rattled.

'Ye'll do what any other human being'd do for yer own sister. Ye'll send the gerrl for the Reverend Weldon and for me at the same time, and you'll stay with her till she's past the need of ye.' They had reached the door of Daisy's room. He opened it, shoved her inside, and made off quickly.

Neither Katharine nor Olivia was allowed to attend Daisy's funeral. Doctor O'Brien's statement that far more people were killed at funerals than were ever buried at them prevented any argument.

Charlotte succeeded in bringing herself to a condition of near collapse, but Eustace and Harriet insisted on her going with them. Her resentment at being pushed into actions that she considered over-demanding mounted hourly. No one guessed how she suffered, she was misunderstood, everyone was so unkind. She could stand it no longer.

She was genuinely upset by Daisy's death; they had been companions for so many years, allied against the claims of duty and necessity, that without her support she found it difficult to avoid the demands of her convalescent sisters. The wretchedness of her lot was constantly being borne in upon her. She wept often. On the day after Daisy's death she shut herself into her cold bedroom and wrote a letter to Pongo Bates, accepting his proposal. She was coming to England at once, she said, and would be glad to accept the invitation of his mother to stay with the family. She would prefer the wedding to be in London and would not return to Ireland before they sailed for Australia as her sister 'the Pope' was very difficult. She then wrote a note to leave for 'the Pope'.

She said nothing of her plans to anyone. Eustace and Harriet drove her back to Fellowescourt after the funeral. Depression settled upon the household as they set off again for their cottage, Charlotte shut herself into her bedroom again. No one disturbed her: they all thought she wished to be alone in her grief. They did not even fetch her for tea.

She packed her few valuables breathlessly; she crossed into Daisy's room and gathered up her few little bits of jewellery; she knew that Daisy would have liked her to have them. Flitting back to her own room, she put her best clothes into a suitcase, dressed herself for the journey and counted out her little store of money. It was enough to get her to London: after that, Pongo would support her.

While the others were at tea in the drawing-room, the curtains closed against the encroaching menace of the darkness, she slipped out of the door, down the flagged path, and stood outside the little iron gate in momentary hesitation. She was going to stop the first trap going out of the village and offer money to the driver if he would take her to Inish. From there she must hire a car to Cork; it would cost the earth but the train had gone and she was desperate.

She let two carts go by; farm carts were too uncomfortable for her. At last she heard the lighter trot of a pony and hailed the driver in the dusk. The pony shied but the man brought it to a halt. He was Michael Maguire, the widower with six small children, who with his sister Brigid was so devoted to Harriet and Eustace.

'I'll take ye, of course, Miss,' he replied when she begged him to drive her to Inish. 'Sure, it'd be a pleasure.' Charlotte did not know who he was but was gratified that he should be so anxious to help her. She pointed to her bag which he picked up and placed on the seat beside her.

'Brigid and meself was terrible sorry to hear of your trouble, Miss

Fellowes,' he said. 'I'd be grateful if ye'd tell Mrs Willoughby we was thinkin' of her.' His voice was rich and strong; he was not looking at her but she was aware of his sincerity as he spoke.

'Thank you,' she said. 'I'll tell Mrs Willoughby.' She knew quite well that she never would do so, but felt it impossible to explain the reason. Besides, this was what she considered a white lie and of even less importance because it was told to a peasant. It did not matter if you were a little untruthful with servants and children; in fact, it was very often necessary to deceive them so that they should not pry into things that did not concern them.

Maguire hesitated for several seconds before he spoke again but Charlotte knew that there was more to come; his voice was feeling for expression; she could hear it grating in his throat.

'Perhaps while ye're at it you'd tell Mrs Willoughby we're in a bit o' throuble ourselves, Miss, if ye wouldn't mind,' he managed to say. Speaking of his troubles seemed to agitate him and he was breathing heavily.

'Oh,' said Charlotte, not at all pleased, 'what's happened?'

'Well, Miss,' said Maguire, pushing his hat further back on his head as his hand ran over his hair, 'we had a long 'spell o' bad luck after me wife died, God rest her soul, and I had to mortgage the farm to Pether Cavanagh below in the public there. Well, what with one thing an' another, an' illness and a couple o' bad harvests, we're in a poor way for money and can't seem to be able to keep our heads above wather at all. And he tells me now he wants to foreclose on the farm.' His broad shoulders shook as he brandished his clenched fist at the starlit sky. 'If ever I git the chance o' gettin' even with that little dirrty rat, may the Lord help him!'

Charlotte disliked this conversation; she had an uncomfortable feeling that the man was trying to ask her for a loan of money and decided that it would be fatal to show him any sympathy.

'Oh,' she said in a tone of cool surprise, 'and what do you expect Mrs Willoughby to do for you?' She stared at his outline in the darkness with antipathy, sitting very straight up.

'Well, Miss,' said Maguire huskily, 'I wondhered if Mrs Willoughby, or the Captain'd ever . . . say a word for me to Pether Cavanagh the way he'd think again and maybe not treat me so harshly. We'd be all right if he'd give me a bit o' time.' He spoke with diffidence as if he were asking a tremendous favour. 'They've always been that good to us, d'ye see, Miss. Ye'd almost think, well to tell ye the truth I do think they take a kind of an interest in us. Ah, it was great news when the Captain come home from the war, now wasn't it, Miss?'

'Yes,' said Charlote stiffly, pondering his request. 'You'd better go and see Mrs Willoughby yourself,' she advised. 'I shan't be seeing her for some time; I'm going away.'

He was horrified by his own presumptuousness.

'Oh, I'm terrible sorry, Miss, sure I ought to ha' thought o' that meself and not be bothering ye with me throubles. Sure ye have plenty o' yer own.' He continued to apologise for some minutes. Then, as they reached the approaches to Inish he asked her with great concern, 'Ye're not thinkin' there's a thrain to Cork tonight, Miss, are ye?'

'No,' answered Charlotte guardedly.

'Ye'll be stayin' the night here, so.'

Charlotte made no reply. He cleared his throat to offset the rebuff.

'Where'll I dhrop ye, Miss?' he asked tentatively.

'Somewhere where I can hire a car,' said Charlotte grandly. She pushed ten shillings into his unwilling hand, ignoring his protests that he would take nothing for his trouble, and waved him away.

She had no regrets. She wondered if 'the Pope' had found her note and would obey her instructions not to search for her. She even felt as if Daisy's loss had been left behind with all the difficulties and burdens from which she would now be free for ever. For she was quite determined that she was never coming back. In due course she would write to Katharine with instructions about forwarding her income from the Trust Fund.

CHAPTER THIRTEEN

For nearly two years Katharine, acting for Harriet and Olivia as well as for herself, had implored Mr Blair to draw up an agreement allowing a ninety-nine years' lease of the little field to Peter Cavanagh in exchange for the repair and decoration of the house. In the end he had come down to Glenmacool to assess for himself the urgency of the need, pretending that he had really come to interview a client in Inish so that Miss Fellowes should not feel obliged to offer him a fee and his travelling expenses. The extent of the dilapidations had shocked him deeply, but he remained immovable; there could be no dealings with a slippery scoundrel like Cavanagh.

Katharine was very put out. She wrote a scathing letter to poor Mr Blair upbraiding him for his obstinacy and asking him what alternative means of having the house repaired could be in his mind. An astute lawyer, she wrote, should be able to foresee whatever trickery might be in the mind of even a scoundrel and prevent it by the wording of his agreement; that was what lawyers were for. However, if he would not do what she and her sisters desired, there was only one course open to them. They must seek advice elsewhere.

Poor Mr Blair wrote back in a dreadful state, but he did not give in. He besought the ladies to be guided by him, to believe that he knew best, and if they must act through another firm, to make sure that it was a reputable one. He could not himself advise them to take advantage of Cavanagh's offer under any circumstances: it was a hare-brained scheme put forward by a swindler. But if they wished to accept it, he could not prevent them. The whole thing made him very uneasy indeed.

There were two firms of solicitors in Inish. One was a Protestant firm called Darling and Love, old-established, honest and inefficient, run by a clerk since the retirement of the decrepit Mr Darling, last survivor of the partnership. The other was a Roman Catholic firm, named Herlihy, Keogh and MacSwiney, which had a reputation for shrewdness in their business and a particularly sound grasp of the intricacies of land tenure. Katharine could not make up her mind which to employ. Her natural inclination was to go to Darling and Love, but she feared that the clerk in charge might not be able to outwit Cavanagh. She did not like dealings with underlings. On the other hand, if she went to Herlihy, Keogh and MacSwiney, could she trust them absolutely? None of the three partners had a very high local reputation. Herlihy was an inebriate, Keogh a poacher in his spare time and MacSwiney supported a seditious newspaper.

In the end, however, she had decided that they would conduct her business better than Darling and Love. She whirled into Inish on her bicycle without waiting to enquire or consider, and within an hour of making up her mind had given her instructions to Mr MacSwiney junior, a shock-headed young man with a very knowing habit of talking to her with one eye shut. Had she known that young Mr MacSwiney owed a considerable sum of money to Peter Cavanagh which he had no prospect of repaying, she might have taken her business elsewhere.

She had made it clear to young Mr MacSwiney that the agreement must preclude the erection of any house, shop or place of entertainment on the little field that skirted Fellowescourt. Mr MacSwiney understood perfectly; he would prepare a lease and submit it to her for approval very quickly. With great deference he showed her out, wiping his clammy fist on the seat of his trousers in case she might wish to shake him by the hand. She spared him this ordeal, however, and he watched her mount her bicycle and ride off with his eye still closed in artful appreciation of the good fortune that had come to him.

Peter Cavanagh's men arrived in the spring of 1921 with sand, cement, paint, ladders, slates, putty, scaffolding and all the impedimenta of a building yard, which they laid out on the grass, the flagged path, the window-sills, flower-beds and steps, alongside the hedge and up against the house. The mess was universal.

As soon as the men had set to work, the village had become the centre of a battle between the Black and Tans and the Sinn Feiners, and the workmen had melted away to take up arms against the foreigners, as they considered the Black and Tans to be. Thereafter, their labours at Fellowescourt had been spasmodic until the signing of the Treaty with Britain in 1922 when they had returned, the fighting over, to a leisurely resumption of work.

Now it was 1923 and there were still ladders up against the house, mounds of sand and empty paint-pots lying about in the garden, and unutterable disorder throughout. Eustace had been heard to comment drily that a shell-hole in France was tidiness itself by comparison.

Peter Cavanagh was in the habit of pottering in to inspect progress, his bowler hat pushed back on his head as he gazed upwards at his workmen, or downwards at the chaos they had created. He watched open-mouthed, his dim blue eyes watering copiously. He had come to look a very old man.

Katharine raged and fumed at the delay in completing the work. But what, he asked her, could he do if his workmen chose to down tools and join the Sinn Feiners for a spell? Was it his fault if paint that had been on order for months did not arrive because the railway bridge had been blown up?

'I wish to goodness,' mumbled Nanny toothlessly to Susan every holidays, 'them fellas'd clear out wit' all that old mess. Sure, they have Miss Kat'rine frettin' like a kittle on the boil.'

By the month of April there had still been little progress, for as soon as the Treaty had been signed with England, the Sinn Fein party had split and former comrades were now fighting a civil war exceeding in bitterness even the recent war against the British.

So far, the workmen had not actually left, but there was a tendency for unknown callers to visit the men at their work and fetch them off their ladders for secret conversations in the hedges. The fighting was sweeping the immediate countryside and Inish was reported to be in the hands of the Irregulars, the troops opposing acceptance of the Treaty.

Katharine stood at her bedroom window surveying the desolation without and observing Peter Cavanagh as he directed his men. She suspected him of being a Republican, or Irregular, but he was at great pains to persuade her that he was a man of peace, a mere spectator watching with Olympian calm the futile struggles of lesser men. The more he emphasised his aloofness, the more sure Katharine felt that he was an active participant in the contest, probably engaged in gathering intelligence. She did not like to think of Fellowescourt as a spy centre, but that was what she now believed it to be. And to worry her even more, Nanny had come to her with the rumour that young Barry O'Brien, having survived the war against the British, had now joined the Irregulars and was the officer in charge of the defence of the Railway Hotel at Inish, which had changed hands several times but was currently held by his troops.

Katharine, a loyal supporter of the British by descent, tradition and inclination, was deeply shocked to think that this friend of Susan's, who had so often been to the house, was an enemy, a viper in their midst. She wondered what poison he had contrived to drop into Susan's ear. She had not known before that he had fought against the British; she suspected that Nanny had known for a long time but preferred not to tell her. That he should now be a Republican struck her as even worse: he might as well declare himself an anarchist right away.

Like most of the Anglo-Irish, Katharine had watched the British leave with a sinking heart. To her, British rule meant justice, stability and order, established on firm foundations; once it was removed, anything might happen. But since it had gone, she believed that the only hope of creating a new stability lay in supporting the Free State government brought into being by the Treaty. The Republicans were now working for the overthrow of the new Free State, which was too moderate for them.

She heard a cart coming slowly over the rise, as if it carried a load too heavy for the horse. As it came over the top, she saw that it was loaded with breeze blocks. It stopped in the middle of the road and the driver shouted to the painters for directions. Then Peter Cavanagh hurried forward unsteadily and waved the man in at the gate of the little field.

Half the field was ploughed, ready for potatoes, so Peter Cavanagh had told her; the half of it nearest the road was under rough grass and weeds as it had always been. The driver of the cart dumped his load in a corner, near the hedge. He threw the reins on to the horse's back and, looking up at Fellowescourt, gave a low whistle. Katharine heard the painter's blow-lamp make a continuous noise instead of the broken sound it had made while it was being worked up and down the woodwork. The driver jerked his head quickly and turned his back while the painter climbed down the ladder to join them. After a quick look up and down the road they began to talk. Peter Cavanagh wandered in an aimless kind of way to the gate of the field, gazed up at the face of Fellowescourt as if he were appraising the quality of the work done by his men, and seeing no one at the windows, for Katharine was concealed by the curtain, turned with surprising agility to join the two men in their talk.

Very soon they drifted away, the carter to his horse, Peter Cavanagh to his Select Bar and the painter to the flagged path outside Fellowescourt where he prepared to abandon work for the day. The carter did not drive off; he placed himself, still on his cart, where he could watch the Inish road from over the hedge, and there he waited.

Katharine felt sure that the fighting must be coming nearer. She also felt, a little grimly, that she had caught Peter Cavanagh at last; for all his apparent innocence, he was deep in the game.

She hurried downstairs to survey her storeroom. If there was going to be fighting in the village it was important to keep a reserve of food in the house. She put on her hat and coat and went to Quinn's Universal Stores to order, for immediate delivery, flour, sugar, biscuits, tea, tins of milk and a piece of boiling bacon. Mrs Quinn sent Malachy flying up the hill after her with the goods in a wheel-barrow.

This curious little procession encountered another which was coming into the village from the direction of Inish. It was formed of two Ford cars full of green-uniformed men, followed by several lorries loaded with troops. They moved at speed, raising tremendous clouds of white dust which coated the hair and faces of the men, giving them a thick and stupid air. Outside the gate of Fellowescourt the first car stopped with a screech of brakes and churning of dust. The only inhabitants to be seen were Katharine and Malachy on the steps of the house, watching fascinated, yet ready to bolt for shelter if necessary.

An officer stepped out of the car and walked up to Katharine, covered by the revolvers of his fellow-officers in the cars.

'Do you live here?' he asked. His voice was hoarse with embarrassment.

'Yes?' said Katharine, the query in her tone asking him his business.

'Is there anny troops in this house?' His eyes darted continually from danger-point to danger-point which might conceal an enemy.

'No.' Katharine knew quite well what was coming. Her only satisfaction was that these soldiers were Regulars, not Republicans.

The officer jerked his head to summon the rest from the car. They crowded up to the door, hot, dusty and dangerous, their weapons ready to go off at a touch.

'I'm afraid we'll have to take over this house,' said one who seemed more responsible than the first. He raised his hand to stave off Katharine's objections. 'I'm very sorry, Ma'am. We'll give you as little trouble as we can but it's bound to be a bit awkward. You give the house the once-over,' he ordered one of his juniors who set off immediately to make sure that they were not being led into a trap.

'Do you think you'll be here for long?' said Katharine. 'I hope,' she added, 'that you've got your own stores with you and aren't expecting me to cook for you.'

He preferred to ignore parts of this speech. 'How long'll we be here?' he asked rhetorically. 'Sure, till we go, Ma'am, and now you know as much as meself. How many people is there living in this house?' He had iron-grey curly hair, a long red face and cold, shifty green eyes.

'Myself and my niece,' snapped Katharine who had taken a dislike to the man, 'and two servants, one of them very elderly. I hope you will see that your men don't frighten them.'

'Tch tch! Some o' them gerrls is very nervous!' he said with a look of surprise. He signalled to the waiting troops that it was safe for them to enter.

The troops settled into the drawing-room and the attics. They rolled up the carpet, kept up a roaring fire and brewed tea by the gallon in the drawing-room, strewing the floor with cigarette ends. They slept on the floor in the attics, spreading old mattresses on the boards, adapting what they found up there to make themselves comfortable in the way of all soldiers. Their serious cooking was done in the kitchen in co-operation with Julia who regarded the whole affair as a sort of picnic. Squeals of kitchen laughter and male guffaws echoed continually through the house, offending Katharine's sense of propriety so that she used to send Nanny to act as duenna.

Katharine was surprised to see that load after load of building materials were being dumped in the corner of the little field next door. At first she had imagined that these were for the repair of Fellowescourt, but soon there was too much there to be used for anything less than a house. She could not understand it. Cavanagh could not build there, it was one of the terms of the lease that he should not use the land for building. Nevertheless, she felt uneasy. For the first time she wondered if she had been foolish to dispense with the services of Mr Blair. Supposing she had been tricked: how could she ever look Mr Blair in the face again? She determined to discover, by asking Peter Cavanagh himself, what he intended to erect in the field. They were on speaking terms now, after many years of communicating only through a third person: it had been too difficult to maintain this arrangement while the house was being repaired by Cavanagh's men.

Katharine tried to keep Susan with her in the study, out of the way of the soldiers.

'I don't think you ought to smile at them when you meet them in the house,' she said anxiously. 'They will only get familiar. And soldiers are very quick to take advantage, especially in a household of women.'

'But they all smile and say good morning to me: so what am I to do?' asked Susan, smiling as if she thought Katharine ridiculous.

'I know what I'm talking about,' snapped Katharine. 'I've had a good deal more experience of the world than you have. Keep them at a distance, that's all I ask.'

Susan continued to smile in a maddening way. Katharine and she were not on good terms; to protect herself from questions and advice she assumed an air of complete superficiality that baffled Katharine. She had developed a capacity to sit through lecturing, instruction and accusation for any length of time without taking in a word of what was being said. If Katharine tried to interest her in the things that were close to her own heart, Susan's face assumed an expression of sullen resistance. Her complete detachment in matters of faith, morals and the things of the spirit was a source of grief to Katharine who would have loved to be consulted, to assist, suggest and reinforce, and who had to make her own opportunities instead of being offered them. She felt that she knew Susan no better than she knew the cat, being aware of all her faults, yet unable to perceive her virtues because she was not allowed to know of them. So aloof was Susan with her that Katharine did not know what she thought, what she liked to do, how she felt on any matter, or even what she hoped to do when she left school; all she had said, to Katharine's great disappointment, was that she would not be a missionary, but Katharine refused to believe that she could be quite sure of her intention and kept trying to persuade her to change her mind. This only intensified Susan's resistance to every approach.

Susan was nearly seventeen and would soon be leaving school. Her fine mouse-coloured hair was tied in a bow at the back of her neck and fell in a shining bunch below for a few inches. Her face had grown so that her eyes looked less enormous than when she had been small. She was of medium height, slim, and held herself well. She had a great look of Katharine, except when she smiled, for then her expression had a warmth not apparent in her aunt. She had the same straight, practical nose, cleft chin and thick, rounded eyebrows, but her mouth was mobile, whereas Katharine's was set, and she showed her feelings more readily. She lit up more prettily than Katharine and looked sad with more pathos. Hers was a more touching face, altogether softer, less certain and more receptive.

Katharine's exasperation drove her to ask Susan the question she had been wording and rewording for days.

'I hear that Barry O'Brien's joined the I.R.A. Is that true?' She flung the words at her, to take her by surprise. Her voice was loud and clear.

Susan glared at her in a horrified way and hissed furiously in a half-whisper, 'Don't say that now, here, Aunt Katharine, the soldiers'll hear you. D'you want to have his whole family shot?' She was breathing quickly in sharp little angry gasps. 'You must be careful what you say,' she added indignantly.

Katharine saw how unwisely she had spoken but she resented the rebuke.

'Ah, so it's true!' she said, with a gleam of triumph in her eye.

'I didn't say so.'

'You didn't deny it.'

'Supposing he has, what's it got to do with us?'

Katharine shrugged distastefully. 'I always thought they were quiet, decent sort of people, but it seems I was wrong. You must keep away from them, Susan.'

'Why?'

'Because decent people don't belong to . . . that movement.'

'They're the nicest people, all of them,' protested Susan. 'I'm not going to keep away from them just because of . . . what you say.' Her chin jutted contentiously, but she drew a deep breath, appalled by her own daring.

The violence with which Susan was defending the O'Brien family made Katharine instantly suspicious: it must be the produce of deep emotion. Susan must be in love with Barry! She must find out the truth. Ignoring the flagrant rebellion of Susan's words, she patted the chair beside her own invitingly and said gently, 'Sit down, Susan. I want to talk to you.'

Susan, surprised into acquiescence by this quiet approach, sat down. Katharine peered into her face with compassionate concern. Choosing her words with difficulty, she laid her hand upon Susan's.

'Tell me, child,' she began. 'How do you feel about Barry?'

'What do you mean?' said Susan, mystified.

'I mean . . . are you in love with him?'

The clatter of Susan's laughter shocked her. 'Good heavens, no!' she exclaimed. 'He's going to be a priest!'

'Oh!' Katharine's relief was offset by her indignation. She felt furious that Barry, knowing Susan, should not be head over heels in love with her; it was another shortcoming revealed. She murmured in a shocked voice, 'A priest!' as if he were a serpent turned holy. 'A priest, with those politics? Tch tch tch!'

'You don't know anything about his politics,' countered Susan unpleasantly. 'You only know the rumour.'

'I know what to believe,' said Katharine crushingly. She could not understand Susan's affection for the O'Brien family; if she were not in love with Barry, nothing could explain it. Once more, Susan's face assumed the look of blank resentment that meant she would reveal nothing.

The heavy thump of a fist on the door made them both jump. There had been no preliminary footsteps. Katharine moved quickly to open the door. A soldier stood there.

'There's a lady wants to see ye, Miss. She says she can't get to her own house because there's some kind of an obsthruction in the way.' He scratched his head apologetically.

Katharine put her head out of the doorway. Dithering on the threshold was Esmé Weldon, being kept at bay by an embarrassed soldier. Beside her, gazing up at the unfinished work left by his labourers and painters, was Peter Cavanagh. He raised his hand to the brim of his hat in salute.

Esmé shrieked across him, 'My dear Miss Fellowes, you must forgive me for intruding, but this kind man brought me in as there is shooting further along the road and I simply cannot get home. So here I am, come to beg refuge from you!' She laughed, as if it showed great feminine weakness to dislike passing an ambush.

'Come in, Miss Weldon,' said Katharine, going into the hall. 'Will you let the lady pass, please!' she commanded the soldier. He stood aside at once and Esmé fluttered past him.

There was great activity in the drawing-room; men came in and out and some of them went to the upstairs rooms from which there was a better view of the road. Stores and equipment were checked, orders issued, uniform hastily put on, weapons re loaded, ammunition issued.

Esmé looked quickly through the open door and gasped, 'Well, I do feel I've come to a safe place!'

Her face had the cement-coloured pallor and her body the unstable look of a fractured stalk, characteristic of the confirmed neurotic. She was tall and painfully thin, given to curious contortions of the face and limbs when she knew that she was being observed. Ceaseless worry about her condition had long ago made her hair thin and grey. She was not, as Katharine had imagined, dressed in black, but in a dark, unbecoming and hideous brown which accentuated the greenish pallor of her skin.

Katharine led her to the study and begged to be excused for a moment while she spoke to Peter Cavanagh. She called him back just as he was about to bolt from the little iron gate. With a quick glance up and down the road, he sidled back again to the steps.

'Were ye wantin' me, Miss? 'Tis a kind of an awkward moment, if ye'll forgive me sayin' so, Miss, for I doubt I'll be able to cross the road in a minyit, thim Irregulars is closin' in so fast, God help us!' Piously, he raised his eyes to Heaven.

'I shan't keep you a moment. I only want to know what all those building materials in the little field next door are for?'

He looked past her into the back hall with innocent, unseeing eyes. 'Arrah, Miss, thim's only for the little garage I'm puttin' up there. Sure, we need some kind of a garage in Glenmacool, there isn't a pethrol pump this side of Inish, or anny kind of a place where they'd mend a puncture for ye. It'll be a great benefit to the community, Miss. Sure, I always was one to be doin' good to me neighbours! If I'd thought o' meself a bit more I'd be a rich man this long while.'

'A garage!' shrieked Katharine at him. 'A garage! But you can't do that: it says in the lease that you can't.'

He passed the back of his hand over his long upper lip.

'I t'ink ye'll find ye're mistaken, Miss,' he said humbly. 'Annyway, me lawyer tells me there's nothing against it, so he does. If it was a dwellin' house, or a shop maybe it'd be different, Miss, but a little garage is all right. Ye'll forgive me, Miss, if I run for it now.' He turned and legged it for the gate with astonishing speed, shot his head out like a lizard to see what was happening along the road and slipped out quickly.

Katharine stood raging at the door, imagining the full horror of a shoddy cement garage next door to Fellowescourt. She saw the pools of oil, the piles of moribund tyres, rusting metal, spare parts and disintegrating motor-cars, the general chaos of a slipshod establishment. There would be ceaseless noise and disturbance, coming and going, and unattractive smells. Young Mr MacSwiney had let her down; he had not drawn up the lease properly, and Peter Cavanagh had got what he wanted. And what, oh what could she ever say to prevent Mr Blair's warranted 'I told you so!'? She felt so angry that she shook her fist at the now invisible Cavanagh, provoking the soldier at her elbow to make the sympathetic comment 'I'd say that ould fella'd be a slippery customer, right enough!'

She did not answer but with a venomous look at him turned quickly and shut herself into the study with Susan and Esmé.

She and Esmé were not strangers. After Daisy's death and Charlotte's disappearance, which Katharine had found more difficult to explain than to endure, Mrs Weldon had called at Fellowescourt with Esmé to offer her sympathy and understanding. She had been so sincere and so kind that Katharine had been compelled to like and admire her, against her will. But Esmé was a different matter; Katharine could only observe and despise, marvel at and detest her. In due course she had gone with Harriet to pay a state call upon the rectory ladies, having chosen a day on which she knew that Lawrence would be absent. The occasion had been painful, but she had had the satisfaction of seeing that she had been right to break off her engagement. Esmé would have driven her either out of her mind or out of the house in no time.

Now she had Esmé on her hands for an indefinite period. The fighting might go on for hours, days or weeks. There was a certain satisfaction in the knowledge that Esmé could appeal to no one if she thought her treatment unsympathetic; she was completely in Katharine's power.

Esmé's excitement had died down. She was sitting in a large chair before the empty fireplace, complaining of the chill of the room.

'We always,' she stated to Katharine, having just said the same thing to Susan, 'keep a fire going well into May. It makes me quite ill to be cold.'

'Sit in the window, in the sun,' suggested Katharine coolly. The sun was indeed flooding through the window on the plush tabby-coloured chair whose seat she stroked encouragingly, aware as she did so of the warm, dry-dusty smell evoked by the warmth.

Esmé drew her clothes tightly around her as she moved to the window. 'There's no draught, I hope?' she said anxiously. 'If there is, I shall have a stiff neck in two minutes.'

Katharine latched the window firmly and smiled. 'No,' she assured her, 'there won't be any draught now.'

'Shall I light the fire, Aunt Katharine?' said Susan helpfully.

'I'm sure Miss Weldon will be quite warm there in the window,' said Katharine firmly.

Miss Weldon, however, was determined to feel the cold and so well did she succeed that Katharine, for the sake of politeness, was obliged to give way and light the fire. Esmé sat as close to it as she was able without scorching her clothes, looking, indeed, wretchedly ill.

'Oh, I do hope,' she said after a few minutes, in a tone of great concern, 'that I have not caught a chill. It is dreadfully bad for me to catch a chill. In fact, the last time I got one, Mother said that another one would be the death of her if it wasn't of me! Mother is so amusing—' Her voice stopped dead as they heard the crack of rifle-fire from the other side of the house, followed by the malevolent rattle of a machine-gun.

Nobody moved or spoke until Esmé suddenly clapped her hand to her brow and shrieked, 'Oh!' in a tone of anguish.

Katharine and Susan stared at her aghast. She must, they both felt sure, have been hit by a stray bullet and be seriously injured. Yet there was no bullet-hole in door or window, and no trace of blood to be seen. Katharine darted to her, leaning over her with anxiety.

'Where are you hurt?' she asked quietly. 'Tell me where you have been hit.'

Esmé opened her eyes roundly. 'Hurt?' she cried. 'No, I'm not hurt. It's far worse than that. I haven't got my pills!' She looked at them with such despair that her dark eyes were pools of misery.

'Pills?' said Katharine shortly. 'What pills?' Her face expressed unutterable scorn.

'My six o'clock pills!' wailed Esmé. 'If I don't have them I'm absolutely finished . . . I can't tell you.' Her mouth drooped. After a moment's thought she asked hopefully, 'Or do you think the fighting will be over by six?'

'Of course not,' said Katharine brutally. 'It'll probably go on for a week.'

'Then I'm afraid that's the end of me!' said Esmé dramatically. 'Not that I'm any use to anyone, a poor sick woman like me, but all the same . . . unless someone could fetch them for me. It isn't far. Do you think one of the soldiers . . .?' Hope gleamed in her eye.

'Certainly not!' snorted Katharine contemptuously. 'They're fighting for their lives. They've no time to run messages for ailing women. It'd be murder to send them out, and anyway they wouldn't be allowed to go, so that settles it. Why don't you go yourself if it's so important?'

'Oh,' shuddered Esmé, 'I don't think you're being very kind.'

'You'll have to make up your mind to do without them for once,' said Katharine briskly. 'It'll probably do you good.'

Esmé looked at her from under her eyelids like a dog that has been punished unjustly. Rocking backwards and forwards she murmured wretchedly to herself, then regarding Katharine vengefully, 'It'll kill me,' she said, 'you'll see.'

'Just forget all about them and you'll come to no harm, I'm sure,' advised Katharine with brittle good humour. 'You'll probably find there's no need for you to take them ever again.' She turned to Susan. 'Tell Nanny that Miss Weldon will be here until the fighting stops. She'd better bring tea up now. It may be difficult to get about in the house later on, you never know. Ask her to bring up that full tin of biscuits I got the other day and a full kettle of water. She must put a big jug of milk and lots of sugar on the tray, then we shan't starve here, whatever happens.'

In the kitchen, Nanny and Julia were sipping oily black tea in the company of the soldier on duty at the back door. He had poured his tea into the saucer and was sucking it up with rhythmic noises. Every now and then he refilled it from the cup. Susan sat on the edge of the kitchen table while she delivered her message and seemed in no hurry to go. Nanny grumbled about Miss Weldon being in the house, her old voice droning cantankerously. The soldier observed them all over the rim of his saucer as he drank. The fire in the range glowed brightly through the bars. It was a very homely, comfortable scene, enormously reassuring.

Upstairs, Katharine and Esmé sat tensely, each contemplating the other with the most earnest dislike.

'I hope poor Lawrence isn't searching for me,' said Esmé suddenly. 'He takes such good care of me that I'm afraid he'll be very much alarmed if I'm not back for tea.'

'He'll guess you've gone somewhere for shelter,' said Katharine. 'Anyway, it can't be helped. We can't let him know.'

There was a pause while Esmé looked affronted. Then she began again. 'What a sweet child Susan is! She's such a favourite with my brother. He thinks it's wonderful how she's turned out, considering.'

Katharine was stung against her will. 'Oh? Considering what?' she said tartly.

'Well, her upbringing, and having no parents, poor child, and all the difficulties about her education. He really thinks a great deal of her.'

'Indeed!' Katharine was sitting up rigidly. 'But of course he hardly knows her.' Jealousy and anger were pricking at her, forcing her to say the very things that she knew Esmé wished to hear from her.

'Oh yes,' protested Esmé, as if Katharine did not know the half of what went on. 'Perhaps he knows her better than you think; she often drops in to see us at the rectory. Mother is very fond of her too.'

Katharine was nearly beside herself: what was Esmé trying to tell her? That Lawrence had fallen in love with Susan? She suddenly realised that, though she would have none of him, the certainty that Lawrence still loved her had been the mainstay of her existence. The thought that he might not love her any longer, and that he might have been captivated by that shallow-minded little minx, Susan, was utter torture.

She saw that Esmé was observing her covertly. She must say something at once: by cushioning Esmé's words in silence she was exaggerating their importance.

'Susan is rather a disappointment to me,' she said drily. 'Her whole outlook is so . . . flibberty-gibberty. She doesn't seem to have a serious thought in her head.'

'I would not have said so at all,' said Esmé stiffly. 'No, not at all,' as if she remembered some incident.

'She can't make up her mind what she wants to do,' complained Katharine. 'I had hoped. . .'

'Oh,' laughed Esmé, 'you were trying to turn her into a missionary but she wouldn't have it. It's no life for a young girl, of course. It would have been madness. She's a pretty child.'

The words wounded Katharine to the quick because she chose to read into them the menace of her fears. So hurt was she that for a moment she was completely silenced.

The firing outside suddenly became much more rapid. Revolver shots that sounded very close were answered by repeated bursts of machine-gun fire. The house shook as three grenades exploded harmlessly. Nanny, carrying a heavy tray, stumbled against the door, and Katharine went to let her in, thankful for the diversion. Susan, also laden, followed close behind.

'What going on, Nanny?' asked Katharine, aware that the latest news would be known in the kitchen.

'The Stater below in the kitchen says his fellas has a machine-gun in the hedge at the front,' announced Nanny proudly. 'He says they can rake the road all ways wit' it. He's a decent young fella, all the same,' she added defensively. 'Sure, I don't believe he's that long outa school, meself, for all his desperate talk. If he knows which end o' the gun to shoot wit', that's all he does know if ye ask me,' she mumbled on her way out of the room. 'Is there annything else ye want, Miss?' she asked from the doorway.

'I suppose no one has seen my brother . . . the Rector walking along the road?' enquired Esmé grandly. 'He may be looking for me.'

'I wasn't sittin' in the front winders, Miss,' replied Nanny tartly. 'The divil himself mighta gone past for all I'd know.'

The door closed disapprovingly behind her.

As the afternoon passed, the fighting became more spasmodic. During a lull, Esmé even tried to go home, so desperate was she for her six o'clock pills, but she was stopped by the soldier at the door.

'No, lady, ye can't go out,' he said repeatedly. ''Tis too dangerous altogether.' There was another burst of firing as he spoke. 'What did I tellya, lady?' he said triumphantly. He drove her back to the study.

Time passed. Esmé abandoned herself to despair, sure that she would be dead before morning. Katharine had given up trying to talk to Esmé; she sat at the great desk, pretending to do the household accounts and gazing morosely into the fire. Susan sat with her embroidery on her knee, exhausted with boredom.

Suddenly there was a tremendous commotion in the hall. The knocker banged and banged as if someone was desperate to enter. The soldier shouted at whoever was outside and the troops poured out of the drawing-room to discover what was happening, but still the knocker was battered and a man's voice shouted, 'Let me in, let me in!'

In the study, they all heard it. Esmé cried, 'It's Lawrence, I know it's his voice!' She rushed into the hall.

Katharine was angry because she had not been the first to recognise his voice; she stayed resolutely in the study.

'Let him in; quick before someone shoots him!' Esmé implored the soldier. 'Oh, quick!'

'Is it someone ye know, Miss?' he asked uncertainly.

'Yes, of course. It's my brother,' she said with impatience. 'You must let him in. Lawrence, it's me, Esmé. They won't let you in; they won't open the door.'

'I'll stand back,' he called. 'Then they can see me.'

The soldier peered through the tiny window flanking the door and nodded to the others.

''Tis some kind of a priest,' he said in a puzzled tone, looking for permission to open the door.

'Let him in,' said a voice, and the soldier opened the door a crack, then a little wider. Lawrence slipped inside and the door was shut again firmly.

Lawrence was greatly agitated and his clothes were plastered with mud. 'Oh, Esmé,' he cried, 'what a relief to have found you! I've spent most of the afternoon in a ditch, waiting for the shooting to stop and let me get home. I had to make a dash for it inside this gate in the end.'

'Then you haven't got my pills?' said Esmé in despair.

'Pills? What pills?' he asked absently. 'Are Katharine and Susan all right?'

'Oh yes,' she said disgustedly. 'My six o'clock pills, Lawrence, you know I can't do without them.' Tears stood in her eyes.

'It's Mother I'm worrying about,' went on Lawrence. 'She's all alone in the house with Teresa. I can't get back there. I tried and they stopped me.' Suddenly he became quite different. 'Oh, my poor Esmé!' he said, deeply contrite. 'Your pills, of course! And we can't get them for you, I'm afraid. Whatever will become of you!'

'Never mind,' said Esmé. 'I know it doesn't matter what happens to me—I'm no use to anyone.' She assumed a look of pious abnegation.

'Now, don't talk like that, please Esmé,' said Lawrence patiently. 'You know it isn't true.' He paused, chin in hand, while he considered for a moment. 'Now, I wonder if I couldn't slip home and get them after dark—they mightn't see me.'

Esmé clasped her hands together adoringly. 'Oh, Lawrence, you are wonderful!' she cried.

But Katharine, who had been listening to every word from the study, called out in an agony of mind, 'Lawrence, you're not to: it's madness!'

And the soldier at his elbow, whose presence he had forgotten, shook his head dolefully. 'I'm afraid, Father, I wouldn't be doin' me dooty if I let you out again. I can't do it, Father, I'm terrible sorry.'

Katharine stood, at the study doorway.

'Come in, Lawrence,' she said, still softened towards him by the thought of the danger only just averted. 'Come back in, Miss Weldon. There's nothing to be done but sit here and wait until it's over.' Never, she felt, as long as she lived, could she call Esmé by her Christian name.

Lawrence took her hand, held it for a second longer than was necessary, looked into her face with concern and said, 'Ah, thank you, Katharine. How good of you to look after Esmé. Ah, Susan, how are you?'

He smiled at Susan in a way that people do only when they have discovered some common way of thought, mutual interest or enjoyment, not secretively, but in a private way. Susan was smiling back at him, a little flustered by Katharine's glance that had settled upon her face, boring into her most searchingly, yet still able to reply with shy, non-committal murmurs.

Katharine's heart hardened instantly. Suspicion soured the goodwill that had animated her only a moment before and when she turned to Lawrence, to whom she had scarcely spoken for nearly five years, it was with a look of accusation that he would dare to look at Susan with sympathy and affection. Like sunken refuse at the bottom of stagnant water that rises when disturbed, bubbling thickly underneath the scum and coming to the surface bit by bit, suspicions detached themselves to rise as certainties in her jealous mind, poisoning the whole area of her consciousness. She persuaded herself, against reason, that Susan had stolen Lawrence from her. Suffer she would, torture herself she must. The cry that had been wrung from her in her anxiety was now to her a foolishness and a regret. She despised herself for her weakness in uttering it and, still more, in laying her heart bare for them all to see.

Drily, she saw them all seated, placing Lawrence close to Susan so that her suspicions might be confirmed by observation. So consumed was she now by jealousy that nothing in the world would have convinced her that she was mistaken.

As dusk fell, the battle broke out again more violently. A running fight developed up and down the road. There was a good deal of coming and going, passwords muttered at the door, a despatch rider roaring off on his motor-bicycle, speed his only hope of survival, the noisy reports from his engine diminishing coldly on the night air until they fell away altogether.

The four people in the study at Fellowescourt had long ago ceased to talk. Esmé drowsed, Susan had dropped off to sleep. Katharine sat near the lamp, sewing away at a shift that would preserve a black schoolgirl from lustful glances and change her from a child of nature to a waif of progress, a vagrant in civilisation. The completion of each of these garments gave her great satisfaction.

Lawrence sat looking at his feet stretched out before him, smoking his pipe. This could have been their secret moment, his and Katharine's, when in a bond of delight they could have become reconciled by wordless glances across the sleeping bodies that separated them. He felt bewildered and hopeless. He could not help blaming Esmé for his unhappiness, yet blamed himself that he could do so.

Nanny had brought them bacon and eggs, soda-bread, marmalade and tea, the meal that any Irish home can produce at any hour, whatever the crisis. That was at about eight o'clock and conversation had not been lively. Esmé refused to eat: she could have faced a little fish, she said, or even a little cold ham, but not bacon and eggs at this hour, and she shuddered.

Katharine had made no comment and offered no substitute, so Esmé had starved. Lawrence had not intervened.

'We shall not go to bed tonight,' announced Katharine. 'It is wiser to stay dressed. If the worst came to the worst, we might have to leave the house and it is better to be prepared.' Indeed, there were soldiers at the windows of all the bedrooms that faced the road, and in corridors and on the stairs. It would not have been easy for anyone to go to bed.

They all had agreed with her and silence had come between them, weaving a barrier between person and person too strong to be swept away by premeditated speech. Gradually it had encased them all.

A stumbling, hurrying step in the passage made Katharine raise her head, ear cocked. Julia fell against the door and into the room, panting.

'Please Miss, they're clearin' out!'

'What—?'

'The Staters is goin', Miss.'

'Why are they going?'

'I dunno, Miss. The one below in the kitchen was sayin' how there's a terrible concenthration o' them about Inish and the place is gettin' too hot for them.'

'I see,' said Katharine. 'Well, as soon as they're really gone, lock and bolt all the doors and latch the windows and go to bed. I hope the Irregulars aren't waiting to occupy the house now?'

Julia laughed uncertainly, unable to decide whether this was a joke or not.

'I'll take Esmé home,' said Lawrence, 'when they've gone.'

Again her anxiety caught at her. 'Oh no,' she cried, 'it wouldn't be safe! Wait until daylight.'

He glanced curiously at her, touched by her fear for his safety. 'You and Susan go to bed,' he said 'We'll be quite all right here.'

Tremendous sounds of departure filled the house; voices, footsteps, the noise of heavy things being hauled about. Engines started out on the road, lorries made off into the night. A fist thumped on the study door. It was one of the soldiers.

'T'anks, Miss, an' I don't think ye'll find anny damage,' he said, saluting with a grin. He left at a run. The hall door banged bleakly:

they were gone. The last of their lorries buzzed away over the rise, out of the village.

Silence closed in upon the village in protective layers, wrapping each house and person in safety. Katharine felt deathly tired and gave a great yawn.

'I'm going as far as the gate for a breath of air,' said Lawrence. 'I'm not going any further than that, so don't worry.'

He opened the hall door and walked slowly down the flagged path, filling his lungs with the clean, chill mountainy air and staring up at the impersonal remoteness of the starry sky. He felt swept away by the release from danger and tension, drawn off his feet half-way to infinity. The peace of the night flooded into him, stilling his private conflict, washing out, like an incoming tide, his reluctance to welcome it, his nostalgia for time past, his dread of the empty future. It filled him with a sense of well-being. Life was still good . . .

Like all hell let loose, murder broke out below in the village. There were shots and screams, racing footsteps and the sound of blows, followed by a cry of sheer terror that dried Lawrence's mouth with fear and horror.

A man was running up the hill from the village and others were after him like greyhounds after the hare. He was gasping and panting, finding the pace too hot yet driven on by his terror. He was within a few feet of Lawrence, through the hedge, each breath an anguished strangulation. Lawrence was immobilised by horror; he crouched on the grass, peering through the hedge and seeing nothing, listening to the pursuers catching up with their prey, almost upon him now.

The hunted man hesitated for a fraction of time, then darted in through the little iron gate and up the flagged path.

'Ah!' yelled a voice from outside. 'Get him, now, get him!'

They had turned in along with him and now one of them stopped. There was a shot and the fleeing figure dropped on the grass with another of those terrible screams, high-pitched as a woman's, fraught with all the terror, despair and anguish of suffering humanity.

There were four or five men round the body now, turning it over to discover whether there was still life in it. A voice said, 'Give him a finisher.'

'No need,' said another. 'He's dead.'

Someone rubbed his hands together. 'Well, that's one thraitor less in the world, annyhow. Thanks be to God, we got even wit' him in the latter end!'

'Sure, wasn't it a great bit o' luck the fightin' was around this house,' said a new voice. 'Now they'll all think that's how he was killed.'

'That's thrue.'

Lawrence, crouched on the grass in the shadow of the hedge, was attacked by sudden cramp. He moved his foot and the sound of his shoe on the grass and his swift intake of breath were heard.

'There's someone here,' said one of the men hoarsely.

They all stood listening for a second, ready to run, to shoot, to do anything that panic dictated.

'Come on!' said one in a whisper, starting to run.

They all ran, out of the gate, down the hill, the thunder of their feet dying slowly away.

Painfully, Lawrence stood up and went over to the body. It was too dark to see anything. He went to the door to ask Katharine for a light. While he waited, he pondered on the identity of the murderers and their victim. All he had seen in the darkness was shape, movement and confusion, but was he right in thinking that he had recognised a voice here and there? Patrick Quinn, Michael Maguire . . . Good men, both of them, incapable of murder. No, he had been wrong, he had no clue to their identity.

Katharine came to the door, a lamp in her hand. As he came round the door, the light shone on his face and she stopped, transfixed with relief.

'Oh,' she said weakly, 'you're safe!' She held on to the hat-stand.

Esmé and Susan crowded behind her, trying to see.

'Did you hear those dreadful screams?' said Esmé, shuddering. 'I shan't sleep a wink for nights.'

'Stay where you are,' said Lawrence with authority. 'Katharine, may I take the light?' She did not hand it to him but seemed to shrink back. 'It's quite all right,' he said gently. 'They've all gone, but there's someone injured here, or maybe worse than that.'

She handed him the light then and he carried it outside. The body on the grass was that of Peter Cavanagh. There was blood on his shiny old serge suit, and the mark of his bowler hat ringed his long grey locks. He was not quite dead, but he was unconscious.

Lawrence rushed into the house and spoke to them from the doorway.

'It's Peter Cavanagh,' he said. 'He's still alive. Help me to bring him in.'

Behind the others he could see Nanny and Julia hovering, thirsting for news. Katharine came forward and blocked the way.

'No,' she said, 'let him die out there as he deserves. Why, only today . . .' She looked at Lawrence with a face as cold as stone as she thought of Peter Cavanagh's final villainy towards the Fellowes family. She stood there for a moment so that Lawrence should realise the full weight of her decision. Then, turning back towards the others she said, 'Susan, come to bed; I'm going up now.'

Lawrence stood looking at her as if she had stunned him, unable to believe that she really meant what she said. As she lit her candle from the one on the table, he called her quietly.

'Katharine!' She turned her head towards him, her face still set. 'Have you no heart, Katharine?'

'Not for him,' she said. 'Come on, Susan.' She set off to climb the stairs, candle in her hand.

Susan did not follow her. She and Esmé looked quickly at one another.

'I'll help you,' said Susan. 'We both will.'

Lawrence turned to go out with them. He looked absolutely defeated. He made no attempt to speak to them.

Esmé was flattered at being included in Susan's offer; someone thought that she could be useful; this was something quite new and made her feel almost confident. Smiling, she bent over Peter Cavanagh. Between them all they lifted the old man into the hall, laying him on the patch of carpet where Katharine had once complained that her father's umbrella had made such a pool. Esmé ran for a cushion to put under his head and water to dab on his face.

'Poor old man,' she said. 'What a way to die!'

Susan came with towels to stanch the blood, but Lawrence stopped her.

'He's dead,' he said, 'and for all I know he did die outside.'

He looked upwards towards the head of the stairs, certain that Katharine was listening. But from upstairs there came never a sound.

CHAPTER FOURTEEN

The unnatural stillness that possessed the house, slipping gradually back into its ancient strongholds now that the troops and the battle had gone away, had brought no peace to Katharine. Trouble from within directed her now that the trouble from without was on the wane; it grew and multiplied, leaping up to terrify her with monstrous apparitions through the night. The coming of daylight, although it drilled these, as it were, into legendary order and discipline, did nothing to dispel them.

Defeat encroached upon her every unguarded moment. As she looked inwards upon herself she knew that there was no strength left on which to draw.

So wrong had she been, so occupied by revenge when she had refused the charity of shelter to Peter Cavanagh as he died, that the enormity of her offence precluded its recognition. She would not admit that she was at fault; she would not even examine what she had done because therein lay condemnation. She supported her wrong and nurtured it, giving it her consent by rhetorical declamations directed only towards herself, like, 'But what else could I do?' and 'Anyone else would have done the same thing; after all, he ruined us.' But even she, 'the Pope', infallible now as ever, could not claim divine authority for what she had done. That source of justification had dried up for the first time. And with it the other which, now that it was removed, she perceived as the wellspring of her probity, the regard and admiration which Lawrence had never denied her and of which she had remained gloriously conscious throughout all her tribulations. It had given her constant illumination and kept her perpetually in countenance with herself. Now that it had gone she had no glimmer of light. She was in a cave without an entrance.

She had no delusions about her capacity to regain his esteem; he was finished with her. Just as for years, made partial by his love he had valued her above her merits, so now, moved by shame and disappointment, he was failing to do her justice. She was the same as she had always been, neither better nor worse; it was he who had altered. And she who had so depended upon his judgement when it was favourable to her, perceived its frailty with contempt now that it condemned her, and despised herself that she could ever have so relied upon its integrity.

Nanny thumped on the door with a cup of tea in her hand, shuffled in and set it down beside her, peering at her to see if she were awake. When she saw that Katharine's eyes were open, she retired to the end of the bed, and without looking at her, mouthed, 'An' what'd ye like me to do wit' the corpse, Miss?'

Her attitude made it clear that nothing but a strong sense of duty had driven her to speak to Katharine at all.

And Katharine, tormented all the night through by unadmitted guilt, put her hands over her face and cried, 'Oh!' as she recoiled from the necessity of making a decision.

Nanny did not spare her; chewing rhythmically on her toothless gums, she stared out at the grey morning, and waited relentlessly.

'Send for Doctor O'Brien,' said Katharine breathlessly, after a hopeful pause. 'He'll know what ought to be done.'

'Yes, Miss.' Still chewing, Nanny turned away without another look.

Katharine felt afraid: the emptiness within her increased its threat as she recognised the isolation surrounding her.

Her life-long habit of self-discipline impelled her to undertake the routine of the day. At breakfast she saw that Susan's eyes were ringed with black; she felt a quick concern for the child and sought to reassure her by a smile, but Susan's glance evaded hers and shifted with embarrassment to the floor, the table-cloth or the knife upon her plate as soon as contact was made. Neither of them spoke after 'good morning' had been said, and the silence became an infrangible barrier, too solid to pierce by mere words. Very soon, Susan gulped down her tea and, whispering her excuses to the toast-rack, left the room.

Katharine shrugged and returned to her unhappy pondering. Everything that faced her in the future was unpleasant, depressing, or worse. For the first time in her life she longed to escape from Fellowescourt, to shed all her troubles and responsibilities and to start a new life in perfect innocence and freedom. But with brutal clarity the truth flashed upon her that whatever else she might discard she must forever carry the burden of herself.

She sighed, and fell to wondering where, in fact, Nanny and Julia had put the corpse. Coming down the stairs, her unwilling eye had been drawn irresistibly to the spot where it had lain the night before but there was nothing there. Ask where it was she would not. She would have to seek it out.

She realised that she had forgotten that yesterday the house had been alive with soldiers, resounding with their heavy tread and loud, jerky laughter, tense with their preoccupation with the impending battle. The house itself had forgotten them; they had left no indelible mark upon its daily ordering. Their disturbance had passed over it like a sudden squall agitating a patch of calm water and left no trace behind. Now that the occupation had come to her mind she sat for a moment savouring the quiet, the ancient succession of silence and familiar household noises that only impressed the ear if they were stilled. Then the hollowness of the peace drove her to make a move, to be busy, at all costs to be active. She left the breakfast table, having eaten no more than would nourish a bluebottle, and went boldly into the hall.

It looked exactly as it had looked ever since time began; there was her father's umbrella still in the elephant's foot, unused since before the war. The coats and hats that hung from the pegs on the stand were of venerable antiquity. Charlotte's and Daisy's amongst her own and Harriet's, and her father's hat reigning over them all at a flamboyant angle that recalled his highly-coloured personality to her with such poignancy that tears sprang to her eyes and she found herself murmuring, 'Oh poor Papa!' in nostalgic compassion for his embedded obstinacy. The light from one of the narrow windows beside the hall door fell greyly on the spot where Lawrence had laid Peter Cavanagh last night but there was nothing to remind her of the fact that he had bled and died there; so impersonal did it appear, with the usual and familiar asserting themselves around her, that she felt inclined to doubt the reality of what had happened until the sole of her foot, on the edge of the patch of carpet, felt a check to its progress and she knew at once that the patch was wet. Someone, working with loving determination, had sponged away all the horror. She stepped back quickly in recoil, turned to open the drawing-room door and stopped in amazement as she perceived that the whole room had been restored to its old condition.

There might never have been a soldier in the house. The carpet had been relaid, the chairs pushed back to their usual places, the folds of the curtains had been arranged with symmetry; a noble and extravagant fire burned in the grate, its core of glowing coals surmounted by a black crust on which flames played and danced in enigmatic flight. Only the sofa was out of its accustomed place, pushed up towards the fire.

Katharine moved over to pull the sofa back into position and with her hand already on it withdrew in sudden terror. Laid out on a spotless monogrammed sheet from her linen-cupboard, and covered in part by another, was the dirty, crumpled, shrivelled body of Peter Cavanagh, so small that the length of the sofa was sufficient for it.

She stood there shaking, her hand pressed against her mouth while the shock abated and gave way to anger. They had done it to defy her, to dishonour her, to shame her for her hardness, using her things in order to make some amends for her want of compassion, as though without her will and knowledge her possessions could repent for her.

She was furious, but prudence warned her against saying a word of protest to Nanny and Julia who must have made all these preparations, sinking their religious differences before the demand to show proper respect to the dead. She must not say a word, she must accept what they had done with good will and appear to approve of it while her heart was murmuring in bitter enmity against giving even Christian burial to such a vampire. From the depths of her being she resented it, and the sight of the magnificent fire blazing in the grate, a fire such as no one had built in that fireplace since her father's day, angered her most of all; flames blossomed and burgeoned from it, heat glowed in its solid heart and the warmth it gave out reached her even where she stood.

She crumpled in sudden laughter, overcome by the sardonic thought that, if she wanted to be warm this morning, she must share the drawing-room with the corpse, for the season of fires was over and the living had to do without them though they were forced upon the unprotesting dead. She laughed more and more hysterically, finding release in laughter, until she was forced to sit on the arm of a chair from sheer weakness, mopping at her eyes and still racked by waves of joyless mirth.

She did not hear the bell, nor did she hear Julia go through the hall though she had not closed the door; so when Doctor O'Brien stepped into the room and took hold of her shoulders to shake her into a sensible frame of mind, she was quite unprepared to see him.

'Take a pull on yerself, Miss Fellowes,' he commanded sternly. 'Sure, I never thought I'd live to see you let yerself go.' He shook a finger at her to give weight to his words.

She stiffened her shoulders and fixed him with a smouldering glare. 'I'm quite all right, thank you,' was all she said and by the subsequent silence made it plain that she would make no explanation or apology. Watching him, her face became serious again.

He was looking terribly ill, as though he were attempting to maintain his normal appearance and behaviour while some secret and hidden affliction devoured him from within, reaching ever nearer to the outer shell. Katharine was so shocked by his appearance that she leant forward in concern and said, 'Doctor O'Brien, are you all right? Would you like me to get you something?'

A quick look of gratitude was his only concession to the existence of personal trouble as he shook his head.

'No t'anks,' he murmured quietly. 'You're very kind, but no t'anks.' He passed a hand over his brow, as if he desired to sweep his distress away while he was with her, so that she might not be further burdened.

'Are you sure you're not ill?' she persisted.

'Ah, no. . .' he hesitated. 'I'm not ill at all, t'ank ye, Miss Fellowes.' He waited again, the words on the edge of his mouth, piled up and ready for utterance. He closed his mouth suddenly and they were swallowed up for ever.

'I hope . . . your family are all well?' Katharine was almost afraid to ask.

'Please God, they are,' he said fervently in a hoarse whisper. He turned blindly away, too deeply moved to continue, put his hand on the back of the sofa and became aware of what was laid out on the seat. 'Oh, my God,' he said quickly, 'I wasn't expecting that.' He looked down for a few moments, his mouth drawn into a line of critical scrutiny as he nodded gravely again and again.

'There's one'll have no mourners, I'm thinkin'. God have mercy on his soul!' he said, and crossed to the other side of the sofa to conduct his examination.

Katharine stayed where she was, answering his questions and trying to solve the mystery of his reticence while she watched him over the back of the sofa. 'Please God, they are,' he had said, whereas the natural thing to have said would have been, 'Thank God, they are.' 'Please God' meant that he did not know, that there was one of them whose circumstances were in doubt and about whom he was terribly anxious. Then the truth struck her with a reproach for her forgetfulness: of course, it was Barry!

Perhaps Barry was missing, wounded, or a prisoner. Something must have happened to him to cause his father such suffering. But of course, she could not ask about him: she was not even supposed to know that he was with the Irregulars. His father was ashamed of that.

Having no doubt whatever in her mind that she had discovered the cause of his wretchedness, she stood up and put it from her mind for the present. She watched him as he made out the death certificate and for a moment looked down at the subject of it on the sofa. There was something so vulnerable and so diminished about Peter Cavanagh in death that compassion stirred her for a moment, but so briefly and with such shallowness that it was gone as soon as recognised.

Doctor O'Brien was beside her again. 'It was good of you to give him shelter,' he said gently.

She almost jumped with the shock of his words.

'It was nothing to do with me,' she snapped. 'The others brought him in.'

'Ah, but it was good of ye all the same,' he repeated, determined that the credit should be hers. But the gleam in her eyes as she held her peace made him hasten his departure.

She wandered through the hall when she had seen him out, past the study, through the morning-room and conservatory and into the garden. She did not feel that she would be able to settle to anything today. Enter the study yet she could not: the hours she had spent there yesterday, the interminable, agonising, exquisite calamitous hours were still contained there, waiting to reproach her, reason with her, undermine her defences and condemn her.

She felt the need to take time off, not in order to think or to reorientate herself, but to exist without thought, feeling or any conscious exertion, in a recuperative vacuum. She was too tired even to be busy, her mind now cold and empty, her only actions reflex. She drifted past the rose-beds, looking but not seeing, her feet making a wavering, uncertain track over the uncharted surface of the dew-drenched grass.

It was spring, yet she felt no surge of delight at the opening of the leaves and the thickening of unfolding buds. She stood before the young chestnut tree which was always the first in the garden to come out in green, and regarded unseeing the grey-green, crumpled, half-liberated leaves, downy as an infant's head, tender and wrinkled as its outstretched hand. Nothing affected her, not even the luminous quality of the sky, grey with a promise of glory, dappled with light, power growing behind the cloud, nor the exciting warmth of the air that pulsed with life. She was quite unaware, like a stone.

Sometimes she stopped, waiting until her thoughts should move her on. She reached, after a certain time, the wall that kept the mountain out, and that part of the garden that was influenced by the Scotch firs beyond it and the primeval mountain itself. She sat on the wall and gazed towards the mountain, seeing nothing but the line of the sky until her eye was caught by a something that moved far away on the slope and she was brought back into herself by its demands on her attention.

It was a figure moving towards the Scotch firs with the exaggerated slowness that distance gives to movement, and for the present she could not tell anything more than that it was human. It was so unusual to see anyone on the slope of the mountain that she felt obliged to discover who it might be. The better to observe without being seen, she moved along until she found a part of the wall where she would be largely concealed by a mound of brambles that heaved spiny tentacles in a writhing mass on the other side; here she sat and waited, pleased to be occupied with so trivial and insigificant a recreation that was nevertheless interesting.

When she had settled herself, she looked again for the figure, but there was nothing to be seen; she thought that it had perhaps advanced further than her calculations would allow, so she let her eye run the length of the whole separating distance, but whoever had been there had taken cover. No living thing was in view.

She lost interest and began to speculate on the inevitable events of the day. The police would be coming, the undertaker, the priest, relatives, if there were any. Peter Cavanagh had been a lone creature and had never married; his brothers and sisters had all died before him and the hag who attended to the bar had also cooked his food and performed the essential minimum of domestic duties. They would all be arriving before long: she must go back to the house. Reluctance to reassume her responsibilities kept her seated for a moment until her will should assert itself again, and she was about to get to her feet when she was aware of something approaching, not from the mountain as she expected, but through the little field that Peter Cavanagh had leased from her, and going towards the slope where she had perceived the first figure.

She stayed absolutely still and peered through her bramble patch; she could hear heavy breathing, trembling inhalations that betrayed intensity of fear, then the footsteps and the breathing stopped while the stranger stood listening, receptive to every vibration, and reassured, released the imprisoned breath in evident relief.

She heard a whisper and a whispered reply, though what was said escaped her. So there was more than one person. Suddenly two forms came into view on the far side of the wall, female forms visible only from the waist upwards, side by side and appearing to carry between them a burden of some bulk.

A gasp of astonishment nearly gave her away as she recognised the untidy plate-like face of Mrs O'Brien, her expression distraught, and her eyes darting this way and that in search of unseen enemies, and on her far side Susan, her own Susan, engaged on a secret enterprise of which she would never have been told had she not discovered it herself.

They sensed danger and stopped again, listening and looking, startled heads raised in tension. Katharine stayed crouched behind her brambles, quite invisible unless they came to the wall and looked over it. She knew what they were doing, she could see it all: the figure she had seen on the mountain slope was Barry, on the run, afraid to go home, afraid to be seen, hiding amongst the rocks on the side of the mountain until darkness covered his escape to some other area where the Regulars might take a little longer to discover him. And his mother and Susan, her two-faced, sly Susan, were taking him food and maybe a change of clothes, imperilling their own lives as well as his and jettisoning the Fellowes' reputation for decent, law-abiding conduct.

Mrs O'Brien put her free hand to her heart and whispered, "Tis too much for me, I can't stand the fright. Oah, what'll be the end of it, child, at all? That's what's destroyin' me, what'll be the end of it!'

Susan shook her head impatiently. 'We must get on,' she said, and they began to move again.

Katharine stood up quickly on the wall so that she overtopped the brambles.

'Susan,' she said in a low voice, 'Susan, come here.'

The two figures separated, dropping the bundle and making for shelter instinctively; then Susan stopped, aware of how useless it was to hide now, and looked up at 'the Pope' on the wall. Poor Mrs O'Brien kept a hand clapped to her mouth as if the scream she had driven back might still escape if it had the chance. When Susan turned, she did the same, then dropped her hand and faced Katharine erect, emboldened by catastrophe.

'Go back wit' yer auntie, Susan,' she said from behind the girl, looking at Katharine. 'Go back wit' her. She's quite right; this isn't a thing you ought to be mixed up wit' at all. I'll manage now, don't you worry, child.'

Susan's expression repulsed Katharine with its unmitigated ferocity and contempt; she could not believe that anyone could so resent her, especially when all her own private hopes and desires, with the personal wealth upon which those hopes had rested, had been sacrificed for the child's well-being, undeclared and heavily concealed though the sacrifice might have been. It was incomprehensible to her that the very fact of her sacrifice, with the love that had prompted it, though that too had never been apparent, should not have softened Susan towards her; she felt it now all thrown back at her without gratitude or acknowledgement.

Mrs O'Brien gave Susan a little push from behind. 'G'wan now, child, wit' yer auntie. You must do as she says. I'd never'a let ye come with me if I'd been in me right mind, sure 'tis no kind of a jaunt for children. G'wan now, there's a good girl.'

'Why do you always have to see what you're not meant to see?' said Susan, her anger and resentment blazing out at 'the Pope'. She had taken a step forward in spite of herself and Katharine knew that this time, once more, Susan would obey her.

With all the authority at her command, she said, 'You can't blame me, Susan, for the wrong you choose to do yourself; if I happen to discover it, you mustn't blame me. Now, come home.' She surveyed Mrs O'Brien in silence and, as Susan slowly began to move, turned towards the house, secure in the knowledge that Susan would follow her.

Mrs O'Brien made a little sound of lament, an almost imperceptible moan, torn between the necessity to conceal the object of her excursion and the certainty that 'the Pope' was entirely aware of it without a word being said.

'Miss Fellowes,' she said wretchedly, groping for words.

'Yes,' said Katharine, turning back to watch the tears rain down the flat, pallid countenance. She felt no emotion; she wished that Mrs O'Brien would hurry up; she wanted to attend to Susan.

'I ask ye for the love of God, Miss Fellowes, to not say a word to any soul on this earth about you seein' me here: will ye do that for me, Miss Fellowes? Arrah, sure ye will,' she added reassuringly, in a pleading voice. 'It's not for meself, d'ye understand? If it was for meself ye could do what ye liked.'

'I must do what I believe to be right,' said Katharine coldly, 'but I'm not a spy,' she added more gently, 'or a gossip.' She looked back to see how far Susan had progressed and saw that she had stopped to listen. Without another word she turned again towards the house and propelling Susan before her by force of will made her way back to the house.

She wanted to corner Susan, to exact from her an account of every detail of the morning's work. How had she known that Barry was on the mountain unless she was in constant communication with him? How could she still say that she was not in love with him when she was content to risk her life by carrying food and clothes to him? Had Doctor O'Brien known Barry's whereabouts when he called earlier, or did he know, even now? And how dared that foolish, besotted woman, Mrs O'Brien, lead a young girl astray, perhaps even to her death? Suspicion and anger, doubt and amazement pursued each other in the vortex of her mind, until she did not know what to think. She did not even know that she would ever succeed in making Susan disgorge the truth, and this grieved her more than anything else.

She had wanted to ask Mrs O'Brien how Susan had come to be with her, so as to have a check on whatever story the child might tell her, but Susan had been listening and she had said nothing. Now there was no way of finding out whether Susan was deceiving her or not without resort to interrogation so severe as to suggest the Inquisition. But Katharine was determined to wring the truth out of her if this could be done, and she followed Susan quickly through the conservatory door in order to catch her before she took refuge with Nanny.

In the hall, however, she was waylaid by Julia who had been looking everywhere for her. The police were here, Mrs Cassidy, the barmaid-housekeeper, was here, the painters had been and gone as soon as they heard the news, Mrs Weldon had called and the undertakers were busy at that very moment. The hall seemed to swarm with people and Katharine found herself surrounded while Susan walked slowly up the stairs. She had a feeling that with her went all hope of finding out the truth, that if time passed before she could question her, Susan would evade her altogether. But it was already too late to prevent that. With a sigh she invited the police to follow her into the study.

It was late afternoon before she had finished seeing people; as soon as one lot left another arrived. Mrs Weldon called again to thank her for looking after Esmé; Lawrence was not mentioned. 'The Pope' enquired whether Esmé had suffered as a result of missing her six o'clock pills and her mother was able to give a reassuring reply; Katharine smiled enigmatically and looked gratified. Nanny appeared with a tray of tea for them and the news that Susan would have hers by the nursery fire today. Nanny looked old and ill and utterly wretched; she had left important things off the tray and Katharine had to call her back twice.

'My dear,' said Mrs Weldon, 'you were so very good to Esmé. I really am grateful.' She stood up to leave. The warmth of her voice and the gentleness of the words moved Katharine as the contempt and condemnation of her own household, of Esmé herself and of Lawrence had failed to do. She shook her head, unable to speak, as she held out her hand; Mrs Weldon grasped it firmly and pressed it with affection.

'My dear,' she said again, moved this time herself, 'you have had a very great deal to bear but you are not as hard as people think. You are not hard at all, at least I don't think so. I . . . I am so very sorry things never turned out well for you. . .' With a final squeeze of her hand she was gone, leaving Katharine quite overcome with emotion.

She went back to the study and poured out another cup of tea to tide her over until her voice should be firm enough to call Susan, lifting the cup to her mouth with a shaking hand, trying desperately to steady herself.

There was an angry sort of thump on the door and Nanny appeared without waiting for an answer. She made a pretence of having come to fetch the tray, then faced Katharine across the little table, hands clasping and unclasping in front of her apron.

'That's a terrible thing is after happenin',' she said accusingly. She seemed to be bringing a charge against Katharine without stating it in words.

'What . . . terrible thing?' repeated Katharine in a small voice.

'D'ye not know then?' Nanny's ancient voice was rough. 'Is that so, Miss?' She so obviously believed that Katharine knew but would not admit that she knew, that an incredulous leer spread over her face which she made no attempt to hide.

'Nanny,' demanded Katharine sharply, 'tell me at once what has happened. Why are you looking at me like that?'

Nanny's mouth opened in surprise; it was beginning to dawn upon her that perhaps she had misjudged 'the Pope'.

'The Reg'lars is afther takin' that little Barry and his poor mother, out beyond on the mountain. They closed in on them, like, from dinnertime on, and they cot them about three o'clock, so I'm afther hearin', Miss.' Shamefacedly, she explained, 'Susan would have it it was yerself set the polis on to them, though how you could 'a known they was there I couldn't make out at all. But isn't it a terrible thing, Miss? That little Barry only outa the nursery this short while, and that poor woman wit' him, an' she wit' a houseful o' children.'

'Are they alive?' asked Katharine, horrified.

'One says they are and another'd tell ye they're not. Ye can't find out the truth. But when I think o' that poor woman . . .'

'Nanny,' said 'the Pope' sternly, 'I had nothing whatever to do with them being taken. Ask Miss Susan to come to me now, this minute.'

Nanny looked guilty and ashamed. For nearly a minute she was speechless, and Katharine imagined that she was trying to word an apology for having believed her capable of the infamy of informing.

'Never mind, Nanny,' she began; 'just ask Miss Susan—'

Nanny gave her a terrified look. 'Susan's gone, Miss.'

'Gone?' echoed Katharine. 'Where's she gone?'

'She said she'd never sleep under the same roof wit' ye again,' said Nanny, and pulling the apron over her face, sobbed bitterly into it. 'Oh, my poor lamb,' she wept, 'my poor, poor lamb. And I helped her to go, I thought she was right. God forgive me.'

It took many minutes to discover anything about Susan's plans. She had set off on her bicycle, which had once been Charlotte's, for Brandon Cottage to borrow money from Harriet for her fare to England.

'To England?' queried Katharine in amazement.

'Yes, Miss. And she promised me faithfully she'll go straight to Miss Olivia's; it wasn't till I had that promise outa her that I said I'd help her. I thought she'd be all right wit' Miss Olivia . . .'

Katharine's relief was tremendous. 'She'll be all right with Miss Olivia,' she said. 'We shall hear from her in a day or two.'

Nanny had been gone for some minutes before she began to realise the extent of the blow that Susan had dealt to her self-esteem. What was she going to tell people? Was she going to try to bring her back? Was it possible that Susan regarded her with such loathing that she would not live under the same roof with her?

Impatience at her niece's stupidity swelled into anger, anger into brooding resentment. She had done her best for Susan and been repaid with nothing but rebellion and evasion; the child was ungrateful, shifty and good for nothing. She had chosen to run away; well, she could stay away. She would not come back to Fellowescourt while she, Katharine, was in possession. She must fend for herself, or persuade Olivia to support her.

It was not until Katharine went to bed that night that she began to consider the extreme loneliness of her own position: no one would live with her; she was quite alone. What was it about her that seemed to drive everyone away?

Her heart grew cold again, alone in the chill of the night.

PART THREE

CHAPTER FIFTEEN

Mrs Lowndes treated telegrams with a deference which she begrudged ordinary letters. Telegrams cost money, they demanded attention at the door and they heralded crisis, thereby raising her own prestige and providing her with an object for her insatiable curiosity. So, instead of shoving them at any angle into a free space on the green baize letter-rack, she always placed them in the top left-hand corner, absolutely straight.

Susan Fellowes was so familiar with this procedure that when Mrs Lowndes telephoned to her at the office to say that a telegram had come for her, she was able to envisage the scene in the dark, narrow hallway of the Chelsea lodging-house where she had rented the same room for twenty-five years, except for a period during the war when she had been in the Services. Mrs Lowndes, a duster on her head, a mop handle propped against her unyielding bosom and the telegram in her hand, was reaching up to the light switch so that she could describe the envelope in detail and stimulate Susan's interest to the point of gaining permission to read the contents.

'Ah,' said the voice with satisfaction, 'there now, that's the light on. Now, let's 'ave a look.' There was a pause while Mrs Lowndes scrutinised the envelope. With a sense of injury, and indeed of deprivation, she continued, 'I've turned it every way but you can't tell where it's from just by looking at the outside.' There was a pause calculated to provoke in Susan an unbearable itch for more information. 'P'raps you'd like me to open it, Miss Fellowes, and read it to you? It'd put you out of your misery, that's one thing.'

'No thank you, Mrs Lowndes,' said Susan with unwonted brutality. 'As a matter of fact I know what it's about.'

This was, of course, a lie. Susan had never expected a telegram less and her anxiety to know its message was exceeded only by that of her landlady; her sole motive for preventing Mrs Lowndes opening it was the pleasure, so rarely granted, of exercising a momentary power over a person against whose benevolent despotism she had long ceased to struggle. Mrs Lowndes had an intimate knowledge of the private affairs of each of her lodgers, acquired by the handy use of a steam kettle, determined scrutiny of the contents of waste-paper baskets and a knack of being always about whenever any of them used the telephone, but she never used her information malevolently.

The poison, however, was beginning to work. Susan was suddenly assailed by a need to know what the telegram was about; it might be something unexpected and exciting. An invitation? The offer of a highly paid job abroad? Someone wanting to marry her? She knew that she could not wait until the evening to discover.

'Aoh? Not bad news, I 'ope, dear?' There was such concern in the tone, mingled with a kind of effort to draw back from the making of a declaration, that Susan instantly knew two things: that Mrs Lowndes had already read the telegram and that it announced the death of the last and most formidable of her five aunts, 'the Pope'.

She had to think quickly; if she allowed Mrs Lowndes to read her the message, she would consider it her privilege to repeat it to everyone else in the house as they came home, but if she muzzled her by a refusal she would herself have to spend the rest of the day miserably wondering if her swift moment of perception had, after all, not been baseless. She gave in.

'I'm afraid it probably is, Mrs Lowndes,' she said. 'Perhaps you'd better read it to me after all.'

'Aoh, all right, dear,' said Mrs Lowndes with relish. 'Just 'arf a mo' till I find me specs.'

The receiver was laid down and Susan could hear carpet slippers shuffling along the linoleum; the paraphernalia of preparing to open the telegram was so impressive that, if she had not known her landlady so well, Susan would have been convinced that it was genuine. She knew, however, that Mrs Lowndes' pince-nez were forever pinned to her bosom so that this little expedition must be for something different. When, a moment later, she heard a minute clink of cup on saucer as Mrs Lowndes put down her elevenses within reach, she realised that this was to be a prolonged session, involving expressions of sympathy, offers of help and much advice.

Mrs Lowndes was chewing a biscuit when she picked up the telephone receiver again; Susan could hear this as she could also hear an important rustling and exclamations of annoyance at the inanimate obstinacy of the paper in refusing to stay unfolded. Some seconds passed while Mrs Lowndes allowed herself time to read the message she already knew by heart, then she drew in her breath sharply, clacked her tongue and spoke.

'Oh dear, I'm afraid this'll be a shock to you, Miss Fellowes.' She paused with portentous solemnity. 'Yes, it is bad news, tch tch tch. Oh, I say!'

With excusable impatience, Susan said quite crossly, 'Come on, Mrs Lowndes, read it out, will you.'

'It's from Glenmacool, Miss. That's where your people are in Ireland, isn't it? Or where they was, I should say,' she added with pious and emphatic gloom. 'I'm going to read it out now; it says, "Your Aunt Katharine killed by Nbu (it's a name, I suppose, it's spelt N-b-u) tribesmen while returning from tour of villages to Mission Station last Friday." Oh, I say, isn't it awful what they do to people, these savages, not but what people ask for it going out there amongst them. Missionary, was she, dear?'

'Yes,' said Susan shortly, more moved than she dared admit lest tears overcome her and Mr Hastings in the next room feel the delicious necessity to comfort her. 'Is that . . . all it says?' she gulped, in spite of herself.

'Well now, if I 'adn't forgotten! Nao, there's some more of it. Listen now: "Funeral took place at once. Expect more news by letter. Grateful you come Glenmacool meet Blair. Glad put you up rectory." Aoh, I say Miss Fellowes, I am ever so sorry. Isn't it awful, I mean to say, reminds you of General Gordon and those days, don't it? You can't ever tame savages, that's what I say, it's like tigers, you can't trust 'em 'owever much you . . . Wot's that, Miss?'

'Who's it signed by?'

'Aoh, 'ard to see, oh yes, Weldon, that's the name, W-e-l-d-o-n. A relative, is it, Miss? I suppose so, yes. Anyway, that's the name, Weldon.'

'Thank you, Mrs Lowndes,' said Susan briskly. 'I think I shall have to go over. I shall have to see what arrangements I can make here. Goodbye.'

'Goodbye, Miss. Tch tch tch! Fancy a thing like that 'appenin' in 1948! You won't fret, now, will you, dear? I'll 'ave a nice cup o' tea for you when you get back. Old, was she, dear?'

'Not much under seventy, I should think,' replied Susan in a practical tone. 'Goodbye, Mrs Lowndes.' She put the receiver down firmly before Mrs Lowndes had time to say another word.

She was not a person easily moved to tears, yet the impact of this news of violence done to the person who had dominated her life from infancy, whom for years she had hated and for only one brief moment actually loved, affected her so profoundly that she felt her throat and her eyes smart with compassion. It was the last emotion she would have expected to feel at the death of 'the Pope' and she was angry with herself for her weakness in giving way to it; but the vividness with which her imagination envisaged thy martyrdom of her aunt by Congo natives avenging some ritual infringement or tribal sacrilege forced her to consider how fitting a death it was, how much Katharine herself would have rejoiced in it, and it was this very appropriateness that excited her sympathies.

Susan resented the impulse to grieve for a woman who had bound her with chains that in this life she would never shake off, and whose influence still enslaved her although it was twenty-five years since she had last seen the erect figure and terrifying, implacable eye that penetrated every excuse and laid bare the ultimate, underlying sin. Aunt Katharine, she told herself, was dead and she was free to live her own life, with no one but herself to direct or condemn her. The moment had come for which she had passionately longed, so passionately that the desire had long since spent itself and she no longer cared.

She shut her eyes and pressed her knuckles against them as a child does and felt the strength of 'the Pope' ruling her again as though death had only extended her influence. Katharine's mortal eye, all-seeing though it appeared to be, had nevertheless a limited range; but now her unsleeping spiritual eye was at large day and night to observe secret wishes and unuttered thoughts and to demand penitence with augmented authority. Never had Susan felt so certain of the survival of the spirit as at that moment. She felt oppressed, smothered by Katharine's papal power. She wanted to scream.

She opened her eyes to throw off the terror. The diluted London sunshine was spilt in a wavering pattern on the floor and there was a comforting hum of traffic from the street far below. An unfinished letter confronted her in the typewriter. Everything was normal and reassuring and, quite suddenly, the dread was gone. There remained only the uncomfortable knowledge that for a number of days thoughts of 'the Pope' had filled her mind and refused to be expelled from it; if this became a permanency she would go mad. She refused to contemplate such a possibility and, in proof of this, continued with her typing while half her mind applied itself to reading back her own shorthand. The other half of it, the free and active part, blamed herself that she could so allow a dead women to rule her; even 'the Pope's' own rigid interpretation of Christianity would not have admitted such a principle. She must take the opportunity that had come to her so late and make her own life with the goods and the modest income that she must inevitably inherit. She must return to Ireland, see the house where she had lived until she had run away and that would for ever retain the imprint of 'the Pope's' individuality; and there, or somewhere, learn to be herself, a spinster aged forty-two, of no profession and with no future but that which she could summon from the inadequate resources of her own character.

She finished typing the letter and, before carrying it in to Mr Hastings for signature, took the small mirror from her bag and with a foundering heart examined her face and person for signs of the disturbance that had affected her. Her mouse-brown hair, bent rather than waved into a pleasantly personal, if slightly prim style, was as tidy as it was possible for it to be; her nose did not shine but her mouth needed attention; she applied lipstick to it with care, ran a smoothing finger along the line of her eyebrows and noticed with alarm that the enormous grey eyes that stared back at her looked as if they were haunted. She closed them for a moment in an attempt to screen what they demanded to reveal and, without looking at herself further, took the letter in for Mr Hastings to read and sign.

Standing demurely beside him, noticing for the thousandth time the unruly tendency his black hair had to curl above the unyielding line of his stiff, white city collar almost as soon as he had had it cut, Susan waited until his mind was at leisure to speak to him about herself.

Her last relative had died, she told him, and the family lawyer had sent for her. Mr Hastings, after a quick glance to see if she was inconsolable, remarked that he hoped this meant that she had come in for a fortune. She smiled and shook her head; there was no fortune to inherit, she said, it had all been spent years and years ago.

He smiled at her in his very personal, interested, slightly amusing way. His attention was entirely occupied with her for one brief instant. He was trying to envisage her as she would be in the grip of the family lawyer, back in her old home. He broke off the effort with a tiny shake of the head; it was too difficult.

'Of course you must go, Miss Fellowes,' he said kindly. 'Don't stay away too long, that's all I ask.' His head bent over a report; he had utterly forgotten her.

She did not give him notice; that, she felt, would be cutting off too much, too abruptly. He had been so kind that she felt guilty, because she really knew that she would never come back to this office again. As she ran down the stairs that enclosed the lift-shaft, aware as always of the immense amount of energy she expended in spiralling round the vertical path of the lift itself, she felt that when she reached the boat train that night she would be entering a world where she would have to push the ghosts away with both hands.

It was a curious sensation, this edging away from the race and turmoil of London into the slow, contented timelessness of the Irish countryside. Susan had begun to be aware of it even on the boat train where Irish people talked with leisure in their minds and a relaxed looseness of attitude that sprang from having always had room in which to grow; they were not compressed, tense or jerky, and time seemed not to exist for them. She felt that the peril and excitement of riding the rapids, of being in continuous agitation on the shallowest and most hazardous of currents, had come to an end and that she was beginning to float on slow-moving waters of immense profundity, nearer to the bank where it was possible to catch hold of an overhanging branch in passing and remain static for a contemplative moment or two. She felt the difficulty, as her journey continued, of slowing her own pace to that of her surroundings, of not getting ahead of her physical self and feeling the impatience of the motorist who has to complete his journey on a bicycle.

She felt a tremendous, almost consuming excitement at returning to Glenmacool. For her, all the time she had lived in England, this village and particularly Fellowescourt and the mountain beyond it, had been the native soil to which her roots had travelled for sustenance, as the roots of a vine will thrust out and down until they find moisture to satisfy their needs. She had taken with her imprinted memories of the line of Scotch firs beyond the garden wall, of the old house as it had been in the spacious days, and of the primeval, many-coloured mountain behind it, and these memories had hardened into an inalterable, rather formal series of views that she felt could no longer be valid. She had not allowed for change, she had never considered the form it might take, but she knew that time must have passed a hand over the place, even if its touch had been nothing more than a caress. Other suddenly-recollected and unsummoned memories often surprised her, like leaves falling from a tree knocked or jolted by some outside agency, and these had the spontaneous quality of life itself, infinitely refreshing. But she was a little afraid that the present aspect of Fellowescourt and Glenmacool might reveal the difference between her youthful vision and the actual, unadorned and unidealised.

Fellowescourt had been let for many years, she knew, while 'the Pope' had been abroad; the tenants had been Americans, called Tilsit, and that was all she knew of them. She felt a great curiosity to discover whether their occupation had altered the house, not structurally, but in its essential being; would it still feel like home to her, or would it only be home to someone like the Tilsits? Would it have its ancient smell, compounded of wood-fires, hen-food being cooked, oil-lamps, soda-bread and damp? Or would it be so elegant now, so changed in every detail, that it breathed a different quality of air? Would there be little bits of Tilsit left about, or would every trace of them have been cleared away? She hoped that there might be, here and there, some small personal clue to their nature; but she also hoped, beyond all else, that the house had not forgotten the Fellowes family and given itself altogether to the strangers.

Alone in the ancient railway carriage, bobbing on the seat like a cork on a waterspout, she was so drawn back into the past that she was aware of the feel of woollen school stockings thick between her knees, of woollen gloves laid on the seat beside her, discarded until the first day of the next term because they set her teeth on edge and she would suffer cold, chilblains and chapped hands rather than put them on, and the hollow feeling of apprehension at the thought of 'the Pope'; she had longed to be back at Fellowescourt, yet dreaded Katharine's papal rule; the holidays had been a kind of exquisite torture, liberation tainted by the threat of damnation. 'The Pope' had possessed the knack of bringing her so near to extinction that survival of her own flickering likeness and individuality had seemed beyond the bounds of possibility; no wonder, thought Susan, spanning the gap of twenty-five years with more misgiving than reassurance, no wonder she felt that 'the Pope' would haunt her to the end of her days.

As the train drew into the station at Inish she let down the window and put out her head. It had precisely the same look of serviceable yet moss-grown bleakness, of the junk-room halfway through spring cleaning that she remembered as its distinguishing characteristic, and its familiar smell, compounded of coal smoke, cattle, damp and lavatories. A figure dressed in black was on the platform, tall, shabby and with an enquiring air about it, taking a quick look into each carriage as it trundled slowly past; peering finally into her own carriage and coming up to the door, hat raised and hand outstretched as the train stopped moving.

'Why,' exclaimed Susan, 'it's . . .you.' She broke off in some embarrassment. She had nearly said, 'It's Uncle Lawrence,' and that appellation had been dismissed from current use when she was only above twelve years old, when the engagement had been broken off.

'Ah, Susan my dear child,' he said warmly, looking at her with such interest that she was unable to return his scrutiny with the same frankness. She smiled at him, and felt obliged to divert herself with the need to attend to her luggage. A porter, immature and gangling, as unaware as a grazing dinosaur, stood staring at the volcanic eruptions of the antique engine, turning endlessly round his mouth a ball of chewing-gum; it was inconceivable that he should ever do anything different but at a summons from Lawrence he suffered a change so striking that Susan could not at first believe that he was the same creature. He leapt into action, seizing her suitcases and flinging them on to his barrow as if they were empty paper bags, then, co-ordinating his body and limbs with difficulty, set off at a fast lope across the line.

Lawrence apologised for his ancient car as they drove off, begged permission to pick up some parcels on the way through Inish and politely asked her if she had found the journey trying. From time to time he looked at her briefly, shook his head and lapsed into silence. Susan carefully probed her memory for the names that must not be made a subject for enquiry: old Mrs Weldon was dead, she knew, but what of Esmé? She did not like to ask.

As they drew up outside the butcher's shop, Lawrence seemed to gather from the physical act of bringing the car to a standstill the power of decision to declare something that was in his mind. Pushing his feet stoutly to the limit of clutch and brake pedals and drawing the hand-brake towards him with a gesture of finality, he leant back and, retaining his extended position, turned his head towards Susan with a tentative smile.

'You must forgive me, Susan. Perhaps you won't like what I am going to say, but there is such a likeness between you and your poor Aunt Katharine as she used to be in the early days, before . . . before you started to grow up.'

'You always said so,' said Susan, stiffening a little, so distasteful was the thought to her, 'but it doesn't go below the surface. I haven't got a fraction of her character, I've hardly got a character at all, and she was all character; it came out of her in sparks, like electricity.'

He looked appraisingly at the tidy, slightly prim head, the mouth set in an unconvincing line of hesitant renunciation, the charming intelligent brow and large grey eyes that belonged to a different face from hers, a hungry, unfulfilled face, the face of someone who is unsure, disturbed by incomprehensible restraints and driven by forces that have long been at work without the unqualified consent of the owner. He looked down quickly, withdrew his feet and hand from their outstretched positions, and gathered himself together for the almost explosive ejection with which he always hurtled from the car to the next point he wished to reach, as it were in one prolonged movement, motivated by a single burst of energy.

'The physical resemblance is very striking,' he said gently, 'but I see what you mean. You have not got her . . . rather frightening certainty.' He was gone, already in the shop before she had gathered her wits for a reply; she felt that he would return without having been even aware of any break in their conversation, and continue as if such necessary and arbitrary interruptions did not merit explanation or apology, so inconsiderable was their effect upon the flow of thought and talk.

She did not use this period of solitude to catch up with his advance and prepare something to say that would drive him to reply, but made a little side-step, a personal diversion necessary to her and which would lead her back on the same track in the end. She set free from behind a gate in her mind the dark shape of the tragedy of Barry's capture on the mountain, of the confused grief and self-condemnation of his parents that a son of theirs could so come to his death, and of the share in the blame for his capture that she had then allotted to 'the Pope'; she set it free to wander as it pleased, to find its own way about, to take up, if it so wished, a threatening attitude and block her path; but the mildness of its deportment was astonishing and she felt that now she need no longer drive it back behind the gate but could leave it harmlessly at large.

The seething, consuming indignation that had driven her to run away from 'the Pope' as soon as the news had become known had, to some extent, dwindled when Olivia had relayed 'the Pope's' reassurance to her that Barry's capture was none of her contriving, and this assurance had been verified in passionate terms by Mrs O'Brien who begged her to return in charity to Fellowescourt and Katharine. But Susan had broken away in hot blood and knew, as well as she knew anything upon earth, that if she went back another occasion would arise which would make the same demands upon her without, perhaps, bringing her courage to the pitch of making the breach. Besides, Katharine would not have her back: this she had stated, and this Susan had been told. So, although 'the Pope' was told that Susan absolved her from blame in this respect, she had to make what excuses she could for her failure to return, and these she chose to base upon the depth of her attachment to Barry, painful though it was to herself to drag this into the light of day.

It had been a temptation to Susan to make a big thing out of her loss in Barry's death, to give their immature relationship an aura of immortal attachment and her own sense of bereavement the grandeur of being inconsolable. But, angry and horror-struck as she had been, and personally stricken by the waste of his goodness and strength and the sacrificial devotion with which he had turned his face to the light and away from the normal pleasures of the young, her battle had been fought while she was still almost a child, when his mother had told her with joyful pride that he was going to be a priest. She had renounced him then, prickingly aware that he had never considered her sufficiently interested in him to be in need of such a warning from himself. So she had mourned, not a lover, but a flame extinguished, youth unfinished, promise unfulfilled. Her larger, more compassionate grief had been for his mother and father in their perplexed affliction. But always she had kept this memory of her last day at Fellowescourt confined, afraid to set it at liberty lest it torment her beyond bearing; now that she let it out and found it almost friendly, she could continue on the direct path of Lawrence's progress through the intervening years without looking in alarm from one side or the other lest the gate be accidentally unlocked.

She felt reassured and much more at her ease. Her mind ceased to dwell on the remote and she began to notice the people moving along the street, the air of unluxurious prosperity alongside the unmistakeable look and smell of poverty, the light-hearted effervescence of the robust and confident shown up by the pallid resignation of the very poor.

Lawrence handed her a sodden parcel, red and amorphous, the contents sliding within the limits of their containing string.

'Liver,' he announced. 'Don't let it get on your clothes. I won't keep you a moment.' He was gone again, out of sight; her eye had been unable to keep track of him.

How like a man, she thought, to tell you not to let it get on your clothes yet to make no provision against this! She held the parcel from her, looking round the car for a piece of newspaper, an unimportant cloth or even a plate provided for just this emergency, but there was nothing. The parcel began to drip watery red drops between her fingers onto the rubber flooring at her feet and she smiled at the thought of the relish with which any British housewife would have endured such small unpleasantness for the sake of having a bit of real, home-grown liver to cook.

She forgot the fact of the parcel in her extended hand as she watched and listened to the coming and going of the country traffic, so expressive of the ancient busy-ness of remote communities still on the fringe of the evolutionary process. Donkeys and horses, carts rattling and shaking over roads that would jolt the insides out of city dwellers, bicycles and venerable motor-cars shivering and vibrating, yet somehow holding together, these and Shanks's pony were the means of transport here. She watched the way the horses stood: a half-schooled colt with head thrown back nervously and a white streak in the eye, his legs stuck outwards in the effort to hold his ground against the march of civilisation; the resignation of an old black pony, dusty in the sunlight, ears unalert, rope reins thrown over his back; and the engaging interest shown by a small brown donkey in the passers-by, her head turned towards the pavement, dark velvet ears set up and forward in a gesture of pleased enquiry; while, across the street, stood in immobile abstraction another donkey as old as time itself, as light in colour as bleached bones, its long, soft ears laid sideways as though depressed by the weight of years on the bony head, taking time off from living until the shake of the reins should jerk it to life again. Even while she watched, a little wizen of a woman hopped on to the cart and the old donkey broke at once into a trippling gait, its tiny hoofs on the hard surface making a swift, light tune like the sound of a tinkling piano through an open window.

'Ah, look what I've done to you,' said Lawrence's voice at the window, filled with disgust at his thoughtlessness. He was gone again, back to the butcher's shop in a single bound and back again on the instant with a whole newspaper in his hand. He took the blood-stained parcel from Susan and laid it on the paper on the back seat, contritely offering her his unused handkerchief on which to wipe her fingers. Then, this having been only another of those essential breaks in the train of thought on which it is waste of time to comment, he returned without warning to the point he had reached earlier.

'You have not got her eyes,' he stated, and made no observation beyond this. The car was already under way and they were weaving their way out. On the edge of the town, where the street became a road, Susan saw with delight how slight had been the changes and how enduring was the character of the countryside. The grass, of surpassing brilliance, was shaggy at the roadside, the black iron pump with its fluted top was surrounded by tiny children with vessels to be filled while those with brimming cans staggered homewards, water spilling over their bare feet, the boys' heads cropped close but for a quiff of hair in the front, the sound of their heels on the road staccato as the tripping of goats. New concrete houses had been set up here and there, slate-roofed and with oak-grained, hideous hall doors, but they were sub-merged by the beauty of the long slant of the light on the gorse bushes in flower, on the gleaming bog pools and the shimmering willow leaves above the ditches.

Lawrence stole a look at her. 'Ah,' he said with satisfaction, 'you're glad to be back.'

She did not answer, feeling a tinge of annoyance that he should find her expression so easy to interpret. But he was undeterred by this, or indeed unconscious of it, and went on, 'Your aunt was home on furlough only two years ago, camping out in Fellowescourt. But she was glad to be off again. She felt that her life was . . . out there by then. In a curious way she transferred her entire being to that country, not just her physical presence, to the Nbu people. Yet, you see what happened . . .? A terrible death, it must have been, to be cut down by the people on whom she had spent herself.' His voice sounded as if he had more to say, but Susan, after a moment's pause in which he might have continued, spoke firmly.

'I'm certain she would rather have died like that. She was a born martyr; it was more fitting than anything that had ever happened to her. I'm sure that the way she died made converts of every one of her assassins, they could not have resisted it, and it would have made her even with them in the end.'

He glanced at her with respect. 'I had not thought of it like that, I must confess,' he said humbly. 'I had only thought of her as a woman alone, surrounded by hostile savages and gradually coming to realise that there was going to be no escape.'

'Is it worse for a woman to die than it is for a man?' said Susan with a little sting in her voice.

'Perhaps she is less accustomed to being unprotected,' he said quietly.

'Not Aunt Katharine,' said Susan. 'She always had to fend for herself.'

'Yes, poor girl, she did,' he said reflectively, 'and it was perhaps partly because of that that she expected so much of other people who had not her independence of character.'

'Like me,' said Susan, looking straight through the windscreen and blushing after she had spoken, because to say such a thing now sounded vengeful and ungenerous.

'And me,' he said, surprisingly. Susan was so disarmed by this admission that she looked quickly at him and away again, but he was aware of her eye upon him and answered with a swift smile whose warmth for her was tempered by ruefulness at his own weakness. 'You don't feel embittered about her,' he went on. 'I can see that and I am so glad, so very glad.'

The statement was so untrue that Susan recoiled and nearly spoke in protest against what she could only think of as a deliberate and premeditated lie, but the intention behind the words affected her so that she began to feel that they were beginning to be true and might be altogether so if she did not deny them. And suddenly she felt ashamed that she could believe words spoken in such obvious sincerity to be a mere device to bring about in her a condition that had not existed before they were spoken; no, he had meant them and the fact that he had meant them took the ground from under her feet and left her abased.

'You see,' he continued, 'she was really very fond of you.' He leant a little forward over the driving wheel as if to emphasise this. Susan drew in her mouth and gave an almost inaudible sniff, so preposterous did she find this statement, having with difficulty swallowed his last one. But he hammered on the rim of the wheel with his fist and insisted, 'No, don't sniff. It's absolutely true. You must not be under any misapprehension about it: she was genuinely fond of you, I know it.'

Susan sat stiffly, refusing to credit it. 'How do you know?' she said, feeling obliged to listen to the evidence yet unwilling to dispel the prejudice that fortified her mind against it. But the very intensity with which Lawrence had stressed his belief made her think him equally biased, but in Katharine's favour.

'Because she denied herself everything so that you could go to school. She was determined that you were going to be properly educated, whatever became of herself. You must believe this, I know it to be true. She endured real sacrifice for your sake.'

'But I got a scholarship,' objected Susan.

'I know you did, but she still had to find more money than she could afford. She was in very difficult circumstances at that time, she had nothing to spend on herself. She even,' he hesitated, as if he were unsure of his authority to reveal the next fact, and of his wisdom in doing so, 'she even . . . postponed our marriage on that account. As you know, in the end it never took place, but that was for a different reason.' He relaxed again, sitting back.

Susan was silent for a little while she considered all this. Then she said slowly, 'I believe you are right, but why did she take such immense pains to make it quite impossible for me to know? I always believed she loathed me. After that scholarship I never did anything to make her proud of me, and she needed something out of the ordinary to gratify her. She was always disappointed in me, from the moment I first remember her until I . . . ran away.'

'Her reserve was like iron. It encased her compassion, refusing it expression. It was like a scourge to her, this inability to show affection.' Lawrence gripped the wheel tightly, seeming to shake it with the vehemence of his conviction. 'I have known her appear very hard, reprehensibly hard, but I believe that was because she demanded as high a standard from other people as from herself. No, it was not that she didn't feel, but that she was incapable of showing it.' He darted a quick, enquiring look at Susan's face to see how his words were being received, and saw that it was thoughtful and composed.

'You're not just making excuses for her?' Susan looked straight at him.

'I am *not,*' he said in the local idiom, for emphasis. 'I believe her to have been gravely misunderstood.'

'She misunderstood too,' insisted Susan, her voice and expression so deeply serious that Lawrence knew that she was about to put into words some ancient and fundamental incompatibility. 'She wanted to turn me out in her own mould, like a cornflour shape of herself, if you understand me. Anything different was wrong, and when I say wrong I mean sinful, against God, and had to be eradicated; and my deficiencies, because they weren't the same as hers, had to be altered until they were like hers, and therefore excusable. She very nearly annihilated me. I grew up feeling so wicked that I couldn't be in the same room with her without it being driven in upon me how despicable I was, and how intentionally I was falling short of her designs for me. I had to be remade by her and the credit for me had to be hers too, but there never was any credit, so . . .' She shrugged her shoulders and gave a tight little smile, 'so I was a continual disappointment to her.'

Lawrence did not say anything for a moment; he looked most gravely concerned and hovered, as it were, over his distress, assessing the value of Susan's assertions, calculating their validity. His head was bent a little forward so that he had the appearance of looking through the thick jutting hedge of eyebrow that accentuated the structural cavity framing the eyes.

'Was that really the case?' he asked incredulously, yet his tone was rhetorical and the question was a general one implying amazement that such things could be, rather than doubt that she was speaking the truth.

'It's true,' said Susan with finality, 'absolutely true. That's why I'm such an uncertain sort of creature now. I still have to find myself out, you know; I'm hardly a person at all.'

'But it's twenty-five years. . .' protested Lawrence.

'Yes, I know, but she had got such a hold on me that she still went on moulding me even though I never saw her. I never lost that awful sense of guilt about anything that was personally pleasing to me: if I wanted it I felt it must be wrong. And I could only make amends for wanting it by doing without it, it doesn't matter what.'

'But, my dear child, that is terrible, really terrible.' He seemed so shocked by this revelation that he had difficulty in saying the words, as though their weight might leave heavy footmarks on the vulnerable surface she had exposed, so he said them lightly, quietly, and in a tone of shocked wonder. 'Had you,' he said diffidently, 'had you no resources with which to repel her . . . invasion of your personality? Had you no resistance?'

'Not when I was small, but then I had Aunt Olivia and Aunt Harriet to back me up sometimes, but she made me feel that they were wicked too if they took my side against her,' said Susan, thought following

thought haphazardly. 'It wasn't till I was about twelve that I had any
glimmering that anything I thought or felt could possibly have the
slightest worth or be authentic for me because it was *mine.*' She laid
such emphasis upon the 'mine' that she was obliged to pause after it.

'And then?' he said, with gentle enquiry.

'And then it was a little better, but very often she nearly extinguished
it. It has never quite left me. I've always had a spark left; otherwise, I
think I should have gone mad.'

'What brought you to this realisation—that there was something in
you yourself that demanded recognition?'

'Ah!' she said, smiling at last, expanding in this warmer climate of
recollection. 'Do you remember the Christmas just after the Armistice,
in 1918?'

'I do indeed,' he said, as if she had struck him a mortal blow. She
remembered, with regret at having stirred up painful memories, that
it had been then that his engagement had been broken, and she could
not help wondering as she hastened to slide over the dangerous patch,
whether he still felt it as deeply as all that.

'It was in church, on Christmas Day, and all the aunts were there.
You had just come back and it was the first time that everybody who
had been there before the war was there again—it looked just like that
. . . old days, only . . . it wasn't,' she added quickly, 'because things were
different inside everybody. Anyway, I was sitting between Nanny and
Aunt Harriet. The rest of them were all in the choir and of course Aunt
Katharine was playing the harmonium.'

'Yes?' he said sombrely.

'Well, something just happened to me, I think it was Aunt Harriet
who did something to me because she didn't know I was there, she
didn't know anything was there. You remember Uncle Eustace was still
missing then.'

'Yes?'

'Well, I knew quite suddenly that she wasn't there at all, she was really praying, and that was the first time I had the slightest notion what religion was all about. It meant something to me, not the sort of thing Aunt Katharine had always told me about God hating this or that, but it was like a light that suddenly made me see everything right. I was so excited I felt I couldn't ever be quite the same again.'

'And?

'And . . . it never quite went out. Mrs O'Brien helped me, but it got pretty low.'

'You should thank God that you had it,' he barked at her with ferocity. 'It is the most precious thing that you can have, the very flame of life, and the only thing that really matters.'

Without saying another word he managed to convey to her that this conversation was at an end. She was aware of it but unable to account for it. Had it been in his voice, a practical inflexion as he broke off? Or in his way of sitting—an alteration in his attitude, a stirring of the shoulders, a kind of shaking off of his mood, not from impatience but because other things were beginning to press for admission to his consciousness? She sat in companionable silence, gradually returning to awareness of their surroundings. They were nearly at Glenmacool and she had not asked one of the essential questions.

'Oh dear,' she said breathlessly, 'there is so much I must ask you about everybody, and now there isn't any time. Is your sister . . . does she . . .?'

'Yes,' he said, with casual good-humour, as if they had just been discussing tennis or a musical comedy, 'Esmé lives with me still. You will find her very altered, I'm afraid,' he added warningly. 'She's a complete invalid now, you know, but she loves to talk to people.'

'And the O'Briens?'

'Ah, poor Mrs O'Brien. She's still at Myrtle Lodge, poor thing, when she's at home, but she's gone out to Uganda to visit the daughter who married a forestry man out there—she was the clever one, Teresa, the one who went to college. The doctor died, you know; he was never the same after that boy was killed. You could see him being eaten away by it.' He shook his head slightly as though he had been reluctantly obliged to grant some unpleasant memory access to his mind.

'I didn't see him,' said Susan thinking back, 'but I thought it would kill her if anything happened to Barry.'

'Women are tougher than men at survival,' he said.

'And the children?' she asked.

'Ah, they're men and women now. All the girls are married; Kevin—the baby, you know—he's building one of these terrific great hydro-electric dams out in Africa somewhere.' There was amused admiration in his voice at the achievements of one so recently an infant. Susan remembered Kevin only as a nuisance, an insistent child who wanted to climb up Barry's legs and be thrown in the air by him while she wanted all his attention for herself.

'Who's the doctor now, then?' she asked.

'Oh, Cormac; he was the second boy, I think. Anyway, he's a first-class doctor. He lives there with his mother; he's never married yet, so it suits them both. Bridie looks after them.'

They were approaching the rectory gate, slowing down to make the turn. Straight on was the road to the village, over the crown of the hill. On the left, the cement wall of the convent had been weathered to shabbiness, moss-green lines of ugliness marking where the water drained off it, cracks seaming it unbecomingly. Beyond the hill and out of sight lay Fellowescourt and the village. It was with a sensation of being diverted from her real purpose that she consented to be driven up to the rectory; she felt that she was falling short of her objective.

'How does Fellowescourt look?' she demanded with great urgency, needing to know before she was involved in social chatter with Esmé. 'And what were the Tilsits like?'

'They did the old house a lot of good,' he said. 'It looks as sound as a bell. You'll find it different inside. The garden is neglected and looks shocking now; they maintained it admirably, but it's gone to pieces since they died.'

They were there, without time to say another word. She was swept into the hall on a wave of apprehension.

'By the way,' he said, opening the drawing-room door and propelling her gently forward, 'Blair is coming tomorrow, for the day.'

Mr Blair had been more a name to her, a target for her aunts' censure because he had been the means of restricting their creature comforts and it pleased them to consider him the cause besides, than a person of whom she had any knowledge. He had been a shape in the corridor, a voice in the study, a reason for putting on a dressing-gown when she went to her bath from the nursery, but beyond the politeness of 'Good morning' and 'How do you do?' he had had no existence for her. She wished she did not have to bother with him now; he must be very elderly: when she had been eight years old he had appeared venerable; it was astonishing that he could still be alive.

She was well into the room by this time and only beginning to perceive its nature. It was very warm indeed, with a blazing fire in spite of the May sunshine, and a carefully measured crack of window lifted from the bottom to admit only a whiff of air, a minute infiltration whose range was limited by its very minuteness. Flowers and pot plants were grouped on a single table at the far end of the room, out of reach of the fierce glow from the fireplace, and just beyond the fire, surrounded by magazines, novels, patent medicines, little wraps and rugs and all the impedimenta of invalidism, lay Esmé on a sofa.

She was disconcerted because Susan had not at once perceived her, and all her show of welcome and its accompanying revelations of suffering and handicap and heart-rending courage must now be gone through all over again. She had to pretend to make the effort to rise and to discover that it was too much for her, to apologise in gestures for her frailty and inadequacy and to make a brave little comment on her wretched state that would excuse her from all further exertion. She did it most convincingly and Susan advanced towards her quite overcome with pity, especially as her appearance gave every possible support to her claims for sympathy.

Esmé looked dreadful; she was really so depressing to contemplate that the eye sought refuge at once. She was so thin that her sleeves hung upon her arms as if they were on sticks and her wrists looked enlarged out of all proportion; the rug over her legs fell with a knife-sharp line from knees to feet and her face, neck and shoulders seemed to have been pared of flesh down to the bones and sinews. Her hair was still not white but of that kind of yellowish-grey mixed with white that is so unbecoming to a cement-coloured pallor; what flesh remained on her looked as if no blood had ever been through it and her mouth was curiously twisted on one side; only her eyes looked as if they were alive; huge, dark, burning pools of suffering for human misery, her own. And she still wore the one colour calculated to accentuate the most distressing features of her affliction, dark brown, unrelieved and hideous beyond belief.

'Dear Susan,' she said in a weak voice, smiling her pleasure and feebly extending a hand to be shaken. 'How very nice to have you back again.' She patted a portion of the sofa not occupied by her legs so that Susan could sit close to her. 'I can't talk to people far away, my voice isn't strong enough,' she explained, 'so they have to come and sit right on my sofa. So tiresome for them, but it's just one of the wretched things about my illness. However,' and she made a gesture of renunciation, 'don't let's talk about me, I'm so dull. Let me look at you, dear child—though of course you aren't a child any more, are you?'

'Well, hardly,' said Susan, aware of her cheek flushing from the blast of heat that struck it like a solid thing. She could feel her skin protesting, cracking and drying, becoming tauter every second. It was almost intolerable, an outside thing that became more important every moment until it dispelled every other thing from her mind. She looked about her in desperation until her eye fell on the pile of magazines. Picking one up, she said, 'May I hold this up? It's just that the fire on my face. . .'

'Oh!' cried Esmé, clasping her hands together in distress. 'It's always the way; the fire's too much for everyone. You see, I feel the cold so dreadfully, even if the fire screen's put out I begin to shiver. It's too silly, I know, but there it is.' She gave a deprecating little laugh.

Lawrence was smiling at them from just inside the door, his coat open; he was not really with them because he was just going to put the car away, but with a tiny frown of recollection he landed, as it were, amongst them.

'Have you had your rest?' he demanded peremptorily, as if the last thing he expected to hear was Esmé's affirmative, and the rest was a daily necessity only brought on by fear of his brutal questioning.

'Well,' she said apologetically, 'I didn't seem to be able to drop off. Philomena made such a noise washing up, and then the clock in the hall has such a loud tick that I didn't seem able to settle down, somehow.' She extended her suffering towards him for sympathy, as a child does with its face to be kissed, and his response was immediate and satisfying. He looked distressed and angry with everything that dared to frustrate or disturb her. Both of them had forgotten Susan. With a grunt of annoyance he turned on his heel and left the room, shutting the door carefully so as to maintain the temperature evenly.

Esmé's concern with her annoyances had carried her so far out into the room that Susan could almost feel her shrinking back into the confinement of her physical immobility. She was not instantly able to remember that she had a visitor, she needed momentary adjustment. Even her eyes had to become accustomed to focussing on something so near to her.

'Oh!' she exclaimed, with one of her little laughs, 'how stupid of me!' This made her excuses for temporary absence, for her unavoidable rudeness, for all her deficiencies; it emphasised the importance of remembering that she was not quite like other people and needed special treatment. There was a little pause while she sighed and then, making an obvious effort to be cheerful, she said, 'Now, let me look at you, Susan! Who are you like, let me see!'

She closed her eyes suddenly and opened them again very wide, bending her head this way and that, the better to make her inspection.

'Did anyone,' she began, and paused; then, with a little run at the words she tried again, 'Did anyone ever tell you that you were like your aunt? Your Aunt Katharine?' She blinked several times.

'Yes, often,' replied Susan. 'I've never been able to see it myself.'

'Then it doesn't distress you?'

'Not particularly: I'm not like her in any other way.'

'Oh?' Esmé sounded unconvinced.'If that's the case, I must say I'm glad: I never could take to your aunt, I'm afraid.' With a rush she continued in a confidential tone, 'You know, I must tell you what a relief it was when that engagement was broken off. I don't expect you even remember it. She and my brother were to be married, you know, but I never thought it a good thing. Such a dominating woman! She would never have made him happy, and he deserves the very best. He was heart-broken, of course, but it was all for the best, and now I suppose he'll never marry. I must say, I've yet to see the woman who's good enough for him. He's been a wonderful brother to me, kindness itself!'

'I'm glad he's still here: I didn't expect he'd spend his whole life in the same parish,' said Susan.

It was clear that Esmé was displeased by this observation. The twist in her mouth became more pronounced, and her eyes were withdrawn instantly from Susan's face and turned towards her own knees. She brushed an invisible crumb from the rug as she said stiffly, 'Of course he's been offered several other parishes; did you know he's a Canon now? They couldn't let qualities like his go unrecognised.'

'Yes, but there are fewer and fewer people here every year, I should have thought a big, busy parish. . .' said Susan, looking puzzled.

'He turned them all down,' announced Esmé; her voice was sharp. 'He knew that I'm never well anywhere else, so he . . . did what any good brother would do, and turned them down. Of course I tried to make him accept them, but he simply wouldn't hear of it.'

'Oh!' said Susan, beginning to perceive the extent of Lawrence's enslavement to his sister's ill-health.

'He'll never move now, while I'm alive,' said Esmé with a sort of fierce satisfaction. 'And really,' she added, smiling wistfully, 'I think we are as happy as you could expect.'

Susan looked at her with incipient scepticism: was she aware of the relative nature of this statement, of the fact that perhaps one might not expect them to be happy at all? Esmé's face was tortured and full of innocence.

'He has the two parishes, now,' added Esmé. 'Glenmacool and Kilmichael. They joined them together when old Mr Poer died, so he has enough to keep him busy. That's why he has a car; he needs it to get round all that distance, but he gets so little petrol, you've no idea.' She gave Susan a sly look. 'He really hasn't enough to go into Inish meeting trains and that sort of thing, but he would insist that he must go and fetch you, so you're highly honoured.'

'Oh dear, I'm sorry, I'd no idea. . .' stammered Susan. 'I'd no idea it was still rationed over here.'

'Petrol is very difficult,' said Esmé severely. 'He really hasn't got enough for his needs. I hope you won't expect him to drive you about?'

'Oh no, of course not,' insisted Susan. Nothing had been further from her thoughts.

There was a thump on the door and Philomena staggered in with a heavy tray, rushing forward with terrifying impetus. It was difficult to imagine what might bring her to a halt.

'Quick,' screamed Esmé, 'the table!' She pointed to a folding table and Susan ran to fetch it, open it out and put it beside the sofa before Philomena's progress turned to disaster. The tray was banged down on to it and Philomena stood back, panting.

She was a huge woman with a square body and face, iron-grey hair waved in rigid lines and enormous red hands. Her nose and mouth were in straight lines, like her brow; there was not a curve apparent on her entire person. Even her bosom was like a thick, deep shelf. Her shiny black frock was well worn and her celluloid cuffs and collar were yellow from long use; her cap looked as if it might take leave of her head without warning.

'Oah,' she said resentfully, 'that thray'll be the death o' me one o' these days!'

'You've no right,' stormed Esmé, 'to come in here with it like that. Haven't I told you again and again to put it down outside, open the door and get out the table first. Then you wouldn't have any trouble. But no, you won't do what you're told, Philomena, and besides making it difficult for yourself you do me a great deal of harm: it's not good for me to have frights like that, it's very bad for me.' She glared accusingly.

'I'm sorry, Miss,' Philomena said, humbly enough, and went out to fetch the cake-stand. She tried to move quietly but concentration on her movements made her breathe with a kind of bulldog snore which was even more trying than a heavy tread.

'I'm afraid,' commented Esmé tartly when she had gone, 'that I shall never make anything of Philomena!' She glanced round impatiently. 'Now, where has Lawrence got to? The tea will be stone cold.'

Lawrence came in at that moment, bland, patient and smiling again. 'I hope you haven't waited for me,' he said.

'You know I never start without you,' replied Esmé sharply.

'I wish you would. I can't always be sure of getting in at the right moment,' he said persuasively.

Esmé glared at them both. Susan was aware of an age-long division between them, a perpetual fount of ill-feeling that probably bubbled up three, if not four times every day; he, preoccupied and blandly unalive to the significance of the precise minute to her, to whom meals were mile-stones in time, a matter of moment, the great events of her barren life.

Lawrence sat down without any sign of irritation; Susan wondered if Esmé's waspishness had long ago ceased to sting him, if he had developed an immunity to it, or whether he made allowances and refused to allow his distress to show from sheer goodness and Christian charity; she suspected the latter; he was patient with such determination that it was plainly not natural to him. She felt great admiration for his self-control and marvelled at his affection for a creature so unlovable, but the ugly thought pushed its way through, like a weed from under a stone, that by such self-effacement he was only making her worse: Esmé would grasp and use every means of bringing him utterly under her power.

'You pour out, Susan,' suggested Lawrence. 'Esmé can't, and men are no good at that sort of thing.'

'No, Lawrence, no!' hissed Esmé, words seething voluminously in her, yet unexpressed.

'Oh, very well,' he said mildly, picking up the teapot. 'Milk and sugar, Susan?'

'Just milk, please.' There was a pause while she hoped for courage to ask something necessary. She said, 'There's just one thing I must ask you . . .' She was blushing with embarrassment. 'What would you like me to call you both? I mean . . . Miss Weldon and Canon Weldon, or . . . I know I'm a lot younger than both of you, so perhaps . . . I just want to know what you'd like, yourselves.'

Lawrence sat back in his chair and smiled at her with affectionate regard; to her relief there was not a hint of amusement in his expression. He opened his mouth to speak, but Esmé was before him.

'You can call me Esmé,' she said without geniality, 'but I think you should call my brother Canon Weldon; you owe it to his cloth.'

CHAPTER SIXTEEN

The nuns were walking about inside the convent wall as Susan passed on her way to Fellowescourt. The wall was too high for her to see very much but now and again a black wing of veiling would lift on the wind, flutter and fall. She could hear their eager chatter, and the up and down swing of local intonation without hearing a word of what they said. The convent had been there since long before she first came to Fellowescourt, yet the fact of it had affected her little as a child; the nuns had been an object of interest because of their conspicuous form of dress and their magnetic attraction for stray cats; cats seemed to be drawn there in droves, to settle down in perfect contentment and issue forth on far-flung marauding expeditions to the rage of 'the Pope', whose baby chicks had regularly been carried off by them. Now Susan saw the place with a different eye, as a remote oasis of life in life, the continuing in the transitory; she wondered if any of the women now behind that wall had been there when she used to run past in childhood on her way to Myrtle Lodge, and if so, whether their ordered, dedicated spirituality had ever led one of them to rub shoulders, as it were, with her for a fleeting instant of eternity, in her own progress by her different route.

She hurried on to the crown of the hill, and only a little beyond, on the left, was Fellowescourt, its genial brown stone warmed and glowing in the sunshine behind the straggling indiscipline of the yew-hedge. She stopped for a moment, taking it in, then went on to the gap in the hedge that marked the entrance to Peter Cavanagh's little field. Through it and beyond she could see the line of Scotch firs that backed

Fellowescourt and the mountain itself, glistening and glinting in the sunlight after a wet night. The little field had been a black path to her the last times she had crossed it, twice on that one deadly morning when, after she had discovered Barry, cold, hungry and hunted on the mountain, she had rushed to his mother with the news, then back again with her and the load of food and clothing for him, taking the short cut in the hope of secrecy. Even now, it grieved her to see that path, but with an endurable, recollected ache of suffering long ago, not the frenzied, engulfing agony of the day itself.

The little iron gate was painted black and had been rehung, but the yew sprigs had grown downwards from the archway, making it difficult to pass under it without bringing down the diamond shower of raindrops that Susan had so often dislodged upon one or other of her aunts. She closed the little gate and went slowly up the path, deliberately brushing her feet against the brilliant fringe of grass that framed each flag-stone. The little lawns on either side and the once trim grass borders surrounding the two large beds were rough and tussocky; it was clear that they had not even been scythed for a long time and the grass itself had spread over the beds, making a matted surface pierced only by the pale blades of the purple irises, even now leggily in bud, and the more robust weeds. The hall door, still white, had lost nothing in its grandeur. The great, long white-framed windows of dining-room and drawing-room looked on at the disorder like maidens lining a ballroom in prim disapproval of the goings-on.

Susan fumbled in her pocket for the key, carefully labelled by Lawrence, and opened the front door.

She stood there in the doorway, smiling with the pleasure of being in the house again and letting the warm, dry, daytime air into the hungry chill of the unoccupied building. She made no attempt to go any further until the smell of the house and the shapes of familiar things made her conscious that she was home again.

Her first impression was of light and space, which was odd, for the little narrow hall had always had a gloomy, cave-like quality in her memory, intensified by the crowded sporting relics on the walls and the over-burdened coat-stand from which nothing was ever discarded. She saw now that the walls were clear of all the weapons and the stuffed heads, the kayak and the hunting trophies, and were painted a very pale sea-green, with the ceiling and frieze brilliantly white. The elephant's foot, with its seedy collection of disreputable umbrellas, faded parasols, down-at-heel walking sticks and forgotten riding crops, had been removed with the coat-stand. The hall looked elegant now, with only the long narrow table, a couple of chairs, the great clock and the big pot-pourri bowl remaining from the old days. Susan could not but approve of its present aspect; it looked so classical, so right and simple, and so obviously as it had been designed to look when Thomas Fellowes had built the house. But she did wonder where everything that had been there in her childhood now was.

She went into the drawing-room with the sensation of having to cleave the atmosphere with every step she made. It seemed to be petrified, to have solidified silence and stillness into perceptible matter, a sort of tangible inertia. She went to the windows and opened them wide, but even so the life and movement of the outside air did not at once overcome the timeless resistance to motion that now characterised the room. But again, as she stood there, she was aware of the lightness and the surprising extent of the room, the beauty of bas-relief on frieze and ceiling brought out entirely by clever decoration.

The walls and the base of the frieze were the colour of the sky behind the mountain on a winter's morning, neither blue nor grey, yet made up of both, with a shimmer of light on the wallpaper that was not repeated on the matt surface above it. The relief-work and the ceiling were white, as in the hall. The scheme accentuated the best and previously invisible features of the room with such success that Susan was charmed by what she was discovering about the Tilsits. They had consulted the house, they had loved it and whatever they had done had brought forth grateful response; Fellowescourt had enjoyed having them.

Leaving the hall door and all the windows open, Susan went upstairs treading on the repeats of the carpet pattern as she had used to do on her way to bed after saying goodnight to 'the Pope'. She stood at the nursery window, loving the sight of the tall, glowing golden-pink trunks of the fir trees under their tops of virile green, saying to herself, 'I must go out there,' yet feeling that she was already there and imprinting them on a special, sensitised surface in her memory for some future day when she might need to bring them back.

Suddenly she wondered how the Tilsits had dealt with Katharine's bedroom, that museum of discomfort and austerity. She hurried along the passage and, opening the door, put her head round it.

Understandably, because the furniture was unchanged, this room had defeated them; the pious shade of 'the Pope' had contrived to repeal every attempt to make it comfortable or human; its chill still pierced to the marrow, the narrow bed with its uninviting contour and the hard-backed, hard-seated chairs discouraged idleness as much as ever they had; the sepia reproductions of pre-Raphaelite religious art were only waiting for the draught from the open windows to shake them in constant and disturbing movement against the newly-papered walls. Without a doubt the Tilsits, that genial and friendly couple, must have been frozen out of this room from the start. Susan wondered, with some amusement, if they had ever realised the potency of Katharine's resistance to their benevolent infiltration.

She looked into every room on that floor, admired the beautifully fitted bathroom, and, constantly aware that the whole interior of the house seemed to have been lifted into the air and to be floating on wings of lightness and brightness, decided not to explore the attics yet but to go downstairs and out into the garden. She stopped on her way through the hall to go into the study, that other papal stronghold, anxious to discover if the Tilsits or 'the Pope' were now in possession.

Surveying the room critically for quite a time, she decided that here there had been achieved a sort of *modus vivendi* in which neither party could claim superiority. The Tilsits dominated the walls, which were covered with a pale grey-green paper, but 'the Pope' still ruled over the great, hideous, forbidding roll-top desk. The old leather-covered chair was papal but upon it was a cushion covered in brilliant cherry-coloured Tilsit silk; the tabby chair in the window was as it had always been, dry, dusty and warm from the sun that shone through the window, having a smell all of its own that neither 'Pope' nor Tilsit could dispel, but one of the armchairs by the fire had a loose cover of pretty, printed linen.

The morning-room was all Tilsit; they had made it really charming, but then they had been succeeding not Katharine, but Charlotte and Daisy there, a much less formidable proposition. Susan found herself taking more and more to the Tilsits, appreciating their careful and loving co-operation with the house in discovering its own character.

She wished that she could find some personal thing belonging to them that would reveal them to her more fully, a letter to 'the Pope' in the handwriting of one of them, an abandoned pipe or a pair of old goloshes, any little thing that would disclose the identity of either of them; but she found nothing at all beyond their embracing affection for the house, their generosity in fulfilling its needs and their evident delight in inhabiting it.

She went through the conservatory to the garden, shocked by the roughness of the grass, the encroachment of weeds upon flower-beds and paths, the inability of the flowers to hold their own against this invasion, and the straggling, elongated shoots on everything that should have been pruned but had been allowed to grow unchecked since the death of the Tilsits.

In spite of the neglect, it was good to be out in the garden; there was such an easy warmth in the air, such life in the brilliant green of grass and leaves, the thrusting of the weeds, the free, lifting flight of the birds and the transforming brilliance of the sunshine, that nothing was ugly. A little breath of wind from the mountain spent itself caressingly against the house, just giving a gentle shake to the tops of the Scotch firs in its passage. There was a cloud behind the mountain, an approaching threat, but it was too distant to be taken seriously. Susan smiled in the sunlight, drawn here and there to look at one thing after another, undeterred by the evidence of decay.

She heard a noise from the direction of the house and made a quick turn about, wondering who could have dared to observe her. An elderly figure stood at the conservatory door looking not at her but at the wilderness in which she stood and punctuating his expressions of disgust with exploratory prods of his walking stick against the woodwork near him.

It could only be Mr Blair, her lawyer, come to torment her with formalities, goad her into making decisions and alarm her with his good advice. She did not like the look of him; he was too anxious to discover the extent of the dilapidations and to protest at the neglect; he would bully her into agreeing with tiresome suggestions of his own and make her feel a helpless, useless, brainless fool.

Mr Blair had been waiting until she became aware of his presence to make himself known to her; he had plenty to do looking round and taking note of necessary repairs, so that he felt that there was no hurry. He had, in fact, been there for several minutes and had made a quick assessment of Susan's character from the way she behaved before devoting himself to an inspection of the fabric of the house.

Ladies had always been a source of great dissatisfaction to Mr Blair; they had so little aptitude for business that their grasp of affairs was rarely divorced from a sadly material desire to get immediately at such money and goods as came their way. They were never able to wait, they had the most immoral propensity for dodging procedural delays and asking unanswerable questions, and their mental powers were very limited. All his life, poor Mr Blair had dreaded having to inform, advise or admonish ladies. But the sight of Susan had been reassuring in one respect; he could see from the way she stood and walked, from the set of her head and the rather diffident reluctance with which she came to meet him, that she was very much less alarming than her late aunt, Miss Fellowes. The very recollection of that formidable personage made him feel uneasy, but, secure in his perception that he had here a different kettle of fish, he advanced with some confidence to greet his new client.

'How d'ye do, Miss Fellowes,' he said, extending a dry, dust-coloured hand for her to shake. His astute grey eye observed her narrowly and he missed no opportunity to fasten it upon her.

'I think Mr Weldon has warned you to expect me: my name is Blair.'

'Oh, how do you do, Mr Blair?' said Susan, fishing the words out with difficulty, so alarming did she find him. 'I . . . I remember . . . you used to come sometimes when I was a child.'

'Mm, yes. Your Aunt, Miss Katharine, that is, was very strong-willed. . .' Mr Blair paused weightily, so that Susan should realise the terrible implications of being strong-willed; that she should, in fact, understand that he meant merely wilful, but was not in a position to speak plainly. Susan understood all this by the time his pause had come to an end; he was adept at driving home meanings that had never been expressed. Besides, she knew her Aunt Katharine as even he had not.

'Tragic, her death out there,' he continued. 'Unnecessary, too, if you ask me: women who go out to outlandish parts and get killed are only getting what they ask for. Besides, it isn't fair on the Government. Just think of all the poor devils who'll have to be strung up for that crime! However, when her mind was set on anything she wouldn't ever listen to reason. I warned her, I warned her very seriously against embarking on such a life at her age, but she felt she had a mission and called me a pagan for trying to stop her!'

Susan had to smile at the thought of this interview; she could envisage poor Mr Blair's determination to caution 'the Pope' even though she might slay him, and her contempt for this prudent little lawyer standing in her path to frustrate her divine purpose.

'She never listened to anybody,' she said.

'Hm. Yes, she was very strong-willed,' he repeated, uncomfortably aware that he had enlarged rather more than he had intended on the nature of her wilfulness. 'Hm. I wonder if there is somewhere inside where we could have a little talk, Miss Fellowes? As you know, I have been in charge of the affairs of your family for a number of years except for a short period, er . . . perhaps you don't know about that. It was in 1923. Your aunt had her own ideas, but they did not prosper . . . She had to climb down in the end. And I want to acquaint you with your present er . . . circumstances.'

She led him through the morning-room and into the hall, hesitating because she could not make up her mind where to take him; the study was too closely linked with 'the Pope', she hated the room; the drawing-room was icy cold, the dining-room equally so. Mr Blair, however, took it for granted that they would go to the study and, opening the door, held it for her until she had gone inside.

'You did mean to come in here, I suppose?' he said, surprised at the reluctance with which she prepared to settle into a chair. 'Your aunt and I always talked business in here and I took it for granted.'

'Oh yes,' said Susan blushing, 'it's quite all right.'

Now, what on earth could be the matter with the girl? thought Mr Blair; she was odd, very odd. At her age, she should know her mind better and not be so easily upset. She was looking thoroughly wretched now, and for no apparent reason. Ladies again! he thought resentfully; they were utterly unpredictable: hard as nails when you expected them to break down and sensitive about silly little things that never even entered your head.

'Hm,' he began, thus announcing that he was about to mention business. Susan quite understood this and looked up at him with a face of alarm. He drew his overcoat closer round him, put on a pair of horn-rimmed spectacles, pulled some papers out of his brief-case and began to speak in the flat, even voice that he imagined would combine with slow speech and simple words to make him comprehensible to ladies.

'I don't know quite how much you have been in touch with the goings on here since you . . . since your break with Miss Fellowes?' he began, lowering his head so as to observe her over the rim of his spectacles.

'Well, hardly at all since Aunt Olivia died,' said Susan. 'You see, Aunt Katharine never wrote to me direct.'

'That was a dreadful thing,' said Mr Blair in his most severe tone.

'What was?' Susan looked startled. 'Her being killed by a bomb, you mean?'

'No, I mean Miss Olivia becoming a nun.' He glared at her in an effort to provoke a reaction similar to his own, but she seemed quite unresponsive, so he was obliged to enlarge. 'Unnatural!' he said in a shocked voice. 'Miss Fellowes was horrified. I don't think I ever saw her so upset. I don't blame her either. Dreadful! And she used to be so jolly!' His voice grew reminiscent as he went on. 'Why, I remember her here, in this very room, when your grandfather died and I had the very unpleasant duty of telling your aunts that they had almost nothing to live on. She was so sensible and such a very beautiful young lady then, such a help to your aunt and me in trying to convince Miss Charlotte and Miss Daisy that they were poor! I'd never have thought it of her,' he ended accusingly, as though Susan were in some way to blame.

'She was still jolly, even after she was a nun,' said Susan. 'She was just the same, really, only I think she was much happier.'

Mr Blair was hard put to it not to snort with disgust, but he passed on to the discussion of business.

'Hm. Well, you know that when your Aunt Katharine went . . . abroad she let this house for quite a number of years?' He was still darting angry glances at her and his voice was so peremptory that she would never have dared to contradict him if she had not known this.

'Yes, well I knew something about it, but not much.' Susan was playing with the fringe of her scarf, looking downwards when she was not actually speaking.

'It was let for a very low rent on condition that the tenants repaired and redecorated it; they were excellent tenants, I must say, and it was they who were responsible for the electric light installation and the modern bathroom on the first floor.' Mr Blair jerked an enquiring eyebrow towards her in the hope of perceiving evidence of approval but her attention still seemed to be on her scarf.

'What were they like?' Susan looked up quickly.

'Very good tenants indeed: your aunt was most fortunate. They were here for the best part of twenty years.'

'No,' said Susan firmly. 'I mean, what sort of people were they, and were they nice?'

Now, how like a lady! thought Mr Blair. Interested in all the wrong things: here he was, telling this girl about the improvements to the house and all she wanted to know was whether the people who had done them were nice, not how much they had cost or how the Fellowes would have managed without such good tenants.

'They were an American couple, quite elderly, called Tilsit,' explained Mr Blair coldly. 'They came to Ireland during a trip to Europe in 1925, and expressed themselves as having fallen in love with the country. They wanted to rent a house furnished for a year, and with option to renew; they stayed until Mrs Tilsit died in 1944. He had died at the beginning of the war. It was an admirable arrangement for both parties.'

'What were they like?'

'Like?' Mr Blair repeated with a touch of irritation; had he not just told her what they were like? 'They were like all Americans; kindly disposed, extravagant, fond of their comforts and unable to distinguish between the gentry and the people.'

'Oh!' said Susan, startled. 'I see.' No doubt, according to Mr Blair, they had let the wrong sort of people in at the front door and perhaps used the back door themselves; something must have stung him to provoke a comment as snobbish at this. It was plain that, personally, he had not liked them very much though he had approved of them as tenants. 'Go on,' she said quickly. 'About the house, I mean.'

Placated, Mr Blair continued in the told-to-the-children manner that he reserved for ladies and other people of low intelligence.

'Miss Katharine was most insistent that every penny of her share of the rent and of the family income should be re-invested annually, so as to increase your capital—she lived entirely on her stipend from the missionary society all those years. It can't have been easy for her, but I suppose her wants were few.'

'I never knew that,' said Susan, put out that she had been told of this so late, when she could show no gratitude.

'She did not mean you to know,' snapped Mr Blair, and continued with his narrative. Susan tried to listen to him with attention but his monotonous voice droned on so endlessly that she began to feel drowsy. When, as happened from time to time he jerked his eyebrow at her with a sharply worded question, she had to drag herself from a morass of sleepiness. He seemed quite unaware of her stupefaction and, provided that she made some utterance by way of reply, continued his recital without delay.

She did glean some sense from his disclosure, though the details made no impression on her. She was certainly not rich, but she had a sound old house and enough to keep her in modest comfort—very modest, he had insisted, suddenly remembering Miss Charlotte and Miss Daisy whose ideas of modest comfort would never have approximated to his own. He reassured himself by observing that Miss Susan did not have an air of extravagance.

'Your Aunt Charlotte . . . now that was a curious thing!' he said wondering what this Miss Fellowes knew of the affair. He himself had not been told more than was good for him by Katharine; only enough to enable him to forward her allowance in quarterly instalments to a poste restante address in Australia, starting quite a year after her disappearance from Glenmacool.

'Was it?' said Susan without much interest.

'Oh yes, very odd, very odd indeed. I always thought your aunt . . . Miss Katharine, that is, was a little ashamed of the way she went off like that. D'ye know she had to help build her own house, out there in the wilds of Australia? Yes, every bit of it they built with their own hands. That must have been a shock to your Aunt Charlotte, eh? Of course, she married beneath her, which explains it all. A most persistent man, that husband of hers, never stopped writing to ask if he wasn't entitled to her estate. But of course the money was only hers for her lifetime and then it reverted to the Trust Fund, to be used for her remaining sisters and yourself. 'Pon my word, Miss Susan, from the way he kept writing and from the very ugly expressions he used when I finally satisfied him that he had no right to the money, it wouldn't surprise me to hear that he had . . . well . . . I don't like the word "murder" but . . . let's call it . . . accelerated her departure.' Mr Blair shot an astute look at her and nodded in confirmation.

'Whatever are you saying, Mr Blair?' cried Susan, staring at him with horror. 'If you thought that, why didn't you do something about it? You've no right to say things like that if you're not sure.' She was thoroughly awake now.

Mr Blair suddenly recollected himself with some alarm; he was saying things that were dangerous and actionable, but, thank goodness, there was no witness.

'Not enough to go on,' he said quickly. 'A very clever chap, your uncle! In the end he stopped writing. He went to prison instead— something to do with forged cheques, I believe. Anyway, it shut him up.' He darted a penetrating glance at her. 'Of course, what I have told you is in complete confidence, Miss Susan. It wouldn't do for such conjectures to get about, you understand.'

'Yes,' said Susan doubtfully, 'I see.'

He hastened to pass on to a new subject. 'When your Uncle Eustace died, a few years after the first war, I never thought your Aunt Harriet would have followed him so soon; it seemed she just gave up once he'd gone. Of course the war killed him, no doubt about that, poor fellow.'

'I remember; he looked terrible.'

'Shocking, he looked,' agreed Mr Blair, shaking his head. Then, anxious to discuss something more cheerful, 'Now what,' he enquired, 'are you going to do? I understand you have a job in London. You'll go back to it, of course.'

'No,' she said. 'I'm not going back. I'm going to stay here.' She spoke with a kind of breathless excitement, now that her intention was being stated.

Mr Blair was alarmed. He feared that she might have visions of a considerable establishment with servants, a gardener, perhaps a motor-car, and a way of life far more expensive than 'modest comfort' could permit.

'Remember, you are not a rich woman,' he snapped. 'You'll have to go very carefully; this is an expensive house to maintain.' He glared at her over his spectacle rims.

She was trembling a little; the tremendous drain upon her resources of strength and determination in coming to a decision and putting it into words, had exhausted her physically. If he opposed her now, she thought that, from sheer weakness, she might drop her plan altogether.

'I . . . I don't want to do anything expensive,' she faltered. 'I only want to stay in the house by myself.' She gave him an apologetic look, hoping that he would not quite refuse her.

'By yourself?' he barked at her. 'Surely you don't mean really by yourself, all alone in the house?'

'Well, there might be a village girl who could come in by the day, or something,' she suggested hopefully.

'You mean to say you intend to sleep in this house alone?'

'Yes,' she said shakily. 'Isn't that all right?'

'Certainly not,' he snapped. 'That would never do.'

'But I don't think I want anyone,' she objected.

He snorted with impatience. 'It doesn't do for ladies to live alone these days,' he insisted. 'What with politics, and robberies with violence, and drunks, it isn't right. It's only asking for trouble. It can't be done.'

'I thought these sort of things only happened in England—except for politics, of course.'

'They happen everywhere, especially when people ask for trouble. Remember your aunt. Ladies always like to think they can do all sorts of things and when they discover they can't it's too late to help them.' Mr Blair looked at her very sternly.

'I see,' said Susan non-committally, and then, 'Had the Tilsits any family? This was a big house for just two of them.'

'I believe there were both sons and daughters on the other side of the Atlantic, but the only one who put in an appearance here was an American officer who arrived here after the war and wanted both coffins exhumed and taken back to the States. He said he was their son,' added Mr Blair in a voice which indicated that this stretched his credulity too far.

'That must have been quite a business to arrange,' said Susan sympathetically.

'I stopped it,' said Mr Blair with pride. 'It wasn't decent, and I told him so. I soon made him change his mind. Hm. D'ye really think you're wise to settle here, Miss Susan? You won't meet anyone here, y'know; Glenmacool's a desperate dull old place. You'll find yourself hankering after London. You'd be better off if you went back there again.'

'No,' said Susan miserably, 'I don't expect so. I know what Glenmacool's like—I know what to expect.'

'Glenmacool's all right for growing children, but it's no good for young ladies—no young men for them!' he announced triumphantly. 'At least, none of the right type. You'll be making a great mistake if you stay here, mark my words,' he said emphatically, wagging a forefinger at her.

'But I don't expect I shall ever marry, if that's what you mean,' said Susan. 'After all, most people are married at my age if they're ever going to be.'

'There is no age at which a lady is too old for marriage,' said Mr Blair with gallantry, looking a little ridiculous.

Susan could think of no reply to this and there was an uncomfortable silence. Susan smiled at him to show that she felt no annoyance, and began playing with the end of her scarf again.

'Hm. I remember, years ago, warning your aunt, Miss Katharine, against . . . young men on the make. I feel it my duty to repeat that warning to you now. You come of a good family, Miss Susan, you own a fine old house and you have a little means; all that, added to your . . . pleasing appearance is enough to put the wrong sort of ideas into the head of any unscrupulous young man. Be careful. Miss Susan, you are very vulnerable. . .' The years had brought considerable self-assurance to Mr Blair; he felt he had made a more convincing appeal now than he had done to Miss Katharine, many years ago. But then Miss Susan was considerably milder than her aunt had been.

'But you said there weren't any young men,' objected Susan.

'A hypothetical warning,' he replied quickly. 'Your aunt told me she was going to marry a penniless clergyman, but it never came off. He seemed a nice young fellow, too, but poor, much too poor to be pursuing your aunt. She was well out of it. I see he's still here: can't have been a great success at his job or they'd have moved him on somewhere.'

'It's his sister,' explained Susan. 'She's an invalid and says she'd never be well anywhere else. He's had several offers of promotion . . .'

'The man must be a fool!' snapped Mr Blair. 'His sister'd soon find she'd be all right if she had to be. These women, the . . .' He was fumbling for his watch while he spoke, and exclaimed, 'Good Heavens, I'm due in Inish this minute!' He collected his papers and shoved them into his briefcase, hunting for his shabby leather gloves and dirty old scarf. With everything found and distributed about his person, he stood up. 'Remember,' he said. 'Think twice before you settle down here.'

'Yes,' she agreed, smiling vaguely at him as he took his leave.

She watched his car disappear over the rise towards Inish, then went back into the house to fetch her handbag. Leaving the hall door open, she wandered out to the street, standing for a moment outside the little iron gate to stare across the road at the ruins of Peter Cavanagh's Select Bar, now broken down and overgrown with nettles and briars. Then, with a determined air, she made for the post office.

Malachy Quinn was behind the counter, doing duty for his father. He was himself a middle-aged man now, with the same flaming exuberance of hair and beard, the same look of gentle power that had characterised Patrick. He smiled at Susan, putting out a hand to be shaken and murmuring a greeting which made it clear that he knew who she was. She smiled back and asked for a telegraph form.

She chewed her pencil for some minutes while composing the message. Then, smiling again, she handed the form to Malachy Quinn.

It was for Mr Hastings, her London employer. It ran, 'Greatly regret unable return your employment stop my apologies inconvenience Susan Fellowes.'

She imagined him opening it, as if she were standing behind him, observing the way the hair grew at the back of his neck and aching for him to turn round to her with that amused, kindly, interested look that she found so endearing. She shook her head; she had worked for him for nine years and he had looked at her in the same way on the very first day as he had on the last. Even when he had, on rare occasions, taken her out to lunch or driven her home after keeping her late at the office, he had never seemed continually aware of her; he would glance at her through his horn-rimmed spectacles, ask an astute question and take his answer from her face rather than from what she said, and then dart off on some other interest and forget all about her. Even when he had come back from the war, once he had told her how wonderful it was to have her back again and how much he had needed someone like her when he was in the Army, and teased her about the cadaverous General for whom she had worked, he dropped back to where he had left off in 1939, quite oblivious to the response these few remarks had incited in her. She had felt suddenly uplifted with excitement, flushed and eager, glowing in the knowledge that he was glad to have her back. For quite five minutes she had been unable to do a stroke of work. But when he next called her in, it was as a slave to find a misplaced file, a machine to prepare his mail and a cushion between him and the technical difficulties of running an office. Thereafter, her exalted moments had been brief and rare.

Walking slowly home, up the hill from the post office, she shook her head wisely at herself again. It was no good trying to pretend that it would ever have come to anything. He thought about her no more often than he did about the lift-man, or the man from the garage who cleaned his car. They were all human and therefore of absorbing interest until something more fascinating captured his attention. His affection for the human race seemed to be allotted with maddening equality to each member of it. She felt that he was incapable of falling really in love: his interest was too general, his emotions were too detached.

With every clock in the house silent, she had taken no account of the time. Back in the hall again, staring at the old grandfather clock in repose, she had a sudden memory of the constant noise there had always been in the house of the seconds flying off as tick succeeded tick on clock after clock. The silence pressed upon her now. She felt for the key of the old clock, wound it and set it going. She looked at her watch to find the right time and saw that it was a quarter to two. Lunch at the rectory was at half past one.

She made no attempt to put the clock right then, but grabbed her belongings and ran. Esmé would be so cross! If people scolded her, or even let her know that they were not pleased with her, Susan suffered out of all proportion to the importance of her offence: to be liked and appreciated was as necessary to her as the light of day. She felt miserable now as she hurried along the road.

Esmé was very put out and did not conceal her irritation. She was wrestling with a piece of gristle on her plate, punishing it with her knife as she held it down with her fork, pursing her lips as she thought of how she would rebuke Philomena for allowing such a bit of meat to go into the stew. She darted a piercing glance at Susan.

'My brother is waiting,' she announced coldly. 'He didn't like to start, though I told him he ought to. Philomena brought lunch up and he made her take it down again. You know how much she hates carrying heavy trays. Does she know you're in?' With a triumphant wrench she detached the gristle from its meat and ranged it with the other discards on the edge of her plate, then impaled the meat with her fork and ate it with exaggerated satisfaction.

'I don't think so—at least I'm not sure. She may have seen me come in. I'm most terribly sorry,' apologised Susan. 'I forgot all about the time. You shouldn't have let him wait. Oh dear!' She turned to go so that she could tell Philomena that she had come in, but Esmé made a gesture which showed that she had more to say, so Susan waited until her mouthful was finished.

'We must change our butcher,' she announced firmly. 'I keep telling . . . er the Canon, but he won't do it: he says the man has an idiot child, as if that was any reason for putting up with bad meat! But what can I do from an invalid chair? I'm quite helpless, so nobody takes any notice of what I say.'

Lawrence put his head round the door. 'Ah, so you're in! We'll have lunch then,' he said genially. He went to call out to Philomena, then returned, smiling.

'Did you think Blair much aged?' he asked Susan, then, without waiting for an answer went on, 'He's an awful old tyrant, you know. You mustn't let him lead you by the nose! But he's a very sound lawyer; he knows what he's talking about. Did you find him civil?'

'Oh yes, very,' Susan assured him. 'But he does go on and on. I'm m-m-most awfully sorry I'm so late. I'm afraid I've really no excuse at all, I just forgot about the time.'

He laughed. 'Time never matters here—unless I've got to take a wedding or a funeral.'

'Yes, but you shouldn't have let poor Philomena take lunch down again when she'd gone to all that trouble. . .'

His face clouded over with annoyance. 'Who told you about that?' he demanded. 'Was it Philomena?' A red flush crept upwards towards his hairline. 'It was most unkind of her, but she never thinks. She doesn't mean any harm.'

Esmé sat looking at him with her mouth twisted to one side. She said nothing and Susan felt obliged to defend Philomena.

'No,' she faltered, conscious of Esmé's glare blackmailing her into silence, 'it wasn't Philomena. Esmé and I were talking, and it . . . just came out.' She felt miserable, as guilty as a schoolgirl who implicates the culprit by the act of exonerating the innocent.

Lawrence controlled himself with difficulty. He looked at Esmé with such unspoken accusation that her thin shoulders wriggled as she turned her face to the window to avoid seeing his. He said nothing and there was a most uncomfortable silence.

'Oh, look, look!' cried Esmé suddenly, pointing towards the window with an expression of rapture. 'My little blue-tit!' She was smiling as though nothing unpleasant had happened.

Susan stared at her in amazed relief. Esmé's face was serene and almost gentle. Lawrence was looking at her too with so much exasperation in his expression that Susan knew that this must be a favourite trick of Esmé's when she was in the wrong. With almost a snort he turned and left the room. Esmé kept on talking about the blue-tit, which was eating a piece of suet outside the window, until the bell went for lunch. She begged Susan to come in again after lunch, before returning to Fellowescourt.

'It's such a treat,' she said, 'to see someone who hasn't lived in the village all their lives. It's like a breath of fresh air to me!'

Susan felt greatly sobered by this encounter; she found Esmé unpredictable, sly, waspish and dominating, yet able to become gentle, wistful and dependent at a moment's notice. Her behaviour made

Susan feel bewildered and frightened, ashamed because she felt no compassion for her, and resentful because Esmé made use of Lawrence's goodness, pity and forbearance to enslave him more and more to her will. The thought that for thirty years he had humbly submitted, without complaint or protest, to her tyranny filled Susan with such marvelling at his self-discipline that she felt almost prostrated by it. That patience was not natural to him had only just been demonstrated.

At lunch, he was again easy and delightful to talk to, full of stories about the changes in the neighbourhood, newcomers to the village and old residents who had left or died.

'Are you going back to Fellowescourt this afternoon?' he asked her. 'If so, I can drop you there. I've got to go past there anyway.'

'Have you really? Oh, yes please,' Susan hesitated. Esmé was not going to like this. But she made up her mind that Esmé should not dominate her as she had dominated Lawrence all his life. She smiled with a little more confidence and felt suddenly emboldened to reveal her plans.

'I sent a telegram to my employer this morning,' she said, with an air of laying bare her most secret heart, a sort of excited reluctance.

'Yes?' Lawrence was observing her quietly.

'I told him I wasn't going back.'

'You did?' There were pleasure and surprise in his voice and expression. 'Well, and what are you going to do, then?'

'Live at Fellowescourt.'

'What, all by yourself? Are you sure you won't regret it?'

'I hope not. Why should I?'

He was looking at her from across the table, head down so that the jut of his eyebrows made a kind of ceiling to his vision. He picked up his napkin and began to fold it reflectively.

'It's a bad thing to live alone,' he said slowly. 'It does something to people, even to the strongest characters.'

'Doesn't it depend on whether they do it from choice or because they have to? If they want to do it, they're contented, but if they have to do it then they're always striving after what they've missed. I'm sure that's what does things to them.' Susan spoke with such conviction that his mind was jolted into the reflection that for twenty-five years this girl, now approaching middle-age, had lived out of touch in an unfamiliar world, living alone and earning her own living, making her own life and learning to reason from her own experience.

He sighed. 'People who live alone tend to forget that one of the basic human needs is to expend oneself on other people. They feel gratified that they're being no trouble to anybody but they don't realise that they're annihilating themselves. And because they are no trouble to anybody they come to think that that gives them the right to keep out of other people's lives. Have you ever met anyone who was absolutely self-centred?'

Susan's face, watching his, expressed horror. Was he thinking, as she could only think, of Esmé? She nodded, feeling guilty, but he went on so naturally that she knew he had not had Esmé in mind. And again she was struck with admiration that he could exempt an instance so obvious and so close to both of them from scrutiny.

'You see what an appalling condition it is? I can't help feeling that it's one of the things that threaten people who live alone. They tend gradually to break all the threads . . . But I'm sure you won't let yourself get like that.' He stood up to say Grace. Before she could say another word he had swept her out of the room and across the hall to say goodbye to Esmé.

Back at Fellowescourt, she slipped the key into the lock with a feeling of secret satisfaction. Lawrence came in for a quick look round.

'Ah,' he said, 'you've got the old clock going!' He watched it in silence for a moment. 'Would you like me to put it right?'

'Oh, yes please! Tell me, where did the Tilsits put all the junk?'

'Junk?' he said, standing back to look at the clock-face. 'Oh, you mean the things from here? Dear me, how different you must have found it all! I believe you'll find it all in the attic. They never used that floor. You don't want to put it back down here, do you?

'Goodness, no! I was just wandering.' Susan opened the drawing-room door and led the way into the room.

The warmth and stir of the outside air were beginning to disperse the icy chill of the rooms; genial currents were starting to circulate and break up the resistance. She went to the mantelpiece and, searching under the china sitting hen for the key, began to wind the old French clock. As she set it going and heard its confident tick, she felt that she was making the heart of the old house beat again; she could sense it coming alive, rousing itself from hibernation, communing with itself as old houses do in little secret creaks and rattles and tappings. She experienced immense pleasure at this, recognising sounds and stirrings that had been the background to her childhood and of which she had never before been consciously aware.

'The Tilsits were remarkable people,' said Lawrence's voice from just inside the door. From the way he spoke she knew that his head was thrown back and that he was looking round the room, appreciating the lightness of the Tilsit touch. She turned round, smiling her pleasure and reassurance.

'Oh, tell me about them,' she begged. 'What were they like?'

'Like?' he said. 'It's difficult to say. American, of course, very kind, very generous, very friendly. They belonged to some curious sect but they used to come to church all the same. You would have liked them: they loved this house and they did a lot more for it than they need have.'

'They understood this house,' said Susan.

'I'm glad you feel that. I always thought that myself.' He looked at her with a kind of gratitude for her happy acceptance of changes made by strangers. 'I was afraid that perhaps . . . you would not like to see so many alterations.'

'It was a shock to see all the junk gone from the hall,' she said smiling, 'but how much better it looks!' She began to look round the drawing-room to see how much had been cleared away from there, but found that nothing at all had been removed, except the Victorian watercolours from the walls. Every prism, mirror, ornament and knick-knack was where it had been in her infancy. The little Irish harp and the balancing man from the East were still on either side of the fireplace. 'How odd!' she said. 'This room feels much emptier, but they haven't taken anything out.'

'It's the walls. Don't you remember that terrible old dark wallpaper with the enormous pattern?'

'Of course!' she said, amused by the recollection. She took a little bowl from the mantelpiece and held it out.

'Look!'

'What's that?' He came nearer.

'All my aunts' baby teeth.'

Their heads bent over the little bowl as they marvelled at the delicacy and whiteness of the tiny teeth, remembering that the owners of them were now all dead.

'Well!' he exclaimed, saddened a little, but amused. Susan put the bowl back carefully.

'I used to try to imagine Aunt Katharine with no front teeth when I saw these,' she said, 'but it was too much for me.'

He laughed. 'Yes, indeed.' He moved over to the window to look out on the unkempt grass. 'When did you think of moving in?'

'Tomorrow.'

'Tomorrow?' he repeated, aghast. 'But nothing's connected, water, electricity, nothing! You can't possibly come in as soon as that.'

'Well, as soon as they are, then. After all, what am I waiting for?'

He sighed. 'I'd hoped we'd have you with us for a little time at the rectory.'

'Don't you think Esmé'd be happier if—'

'Of course not,' he interrupted. 'It's done her all the good in the world having you here. She loves it.'

She looked quickly at him to see if he was serious. His sincerity was obvious. He was mystified that she should have had such a notion.

'Would you like to do someone a charity?' he asked, with a trace of reluctance.

'Yes, if I can,' she answered with equal hesitation, unwilling to commit herself before she knew what was to be asked of her.

'There's a girl . . . a very decent girl. Maybe you might remember her father, Michael Maguire? Well, this Mary Ellen was a nurse in London and was terribly badly burnt in the Blitz. She's been at home since the end of the war, terribly disfigured. She won't apply for any jobs because she feels it frightens people to look at her, especially children, and she's not really getting enough to eat there on the farm. She'd make you a very faithful servant. . .' he paused, to allow her time to consider the idea. 'She's not one of my flock, as you know, but I'm always glad to do anything for Michael Maguire. If she came to live in, you could build her up a bit: it would be a real kindness.'

'How old is she?' asked Susan, playing for time.

'About . . . let me see, forty, I should say. Indeed, she might be more!'

'Ask her to come and see me,' said Susan, but she knew that, Mary Ellen Maguire was as good as working for her already.

CHAPTER SEVENTEEN

The golden weather had broken and a rough wind threatened the end of summer, tearing the leaves prematurely from the trees and driving them across the grass to add to the disorder in the garden. Jackdaws, like small tattered umbrellas, glided untidily downwind, then folded up, fluttering, with jagged wing and tail edges, once more in control of their direction. Quite suddenly, in a matter of hours, the year had entered a new phase.

Susan had been back at Fellowescourt for three months, after having spent many weeks at the rectory. She had made the morning-room her centre. There she sat, ate her solitary meals, listened to the wireless and read, received her visitors, wrote her letters and frowned over her complicated knitting patterns. It was a charming room, light, almost square, easily warmed in winter and not large enough to be overpowering. Slowly, it was beginning to look like her room, though the predisposition to tidiness and method that gave her a tendency to primness in her person made it difficult for the room to acquire character, so meticulously was everything arranged, put away and, as it were, deprived of its spontaneity.

But she had brought in from the drawing-room the china sitting hen that was so dear to her, and the books in the bookcase were the ones that had followed her over from England, much-read copies of the classics, novels and plays, poetry and biography.

The uniform and sombrely bound copies of the *Cornhill Magazine* that had filled the room in her youth were now piled on the dining-room table, awaiting the next jumble sale. And in spite of the dereliction outside, she had never been without flowers of one kind or another. She arranged them with rather too much precision, producing an effect that satisfied her need for order while it annoyed her by its lack of charm. As when she did her hair, she abhorred the straying tendril, the snaking deviation from the rule, yet deplored the uninspired result.

The gale thrust infiltrating trickles of draught into the room, chilling the back of her neck, her ankles and her wrists. She would be cold until she lit the fire, but it was too early in the year to light a fire in the daytime. She must find some warming occupation instead. Indeed, there was one thing to be done that she had promised herself to do as soon as the weather broke: she must go up to the attic and go over all the things stowed away there by the Tilsits.

She shivered. The weather had broken and she had no excuse to postpone this distasteful job. The thought of poking about up there amongst all the family junk oppressed her terribly. The ghosts, she felt, had been shut up in there with all their familiar possessions, banished from downstairs by the Tilsits. She was afraid to go up. Supposing she heard an echo of Nanny's ancient cackle, or one of Aunt Daisy's heavy sighs?

Chilled to the bone, as much from apprehension as from the cold, she forced herself to start off as if she meant to continue. In the back hall she opened the door that led down a few steps to the kitchen passage and called out.

'Mary Ellen!'

Beyond, in the shadows, Mary Ellen Maguire had made of her kitchen a sort of *oubliette* where she hid her scarred and mutilated face from the sight of every living soul. She avoided contact even with her mistress and only spoke when she knew she was invisible. Her voice floated from obscurity.

'Yes, Miss?'

'I have to go up to the attic. Will you call me if anybody comes to the door?'

'I will, Miss.' The words might have come from the bottom of a well.

Susan had said she was going, so go she must. She toiled up the narrow attic stairs, making much of the climb because she did not want to reach the top. Perhaps someone would come to the door and she would have to go down again. When she had engaged Mary Ellen, her father, Michael Maguire, had begged that she might be spared the ordeal of opening the door to visitors, so Susan had agreed to do this herself.

Along the corridor at the top of the house, the doors were all shut and the air was thick with disuse and the smell of summer heat, almost of scorching, under the roof. No window had been opened up there for years.

She made her way to the tiny window at the end of the landing, as she had always done as a child, and pressed her nose against the glass. From here you could see for miles, out over the rise of the hill to the convent, the church and rectory and even as far as Myrtle Lodge. The white dusty road threaded into the distance towards Inish like a length of tape. There was nothing to be seen that had not been there when she was three years old, except the mound of Peter Cavanagh's building materials, now covered with grass and thistles, in the little field next door where they had lain undisturbed since the day of his death, for he had died without an heir of any kind. She gazed out for a little longer than it took to see that nothing had changed, then turned away to the door of what had always been Miss Flynn's room.

It opened easily enough to start with, but it must have become warped with the years for it grazed the floorboards in its passage, and stuck. She leant against it, heaving with her shoulder, and it suddenly flew open, hurling her with great force into the room.

She fell against the elephant's foot that had stood in the hall as an umbrella-stand until the Tilsits had banished it. It upset backwards, scattering its content of sticks and umbrellas, faded parasols and gone-to-seed tennis racquets in a cloud of dust. Behind it, the coats and hats, cloaks and caps hanging on the old coat-stand, also from the hall, rocked and swayed on their pegs as if this were a ship's cabin in a rough sea, and some of them collapsed onto the floor to lie there inanimate, hollow little corpses of the real people they had clothed.

Charlotte's motoring veil, bought hopefully while she had been nursing in Dublin during the first war and scarcely ever worn, draped Katharine's shabby old goloshes, their rubber dull and perished. Harriet's ancient navy-blue mackintosh that had gone as stiff as a board tottered to rest against a table-leg, slid sideways and fell with a sigh to the floor, as unbecoming in disuse as it had been upon her dumpy little person. Olivia's tiny pink lace parasol, once so frivolous and fashionable and the envy of all her sisters, except Katharine, sailed into a discarded brass fender, tarnished and coated with dust, where its little form, opened a few inches by the stir of the flight, closed slowly in a dying breath to lie, wretchedly bedraggled, faded to the dinginess of old newspapers. And old Captain Fellowes' hunting boots, unworn since the turn of the century but still preserving, with the help of trees, the comely outline of his leg, knocked and jostled one another noisily as his heavy check overcoat plummeted upon them from above.

Susan was unhurt, but the sight of all these dispossessed garments in motion, advertising as it were their aching vacuum, stabbed her with an intuitive terror lest they continue to move after they should come to rest. Drawing in a quick, noisy breath, what would she do, she asked herself in panic, if they would not lie still? Her hand pressed against her wildly beating heart, she watched them slowly settle, the pendulum action of those still hanging diminishing with each swing.

Now that she was thoroughly frightened, their immobility alarmed her as much as had their movement. Sitting on the floor where she had fallen, she watched them with an unblinking stare for any sign of life. But as the moments passed, reason returned and she picked herself up, brushing the dust from her clothes and even forcing herself to touch the fabric of Katharine's old garden coat that had been the last garment to stop swaying and now hung, erect and rigid, from the same peg as Daisy's wide-brimmed garden hat of coarse, discoloured straw. Disturbed, the hat flopped swirling to the floor.

With a quick gasp, Susan decided that she could do no sorting today. She was still so much under the influence of her fright that she did not like to breathe in case that sound might drown another and the things in the room take command without her knowledge. She backed to the door and out onto the landing, keeping her hand on the door handle as she paused to listen, before pulling it shut with a sharp tug.

She could hear footsteps, and she had the sensation of being surrounded with every way of escape blocked. She stood, back to the closed door, tightness in her throat, and sought some path of flight from the invisible, intangible and ever-encroaching terror.

'The bell, Miss Susan. Are y' there, Miss?' came Mary Ellen's voice from the foot of the attic stairs.

She slumped with relief against the door, quite unable to speak. Mary Ellen called again.

'There's someone at the door, Miss Susan!' Her voice was perturbed, as if she had been calling for some time without any reply. To Susan, it was the trumpet-call of liberation, heralding release from the world of departed spirits.

'Miss Susan?' She heard Mary Ellen take a couple of steps up the little staircase.

She took a deep breath. 'All right, I'm coming. Thank you, Mary Ellen.'

The footsteps tripped rapidly away. Susan went down slowly, weak at the knees.

From the top of the main staircase she heard the bell being rung again. The pressure was prolonged and steadily maintained without diffidence or delicacy of touch, and the knocker battered the door with such homely directness that she knew the visitor could not be one of the county ladies come to call and discover what was going on at Fellowescourt; they had gentler hands and sounded less determined. It was not Lawrence; his knock and ring were short, direct and instantly recognisable. It must be a country person. Susan opened the door and looked round its edge with some apprehension.

Mrs O'Brien was standing there, looking at her troubled face with an expression of amused enquiry.

'I wondher now, who ye thought I was?' she said with a little chuckle.

Susan was overcome with relief and delight. She flung her arms round the well-cushioned figure and kissed the smooth, flat face with such vehement affection that Mrs O'Brien was nearly thrown off her balance.

'There, there,' she murmured, returning the kiss warmly, then holding Susan away from her so that she could look well into her face. 'Is this the way ye go on when I doll meself up to pay you a grand afternoon call? Are ye not going to let me in at all?'

'Come on in. Oh, it's lovely to see you! I didn't know you were back.' Susan drew her inside the door and Mrs O'Brien wiped her feet methodically on the mat while observing with evident curiosity the interior of the house.

'I got back yesterday,' she said, craning her neck in order to look at the plasterwork on the ceiling, then suddenly beaming at Susan, continued, 'so, says I to Cormac, the first thing I must do is to go and see Susan. D'ye know, I never set foot in this house before, never in me life! So I squeezed meself into me corset, and here I am, in agony!' The flat face creased into countless wrinkles as she laughed.

It was evident that she had taken a great deal of trouble with her appearance. The hanks and loops of hair, now a yellowish-grey in colour, had been stuffed almost out of sight under a black hat whose diamanté ornament had lost several of its gems. Her undisciplined form, only partially controlled by the corset, was contained in a loose, black velour coat which sagged and filled with her movements like a wind-sock in a slack breeze. A purple scarf had gone astray round her neck and her feet bulged painfully over strapped shoes a size too small. With near desperation, her left hand gripped a handbag of black plastic, marked to look like crocodile skin, and a pair of black rayon gloves with holes at the ends of the fingers, as if once put down they would be left behind and lost without trace.

Impressed, Susan asked, 'Did you have a lovely trip? And how are Teresa and the baby?'

'Gorgeous! And Teresa's great, and the baby's twins, no less. Twin boys, near as big as herself. Haven't I a wonderful family of children, now I ask you? They saved up an' saved up between them and gave me this trip, an' not a penny did I pay of it meself. Oh, I had the time o' me life, black servants an' all!'

Still looking around her with unflagging curiosity, Mrs O'Brien followed Susan towards the morning-room, but in the back hall she stopped and burst out, 'My, isn't this a desperate great house, and you all alone in it! What have ye behind all them doors at all?'

Susan opened in turn the doors of the drawing-room, dining-room and study, each room chill with disuse.

'An' you alone in it? Well, glory be to God!'

'I've got Mary Ellen.'

'Sure, I know that,' scoffed Mrs O'Brien, 'an' she below in the kitchen an' you above, freezin' to death in one o' them great big rooms! Ye might as well be alone in it, so ye might!'

Susan laughed. She was feeling much better. Her feet were once more on the ground and her experience upstairs in the attic seemed so fantastic as to be incredible. She was back in a different world.

In the morning-room, Mrs O'Brien refused the armchair offered to her and looked round for something more suited to her, finally settling on the sofa where Charlotte and Daisy had spent so much time.

'If I sat on that old low chair, I'd burrst!' she explained, adjusting her person to the contours of the sofa with little restless movements, like a hen about to sit on a clutch of eggs. 'Oh! isn't a corset a desperate conthraption, though? Oah, ah! Aah! That's better now.' She gave Susan a penetrating look. 'So ye never married?' she said, with evident surprise.

'No,' agreed Susan warily. 'I never married.'

'You would have liked to, though.'

Susan looked confused. The truth of Mrs O'Brien's assessment of her circumstances was startling, but still more so was the fact that since her return to Fellowescourt she scarcely ever thought of Mr Hastings at all. He remained a part of her life across the Irish Sea and now that that was over, so too was her ceaseless preoccupation with him. Her faithlessness disturbed her; she was ashamed of the transience of her devotion. At last she was able to see him slightly smaller than life, and shrinking rapidly, to suspect that his engaging effervescence masked an inability to give his attention to what was not, for the moment, of absorbing interest, and to discern the indiscipline that permitted him to be blind to what was distasteful or dull. With devastating clarity she saw him as if he had been there in the room with her; vital, gay, impersonal and restless, handsome and appealing, with the quality of being untouched by emotion, trouble or suffering that she had once found so infinitely endearing and now perceived to be the result of selective evasion. To her amazement, her heart had not foundered at the thought of him for months. With a jolt of dismay she realised that it was Lawrence who now filled her consciousness.

Watching her face, Mrs O'Brien said, 'You are well out of it, I'm sure so.'

Susan was alarmed at the acuteness of her perception. 'I think you're right,' she said quickly. 'Being married to him would have been like paddling in the shallow end of the swimming pool. I'm thankful, now, it never came to anything.'

'I'd like to see you married, all the same,' said Mrs O'Brien warmly, 'to some nice, good man who'd look after you and make a bit of a pet of you.'

Susan laughed. 'I'm not pretty enough to be anybody's pet.'

Mrs O'Brien surveyed her, head on one side. 'I don't know as much,' she said. 'If you could loosen up a bit in your hair-do, be a little bit untidy and let yourself go more, I think we might nearly make a beauty of you.'

'But I can't bear untidiness, in anything.'

'Don't be spinsterish now. That's prim talk. Ye might be yer aunt, Miss Fellowes, when ye talk like that. Ye looked the dead spit of her that minute.'

'Well,' retorted Susan, 'didn't she spend the best part of seventeen years trying to make me like that? Discipline, control, method, it's wrong to enjoy yourself, it's wicked to try and make yourself look nice, if you like anything it must be wrong! How can I help being like her?'

'Now, listen to me,' said Mrs O'Brien with great firmness. 'That excuse is wearing a bit thin. She did try to do all that to you, I'm not denying it, but it's twenty-five years since you last saw her and that's long enough for you to have made something of yourself. It's time you asserted yourself, did the things ye want to do yerself, and to hell wit' her! Haven't you got yer own conscience? She may have tried to put her foot on your soul, but it's time ye wiped off her heel-mark.'

Susan flushed scarlet with indignation. She had never thought that Mrs O'Brien could turn on her like this, blame her for what was not her fault and expect her to throw off an influence that would be with her all her life. It was unfair of her not to understand that an unhappy childhood excused all her shortcomings. Lawrence understood that and it was stupid of Mrs O'Brien not to do the same. She seethed speechlessly, too hurt to express her anger and reproach.

Mrs O'Brien regarded her with a gimlet eye, sharp as Susan had never seen it.

'Oh, I know ye're ragin' with me, but it's time ye grew up. Here y'are a woman of . . . well, over forty anyway, puttin' the blame for everything that's not right wit' ye on a woman ye never clapped eyes on since you were seventeen! If that's not nonsense, I'd like to know what is!'

'It's not nonsense,' blurted Susan, almost in tears. 'I thought you understood what she did to me.'

'I did, and I do,' said Mrs O'Brien with dignity, 'but ye can't live under the heel of a ghost. It's wicked, it's reelly wicked, so it is. So don't ever speak to me again in that self-pitying way about what she did to ye!' There was a hint of mimicry in the way she said the words that made Susan wriggle. 'Now,' she went on more gently, 'I've had me say.' She paused. 'Think it over an' ye'll see I'm right.' She grabbed at her bag and gloves. 'D'ye want me to go?' She shifted her weight delicately as if in preparation for a move, then smiling with great kindliness leant forward and touched Susan's hand. 'Ah, don't be angry wit' me, lovey!' she said. 'Sure, haven't I known ye long enough to tell ye the truth?'

'But it's not the truth,' said Susan passionately.

'Believe me, it is. Think it over slowly.' Mrs O'Brien gave her an emphatic nod and put her bag and gloves down again. After a short pause she began, 'And what's it like to be home again after all these years?'

Susan's anger began to ebb away; she felt too tired to keep it going any longer. She leant back in her chair, almost smiling.

'Lovely,' she said quietly.

'This wasn't yer aunt's room, surely?'

'No. She always used the study. My frivolous aunts sat here.'

Her head against the chair-back, she smiled, savouring the peace and stability she had found now that she was back at home. The big, solid old house gave her a sense of permanency. The things in it had been there since . . . well, as far as she was concerned, since before time began. More and more, since her return, she had caught herself dreaming, slipping out of the race of her London existence; breathing more slowly, sensing the fullness, the three-dimensional nature of space around her instead of being drawn onwards ever onwards at a pace that precluded familiarity with the ground covered or even awareness of what lay round. Before, she had been slow-witted as a winter fly, dragged to destruction on the cloth that is being pulled off the table.

'I was thinkin',' she heard Mrs O'Brien's voice saying, 'there wasn't much cosiness about her room, I'm sure! Ye're tired, child. Tell me, were y'in the raids much—the air raids?'

'A bit.'

'Were ye frightened?'

'Terrified.' She felt better for the admission.

'God, it must have been awful! No wonder ye're glad to be back here where nothing's changed in centuries o' time!'

'Everything here seems so secure, it's wonderful. You can hardly believe that awful things happen to people here, but of course they do.'

'They do indeed,' said Mrs O'Brien, very quietly, and Susan knew that she was thinking of Barry. Her admiration for her increased enormously. Here was a woman who could have made herself into a tragic figure with every justification, but she refused to do so. She was so robust in her outlook, so quick-sighted and jolly, and so intensely interested in the rest of humanity that she had never had time to cultivate an air of affliction.

Susan could hear the bell ringing again and Lawrence's tap on the knocker. She knew that her pleasure showed in her face as she excused herself to Mrs O'Brien and went to let him in, but there was no sign on the smooth face that this had been observed. Susan felt grateful to her for her reticence, for blindness it could not be.

'Ah,' said Lawrence, 'may I come in for a moment?' He held up an air mail letter. 'From the Mission in the Congo.'

'Mrs O'Brien's here. Come in.'

He stopped dead. 'Shall I be in the way? I'll come another time.'

'No, of course not. Come in.'

He followed her into the morning-room. Mrs O'Brien held out a puffy, capable hand, pivoting on her seat.

'An' how's Miss Weldon?'

'Not up to much, I'm afraid, at present. She suffers when there's a sudden change in the weather.' He looked depressed.

'Ah, it's too bad!' said Mrs O'Brien sympathetically. There was a pause. Discussion of Esmé's sufferings necessitated a respectful hush before anything more cheerful could be mentioned. Lawrence gazed through the conservatory at the garden in complete abstraction, tipping the letter over and over in his hands.

'We were just sayin', Misther Weldon, how secure it all seems over here, compared to England.' Mrs O'Brien spoke loudly and clearly, rather as if she were making a long-distance telephone call.

'Secure? Secure?' He seemed to be drawn back from infinite remoteness. 'Oh, security! I beg your pardon.' He looked at them both, a quick, live, interested look. 'Surely security, physical security has been proved to be a complete illusion. These last two wars have taught us that. Material security does not exist, anywhere. . .'

'Ah, don't be talkin', Misther Weldon,' said Mrs O'Brien comfortably. 'All the same. . .'

'All the same,' he gave her one of his charming, very personal smiles. 'All the same, I'm sure that our only stability lies in recognition of that fact. Nothing is safe. When that is understood, our security is complete.'

'Thank God ye're a Christian annyway,' said Mrs O'Brien happily, 'or it'd be a poor lookout for ye with nothing in this world or the next!' She stood up gingerly. 'I'll be off, now, Susan. No, I can't stay to tea, I promised Cormac I'd be back. I'll let meself out.' Waving them away from her, she was gone, sweeping back a moment later for her bag and gloves which she picked up and brandished at them in despairing silence. The hall door clicked behind her.

'You really meant that, didn't you?' said Susan, smiling at him.

'I never meant anything more.'

'Isn't it a counsel of despair?'

'Anything but. The last generation lived in much a settled period that it never occurred to them to doubt the permanence of their material surroundings; we have had to discard that kind of stability as unreliable and it has made us look further for our, security, finding it where it is indestructable. I think it's even a mistake to hanker after material stability, yet such is man . . . we all pursue happiness, not knowing what it is, mistaking its nature.' He leant back, crossing his legs. 'I'm sorry, I didn't come to lecture you. Read this.'

He handed her the air mail letter. She took it, preoccupied, holding it loosely between finger and thumb.

'What is the nature of happiness? Is anybody happy, really?'

'May I smoke a pipe?'

Susan nodded and he began feeling in his pockets for pipe, tobacco pouch and matches. Pressing tobacco absentmindedly into the bowl of the pipe and looking, not at what he was doing, but far away out of the window, he began.

'Of course, for a start we miscalculate the essential equipment, which is an absolute disregard for happiness as a goal, so the pursuer is foiled from the word go. As I see happiness, it is a by-product, never obtained directly. The conscious pursuit of it must fail because only by entire subjugation of the will can it be attained. There must be complete liberation from the ego, its demands and exertions, and this is an operation both arduous and unattractive to those who confuse happiness with pleasure, or with the satisfaction of their physical desires.'

He paused to light his pipe and puffed contentedly for a moment before continuing.

'The ruthless whittling down of personal requirements until the minimum is arrived at, and the consequent state of simplicity reached thereby, seems to be the beginning. There follow constant preoccupation with the well-being of other people and absolute concentration on discovering the will of God. In the view of most people, neither of these pastimes is calculated to lead to happiness, but I think they are the basic necessities without which it is unattainable.'

He smiled at her, suddenly looking towards her with extraordinary sweetness and interest. She, her head against the back of her chair, smiled, appreciating what he had been saying, but not speaking herself for the moment.

'It's only another way of saying that happiness is never to be found in oneself,' he said, as if he had not made this clear.

'Yes, but there are times when one is suddenly perfectly happy without any reason, or without any of the requirements you lay down. When I was a child here, the only times I was really absolutely happy was when I was alone on the mountain, not thinking of anyone else, or about God, but just being happy.'

'Ah, but you were not chasing happiness as an end. You were not even aware of what was happening to you, but just of your state. And surely in that state you were, so to speak, turned inside out, looking outwards and suddenly conscious that you were in accord with the living creation, entirely vital, with none of your perceptions wasted. Therefore, at a stage of growth in the awareness of God. Perhaps now, that kind of happiness is insufficient for you? Or you may have discovered other conditions which only progress can make compulsory. Susan, my dear, you mustn't let me lay down the law for you. It is preposterous.' The matter-of-fact voice in which he spoke made it difficult for her to return to the same subject.

'Tell me one thing, Lawrence,' she said, using his Christian name deliberately. 'Are you happy?' She had not moved and was still watching him with her head against the chair-back, smiling with pleasure at his serious consideration of her question, at the natural way in which he accepted her use of his Christian name though he was perfectly aware of Esmé's edict on that matter, and at her knowledge that of all her acquaintances he was the one who best fulfilled his own requirements for happiness. She felt much affectionate respect for his goodness, such astonishment at his self-abnegation in his human relationships, that it was a shock to see him shake his head.

'Occasionally and briefly, like you,' he said, smiling. 'It's a long road and, as I say, one does not seem to cover it directly.' He looked at the clock. 'We must consider that letter. Esmé will be waiting for her tea.'

Resentment of Esmé's possession of him smouldered inside her as she drew the letter from its envelope. She began to read, then broke off.

'Stay and have it with me. I'll send Mary Ellen with a message.'

He thought it over, then shook his head with evident regret.

'She counts on my being there,' he said. He stopped suddenly, looking at her with some uncertainty. 'Perhaps. . .' he began, 'Perhaps I could come back here after tea? Or would that be a nuisance? No, I'm sure you don't want that; it was just an idea and not at all a good one. Goodbye . . .' He stood up, about to go.

'Oh, do come back,' she said with such sincerity that he was reassured. 'Please do.'

He looked delighted. 'Very well, if you're sure you understand. Thank you. Don't get up, please.' With a grateful glance at her he was gone.

She sat up straight, about to ring for Mary Ellen to bring her tea, to read the letter, to light the fire, but for the instant considering this elderly man whose company she found so stimulating. Part of his attraction for her was certainly due to his elusiveness, his intangibility, to the way he stood beside the road and let the rest of the world pass on, and part to his compelling integrity, of which she was constantly aware. And suddenly she hit upon the difference between his rule of life and 'the Pope's', for both had preached renunciation. His concern was with goodness, whereas hers had been with sin. He did not think it wrong to enjoy the pleasures of life, but felt that in time people might progress beyond the point where they afforded satisfaction. Katharine, on the other hand, had regarded the gratification of any earthly desire as flagrant disobedience of the law of God. Poor Aunt Katharine, she thought, forever haunted by damnation! How bare must have been her spiritual landscape; like a no-man's land, raked by shell-fire.

Pleased at having made this discovery, she rang for Mary Ellen and began to read the letter from the head of the Mission in the Congo.

'Dear Mr Weldon,' it ran, 'It is with some hesitation that I write to you as Miss Fellowes' executor rather than to Miss Susan Fellowes who, I understand, was estranged from her family and may be difficult to trace. If you have been able to discover her whereabouts, perhaps you would be so kind as to acquaint her with the contents of this letter, at the same time making my apologies for not writing direct to her.

'We have had a most melancholy time reconstructing with the Police the crime in which poor Miss Fellowes was martyred but I am happy to tell you that these splendid fellows have at last succeeded in tracking down the criminals, of whom there are seven. These evil and impenitent men are now in prison awaiting sentence, which can be nothing less than hanging. They are Leopard Men, members of a secret society pledged to kill their victims in the same way as does a leopard, being possessed of a set of metal claws for this very purpose. I do not want to cause you unnecessary pain by describing this dreadful crime in detail, but feel sure that you would wish to know the main facts.'

At this point, Mary Ellen brought in the tea-tray, contriving with great skill to keep her face out of sight while she brought up a little table and put the tray upon it. In an instant she was gone. Susan returned to the letter.

'The reason for the crime, admitted by the assassins, was revenge for her interference with a *ju-ju* (or symbol to which magic powers are ascribed) which was regarded as sacred. She was perhaps a little reckless in the destruction of what she described as "idols", but when one realises her hatred of such things her action is understandable and her courage commendable. The Police, however, implore the rest of us not to follow her example as the responsibility for our safety, were we to do so, would be more than they could assume.

'Looking through poor Miss Fellowes' papers, preparatory to packing up her belongings for their last journey, I yesterday came across these two letters, marked, "Not to be opened until after my death", one addressed to you and the other to Miss Susan Fellowes. I enclose both of them, as I feel that you are the person most likely to be in touch with the niece and feel complete confidence that you will see to its delivery at the first opportunity. I pray that Miss Susan Fellowes, whose resistance to the Call was a great grief to her aunt, will be influenced by her glorious example and perhaps, who knows?—be led to take her place with us here.'

There followed a polite phrase of dismissal and the bold signature: Cicely Manning. Inside the cover was a smaller envelope addressed to herself in Katharine's erect and uncompromising hand. The sight of it made Susan straighten her back.

Even as she opened the envelope containing 'the Pope's' last message to her, Susan had a vision of the undefeated Miss Manning, white hair gathered into an untidy bun under a large white pith helmet, trotting tirelessly through the African forest and suffering agonies of frustration at the forced suppression of her iconoclastic zeal.

Katharine's letter had the musty smell that impregnates everything in West Africa, although it was dated only in January, of the current year. It was quite short.

'Dearest Susan,' it began, and Susan jerked backwards with the shock of being so addressed by 'the Pope', and gave a cynical little sniff of amusement before she read any further. 'For you will always be dear to me in spite of the way you shrank from my help and advice all through your life, preferring to trust to your own unformed, and often rebellious, judgement. I have often wondered if my work and, I hope, example, had any more effect upon your character than a footprint upon water, but perhaps wisdom has come to you with the years. Believe me, everything that I did was meant for your good and I freely forgive you now the bitter unhappiness you caused me many times by your resistance to every effort of mine to bring you to a proper state of mind. Whether you have made your peace with God is another matter that I hope you have not neglected.

'I am writing this because I feel that I may be called to give my life for the Faith. I have had warning which I choose to ignore. If I die by the hand of man out here, I charge you by all that you hold sacred to take my place out here and continue the work begun by me for the conversion of our African brothers and sisters. In this way, the only way open to a Believer, you will avenge my death. I lay this upon you with an Authority greater than that which I exercise as Head of the Family. You cannot refuse without imperilling your immortal soul. Remember, there can be no excuse for rejecting the Call! Your loving Aunt Katharine.'

As she read, Susan felt a hot surge of terrified indignation flooding her face and neck. She pushed the letter away from her on to the tray and stretched out her hand for the box of matches on the mantelpiece. Then, trembling, she knelt to light the fire, driving out of her mind the demand in the letter, concentrating fiercely on the insignificant matter of making the paper and sticks ignite. She would not admit 'the Pope's' demand, she would resist even understanding its nature, taking in its magnitude. She would pretend to herself that she had not even read it.

The fire was not doing well; the paper felt damp. Probably the night's rain had dripped upon it down the chimney. She tore it out of the grate, laying the sticks on the hearth, and replaced it with that day's newspaper, crumpling it furiously and laying the sticks against it with shaking hands, scarcely able to see what she was doing, so intense was her resistance to 'the Pope's' onslaught. When she opened the box of matches again, she pulled it out too far and spilled all the contents on to the hearth. This enraged her and she clenched her fists at the empty box, breathing fast and loudly. She swept the matches impatiently into the shovel, refusing to submit to the discipline of replacing them one by one in the box, heads all pointing the same way. Her emotions were so enlarged that she felt incapable of an operation of such minuteness. With ferocious concentration she lit a single match. It burnt with an impoverished blue flame and she had to shield it in its passage to the grate. It fell harmlessly from her fingers when it touched the paper, and went out.

She felt consumed with anger at its inanimate mutiny. She picked it up and threw it amongst the sticks and paper, broken in pieces. She tried again with another match, fulminating against the draught, the damp and the inferior quality of the matches. Her hands would not obey her; they shook feebly, refusing to grasp.

'Damn you!' she cursed the second match as its flame died, and 'Damn you, oh damn you!' she cursed the sticks and paper, infuriated by their obstinacy.

Behind her rage, battering at her defences, screamed the thought, 'She's got me! She's got me at last!' But scream as it might, she would never let it in. Once it had access to her mind she would be finished.

Quire suddenly she sat back on her heels and gazed at the unlit fire. 'Quiet,' she thought, 'I must be quiet. Being frantic isn't going to get me anywhere.' She forced herself to stay motionless until she felt her hand would be steady enough to carry the lighted match to the paper. Then, carefully and slowly, she lit a match, holding it downwards until it flamed brightly, and touched it gently against an edge of paper. In a moment the fire was lit. She laid small pieces of coal upon it and built it up with logs. Then she picked up every match, laying them singly in the box.

That completed her activity for the moment. Now she had nothing but 'the Pope's' letter to occupy her mind.

'I won't do it,' she assured herself. The thought had forced an entrance. She felt as unprotected as a small wild animal seeking cover on the bare earth, aware of the kestrel hovering above, running desperately in frantic, unavailing circles.

She tried to eat some bread and butter but could not swallow. Her throat felt thick. She poured some tea but could not drink it. She reached out and picked up the letter as gingerly as if it had been a snake.

She read it through once more from beginning to end, forcing down her anger and terror so that she could think more clearly.

'"Footprint upon water"!' she thought. 'If only she had known! More like a footprint upon wet concrete, set there for all time. How little Aunt Katharine knew me! Had she no idea of the bitter unhappiness she caused me, ceaselessly and unremittingly? Perhaps unhappiness was a contributory factor of repentance with her, and therefore necessary; she did not cause it malevolently. Of course I must have been a maddening child, enough to drive a saint to drink! But I do think I have every bit as much to forgive as she.'

Suddenly she remembered Mrs O'Brien's advice to her, less than two hours ago. She must be herself, make her own decisions.

'I won't do it,' she said aloud. This time the words expressed intention, not frenetic revolt against authority.

Again she picked up the letter and read it through. Suddenly the colossal presumptuousness of Katharine reared up at her. How could she dare, how could anyone dare to claim divine authority in this way and attempt to exercise it? All her life, Katharine had managed to convince her that only she, 'the Pope', could interpret the mind of God; no one else could be trusted to do so lest they interpret it differently. And at last Susan had seen through her fantastic egotism; at last, after all these years.

She began to laugh. She laughed as she thought of the holy terror in which Katharine had kept her throughout her childhood and of her own naiveté in believing that 'the Pope' really did have access to the mind of God. She laughed when she remembered Nanny defying Katharine's authority, and Charlotte and Daisy's nervous anxiety to escape from her strictures which made them feel uncomfortable without stirring them to mend their ways. She laughed as she thought of the hideous grey crossover shawls which she and her aunts had been forced to crochet on Sundays for the poor and of Olivia's disgusted comment that all they were good for was the cat's bed. She laughed at poor Mrs O'Brien's bewilderment when she had said that she could never kiss Katharine. She laughed until she was weak, and then she began to remember things that were not funny at all. Katharine's broken engagement, her refusal to give shelter to the dying Peter Cavanagh, the way in which Charlotte had escaped from her enslavement. One single kink of character had brought about so much.

She ate her tea. She felt liberated, as never before. At last she was a person in her own right.

She wished that Lawrence would come back. He had been away far longer than could be accounted for by simply having tea with Esmé. Perhaps, she thought regretfully, he had changed his mind and did not mean to come back after all.

She had never met anyone in the least like him. It was something quite new to her to observe a brilliant man who did not consider himself wasted in a backward and sparsely-populated area where the souls in his cure could be counted in double figures. His unselfishness led him to ignore his own interests to the point of neglect. His patience with Esmé and, it seemed, his affection for her, were almost frightening. In spite of living in a remote part of the country, he was aware of global trends, as fascinated by the uses of penicillin and atomic energy, diesel power and supersonic flight as anyone in close touch with these developments. His opinions on everything, from the Colour Bar to the Welfare State, self-government for India to the future of Communism in Western Europe, were informed, balanced and unprejudiced. He had chosen to learn Irish when it became compulsory to learn it in the schools, and was now the local authority on it. Yet he seemed to be absolutely without personal ambition, content to be poor, obscure and unappreciated, becoming daily more withdrawn from customary human aspirations so that he had come to have a kind of spareness about his demeanour that at once conveyed the great simplicity of his life. Susan, in his company, felt herself so very much less than he, so much at the mercy of needs and desires that he had discarded yet did not blame her for retaining, so complicated and confused in the light of his integrity that she found him alarming. She was continually afraid that he would discover her appalling spiritual poverty and despise her. Yet she longed for his presence and admired him more than any man she had ever known.

She had not wanted to fall in love with him. To begin with, he was sixty-five years old. He had been engaged to her aunt for many years, which would give a smack of the ridiculous to any attachment to herself. He was inescapably burdened with Esmé, not only in the matter of supporting her, but because she played on his pity and made a slave of him. And she was afraid to love a man like Lawrence: there would always be so much of him that would be inaccessible to her, not even aware of her; in fact, she wondered whether falling in love, for him, was not one of the human consolations that he had left behind. It annoyed her that she had fallen in love with him; he was at everybody's call. His time, his attention, his sympathy were permanently on loan. And what would there be for his wife, but Esmé to care for and him to wait for? Whoever married him would need to annihilate all personal needs and desires, expect nothing and hope for very little. No wonder, she thought, that she had fought against falling in love with him.

It was after six o'clock when she heard his knock on the door. She had felt sure that he would not come. She bounded from her chair, put out the tea-tray for Mary Ellen to remove, tidied the grate and then made frantically for the door, afraid that he might be tired of knocking and have gone away.

Great rain-clouds were piling up from the south-west. Darkness was gathering prematurely. There was a chill at the back of the wind and she was glad that she had lit the fire.

He gave no reason for his delay: it was clear that he did not think she had expected him earlier.

He smiled when he saw the fire. 'Ah,' he said. 'May I stand? I've been sitting far too long.'

She handed him Katharine's letter. 'Read that.'

Before he opened it, he said, 'Tell me, what did you think of Miss Cicely Manning?' He gave her an astute look.

'Could you see her?' said Susan. 'I know exactly what she looks like.'

'I could: very small, very dark, with luminous brown eyes and rather frizzy hair. A sort of Mrs Mouse.'

'Oh!' she exclaimed, infinitely disappointed. 'I don't see her a bit like that. I think she's pink and white, plump, with rather wild white hair, and she wears a huge white helmet and an 1890 white tropical suit. . .' her tone was persuasive.

He shook his head, laughing. 'I can't change her,' he said, 'however much you try to make me. Oh, and she is a Cambridge graduate.'

'I wonder which is right.'

'Neither, I expect. What did you think of her letter?'

'Ah!' said Susan. 'Read that.'

She watched his face while he read. She could see the colour rising in it as it had in her own. He stopped to give her an enquiring look but continued reading when she made no response. When he had finished, he shook the thin piece of paper as if he found it incomprehensible, re-read it and put it away in its envelope.

'Well?' said Susan.

He looked terribly upset, almost afraid to look at her. 'It's dreadful, of course.' He drew in breath as if he were about to say more, then decided not to speak.

'Of course I shan't do it,' she said quickly. 'Ah!' He looked enormously relieved. 'I'm glad you don't feel you have to yield to her . . . compulsion.'

'It's taken me all these years,' she said, a slow smile lightening her face, 'to discover that she was only a woman like myself. Her letter nearly finished me, until about the third time I read it I suddenly saw how fantastic it all was, and always has been. I mean, the way she ruled us by threats of damnation and so on.' With what seemed complete irrelevancy she added, 'And I'm going to clear out the attics and get rid of all that junk up there.'

'What have you been up to, Susan?' he asked with a trace of amusement. 'Laying ghosts? You're quite different.'

She was astonished at the quickness of his perception. He had grasped everything, the change in herself and the reason for her last sentence, without a word of explanation.

'I am different,' she said, a little distantly. He looked down at once, no longer amused, aware of her unwillingness to discuss her difference. After a moment she said, with almost exaggerated gentleness, 'Are you going to answer Miss Manning? I suppose I should write too.'

'I must, and I think you should too, if only to announce that you have been traced at last. And it would be a kindness to put her mind at rest about joining the Mission: otherwise she'll probably feel she had to meet every boat.'

Susan was aghast. 'Do you think she seriously expects me to go out there?'

'Her letter was certainly serious and she strikes me as a most determined expecter.' His tone was perfectly solemn but there was a gleam of humour in his eye. There was an answering gleam in Susan's.

'Do you think Aunt Katharine really thought I'd go?'

'I think she thought she could blackmail you into it.' This time he did not look amused.

'Wait a minute,' she said. She went to the dining-room and returned with a bottle of sherry and two glasses, which she filled.

'Thank you, how very nice,' he said as she handed one to him. He turned it this way and that between himself and the fire, watching the pale gold of the wine light up and glow against the flames.

Susan took a quick gulp of sherry to give her courage.

'Lawrence?'

'Yes?' The expression on his face encouraged her to go on.

'Do you think you would have been happy—you and she?'

Now that she had said it she dared not look at him; she frowned at the fire, feeling wretched. There was complete silence, but she could sense that he was not angry. She glanced quickly at him and away again. He looked thoughtful, hesitant and unhappy.

'It's not a fair question,' she said penitently. 'You don't have to answer it.'

He ignored this. 'If we could have been married in the beginning I think we might have been,' he said slowly. 'We ought to have had the courage to do it in spite of everyone. Putting it off and off changed both our characters utterly. By the time it was broken off we had grown so much apart that it would have been a disaster.' He showed no resentment at being asked so intimate a question.

'You don't think that perhaps at first you didn't really know what she was like . . .'

She could see that he was torn between loyalty, the undiscerning approval of every action of the person concerned, and truth.

'When I first knew her,' he said with some reluctance, 'I don't think she was as you remember her at all. All that domination and intolerance sprang from her unhappiness. If people do not complain, it finds expression some other way.'

'Was she more unhappy than anyone else?'

'It seems to me that her own strength of will was the one thing that was on her side of the balance. Against her she had her father, the money crisis at his death which made her responsible for four quite helpless, uneducated women. Then there was the war, your education and, when things looked like coming right at last, my father died and my mother and Esmé came to live with me. She and Esmé never got on and she refused to live in the same house with her. So, in the end even I had to be against her. We had no choice but to part. Don't you think that she was indeed a most unhappy woman? Is it surprising that she became . . . difficult and eccentric?' His look and his voice were quite fierce.

'No,' Susan was obliged to concede. 'I never realised so much was against her. All the same, if she wouldn't live in the same house with Esmé, she had only herself to thank that she never married.'

He shook his head. 'With two such temperaments flung together at close quarters, there would have been no peace. I can't blame her.'

'If she really loved you, she'd have thought it was worth it.' Susan looked up at his face with a sort of desperate boldness. 'She'd have put up with anything.'

She spoke with such feeling that he was startled out of his half-nostalgic mood into a wide-awake consciousness of the actual moment. He perceived instantly what his mind could not permit him to accept. Looking at her face for confirmation of this intuitive communication and watching the effect of each word, he said, 'I have learnt that it is too much to ask any woman. There is not one who would be willing to face it.'

There was an expression of incredulous hope on his face as he saw Susan's face being raised, smiling, towards his.

'Yes, there is,' she said quietly. 'Me.'

'You?' he said, as if stupefied by his good fortune. He bent towards her and took both her hands, looking into her face as he asked her gently, 'You?' He put her hands away from him with a little shake and stood up right. 'No,' he said, 'you don't know what you're taking on. You would not do it if you knew.'

'I do,' she said desperately, 'oh, I do! Good Heavens, do you imagine I wanted to fall in love with you? Why, I think it's absolute lunacy, but I can't help it.' She shook her closed fists at him to emphasise her determination. 'But if you don't want me I'll go away,' she added in sudden panic.

'Don't want you? Don't want you? Oh, Susan darling! If you hadn't said that you were willing to undertake my . . . commitments with me, I should never have dared to imagine that you could even consider marrying me. I didn't think any woman in the world would marry me, placed as I am. Are you sure you know what you're doing?' he added incredulously, afraid to believe the truth.

She raised her face towards his, but he did not kiss her.

'I'm sixty-five,' he objected.

'I know. I'm not exactly a child myself.'

'I've got no money and no prospects. And I've got an insoluble family problem . . .'

She nodded energetically as he put his hands on her shoulders to hold her away until he should have set out all his drawbacks.

'People will laugh at us, because I was going to marry your aunt.'

She began to laugh. 'Well, I think that's rather funny myself. Don't you?'

He could not help laughing at this. 'Thinking something is funny isn't the same as standing up to ridicule,' he warned her.

'Do stop thinking of all your disadvantages. I've thought of all those already, and lots more that you haven't even mentioned.'

'And you still . . .?'

'Yes, I still . . .'

'You know that a clergyman's wife has an awful time: she marries the job with the man?'

'Yes, I'd even thought of that.'

He took his hands from her shoulders and drew her towards him to kiss her on the mouth.

When they began to talk again, he stood a little apart from her, not touching her. She perceived at once that this was a reticence, a discipline that he would not infringe because he believed it to be an essential element in their relationship which he expected her to understand without explanation. And she was grateful that he did not feel it necessary to put everything into words, that he thought her capable of sensing what it was right for them to do, in their circumstances, at their age.

'What will Esmé say?' said Susan, suddenly apprehensive.

'Ah, I'm afraid . . . I'm afraid she won't like it. It may take time to persuade her. Will you come and see her; that is, when I've told her?'

'Will it do any good?'

'It can only do good.'

'You may think that. It doesn't mean that she'll see it the same way.'

'Goodwill can never do anything but good.' He looked at his watch. 'That you are willing to live with us both will mean a lot to her. Susan, I must go.'

'But I'm not marrying her,' said Susan.

'My darling,' he said, 'I'm afraid you are.'

CHAPTER EIGHTEEN

L awrence chose a bad moment to tell Esmé that he was going to marry Susan. The day was cold and damp, the fire in the drawing-room was inadequate, Esmé had slept badly and she was depressed by the threat of winter. Her first reaction was, understandably, petulant.

'Oh,' she cried, watching him, 'so she's got you at last! I knew that was what she was after, the minute she came back to the village, but I thought you had too much sense to fall for it. After all, you're nearly seventy.'

'Sixty-five,' said Lawrence in gentle protest.

'There's not much difference: what I mean is you're getting old. Too old to be made a fool of, and too old to marry.'

These remarks were, so to speak, surface ones, provoked by the shock of hearing the unwelcome news. She threw them off while trying to discover some really insuperable obstacles to the marriage.

He waited for this first unpleasantness to pass over before making any further persuasive remarks. After a moment of silence he began again, speaking with real affection.

'We both want you to know that of course there's no question of your going away from here: we want to have you here with us. Susan asked me to make that absolutely clear to you.' He smiled.

'It's kind of her, I must say, not to want to turn me out of my own home!' She turned great dark eyes upon him with reproachful insistence. 'Have you thought what this is going to mean to me, Lawrence? Have you considered my position? I mean, it's not going to make things any easier for me, is it, to have a strange woman in the house?'

He refused to be annoyed. 'You'll enjoy having Susan for company, my dear. You know how much you enjoy it when she drops in to see you.'

'That's not the same thing as having her always in the house, taking you away from me and wishing me out of the way.' Her eyes became huge liquid pools of suffering, tears brimming almost over. 'I believe it will kill me. Lawrence, how can you do this to me? Of course, I know it doesn't matter what happens to me, but I did think you had that much affection for me: I never thought you'd let a stranger come between us.'

He was sitting beside her sofa, leaning rather forward in his chair, answering her slowly and taking his time over his words as if he had all eternity to spend with her and no desire to be elsewhere.

'Because I love Susan I shall not stop loving you,' he said. 'Don't tell me you don't know that, Esmé.' He looked directly at her, refusing to look away until she should have answered him. 'You know I love you and that if I thought this would harm you in any way I should not do it. Isn't that so, my dear?'

'I know that's what you think, Lawrence, but I know that from now on I shall have to play second fiddle. And I know that Susan will want to have you all to herself and will hate every minute you spend with me. And I shall end by being the stranger. I can see it'll be a good thing when I . . . go. I've nothing to live for, now.' The tears overflowed and Esmé's mouth turned down.

'You simply must not let yourself talk like that, Esmé,' said Lawrence sternly. 'You know how wrong it is when there is no justification whatsoever for such self-pity. Consider for a moment and you will see that the good points in this project far outweigh the bad ones.'

'There are no good points,' wailed Esmé hopelessly. 'Oh, why do you have to do this to me when we've been so happy together all these years?' She wept loudly, bowing her head over her up-drawn knees.

Lawrence could only wait for her to be done. It was no good talking to her while she was sobbing so violently. Wretchedly, he looked at the floor, at the ceiling, at the fire and at his own hands, clenched with agitation. Gradually her crying eased, she produced a handkerchief to mop away the tears, and awaited his ministrations with the demanding hunger of the greatly-wronged.

'Try and see how difficult you are going to make it for Susan if you go on like this,' he pleaded. 'It isn't at all easy for her in any case. It would make all the difference if you were to make her welcome.'

She gave him a quick, sly look. 'I haven't ever liked her, really,' she said. 'She's too like Katharine. It's funny, isn't it, first the aunt and then the niece! That you should fall in love with both of them, I mean, one after the other. Are you really in love with her, Lawrence?' she added, as if such folly was both shameful and incredible.

'I am,' he said with dignity, 'and she with me. The fact that we are not young does not make it impossible for us to be in love.' There was an edge of exasperation on his voice and Esmé observed a flush that was beginning to colour his face. The moment had come, she decided, to deal the final blow that would dispel his romantic notions for good.

'No fool like an old fool! So they say,' she said almost with gaiety. 'What a laugh the whole countryside is going to have over it!'

'They will get over it in time,' he observed stiffly.

Esmé's face twisted nervously as she perceived how near he was to losing his temper. With a little further effort she might provoke him into saying something regrettable and in his subsequent remorse would lie her victory.

'I don't know which they'll laugh at more; you, the elderly Don Juan, or her, taking on her aunt's jilted lover!' Esmé ended with a hint of an amused titter, only perceptible to a sensitive ear, a vulnerable spirit.

To Lawrence it had the force of an explosion. It struck him like a physical blow. It was the culmination of all the injustices, the deliberate misconstructions and acts of ingratitude and selfishness, the personal frustration and humiliations that he had suffered at Esmé's hands since she had come to live with him. He stood up, his face very red, and looking so enlarged by his anger that it seemed the immediate space was too small to contain him and he must find an outlet for his emotion. He was making a kind of speechless mutter and Esmé believed that he was about to have a stroke. She tried to scream for help but so frightened was she that her voice made no sound. She agitated her hands wildly and tried to back away against her pillows as he towered over her. For a moment she thought that he might even kill her. Then he turned away and almost ran out of the room.

Esmé lay slackly on her sofa, exhausted by terror, and began to whimper quietly. She had never been so frightened in her life. It was becoming clear to her that she must revise her ideas and be prepared to accept Susan for the sake of expediency. She dared not resist any longer. When, after a few minutes, Lawrence came back into the room, she was ready to capitulate.

He was deeply contrite. He looked deflated and overcome with remorse at his behaviour. He went up to her sofa and spoke gently to her, as he would to a frightened bird cowering against the window-pane in a paralysis of terror.

'Esmé, did I frighten you? My dear, don't look like that. I was possessed, but it is all over now. I won't hurt you.'

She had taken her cue from him. He was ashamed and if she worked on his contrition she might still have her way. She did not move; handkerchief in hand, she lay breathing shallowly, her eye warily upon him.

'Esmé, you don't have to watch me,' he said with infinite reproach.

'Oh, Lawrence, how could you?' she said weakly, and buried her face in the pillows.

Mortified as he had never been before, he stayed beside her, imploring her to speak to him, to take heart, to be more cheerful.

She put out a hand feebly. 'Lawrence!'

'My dear, what is it?'

'I don't think you would be happy for long with Susan,' she said tremulously. 'She's not good enough for you.'

'Not good enough for me? For me?' he looked at her in utter amazement. 'You think she's not good enough for me? My dear, how little you know of us both! It is she who is giving up so much in order to marry me, and you say she is not good enough. . .' He shook his head in bewilderment.

'Oh well,' said Esmé with infinite weariness, 'I only hope you're not making a big mistake. Now I must have a little sleep, all this has made me feel quite . . . odd.' She closed her eyes and stayed quite motionless.

Nothing had been resolved, no agreement reached. Lawrence tiptoed from the room and sought refuge in his study. He sat at his desk and gazed across it at the books in his bookcase, seeing nothing of them, his hands clasped under his chin. He felt opposed by everything, hopeless in the face of all his difficulties. What was the use of pretending that Esmé and Susan could ever inhabit the same house in peace? Katharine had been right: there was no hope of happiness there. Susan simply did not realise the magnitude of Esmé's resistance or the ingenuity of her opposition. If Esmé behaved unjustly to Susan, how would he himself react? As he had done just now, with anger so inflamed that he was not responsible for his actions? That was a pleasant prospect, indeed.

Promise faded, leaving him with an outlook infinitely dreary, devoid of any gleam of hope.

He did not go to Fellowescourt that day. He had neither the heart to tell Susan his conclusions, nor the courage to put them into words. With a sense of deprivation he was aware of her constantly, guiltily troubled by her confidence in their happiness, overwhelmed by the knowledge that he must bring all their hopes to destruction. All through that day he kept saying to himself, 'Katharine was right: she could see how it would go. She was wiser than I in this matter.'

Susan, meanwhile, was mystified because he did not come to see her. She could settle to nothing because at every moment she was sure that he would arrive. As the empty day wasted away she imagined calamities of every kind; she did not go out for fear of missing him.

She would not even go to the rectory lest he call at Fellowescourt in her absence; and she had an uncomfortable sensation, a sort of intuitive fear, that something was happening to him which he could resolve better without her, that perhaps it was necessary for him to be alone. She felt neglected and shut out, and spent a miserable evening.

The next morning she sat down to write him a note which she would send by Mary Ellen. She looked at the blank sheet of paper and felt a fool: she had not seen him for one day and she felt that the end of the world had come. She pushed pen and paper away from her and went out to work with consuming industry in the garden.

She was bent double, weeding, when he came towards her from round the side of the house. She stood erect, muddy hands held away from her clothes, so delighted to see him that her apprehensiveness was forgotten until she saw how wretched he was looking.

'But what's the matter?' she cried. 'You look terrible. Something's gone wrong, hasn't it?' She ended almost in a whisper.

He smiled, lit by the warmth of her pleasure at seeing him.

'There are things we must talk about. Where can we go?' he said.

She looked enquiringly into his face as she wiped her hands on a tuft of grass; he looked exhausted, old and defeated, and the sight of him standing there, so contained in his despair, so undemanding of sympathy, wrung her heart for the loneliness which had been his lot for so long.

She slipped her arm under his elbow and led him towards the wall at the end of the garden, under the Scotch firs. The day was mild, with a hint of sunshine behind the clouds and a tremulous stirring of the air that was not quite a breeze. They sat on the wall in silence, looking back towards Fellowescourt, cinnamon-coloured beyond the lawn.

'What is it?' she asked in a tight little voice.

He kissed her cheek, not passionately, but as if contact with her warmth would soften his despair.

'It won't do, my dear,' he said gently.

'Won't do? Why won't it do?' There was an edge of alarm on her voice.

'Esmé will not have it, for one thing. But that is not the whole of it.'

'What else is there?'

'I cannot express it, even to myself. It seems to be impossible when I am with Esmé. It is not only that she is against it . . .'

'What did she say?' Susan's tone was practical.

'She is all against it,' he said again.

'She'll get used to it.' Susan spoke almost with relief.

He shook his head. 'It is not what she says,' he began quickly, and speaking with great urgency continued, 'I see when I am with her that there would be no peace in the house. Terrible things would be felt and said and suffered. I don't think you have any conception of how poor Esmé can . . . inflame one with the desire to hurt her back, to shake her into reasonableness again . . . with such evil passions that it is very dreadful.' He stopped, throwing out his hands hopelessly.

'You're telling me that when you told Esmé about us, she made you feel like that, and that you can't live in the house to be subjected to such provocation, that it frightened you?' Susan was looking directly at him.

'I was quite beside myself,' he said miserably. 'I could have done her an injury. I had to run away.'

'Do you mean you really lost your temper with Esmé?' said Susan with amazement.

'It was worse than that. I was possessed . . .'

'Was she frightened?'

'She was terrified,' he admitted with shame.

'Then she's never going to drive you as far as that again. Lawrence, you should have done it years ago! I can't tell you how glad I am, honestly.' Words came rushing out, so excited was she.

'You mustn't say such a terrible thing, Susan,' he protested, deeply shocked by her levity. 'I tell you, I could have done her an injury.'

'You think that you might. I am quite certain that you could never hurt anyone, especially Esmé, in anger. There I know you better than you know yourself.'

'How can you tell?' he asked in exasperation. 'Who can speak for any other person when none of us can answer with certainty for ourselves?' Gloomily, he gripped the wall on either side of him.

'Listen, I know Esmé pretty well by now, and you too, I think. She won't oppose our marriage any more now, I'm convinced of it. Has she said anything about it today?'

'No. We have avoided discussion on the matter.'

'She will accept it if she sees that you intend to go on with it. If you start wavering, you're finished. You must let her see . . .'

'It's all very well,' he began hopelessly. His expression changed. 'You think I've been too . . . yielding to Esmé all these years?'

'If you could have been even mildly selfish, I think it would have done her all the good in the world.' She grinned suddenly at him. 'Wait till you see the beneficial influence of my crass selfishness upon her! Why, we'll do each other so much good you won't know either of us in a month!'

He shook his head, smiling. 'You will not be serious, in spite of the gravity of our situation. I don't think we can go on with it, my dear.' He spoke with great tenderness.

'Don't you want to marry me, Lawrence?' Susan looked straight at him, watching his face till he should answer her.

'Not want . . . Oh, my love!' His face was turned to hers in entire devotion. 'More than I have ever wanted any thing.'

'And this time then, I am going to see that you get what you want,' said Susan, and from this purpose she refused to be deflected.

There was a snail-shell, small and elegant, striped like a bull's eye in grape-black and yellow, wedged between two stones of the wall. Susan dislodged it, held it up to see if it was inhabited and, finding that it was, set it on the bare stone so that the emerging snail should walk the wall before reaching food or shelter. They watched it in silence, able to take an interest in this small matter that was so far removed from what occupied their minds. For a time nothing happened, then suddenly the shell rocked slightly and the head and horns appeared; in a moment, the whole thing was in motion, the slight, elongated body arching and dipping in its progress, the horns set forwards and upwards so bravely that the creature had the air of a little ship sailing her course across an uncharted ocean in confidence and safety.

The sight of it delighted both of them, so that they smiled secretly at one another in silence as it reached the edge, reared its head uncertainly for an instant, then plunged resolutely downwards towards the ground. It encouraged them to see the directness of its course, its determination to reach port and the steadiness of its progress. They smiled at one another again, curiously moved, almost to tears.

'What did she remind you of, Lawrence?' asked Susan quickly.

He was still smiling. 'A boat, I think, at sea. Why do you call her "she"?' That she had done so seemed to please him greatly.

'Well, she was so feminine—she couldn't be anything else. Didn't you think so?'

He nodded, half-laughing. 'In this country, all cats are "she", regardless of their sex. It may be the same with snails.'

'No, only elegant ones like that. Lawrence?'

'Yes?'

'I think the thing is to get married quickly, almost at once.'

He considered this in silence.

'Then no one can put us off,' she said. 'And we won't tell anybody beforehand; they would all disapprove too much.'

'We will tell Esmé.'

'Oh yes, of course we will tell Esmé.'

'People will talk.'

'They will talk whatever we do. Once we are married it doesn't matter what they say; they can't stop it then.'

For a moment he said nothing. Then he laid his hand firmly on hers.

'Yes. That's what we'll do,' he said. He looked years younger. Tension fell away, leaving them with a sense of reprieve. It was a moment of extraordinary happiness. They sat holding it, as it were, in experience; grateful for it, yet neither assessing it as might those practised in love-making, nor carried away by it as the very young might be. Smiling at one another, they neither spoke nor moved.

Time did not press upon them, nor any outside force. It was their portion of the actual, spilt out of the morning and spreading as moment after moment dripped into the pool.

Fellowescourt glowed in the half-sunlight, grateful for the warmth on the air like an old animal asleep with one eye open. Lawrence sighed.

'What will you do with this?' he said suddenly.

'With Fellowescourt? It will wait for us, Lawrence. One day you will retire and then we'll come and live here. In the meantime, well, perhaps we can find some more Tilsits.'

He shook his head. 'It ought to be full of children.'

'I wish I had seen it when my father and all the aunts were small. That was the last time it had a proper family of children in it. Of course I don't remember my father, but I think all my aunts, except Olivia, were born grown-up. Can you imagine Aunt Charlotte playing hide-and-seek?'

He smiled wryly; the thing was unthinkable. 'If you would be content with a small rent,' he said tentatively, 'I know of two young war widows, friends, with five children between them, who would jump at it. The father of one of the widows served with me in the first war; he wrote to me about them the other day. They are desperate for somewhere to live, and they've very little money.'

'You don't think they'd want it forever?' Susan felt herself being denied her last refuge; she had visions of Fellowescourt overrun by a tribe of strange children who would consider it their home, not hers, and who would slowly drive her out of its comfortable embrace. She hated the thought of being excluded from what had always been her private world, even while she had been away from it, of having to ring the bell before she could enter the house, of having to stand waiting on the step and be shown into the drawing-room by strangers. But none of these quite natural objections could account for the feeling of alarm that seized her at the thought of letting Fellowescourt. Suddenly she realised that the deep-seated, the most obstinate objection was that she would have no bolt-hole. Quite unconsciously she had felt that if Esmé became intolerable she could always take refuge in Fellowescourt until she was able to endure her company again; with Fellowescourt let she would have to support the intolerable.

'You could let it furnished by the year, or even by the quarter; there need be no permanent settlement,' he said gently, aware of her uneasiness. He looked at her enquiringly. 'Think it over for a bit—no need to decide this minute.'

If she held on to Fellowescourt as a kind of refuge, she would never take up the full commitments of her marriage; she would be running off there more and more often and for less reason as time went on. It would be a sort of drug to her, becoming more and more necessary. She perceived that it would be a menace to the stability of her relationship with Lawrence: if she were to marry him she must make her home in his home, transplant herself absolutely and have no secret hiding-place. She must overcome her exasperation, her bad moments and her unhappiness as they came and where they fell upon her.

'No,' she said, almost nervously, 'no, I don't want to think it over any longer. Write to them, will you? I'd like them to have it.'

He looked at her gratefully. 'Really,' he said, 'it would be a charity. I don't think you'd regret it.'

'I hope it comes off,' she said, so seriously that he was startled.

When he had gone, she sat down and wrote to ask Mr Blair to be a witness at her marriage. Lawrence had a friend, rector of a city church in Cork, who would marry them by special licence, in his church; he was going to write to him today. Susan sealed the letter, walked down the hill to the post office and put it in the box herself.

She had an early lunch because it was Mary Ellen's half-day off. This was a ritual meticulously observed, though in general Mary Ellen spent her free afternoon immured in her kitchen, reading, instead of tearing home on her bicycle, so that it would not have mattered if lunch had been at two o'clock instead of one. After the meal, Susan went up to the attic, resolved to condemn to destruction, sale or charity every relic of ancient times still preserved up there.

She went from room to room, disturbing piles of orderly rubbish, moving things to see behind them. She did not find it frightening to be alone up there today. Dust had settled on all the things again and they looked as if they had lain there undisturbed for ever. Nevertheless, she felt reluctant to destroy them. She made a start of collecting the piles of pianoforte pieces of the 1870s and laying against them the Victorian watercolours painted by her inartistic great-aunts: they could all go to a bonfire. Once she had begun it was not so painful to continue. By the end of the afternoon she had made great progress. She had even sealed the fate of all the garments on the ancient coat-stand. They would all burn, every one of them.

She broke off, determined to do no more that day. Her back and legs ached and she felt coated with dust. She made her way to the little window on the landing and peered out, as she always did, surveying the countryside. It was very beautiful today, green and rolling, warmed by the pale half-sunlight; chequered by dark hedges, stone walls, white lanes and ribs of bare grey rock it lay unfurled before her. A tiny black figure was striding towards the village, about to pass a pair of lovers, arms about each other's waists. It was Lawrence, coming to post his letters; who the lovers might be, she did not know, until suddenly she recognised Mary Ellen's coat.

It was unbelievable that Mary Ellen, the recluse, the afflicted, should be walking out. Susan pressed her nose to the window, waiting till the lovers should come nearer. As Lawrence passed them, they separated sheepishly, answering his greeting with obvious embarrassment. They closed together again as soon as he had passed, then turned and went the other way.

Susan ran down the stairs to the hall door, opened it and hurried down the flagged path, lying in wait for Lawrence under the yew archway. He came along at such a pace that she felt as if she were trying to stop a train.

'Lawrence,' she called, 'stop a moment.' She began to laugh; he had walked right past the gate and had to come back quite a distance.

'Tell me,' she said, 'was that Mary Ellen you passed? What has come over her?'

'It was,' he said, smiling. 'With Michael John Mahoney; they were walking out before the war.'

'But she always hides from everybody; what's happened to her?'

'She doesn't need to hide from him,' he said gravely. 'He was blinded at Arnhem. He's only just come home after being trained at St Dunstan's.' He waved the letters at her. 'I'm missing the post,' he said, and was gone.

From over the rise, Susan could hear the sound of slow footsteps approaching and a murmur of voices: Mary Ellen and her young man must have turned round again. She dashed quickly into the house so that she might not be caught watching them. As she shut the door silently she heard a great screech of courting laughter from the other side of the yew hedge. She peered out of one of the tiny windows flanking the door and watched them pass the little iron gate. Michael John Mahoney was tall, fair and immensely handsome. Susan beamed: Mary Ellen would be no problem to anyone again—she was too happy to be bothered hiding from the rest of the world.

Mr Blair was not content to reply to Susan's letter by post; he arrived by car, in person, without warning, hastening up the flagged path as if any delay might prove fatal to his purpose.

'Ah, Miss Fellowes!' he cried anxiously when Susan admitted him.

'Indeed, I'm greatly relieved to find you in.' He peered into her face as if he hoped to discover whether she would listen to reason or not. Then he grasped her by the elbow and pushed her towards the study.

'No, Mr Blair; in here if you don't mind,' she said, opening the door into the morning-room.

'Ah yes, things are different now, of course,' he said rather sadly. 'Nice room, though,' he added with surprise, 'Of course, the Tilsits did it up.'

She settled him in a chair but he was too agitated to sit at ease. He kept leaning forward, gripping the arms of the chair and moving his feet. Susan offered him a cigarette which he refused impatiently then, as she withdrew the box, decided to accept. He lit it clumsily and smoked it without enjoyment, seeming to resent its interference with his freedom.

'Miss Fellowes!' he said after a few shallow puffs, looking at her with great severity and refusing to say more until she had replied.

'Yes, Mr Blair?'

'Miss Fellowes!' A nervous finger flicked at his cigarette so that the ash fell all over his waistcoat. 'Tch tch tch!' he exclaimed, very annoyed, brushing at his clothes. 'What is this that you propose to do?' he suddenly shot at her.

'To marry Canon Weldon,' said Susan uncompromisingly.

'But whatever brought you to this . . . decision? Have you consulted anybody?'

'About what?' said Susan with a mystified expression. 'About this . . . match. Has anyone told you that it is most unsuitable?' He sounded exasperated by her stupidity.

'Nobody knows, except Miss Weldon,' she said stiffly.

'Ah! And you say she favours the match?'

'I did not say so. As a matter of fact she is against it: but what else could you expect?'

'I must say,' commented Mr Blair tartly, 'it's the first sensible thing I've heard of her.' He paused, looking sourly at Susan from under his eyelids. 'I cannot understand this man, Miss Fellowes; he seems determined to ally himself with the mistress of Fellowescourt.'

Susan was finding it difficult to keep her temper. Trying to make her voice sound civil, she said, 'You mean, you think he's on the make, Mr Blair?'

He grimaced at this and shifted his feet uneasily. 'Well,' he said uncomfortably, 'that's not a pretty way of expressing it, Miss Fellowes, but it does more or less put my point.'

'And what brought you to imagine such a thing? What put it into your head?' Susan glared distastefully at his small, dusty, snuff-coloured person.

He fidgetted on his chair. Miss Fellowes was proving herself true to type: unreasonable, headstrong and obstinate. He could see it in the set of her mouth, the flash in her eye. If he was not very careful he would have a wild tigress on his hands.

'Now you're getting vexed,' he said reproachfully. He took a large, not too clean, handkerchief from his pocket and wiped his spectacles in a meditative way, screwing up his eyes the better to see what he was doing. Then he replaced them carefully, paying great attention to setting them absolutely straight. 'You mustn't resent my saying these things to you, Miss Fellowes,' he pleaded. 'I'm your family lawyer and friend into the bargain. It's entirely for your protection that I'm here.' He glanced at her benignly, half smiling in a deprecating way.

'You can't know Canon Weldon very well . . .' began Susan, but he would not allow her to finish.

'Oh, but I do!' he assured her. 'I have known him for very many years, very many . . . in fact, ever since he was . . . since you were a very little girl.'

'You mean when he was engaged to my aunt, to Aunt Katharine?'

'Ahem . . . yes,' he admitted drily. 'As a matter of fact I had a long talk with him at that time, on this very matter, being suspicious of his intentions, even then. But he satisfied me then that he was not . . . He is a man who can state his case with great conviction.' Mr Blair shook his

head sadly, darting a malignant glance at Susan to watch her reaction
to his next thrust. 'And you see what happened?'

'They never married,' said Susan with composure.

'Exactly! They never married. And do you want to know why? I'll
tell you why!' He wagged an excited finger.

'But I know why.'

'You think you know, Miss Fellowes, because he has told you the
reasons he wants you to believe. But did your aunt ever tell you why?'
He waited for her to answer this and as she said nothing, continued, 'He
was very keen to marry her until he discovered that your grandfather
died almost bankrupt, and then he started putting it off. He went
on putting it off. Miss Fellowes, until your aunt herself began to see
through him and broke off the engagement herself!' His eyes gleamed
triumphantly.

'How you dare say such things, Mr Blair, I can't think!' Susan was
trembling with anger and scarcely able to speak.

'But even clergymen are not always perfect, Miss Fellowes; they
have their ambitions too, you know, and not many openings. If they
want money, they cannot earn very much in their . . . calling: they must
either marry it or inherit it. If they have missed promotion, as seems to
be the case here, though I don't like to say such things, mind you, social
advancement is possible also by marriage. To marry one of the Fellowes
is quite a leg up for an obscure country parson, after all!' He held up a
hand to stave off her protests until he had finished. 'Now I know you're
very cross with me, and it does you credit, but just consider, I beg you
to consider. That's all I ask. Consider this in the light of what I've been
saying to you and see if I haven't something on my side.'

Susan glared silently at him, so amazed at his accusations against a
person so undeserving of them that the power to protest abandoned
her; nothing that she could say, she knew, would alter Mr Blair's
opinion of Lawrence.

He assumed that her silence was an admission of doubt.

'You can see how it all adds up, can't you?' he said persuasively.

'Mr Blair, I really believe you're mad,' said Susan in despair. 'You can't know Canon Weldon if you think he's capable of systematic self-seeking. Do you know that neither money nor social position mean anything to him at all? That he's perfectly happy to be obscure and that he has no ambitions for his own advancement at all? I've never met a less worldly man, and I'm quite sure you haven't either, if you but knew it.'

'Well then, the man's a fool,' said Mr Blair, shutting his mouth with a snap. 'If he's not a knave, he's a fool. Oh, he's very plausible, I'll admit, but he's no husband for you, Miss Fellowes. And look at his age! Tch tch tch, it's a poor business whatever way you look at it.'

'But I want to marry him,' said Susan obstinately.

'That is no sound reason for marriage, Miss Fellowes,' said Mr Blair with equal obstinacy, and Susan sighed hopelessly. She was casting about in her mind for something to say that would carry them a stage further when she became aware of Lawrence's figure at the conservatory door.

'May I come in?' he called, and she beckoned vigorously to him.

Mr Blair shot round in his chair and glared at the doorway.

'Merciful Heaven,' he muttered, 'if it isn't the man himself!' He stood up ungraciously, brushing his clothes down with his hands.

Lawrence smiled at Susan and advanced with outstretched hand towards Mr Blair, grasping firmly the dusty, rather grimy one before him.

'I saw your car outside, Mr Blair, and thought we should have a word together. You don't mind, will you?' he added, turning to Susan.

'I think Mr Blair had better tell you some of the things he's just been saying to me,' said Susan bluntly.

'Ah! So you came down to warn her that I'm after her money? D'you know, I never met a more faithful family lawyer than yourself, Mr Blair. I wish there were more like you.' Lawrence spoke with such good will that Mr Blair was nonplussed.

'Hm hm, Canon Weldon. Well, I must admit there's some truth in what you say. I had something of the kind in mind, I can't deny it, but you mustn't think there was anything personal in it.' A furious glance from Susan made him hurry on. 'I mean to say I should feel it my duty to make enquiries, whoever she married, don't you know. Hm.' He broke off abruptly, conscious that he was not improving his case by much talk.

'You're against our marrying, then, I understand?' said Lawrence. 'I quite see your point. You think I stand to gain too much by it and Miss Fellowes too little, and I must agree that that is only too true. I wish I had more to offer, but I cannot alter my circumstances. And I don't believe it a sufficient obstacle to the marriage of two people who are very much attached to each other.'

'Hm,' said Mr Blair. 'Of course, if you're going to bring sentiment into it . . . I seem to have heard the same reasoning in this house many years ago.'

'I've no doubt of it,' agreed Lawrence. 'It's always a sound reason, and none the less so now than then. Do you deny it?'

Mr Blair fidgetted uneasily. 'Hm. If . . . the sentiment is genuine,' he conceded.

'But you are not convinced that it is, in this case; and no assurance on my part will persuade you. My position is a bad one. Have your arguments had much influence on Miss Fellowes?' He looked at Susan with some amusement.

'No!' exclaimed Susan disgustedly. 'Of course they haven't.'

'I'm afraid not,' admitted Mr Blair. 'She is like all the Fellowes, Canon Weldon, very strong-willed, very strong-willed indeed.' He would have liked to say, 'Obstinate as the devil.' He felt deeply hurt. He had made many journeys to Fellowescourt to advise its ladies that they were making fools of themselves, but never once had they taken his advice. He would have done better to have stayed at home. And he was no longer certain that this penniless Canon was quite the grasping adventurer he had imagined him to be. Certainly, his frankness was most disarming. With a grunt he decided to give him, once more, the benefit of the doubt. He held out a flabby hand.

'I take back my objections Canon Weldon,' he said 'although I don't approve of it, mind you.'

Lawrence took his hand and shook it warmly. 'That's very generous of you, Mr Blair.' He turned towards Susan. 'If I were you, I'd put myself right with Miss Fellowes before you go. I have a feeling that she's very cross with you.' He smiled at her, relishing so much the humour of the moment that she could only laugh.

So it was that Mr Blair agreed, after all, to be a witness of their marriage. Moreover, to make amends for his unpleasantness, he insisted on bringing his young partner to be another, and on entertaining the bride and bridegroom to luncheon after the wedding.

He made far too long a speech. They did not mind; they did not even listen to it. They were both a little dazed by the early start from home, the emotions of the occasion and the effects of a heavy lunch. The party began to fall a little flat; no one seemed to have anything more to say. Lawrence looked at his watch.

'Our train goes in half an hour,' he said.

'Going abroad?' enquired Mr Blair coyly.

'Abroad? No. We're going back to Glenmacool: my sister is not well enough to be left for more than a day.'

'Well, bless my soul!' exclaimed Mr Blair. 'I never met such a hole-in-corner affair as this wedding, I must say. No guests, no presents, no reception, and now no honeymoon! Does anybody know that you're getting married at all?'

'Only the Bishop and my sister.'

'She's so pleased that she and the Bishop are the only ones in the know that you'd almost think it was they who were getting married, not us,' said Susan. She stood up. 'We mustn't miss our train.'

The thankyous and goodbyes began. Lawrence went to fetch their coats. Emboldened by champagne, Mr Blair gripped Susan by the elbow as they waited just inside the revolving doors.

'I bet your Aunt Katharine is whirling in her grave this minute!' he whispered in her ear. 'I'd be frightened out of my life she'd put the evil eye on me if I was in your shoes, I would indeed. But you're like she was herself, obstinate as the devil, so maybe you're a match even for her!'

Susan turned and smiled at him. 'I really think I've laid Aunt Katharine's ghost,' she said. 'I don't think she'll trouble us.'